SOLDIER SON

The Teralin Sword Book 1

D.K. Holmberg

Soldier Son

ASH Publishing
dkholmberg.com

CHAPTER 1

Endric glowered at his father, but the man had already started off, his wide back deflecting the gaze. Endric's hand itched and instinctively found the cold hilt of the sword hanging at his side. There was a momentary urge to unsheathe the blade and attack, but he suppressed it as he took another deep breath. Still, his shoulders didn't relax.

Instead, he stared until his father disappeared, only turning away when he heard the deep roll of far-off thunder. Dark clouds gashed the sky overhead, inky and black, and flashes of lightning flickered distantly. The coming weather did nothing for his mood. Rain was a constant annoyance in the city, but then, they were high enough that they were practically *in* the clouds, so it shouldn't be a surprise.

Why had his father forced this conversation here, in the middle of the street, shops on either side of him? People had given them a wide berth, not wanting to distract the general as he chastised a soldier, let alone his son, leaving the street strangely empty. The second terrace of the city loomed overhead, the sheer rock wall rising toward the barracks level, a reminder of the role the Denraen soldiers played in the city. Above everything rose the Magi palace on the third terrace. He couldn't see it today; the thick clouds obscured it.

A quiet scuffing from behind him—too close to be accidental—startled him, and Endric spun, his sword half out of its scabbard before recognition halted his motion. He resheathed more harshly than necessary, snapping the blade back into place. It should not surprise him that Andril still tried to soothe him, yet it did.

"What?" Endric asked.

Andril snorted as he ran his hand across his chin, scratching idly at a small scar—his first. "That's all you can say?"

Endric met his older brother's eyes—defiance flashing through his—holding his gaze steady as long as possible before turning away. Andril had known he would turn away first.

"What?" he asked again, his tone softer. His shoulders sagged, releasing the tension he had been holding since their father first found him in the street.

"You should listen to him. There is much you don't yet know."

"You heard."

Andril nodded. "I did."

Endric scowled at his brother, and a moment of uncertainty passed through him. "He doesn't understand."

Andril snorted. "He's the general. It's not for him to understand. He asks because you are Denraen. And his son."

"You know I can't be what he wants."

Andril cocked an eyebrow and his mouth twitched in a small smile. "How do you know you aren't already?" He paused, and the words hung heavy in the air. "Besides, he'll find a way to mold you into the Denraen he needs. He *is* the general."

"Are you to help?" Even to him, the question sounded like he sulked.

Andril shrugged. "I'm Denraen as well." He blinked slowly and sighed. "And your brother. I will not lose sight of that."

"That's why you watched." Andril had known of the difficulty Endric had with their father and had not intervened. There was little Andril would have been able to do anyway.

His brother nodded and stared down the dark street.

"Does he know?"

Andril shrugged his wide shoulders. "Probably," he answered. "If not him, then his Raen. Either way, he knows." He slid forward with the dangerous grace of a mountain wolf, and Endric's hand twitched again. The corners of his brother's mouth tugged again, not quite a smile as his eyes flicked to the motion.

Endric inhaled deeply. Andril was not the problem. It would serve no purpose to challenge him. Not that he could win if he did. "What do you want of me?"

Andril again glanced down the narrow street that had swallowed their father. "Father is not your problem." He fixed his gaze on Endric.

Endric grunted, unable to meet his brother's eyes any longer. "Not to you. You will succeed him."

Andril shrugged. "Someday." On another man, such a comment would come off as arrogance. From Andril, it was simply a statement of fact.

"Then I will no longer have a problem. Then you can release me from that obligation. I'm no officer, Andril. You know that as well as I. Let me be the soldier I want to be. Let me *fight*."

"The issue will not go away so easily."

Endric frowned. He should know better than to argue with Andril. "Does he truly need for me to follow you in this? Is it not enough that I am simply a soldier?"

"You are much more than a simple Denraen," Andril said as a small smile threatened to crack his face. "You fight what you should embrace. One day you will learn."

Endric grunted and shook his head. "Or one day you will realize the same as Father."

Andril's face almost became sympathetic. Almost. "He doesn't blame you for Mother leaving. Neither do I."

Endric had to look away. Andril knew him too well. "You can't say it wasn't my fault she left."

An uncomfortable silence settled over them. Endric knew there was nothing he could say. Their mother had left shortly after his birth, leaving their father to raise them. Endric had no memories of her, nothing like the years he knew Andril still savored. Neither Andril nor his father ever spoke of her departure.

Finally, Endric broke the silence. "You still haven't answered why you watched if you weren't going to help."

Andril hesitated, his blue eyes piercing and so much like their father's. "I had thought to discuss something with you." He considered Endric for a moment, then shook his head. "Another time, I guess."

Endric felt his frustration grow. "Now you just taunt me."

His brother spread his arms and smiled, barely a parting of lips. There had been a time that he smiled easily, but no longer. Now he commanded men and directed them in battle. Endric once knew him as happy, but much of the joy that had been a part of Andril was no longer there. That alone would have been reason enough to despise his father.

"There will come a time when you will become more than a simple soldier," Andril said.

"Pray to the gods that day is far off."

"And yet I pray for the opposite."

Endric's eyes wandered, looking past Andril's head to the replica of the Tower of the Gods, which loomed over the first terrace. On this level, there were shops and taverns and temples, including the replica. "I stopped praying long ago," he said softly before turning and meeting his brother's eyes.

A flitter of irritation crossed Andril's face. "Perhaps you are right."

Endric frowned. "About what?"

"I had thought..." He shook his head slowly, not trying to hide his disappointment. "There is much you don't understand." He glanced back at the sword hanging at Endric's waist—his hand still hovering near the hilt—and frowned. "Are not ready to understand," he muttered.

A moment passed and Endric waited, knowing his brother well enough not to press. Andril said nothing. Thunder rolled again, closer, a flash of lightning casting his brother's face in a mask of frustration.

"I had hoped..."

Andril never finished. He shook his head before turning and moving silently down the street, disappearing into the shadows.

Endric watched for a moment. It was not like Andril to show hesitation. The man was infuriatingly confident, and deservedly so, excelling in everything he did.

And Endric pushed him.

A wave of shame flushed through him. Their entire life, Andril had been nothing but short of the ideal brother, mentoring him in a way their father never had. He should not take the frustrations he had with their father out on Andril.

For a moment, he considered chasing after him. Another peal of distant thunder echoed and he took a deep breath, pushing the conversation out of his mind. The anger filling him after meeting with their father had disappeared during their talk, leaving him more troubled than annoyed. He didn't know what he would even say if he caught his brother.

Stepping quietly along the stones of the street—not quite with the silence Andril managed—he moved quickly past the row of drab stone buildings until he reached the one he sought. A muted cacophony of sounds seeped through the stone and heavy wooden door, flooding out onto the street.

The Scented Lover was typical for this part of the city and catered mostly to the Denraen soldiers. Heavy smoke filled the tavern. The sharply pungent aroma of rumbala mixed with the thick scent of the hickory log burning in the fire along the far wall. Flames jumped and cast flickering shadows, leaving the room obscured in swaths of darkness. Tables crowded the floor, solid and worn with grime and spilt drink. Some few rested in the pools of darkness that were coveted in places like the Scented Lover.

Endric pushed his way through the patrons, ignoring the brief glares he received. Most men frowned only briefly, turning away when they recognized him. He might not have Andril's skill and certainly not his rank, but he still had earned a reputation, and it inspired more than a little fear, though as he thought about it, Endric wasn't sure that was a good thing.

Reaching the back of the room where the darkness stretched the deepest and the flickering light of the fire barely penetrated, Endric paused and looked down at the small group sitting around a table. No one looked up, though he saw from the stiffness of their posture that they were aware of him.

"Well?"

"You'll have to sit on me for my seat," the man nearest said. He was stout and his head was shaven, leaving the heavy scars across his head shining even in the low light of the tavern.

Endric grunted and placed a hand on the man's shoulder, sliding him over and sitting alongside him. "One day I will sit on you, Pendin."

Pendin laughed and looked up. "Another scar then." Scars were respected among the Denraen, worn like badges of honor. A playful glimmer crossed his face for a moment while he eyed Endric, disappearing as their gazes met. "Something's wrong."

Endric shook his head, but the others knew him too well. They had been friends since their earliest days in the barracks. Those first months of training bonded men—and women, he decided, glancing over at Senda—in a way few outsiders would understand. "It's nothing." He looked away as he waved for a drink, hiding his eyes.

"Looks like nothing," Senda noted.

The waitress brought a mug over for him, leaning over to reveal a flash of cleavage. Endric ignored it as he took a long drink. The waitress scowled, stalking away with a sway to her hips that turned a few heads. She looked back, the scowl replaced by a satisfied smirk.

"Looks like someone else will need to order my drinks tonight," Endric said.

"Maybe you should at least speak to her since rolling her last week," Pendin said and laughed.

Senda frowned at him and sniffed. Olin, a man whose long face matched his height, smiled tightly but said nothing. He rarely did.

Endric shrugged. "There is that."

"Why the mood?" Pendin asked.

He sighed. "The usual. The weather. This city. My father."

"Those never change."

Endric closed his eyes. *They are friends*, he reminded himself. *And good ones at that.* "I argued with my father and took my frustration out on Andril."

"And yet you still live." Senda still frowned at him, and Endric knew that she would be irritated by his treatment of the barmaid longer than necessary. She flipped her tight braid over her shoulder as she looked away from him.

Pendin chuckled, smiling briefly at Senda. "How is that unusual?"

"Something about him was different tonight."

"Perhaps it's because he's been sent from the city," Olin said, barely looking up from his drink.

Senda shot Olin an unreadable expression.

Endric finished his drink and looked up at Senda for confirmation. Her face was blank, and even though she worked with the spymaster Listain, she would say nothing. She looked away from his gaze, and he knew better than to press.

He turned back to Olin, wondering how he knew about it and wondering why Andril had not said anything.

Olin stared back and shrugged. "Rumors. Skirmishes in the far south. Supposedly some kind of cult of warrior priests. Denraen are deployed to investigate."

And Father sends Andril.

His brother had only recently assumed his command and had yet to lead his men in anything more than simple training drills. Was this Father's way of testing Andril's leadership? It wouldn't be out of character for the general to do so. Something about that felt wrong though, and Endric couldn't place why.

"You could ask to go with him," Pendin said, tracking Endric's line of thinking. He pushed his mug of ale over to Endric and winked.

"Not after tonight." Was that why Andril had found him? To see if he was ready for assignment to his regiment?

Endric closed his eyes and visualized his brother, remembering the hesitation he'd shown before leaving. What had his brother intended to ask him? Knowing that he was being sent from the city cast their conversation in a different light. Disappointing his father was for sport; disappointing Andril was agony.

He downed another mug of ale. "I need to find Andril," he said, deciding it couldn't wait.

"Give it time, Endric," Pendin said.

Endric glanced at Senda.

She sighed but answered. "I'm not sure when he's to leave."

"I can't wait," he decided. "I need to know what he wanted." He stood, knocking his chair down as he did. The man behind him hollered and Endric turned, an apology on his lips, but he never got to say it.

The man swung.

The attack was quick. Nearly too quick. Endric ducked and stepped back. "Listen, friend—"

"You damn Denraen are all the same!" the man spat.

Endric took in the man's soiled clothes and thick arms and noted the dirt ground under his nails. A miner.

The mountain city owned one of the few known active mines for teralin, and the mines twisted throughout the mountain. The metal was precious to the Magi, supposedly because it was necessary to speak to the gods. Most who worked the mines did so because they had no other choice.

"Easy, man. It was an accident." He was annoyed but knew better than to attack one of the local miners. The Denraen had a hard enough time with them as it was; it was surprising that these miners would patronize a tavern mostly filled with soldiers. Besides, he had enough trouble from fights he had started. Better to avoid this one.

The man looked down at Endric's sword and sneered. "An accident like the way you pushed me over getting into the tavern?"

He frowned. Perhaps he *had* pushed a little more than was necessary.

Chairs scraped roughly over the wooden floor, and Endric didn't need to turn to know his friends stood to support him. "No need. I'm going," he said and looked over at Pendin.

And was hit.

Endric didn't know how the man was able to hit him so quickly. If not for Pendin's widened eyes giving away the attack, he would have taken it harder. As it was, he managed to pull away and absorb some of the blow. Still, he felt as if hit by stone.

He reacted as a man trained by Denraen would: he attacked.

Endric lunged forward, closing in on the man. Another quick blow caught him on the shoulder, but he had leapt soon enough to miss the worst of it. He jabbed quickly, catching the man in the stomach, and twisted, throwing his arms out to catch him in the throat and knock him down, hoping to end the fight. The man somehow eluded him.

Movement behind him put him on edge and the attacker took advantage, swinging hard toward Endric's face. He twisted and dropped, grabbing the man's arm as he spun. He pulled it down and over his shoulder. Instead of the expected crack of bones breaking, he was left with a handful of sleeve as the man tore his arm away, revealing a heavily tattooed arm. Endric frowned at the markings, tried to make sense of the dark patterns swirling up his arm, but couldn't.

The man smiled. Stained teeth gleamed dully.

He darted suddenly forward, bringing his arm up and out toward his throat.

Endric turned and ducked, punching up and into the man's flank as he passed. A quick kick knocked the man forward to sprawl on his face on the rough floor.

Endric pounced. He landed on the man's back and grabbed the still-sleeved arm and twisted it back. The man pushed up with his free arm, but Pendin was there, forcing him back down. Olin and Senda stood around them, Olin with his sword unsheathed and staff in hand. Their stance dared others in the bar to interfere.

Most turned away and returned to quiet conversation, sliding out of reach of the Denraen. Two men remained. One was short and thin and covered in dark rags somehow holding together. He stared for a long moment at Endric, pushing ratty hair out of his black eyes before he turned. The small man disappeared without a word and was quickly swallowed by the thick throng of patrons.

The other man waited. He was meatier, heavy in the face, and his thick forearms looked perpetually stained with dark smudges glimmering strangely in the muted light. While he was not as raggedly dressed as the other man had been, his dark clothes were nearly as well worn. He stood staring slack faced at them and scratched his arm absently.

Endric pulled up on his attacker's arm and twisted him to face the other. "Is he with you?" he asked. The words were little more than a grunt and thick with the anger he felt.

His father would hear about what had happened. His brother. Another fight. This time, he had done nothing other than protect himself, but it wouldn't matter. The warning after the last one had been clear. Now they wouldn't be pleased. Further disappointment.

Endric shook his head, not waiting for the man to answer, and thrust his attacker forward. The thick man caught him clumsily, then lifted him. The attacker shook him off and twisted, turning quickly to face Endric. A dark smile simmered on his lips and his mouth parted again slightly.

"Go," Endric said, his voice ragged.

The man paused and Endric noted his shoulders tensing as he slowly eyed the sword and staff held ready. A dangerous glint passed across his face, and for a moment, Endric was sure he would try his luck.

Olin slid forward, just a step, but it was enough.

The man nodded slightly. "Another time," he whispered.

"Go," Endric repeated.

The man turned, pulling his solid friend with him, and they pushed through the crowd. Endric watched until the heavy door opened and then slammed closed, a gust of wind whipping in as it did and sending the dark shadows in the tavern spasming with new life.

"What was that?"

Endric turned to look at Pendin, who stared at the doorway. His eyes were slightly widened and he shook his head slightly from side to side. Senda's face was troubled, her brow furrowed, and she stared at the place where the men had stood. Olin held his sword limply, the point resting carelessly on the floor. The soldier in Endric wanted to admonish him for resting his sword in such a way, but he wouldn't do that to his friend.

"I don't know. Miners, it would seem. Not sure what I did to upset him."

"Tipped your chair back, as far as I can tell," Pendin said.

"You walked into the bar," Senda said, the troubled expression now gone.

Endric watched her for a moment, wondering what she knew, knowing she would say nothing. Her work with the spymaster taught her to keep her lips sealed, so he let the thought go. He needed to find his brother before he left. Perhaps now was a good time to be out of the city.

"I'm leaving," he said.

"We'll go too," Pendin said.

The crowd parted for them as they made their way to the door. The other patrons in the tavern had ignored the disturbance. Nothing was broken, and they had been hidden in the darkness of the back corner. And fights were not that uncommon in the tavern. Especially this tavern. Still, a faint hush met them as they passed on their way out.

The others went out before him, but Endric paused. A strange drumming started behind him, and he turned to see what caused it. He barely saw the heavy board as it whistled toward him, cracking him on his forehead, and he dropped. Something wet dripped into his eyes—tears or blood—and he blinked to clear the sudden flashing lights. He heard the door open again, a muffled whoosh of air.

A dark shape hovered over him briefly and laughed, and then he heard Pendin. His voice was distant, as if coming through the walls, and he heard "Endric—" as he passed into darkness.

CHAPTER 2

Endric awoke to a throbbing head. He blinked slowly, fighting through the dried crust clinging to his lids. A sliver of light overhead barely pierced the darkness. He was on his back, resting on something rocky and cold, and staring at the slight illumination, hoping his eyes would adjust to the darkness. They didn't.

Loose rubble beneath him stabbed into his flesh like dozens of small knives. He focused on his body to ensure that everything still worked, carefully moving his toes and fingers. When he found that he could, he slowly sat up, ignoring the pounding pressure in his head. A momentary wave of nausea threatened to knock him back, but he fought through it.

He couldn't remember what had happened. They were leaving the tavern, and then something had hit him. Or someone. He tried to remember the face of the person who had stood over him laughing, but couldn't. Could it have been the miner? His head hurt worse trying to think, so he stopped.

Though he couldn't remember what had happened, he could guess what had come next. The all-too-familiar cell he now found himself in was answer enough. It didn't explain why, though.

Endric turned to the thin beam of light marking the upper edge of the door. When he could stand, he pounded forcefully upon the door, ignoring the pain in his head that mirrored the movements of his fist.

When the door opened suddenly, Endric nearly fell backward in his surprise. He hadn't expected anyone to answer, hoping mostly to take his frustration out on the door of his cell. A familiar figure stood framed in the doorway, his face shadowed by the lantern hanging on the far wall.

"Listain."

The man nodded slightly. Endric couldn't see the expression on his face but imagined a slight sneer. His father's Raen had nothing but disdain for him, likely sharing the general's assessment. Listain stood a head shorter than he did and was reed thin, but he still filled much of the doorway.

"Where am I?"

Listain snorted. "That should be obvious. Even to you."

He paused, and Endric imagined him peering into the darkness with narrowed eyes. If Listain was here, that meant the barracks jail. Probably better than the city jail, but not by much. Unfortunately, he had known both.

"Perhaps especially for you."

Endric started forward, unwilling to listen to Listain's comments and intending to push past him, but an iron hand gripped his shoulder. Listain squeezed harder than necessary, and Endric stopped and pushed him off.

"That's what got you into the cell in the first place," the spymaster said in warning.

"I didn't start it."

Listain snorted again. "Witnesses say you did."

"Then they weren't watching."

Endric tensed again, thinking about trying again to push past Listain, but reason got the better of him. Like it or not, Listain was the Raen and far outranked him. Only fear—or respect—of the general had prevented the Raen from punishing him more severely in the past. With his father's current attitude toward him, Endric was uncertain he would be protected.

He took a deep breath and stepped back. "What do you want?"

"Restraint," Listain said, a hint of surprise entering his voice. "It's a start." He took another small step, sliding just past the doorway. His posture was relaxed, but that was deceptive. The man was nearly as dangerous as his father was rumored to be and at least as dangerous as Endric knew Andril was. He resisted the urge to step back.

"The general thinks you should stay another night in this cell."

Endric bit off the first thing that came to mind. "Then why are you here?"

"Your brother thinks you should be allowed to speak on your behalf." He paused for several heartbeats. "Fortunately for you, the general puts much stock in what your brother thinks." The emphasis to his words was clear.

Andril knew he was jailed. That thought bothered him the most. He could deal with his father's disappointment. And Listain was right—it wasn't the first time he had been arrested. But something about this felt different. Especially after how he had left Andril earlier.

"When does he depart?" he asked, not sure if Listain would bother to answer. The thin Raen cocked his head and his lips tightened. "Sir," Endric added.

Listain stared a moment longer before answering. "Two days." He paused another moment, as if considering his next words. "It would be better if you went with him."

The fact that he was right didn't make his words any easier to hear. The chance to join Andril's regiment had probably passed. That he had followed up their argument with a tavern brawl made it even more likely. Endric's shoulders tensed and his hand instinctively slipped to his waist, feeling for his missing sword.

"Better for who—my father? The Denraen?"

"Yes."

The word seemed to echo in the small cell.

Endric shook his head, closing his eyes and sighing. It would be, he knew. Perhaps then his friends wouldn't carry his stigma with them as well. None had ever said anything, but he knew. Pendin—such a skilled and promising soldier—would no longer be held back by his best friend. Olin might find his assignments less unpleasant. Only Senda seemed unencumbered by him, rising to work alongside the spymaster, her analytical mind carrying her beyond the handicap of her friendship with Endric. Occasionally, he wondered if she spied on him to Listain.

"I would go," he said.

Listain cocked his head and furrowed his expansive brow. Endric imagined the Raen smiling at the prospect of him leaving the city, but in the subdued light he couldn't be sure.

Listain grunted and motioned to the doorway. Endric stepped past him and into the dimly lit hall. A few of the other cells were closed, and he worried that his friends had been jailed as well. They had gone out before him and none had been more than incidentally involved. For a moment, he considered asking Listain but thought better of it.

Guards stationed near the end of the hall blocked another door. Behind the door were steps leading to another guardroom. Beyond that, the offices of the highest-ranking Denraen.

His father. Listain. And his brother.

His steps faltered. He couldn't help it.

He felt Listain's eyes on him. The man had a way of seeing and observing fear among the Denraen. Most feared his network of spies, which seemed to miss nothing. Endric knew he was weighed and measured—as he was every time the Raen looked at him—and dismissed as no more a threat than the ash beetles that came out each spring. An annoyance. Little more.

His brother stood waiting at the top of the steps but didn't meet his eyes.

"Listain," Andril said, acknowledging his Raen.

Listain nodded. "You may take him. The general is expecting you."

Andril thumped his fist to his chest in salute. He paused a moment, expecting Endric to do the same. He didn't. Andril ignored the slight and led him off.

They had only gone a few steps before Andril slowed. "You started a fight with a miner." The words were laced with heavy layers of disappointment.

"I didn't start it," he said quietly, knowing the comment wouldn't matter. His history of fighting was damning enough. Worse was that this was not his first run-in with the miners.

Andril turned and faced him, his face the fury of a Denraen officer. Little of his brother remained. "His uncle is Mageborn."

Endric blinked slowly. He had not expected that, though many were born to the Magi without the Mage gift. It was only logical the Magi would have miners in the family as well. "I didn't know."

15

Andril sighed and turned away, starting forward again. "Would it have mattered?"

Endric couldn't say anything that would sway his brother, so he changed tack. "You didn't tell me you were leaving."

"You are not of my regiment."

"I am your brother."

Andril tilted his head but didn't look back. "I tried," he said after taking a few more steps.

"I would join your regiment if you would have me." For some reason, those words were hard to say.

"I tried," Andril repeated, then shook his head. Then sighed again. Endric saw it as a slow heave of his broad back. "You are not ready. Or I am not ready. I'm not certain which."

"Ready for what?" he asked.

They had reached their father's office. The door was closed and Andril rapped twice upon it before answering. "For the discipline necessary to be Denraen," he finally said.

The door opened and Endric didn't have a chance to counter, though he was uncertain what he would have said anyway. There was no arguing the fact that he was not the ideal soldier. He was skilled with the sword—few were his equal—but that was nearly all he offered the Denraen. Perhaps Andril was right.

Still, it didn't change the fact that he would support his brother. He would rather follow him and act the Denraen Andril needed than remain stationed in the city. Only Andril would know that he simply pretended. And now he didn't want him.

The door opened fully and their father faced him. He was tall—nearly a full fist taller than Endric—and as broad of shoulders as Listain was slender. His bearded face was scarred and worn, and his gray eyes stared at Endric for long moments. He imagined a fleeting look of disappointment crossed them.

"Come." The word was a command, not an invitation.

Andril pulled him through the doorway and closed it after them with a solid thud. Endric suddenly felt more confined than he had within the cell.

Months had passed since he had last been in the office—then on somewhat better terms—but little had changed.

The huge map still hung on the far wall, with small dots marking something Endric never understood. Beneath it and facing the doorway was a massive desk. Years had worn away most of the stain, but rather than looking old, it simply appeared more rugged. More fitting of its owner. Papers stacked neatly atop the surface hinted at the amount of work the general sorted through. Rows of bookcases lined the wall to his left. No open space remained on the shelves. The books upon them were all neatly arranged. A huge table rested along the wall to his right, where the senior council of the Denraen met.

Endric looked away. Once, his father had dreamt that both his sons would sit around his table with the council. That dream had died long ago. Only Andril sat among them now.

Few things in the office caught his attention any longer. He had seen it since he was a child and, other than the location of the dots on the map, little changed.

Rather, it was the huge broadsword hanging on the far wall that always commanded his attention. The sword Trill was nearly as renowned as its owner. And just as feared.

Endric wrested his eyes away to focus on his father. The man simply stared at him with eyes of stone. The rest of his face showed nearly as much emotion.

"Were you any other man, you would have been expelled from the Denraen by now," he said finally.

The words were soft, but his father's rasp sliced through him. Endric had not expected the conversation to begin like this. Though they had argued only the day before, it had been about his willingness to lead rather than his desire to remain Denraen. He knew nothing other than the Denraen.

All of a sudden, his heart started hammering in his chest. His throat swelled and he feared needing to speak.

Their father turned away to sit at his desk. His broad forearms rested on the surface and he stared at something on a corner of the desk for a moment before looking up again, his face now wearing the weight of his office. "I am undecided as to your fate. Another fight. And with a miner." His father blinked slowly and shook his head. "You of all soldiers should know the struggles we have had with the miners, and now this!"

"General," Andril interjected. "He is a skilled soldier. The Denraen need men of his skill. I believe he can still be rehabilitated."

His brother didn't turn as he spoke. There was a distance to his tone, as if he were speaking of a warhorse rather than a man. His flesh and blood.

The general turned his hard expression upon Andril. "You would take this task upon yourself?"

Endric allowed himself to hope that Andril had had a change in heart. That he would be willing to let him join his regiment as it deployed.

"I think our relationship would make his discipline ineffective," Andril said, dashing Endric's hope.

Their father blinked again and nodded, sighing deeply. "It should not have to be like this," he said, sounding like a concerned father for once. He crossed his thick arms in front of his chest. Then he straightened his back, furrowing his brow as piercing eyes narrowed, once again the image of the stern general. "Andril. You are dismissed."

Andril nodded and thumped his chest in salute. He turned and left without looking at Endric.

"Endric."

Endric turned his attention back to his father. He had been watching Andril leave, hoping his brother would turn, that he would meet his eyes, but he didn't. "Sir."

The general snorted. "Andril speaks truly. Discipline is needed, though I am uncertain what course to take. Because you are my son, it needs to be someone who can act on my authority and not fear repercussions. I had hoped Andril would be willing to see to your discipline, as he saw to much of your training. Perhaps you have burned even that bridge." He glanced down at his desk, shuffling a few papers. "Listain would relish the discipline too much, and that will serve no purpose. That leaves Urik."

Endric said nothing. At least his father acknowledged that it was Andril who had trained him. And that Listain would enjoy disciplining him. Urik was strict—a typical Denraen—but a good man.

"There is more to being Denraen than being a skilled fighter," the general said. "If you choose to ignore the opportunity I have given you, ignore the chance to lead, then you will learn what is expected of my soldiers."

"I know what is expected of the Denraen," he said.

"No. You do not." His father stood and fixed his eyes on Endric. "You have been protected. That stops now." He grabbed a slip of parchment and scribbled something before folding it and fixing his stamp upon it. "This is your last chance, Endric. Do not treat it lightly." He handed the parchment across the desk. "Give this to Urik. You are dismissed."

Endric took the paper and left. His eyes lingered on the council table, sliding off when he reached the door. He felt his father's eyes on his back. Though he had heard no movement, he suspected the general had sat back down, staring at him from behind his desk.

Endric didn't look back as he turned down the hall.

CHAPTER 3

He found Urik in his office. It was smaller than his father's and had room for little more than his desk, but Urik had been en'raen long enough that the office was cluttered with stacks of books and papers. Nothing like the clean organization his father maintained.

Endric stood silently before the desk while Urik read the parchment. Endric had resisted the urge to open it and see what his father had written. Whether it was out of fear or respect, he didn't know. Perhaps he truly didn't care. He crossed his arms over his chest so that he didn't reach for his missing sword.

Urik quickly finished reading it and set it down atop his desk. "You know what is said here?" he asked. His eyes caught the crossed arms and narrowed slightly.

Endric shook his head once. He imagined what the general had requested. Discipline had been mentioned often enough that he knew Urik was expected to dole out some sort of punishment.

Urik smiled. It was a slight turn of his lip. It did nothing to make him more remarkable, and it was this plainness that made him a dangerous opponent. Most didn't expect the keen mind and quick sword behind such average features. Yet his father had seen the whole man.

"You are assigned to me."

Endric frowned. "One of your regiments?"

Urik turned his flat brown eyes upon him. "Me."

"I'm not sure what that means."

Urik chuckled, though it came out as a grunt. "Me neither. Seems you have offended Andril. So Dendril assigns you to me. To 'learn the ideals and understand the role of the Denraen.'" Urik looked up from the parchment and shook his head. "Be easier if you took the commission he offered."

Easier, but not what he wanted. It was simpler to just serve. There was something satisfying in being a mindless soldier. He didn't tell Urik that. Instead, he said, "It's no longer offered, I think."

Urik laughed again. "You don't know your father then. To him, any man can be an officer. He just needs to earn the right."

Endric didn't think there was anything he could do that would regain his father's good graces, let alone warrant earning a commission. Too many years had been spent intentionally antagonizing him. Still, he never let it show. Always the general, never the father.

They were interrupted by a harsh knock on Urik's door. Urik looked over Endric's shoulder and frowned. "Enter."

The door opened to reveal Listain standing on the other side. His face became drawn and tightened even more when he saw Endric. He was clean-shaven, revealing a few old scars along his chin. Most of the officers shaved, but Listain frequently grew out a beard, hiding his scars, though he kept his hair shorn close in the style of the Denraen officers. Only the general wore a beard routinely.

"The general convenes the council," Listain said, flicking his gaze to Urik. "When?"

"Now. New report from the south."

"I've warned of the south, but you have convinced him that it's not a risk."

Listain shot Urik a hard look. As Raen, he outranked Urik.

Urik nodded carefully. Listain glanced at Endric before turning and closing the door. "Seems we will start later. Best that your father assigned you to me rather than the Raen."

Endric looked back at the closed door and nodded. Listain would have tormented him and relished doing so. Even his father had acknowledged that.

"I know the two of you haven't always seen eye to eye," Urik continued.

Endric turned to Urik and snorted briefly before he remembered his place. He was assigned to Urik to learn how to be Denraen. It wouldn't do to offend him already. "He is the Raen."

Urik laughed. Emotion never reached his eyes. "Exercising caution already?" He tilted his head, seeming to weigh Endric before smiling slightly. "The two of you are both misunderstood. It is only natural that such misunderstandings lead to conflict." He hesitated, glancing at the door as he considered his next words. "Listain serves the Denraen well. The intelligence he gathers is nearly irreplaceable. You would do well to remember that."

The implication was clear. Listain was irreplaceable. Endric was not.

Urik chuckled softly, breaking the brief tension. "There are some things his spy network does not help him see. Such as the rumors that spread about him." Urik shrugged. "Or maybe he sees and doesn't care." He met Endric's eyes and held them. "Who is to know?"

Endric shifted uncomfortably, uncertain what to say.

"Perhaps he knows his days are numbered. That may be why he suggested Andril head south," Urik said, the comment strangely casual. "Andril will succeed your father someday, and then—"

Another knock interrupted them, leaving Endric wondering what he'd been about to say.

Urik glanced at the door and then grabbed a handful of papers that he stuffed into a small satchel near his desk. "Council awaits." He glanced up at Endric. "I think for your first assignment, we should focus on the ideals of the Denraen." He smiled, his teeth flashing briefly. Turning to his desk again, he leaned and scribbled something upon a scrap of paper, then held it out for Endric. "Take this to Tildan. You have patrol the next three nights."

Endric bit back a comment at his assignment, feeling a surge of irritation flash through him. Patrol was meant for the earliest of recruits… and perhaps that was the point.

Urik watched his face for a moment, then pushed past him as he moved toward the door, holding it open while he waited for Endric to follow. "After that, we will discuss what is next."

Urik hurried down the hall toward Dendril's office and the council. Andril would be there, sitting alongside their father. Endric had never felt that their father wanted the same for him. Not that it mattered to him anyway. He was happier being a simple soldier.

A thought troubled him as he made his way to find his sword and then Tildan. He had not thought of how Andril's eventual succession would affect others. Andril's promotion to en'raen had come with Tordal's retirement. The man had served the Denraen for thirty years and had left scarred but on his own terms. All knew Dendril intended Andril to be general. None in the Denraen debated the logic of the decision; Andril was nearly as respected as Dendril, if not as unapproachable.

But Andril's eventual promotion would impact others. Each general put their own stamp on the Denraen leadership, and Dendril had been no different. Something Urik had said bothered him. The spymaster was calculating and a skilled planner, traits his father respected and used. But could those same traits complicate things for his brother? Could Listain already fear Andril's promotion?

He started down the hall toward the cells to retrieve his sword, wondering if there was more to Listain's attitude toward him than he had thought and suddenly realizing he might need to be more careful.

CHAPTER 4

The alley was dark.

The clouds overhead let little light through, but the alley would have been dark even on the sunniest day. Not that there were many of those in Vasha. Endric squinted down the alley, looking for motion more than anything else, but saw nothing.

The longer he stood there, the more he wondered what it was Urik had him doing. Endric held little rank, but enough that he had not been on patrol in years. Pendin stood next to him, silent and more relaxed than Endric felt. Tildan had pulled Pendin from his other duties to patrol with Endric, telling him that it was Urik's request. Pendin had not objected, but Endric saw the displeasure on his face, leaving him wondering if that wasn't really the lesson Urik intended.

It was the fifth night of patrols. Urik had only assigned him three, but so far Endric had been unable to find the en'raen, so he kept at the patrol rather than upset Urik. Fear of expulsion from the Denraen was a powerful motivator. As much as he refused the commission his father had offered, Endric didn't know what else he would do if not for the Denraen.

The other nights had been silent and uneventful. Pendin never mentioned his annoyance with the assignment, but then, he wouldn't. Somehow Endric would have to make it up to his friend. Only, he didn't know how. Endric had no influence, and what little pull he may once have had because of his name disappeared as men saw him on patrol.

He sighed, breaking the thick silence between them. Tonight was darker, and they were deeper in the Stahline section than they had patrolled on previous evenings. Endric kept his hand hovering over the hilt of his sword. The shadows along the alley shifted and he tensed, squeezing the hilt. The leather wrapping creaked.

Pendin turned and looked down at him, shaking his head once. "Relax," he whispered.

Endric grunted. "Easy for you to say."

Pendin frowned. "Because I grew up in this part of town?"

"Mostly because you stink. You smell like you belong here." He hoped the words came out as a joke, briefly fearing how Pendin would take the comment.

There was truth to his words as well. This part of the city smelled of rot and decay. Once, he had thought it simply from the trash and waste in the countless alleys that worked through here, but the problem went deeper than that.

Pendin shook his head. "Nice of you to say. Tell me. Why is it that we're here?"

Endric snorted. "I am to learn the ideals of the Denraen."

Pendin narrowed his eyes, considering the comment a moment before he chuckled quietly and shook his head. "And I am here because I know..."

"This part of the city. Dirty Stahline."

Endric looked at Pendin. His muscular friend fairly filled the alley, and Endric sensed his frown. Pendin rarely shared much of his youth, but Endric knew the fact that he had survived to become Denraen after growing up in this part of the city was a feat in itself.

Vasha, the city of the Magi, prided itself on following Urmahne custom. Peace. Fairness. Justice. Still, there were hard parts of town. The Stahline section was one of the hardest.

"Most in this part of the city work the mines," Pendin said.

Endric grunted softly as he looked around. It felt like it. This section of town was dirty and dark like the mines. An air of oppression seemed to weigh over everything. "Not all, though."

Pendin met his eyes. "Not all," he agreed. "Some are thieves. Some women are whores. Few are honest tradesman."

"You are."

Pendin shrugged. "It wasn't easy leaving Stahline," he admitted. "Most here feel abandoned by the Magi. And the Denraen. Most feel that you abandon your family by leaving."

Pendin looked away and Endric didn't push. Pendin rarely spoke of his family remaining in Stahline. Endric knew there was a sister and that his parents still lived, but little else.

A sound came from the end of the alley, and Pendin motioned for him to follow. Technically, Endric outranked Pendin, but barely. That mattered little between the two. Endric followed him into the darkness. It practically swallowed him.

Light at each end of the alley was all he saw. The walls lining the alley were sensed more than seen and pressed upon him like a physical weight. Pendin moved swiftly. Endric followed silently, using the skills Andril had taught him so long ago.

They reached the end of the alley and found nothing. It opened onto a street only slightly wider than the alley. Storefronts were lit with sooty lanterns that smeared the lettering of their signs. Most along the street couldn't afford oil, and Endric didn't want to know what it was they burned instead. Instead, he ignored it like the Denraen had done to this part of town for years, preferring to focus most of their patrols outside the city.

Pendin motioned him to follow out into the street. They wore their Denraen gray, and each wore his sword at his side. Still, Endric didn't feel comforted by that. Perhaps it was the disdain the people in this part of town felt for the Denraen. Or something else. Pendin's presence provided small comfort.

A shuffling sound scratched its way along the broken stones that defined the street. The dim light of the lanterns cast a hazy light—nearly enough to see down the street—but there was nothing. No one moved.

"What is it?" Endric whispered.

Pendin cocked his head, listening, and turned to face Endric. "I don't hear anything."

The strange sound was farther away but still audible, like a stick scratching at a stone. Or nails on stone. Endric could see nothing.

He shouldered past Pendin and stepped carefully down the street. The leather wrapping of his hilt was comforting as he gripped it, now careful not to make a sound. He moved as silently as possible, envisioning Andril as he did, trying to mimic the silence his brother so easily managed. He didn't think he could copy his dangerous grace.

The street ended at an intersection. Endric saw little more than storefronts along the cross street. The lanterns were no brighter. If possible, they put off an even hazier light as the street stretched into darkness. He sensed Pendin's approach and turned. As he did, something scurried off between two nearby buildings.

"What do you see?" Pendin asked.

Endric took a deep breath and relaxed. "Just a rat, I think."

Pendin chuffed and shook his head. "Surprised it came out of the garbage lining the alley. Surprised it didn't attack you." He stared down the street, his eyes narrowed as he tried to pierce the darkness. "Come on. We should be patrolling. Not sneaking."

"You sure?" Endric knew how the Stahline people felt about the Denraen. Pendin had made that clear.

Pendin frowned at him and waved him forward. They started down the intersecting street, moving quietly and staying to the middle. Neither spoke. Their steps were muted along the stone, the sound quickly enveloped by the silence. Little unsettled him, but this patrol somehow managed to do so.

The street eventually opened onto a square. Once, it had been a place of greenery in the midst of the city. Now, crumbling sculptures marked each corner. A stone bench along the edge of the square was tipped over. Grass no longer grew; instead, tall weeds sprouted randomly. No lanterns lit the square, and what light seeped toward the center did so by accident.

"Fits this part of town," Endric whispered.

Pendin ignored him. His eyes were fixed on something on the far side of the square. Endric couldn't make out what it was that Pendin saw. Suddenly, Pendin grabbed his jacket with a firm grasp and pushed him behind a building. Into darkness. He raised a finger to his lips and nodded toward the opposite side of the square.

"What is it?" Endric said. He pitched his words to be barely more than a whisper.

"Not sure. Movement."

"We're Denraen. We're the ones patrolling," he said.

"Doesn't matter. Not here. Gather information first. Then we can patrol."

Endric snorted quietly. "We have the swords."

"They may have the numbers. Trust me—the type of people that would be out at night here wouldn't hesitate to attack Denraen." The whispered words seemed to hang in the heavy, cool air.

Pendin pointed to an area no light managed to penetrate. At first, Endric saw nothing but inky blackness. Gradually the darkness seemed to lighten as his eyes adjusted to the low light and he saw what had caught Pendin's attention.

Two figures stood on the far side of the square. One was cloaked and only distinguishable as a change in the blackness. The hood of the cloak appeared to flicker, a smudge of changing shadows, and Endric imagined the figure looking around nervously. The cloak was pulled tight and the outline of a sword was concealed beneath.

The other person stood casually and appeared dressed in a simple robe. As his eyes adjusted, Endric saw this figure much more clearly. Nearly a head taller than the other—and taller even than most of the Magi he'd ever seen—he didn't carry a weapon.

A Mage.

Endric was surprised to see one of the Magi in Stahline. They tended to avoid this section of the city—this level, really—preferring to ignore its existence. The Magi were the first priests of the Urmahne, and though they no longer served that role, they still held themselves above the common man. And those from Stahline were as common as men could be.

"A Mage," Endric whispered.

He sensed Pendin turn toward him. "You sure?"

"Too tall to be anything else. And the robe is a giveaway."

Pendin stared for a few moments longer. "I'll take your word for it."

They two figures spoke for a few moments longer before suddenly parting. The Magi turned and came toward them, walking quickly but confidently. Though they were Denraen and served to protect the Magi, something told Endric this one didn't want to be seen. Some said the Magi saw well in the dark. Endric was not sure if it was true or not but didn't want to take a chance. He pulled Pendin deeper in the space between the buildings and crouched down.

The Mage passed them without pausing. There was just enough light for Endric to see a smooth jawline and softly angular face. His hair was cut short and his gray robe practically dragged across the stone.

After the Mage was gone, Endric crept back toward the front of the building and peered down the street. The Mage turned down one of the intersecting streets and disappeared. Endric looked back toward the square and the cloaked figure that stood staring after the Mage for a moment longer before spinning and striding out of the square in the opposite direction. There was something about his walk that gave Endric pause.

"What is it?"

Endric suppressed a jump. He had been focusing on the figures and had not heard Pendin approach. "I don't know. Something is odd."

"Like us patrolling in Stahline?"

Endric shrugged, trying to downplay their assignment. He was not sure if he even convinced himself. "If not us, someone else. Father increased patrols here after the last episode." *Episode* was putting it lightly, but *riot* felt like too strong a word. Either way, the people in Stahline had nearly destroyed an entire block. The fires had burned until the Magi had sent help in the form of the Denraen.

"Then what?"

Endric shook his head. "Not sure. I think the other was Denraen." He wasn't sure why he thought that, but something about it struck him as true. The shorter of the two was lean enough that his sword protruded from his cloak. Could be nothing. Or everything. Endric didn't know, but he did know he couldn't let it drop.

Pendin scrubbed a hand across his face and frowned. "What does that mean?"

Endric shook his head. He had no clue what would lead one of the Magi into Stahline at night. And why would a Denraen be meeting the Mage in secret? Unless he had the whole scenario wrong.

"Let's follow them," he suggested.

Pendin blinked slowly, the serious expression on his face making it clear that he considered whether Endric was joking. When Endric didn't say anything more, he shook his head slightly. "Follow a Mage councilor? And some mysterious Denraen? We should get back to what we were assigned. The patrol."

"I'll take the Denraen. You follow the Mage," Endric said, ignoring Pendin's comment.

His friend simply snorted. His wide nostrils flared as he took a deep breath. "You take the Mage."

Endric shook his head. "I can move quieter. Just see where he goes. Even better if you can figure out who it is." He looked at Pendin a moment, waiting for his decision. Not that it was truly in doubt.

Endric wasn't sure what he would chose, but finally Pendin nodded and moved down the street. He kept to the side but made no effort to hide his presence. Still, the shadows hung around him, slipping over the gray Denraen uniform. Soon he was barely visible. Endric watched as he paused at an intersecting street and then turned, disappearing completely from view.

His task would be more challenging, but he knew he was better suited for it than Pendin. While his friend's knowledge of the streets in this part of town would be an advantage when trailing a Mage, silence was important if the other was truly Denraen.

Something about the encounter felt off. Endric couldn't say what it was that bothered him, but instinct hammered into him by years of his brother's training left him with a heightened sense of concern.

Endric felt his heart surge excitedly as he started down the street, and didn't think about what it meant. He was acutely aware of the thrill of the chase. His pounding heart and the nervous energy suffusing him were evidence to that. Distantly though, there was something more, yet he ignored it, focusing only on his quarry.

Passing through the square in silence, the worry over what would happen if Urik discovered he had ignored his order was pushed to the back of his mind. He could argue that he *was* patrolling. Perhaps not in the way Urik intended. Endric tried to shake his misgivings but knew the en'raen would be disappointed and wondered if he would be assigned more patrol. At the least, he would shield Pendin from trouble. Somehow.

Endric followed the path he imagined the other had taken. He wasn't sure why he felt the person was Denraen, but there was something familiar about the way he carried himself, something Endric was certain he had seen in his own training. Not from Andril. His brother was different than most of the Denraen, taught by their father and nearly his equal. This was something else.

The thought troubled him as he clung to the shadows, trailing the memory of the other figure. The streets had narrowed and, if possible, the lighting around him had grown more subdued. Nothing else moved along the street other than a gentle northern breeze. It blew in the stench from this part of the city and was harsh enough that he struggled to ignore it, stealing some of the focus he needed for the chase.

When he was nearly ready to turn back, a flicker of motion slipped around a corner in the distance. The corner was little more than a smudge along the street where shadows seemed to collide. He approached it carefully. Each step fell lightly, his footing cautious and slow so he didn't thud along the broken cobbles. There could be no misstep now.

Peering slowly around the corner, he realized he was on the edge of Stahline. The street widened here, and the shops along the street were different. The shops nearby were dark, but farther along, lanterns burned brightly. And cleanly. The shops were less worn. Bright paint marked the storefronts clearly. No garbage lay unattended. It was as if the people here were trying to look as unlike Stahline as possible.

The sudden change took him aback, if only briefly. Endric let his eyes

31

adjust as he stared cautiously down the street. Just because he neared the edge of Stahline didn't mean the danger had passed. He saw movement at the far end of the street but wasn't sure it was the same figure, though the street was otherwise empty.

But not silent. Sound drifted down the street as a mixture of faint noise, the melody of the night. Several taverns lined the street, and he could no longer be certain where the figure he had followed ended up. Perhaps the movement at the end of the street wasn't even the same person.

Endric closed his eyes and sighed, letting his sudden frustration wash away as he exhaled. The calming trick was one of many Andril had taught him, but it only partially worked.

Finally, he started out of the shadows and down the street, not trying to hide his presence but not announcing he was Denraen. Nothing else joined him as he moved along. It wasn't until he neared another intersection that he saw motion. He fought the urge to freeze and continued forward. His hand inched toward the hilt of his sword and his shoulders tensed. His heart hammered a little more quickly than necessary. Sweat beaded on his forehead although the night was otherwise cool.

He didn't know why he should be nervous, but instinct sent him warnings and Andril had taught him to pay attention to such things. He was on edge when the muted sound of running along the cobblestone street echoed back to him.

Endric quickened his pace. He wondered if the other was already aware of him. Running after would only announce his presence. The other was obviously trying to mask his running and doing so with a trick that was distinctively Denraen. The muffled steps were testament to that. No longer was there doubt that he trailed one of the Denraen. Now he only needed to know who he trailed.

Ignoring the noise emanating from the taverns, he focused on the sound ahead of him. He was able to filter it out and took side streets, hoping to head the other off or intercept him, but he never got any closer. Always, the sound stayed far ahead of him.

And then it was gone, stopped suddenly.

Endric froze, gripping his sword as he did. Waiting. Other than his careful breathing, no sound came.

He had been bested. There was no doubt in his mind that the other figure from the square in Stahline had realized he was followed. And was Denraen. He didn't know why one of the Magi would have a clandestine meeting with a Denraen in that part of the city. Some part of him warned that there was a larger plot going on. Perhaps something his father should know about.

Or did he already? Was that why his council had convened?

Endric hated having questions without answers. He started down the street, recognizing now where he was, and hoped Pendin had better luck.

CHAPTER 5

He didn't find Pendin back at the barracks.

Endric felt a moment of worry, thinking that it wouldn't have taken long to follow the Mage. Unless the Mage had taken some strange route, but there were few places the Magi visited, and Endric figured they would quickly return to the palace.

The huge palace of the Magi on the third terrace loomed over the barracks. When the clouds parted, you could often see the three towers topped by pointed spires framing the large central palace. Now, some thousand years after the first Magi appeared, it was still steeped in mystery, even to those who lived in the city. Perhaps more so.

Endric had never seen the inside, but it was said to be nearly the equal in craftsmanship to the Tower of the Gods in Thealon. Ordinarily, it was clearly built by lesser artisans, but the thin moonlight mixed with the faintly glowing stone of the palace, and low-hanging clouds appeared to circle the upper towers in such a way that tonight, he could believe it was.

"Thinking of the gods?"

Endric spun at the words. His hand squeezed his sword as he tensed. How could he have been so careless as to let someone sneak up on him? A shadowed figure stood nearby. Too tall and muscled to be the person he had been following but still, he felt stupid for his carelessness.

"Andril?" he asked. At least it had been one of the most skilled Denraen sneaking up on him. That still didn't change his irritation.

His brother stepped forward. In his uniform and with his sword, he looked every bit the fearsome en'raen. He didn't smile as he approached, and the shadows seemed to hang on and around him.

"You seem jumpy," Andril said.

Endric considered telling his brother what he had seen but decided against it. Andril would only chastise him for disobeying Urik's order. "It's nothing."

Andril tilted his head as he considered for a moment. Endric worried his brother would press him. He wouldn't lie to Andril.

Finally Andril shook his head. "It's late."

"Urik," he said in answer.

A tight smile crossed Andril's face and he snorted. "Perhaps he will be good for you."

Endric breathed out slowly. In the chill of the growing night, his breath was visible. "I could still go with you." Surely Urik would agree. If only Andril would.

Andril shook his head. "No." The word hung in the air longer than the breath it had taken to say it.

He wouldn't have his brother leave the city angry with him. Bad enough that he was leaving disappointed in him. He opened his mouth, and what came out was not what he intended. "Be careful, Andril."

"Just scouting. There should be no fighting."

Endric shook his head. "Not what I meant."

Andril watched him for a moment. "Do as Urik asks. Promise me you will learn what it means to be Denraen while I am gone."

"I know what Denraen means, Andril."

"Do you?" Andril stared at him a moment, then frowned and shook his head. "No. I don't think you yet understand."

"We are peacekeepers. Defending the Urmahne ideal. That is all." The gods knew there had been battles, though. The Denraen often moved in to settle disputes and too often had to wage war to end war. "Denraen means protector," Endric said. He was growing annoyed that his father and now

Andril thought he wouldn't know this. One thing his father made sure he knew, teaching much of it to him personally, was the ancient language. "The Denraen ensure and protect peace. We protect the Magi and the Urmahne gods they serve." He tried to keep the sarcasm from his voice as he spoke.

Andril didn't miss it though. "Father was right. You have much to learn." He raised a hand when Endric attempted to speak, cutting him off. "You're right. Denraen means protector. But there is more to it than that. The ancient language has many layers to it. In this case, protector is but one." He frowned at Endric, his face somehow managing to look just like their father's with the expression. Both now wore the same mask of disappointment. "Keep your eyes and mind open. Do as Urik asks and you will learn the true purpose of the Denraen."

As he started away, he paused to look back. His eyes flickered to the palace briefly before returning to focus on Endric again. He had stepped just far enough away that the shadows surrounding him made reading his expression difficult, casting a haunted look on his face.

For long moments, he said nothing. Then, finally, he broke the silence. "Know that I love you, brother. That will never change."

Then he turned and walked away, disappearing quickly and silently into the dark night.

Endric sighed and finally shook his head. At least he had not completely burned the bridge between him and Andril. Something good had come of this evening.

"You look lost."

Endric turned quickly, cursing himself again for lack of awareness. Pendin eyed him strangely. Though he respected Pendin, his friend still should not have been able to sneak up on him. That made twice tonight.

"Just distracted."

"Did you find him?"

Endric shook his head. "Followed him out of Stahline and then lost him. I think he knew he was followed."

Pendin took a step forward, moving into the pale light of the moon filtering through the heavy clouds overhead. His face was drawn and a troubled look furrowed his brow. He frowned and scratched a hand over his shaved head. "Do you think you were seen?"

Endric shrugged. "Not sure. Probably not, though I didn't disguise my presence. Would have been too hard." He let go of his frustration with a deep breath. "I think he just sensed something off. I know I did."

Pendin grunted. "Something *is* off here, Endric. I followed the Mage. Thought he would go to the palace and he did, just not straight away. Stopped in a small shop at the edge of town. Couldn't tell from the sign what it was."

"He? Did you get a look at his face?"

Pendin shook his head.

"What did you see?"

"Long face. Thin nose. Short hair. For the most part, they all look alike."

Pendin described everything that Endric had seen. He had not really expected Pendin to recognize the Mage; they didn't have enough interaction with the Magi for that. He had hoped for something more distinctive.

"Anything else?"

Pendin frowned again. "I don't know. His gray cloak had some darker stitching along the collar. Some pattern to it I couldn't make out."

Endric smiled. "That should help."

"Maybe you can ask Urik," Pendin suggested.

Endric groaned. "If Urik finds out, I'll be on patrol for the month."

"You mean *we* will be on patrol for a month. I was supposed to keep you in line."

Endric's face darkened. "Pendin…" He was unsure how to continue. "I'm sorry you were pulled into this because of me."

Pendin opened his mouth to say something but hesitated, finally shrugging. "If not patrol, then something else." When he started to object, Pendin cut him off. "Sometimes you worry too much."

Endric frowned.

Pendin laughed quietly. "I didn't say it was often." He glanced up at the cloudy sky. "So what do we do now?"

"Satisfy our curiosity?"

"How?"

Endric shrugged. "Learn which Magi we saw. Then track him to the Denraen."

"You make it sound easy."

"Isn't it?"

Pendin laughed. "I suppose I did gather critical information to make it a simple matter."

"Yeah. Because they all look alike."

Pendin shrugged. "Prove to me they don't."

He paused a moment as a muted sound broke the silence. It was the muffled sound of boots echoing off the stones, as if dulled by the night. Fog filtered down to settle upon the city as it did many nights; often, it was as if the clouds simply descended toward the mountain city. The heavy mist was thick and moist in the air, filling his nostrils with an earthy odor. The barracks were nearby but now obscured by the fog.

A pair of Denraen approached on patrol and nodded as they emerged from the fog into the wan moonlight. Endric recognized one of them. Tallin was a good soldier and had been friendly in the past. Now he simply nodded. Perhaps Endric's reputation had been sullied further. Or perhaps his father was right when he had said his protection would end. Either way, the Denraen patrol moved quickly down the street without pausing, disappearing back into the thickening fog.

"That was strange." Endric frowned at his friend.

Pendin just shrugged. "Word is out. Most know we're on patrol and what that means."

"How?" he asked, though he already knew. Little kept a soldier's tongue from wagging about one of their own. Especially one they felt received favored treatment.

"You couldn't keep your assignment to Urik quiet, Endric."

He sniffed and shook his head. "No. I suppose not." It didn't explain how word had spread so quickly. "I don't suppose Listain had anything to do with it?"

Pendin shrugged again. "Don't know." He paused and then smiled. "Probably. That would be the fastest way to get the word out."

And probably at his father's command. The Raen was connected better than any among the Denraen. And devious. They were the reasons he was so effective.

"I hope I can find Urik tomorrow," he said. "This patrol will make me crazy."

"Too late for that, I think," Pendin said. "For me too. What was I thinking listening to you when you suggested following one of the Magi?"

"Maybe you can get back to your assignment with Tildan soon. What were you doing there again?"

Pendin glared at him briefly. "I was assisting him with his command."

"You were assisting him with his laundry," Endric said and laughed. Before Pendin could say anything more, Endric grabbed his shoulder. "For your troubles tonight, let me buy the first round."

Pendin frowned at him another moment. "For that, you've got the first two rounds," he grumbled.

CHAPTER 6

The sound of muffled voices came through the stout door.

Endric stood just outside Urik's office with his hand raised to knock, but paused. If the en'raen had the door closed, he likely didn't want to be disturbed, yet patience was never a trait Endric had mastered. Always too eager and impulsive.

It had been an ongoing problem for him. His first lessons with the sword had come at his father's hand and had stopped because of that. The lessons were clear in his mind, even now. He had not known then that they would be the happiest memories he had of his father.

Endric had strength, but none of the other traits Dendril felt necessary to use that strength wisely. He was notoriously quick to anger and far too impulsive. That had led to more than a few incidents; his most recent jailing was but the latest. His father had tried to work with him but had given up. Andril had tried to teach him by example. Endric had been stubborn and ignored the lesson until it was too late. Now his brother was unwilling to teach him as well.

But he remembered what his father had tried to teach as his hand paused in front of Urik's door. Patience. Think about the long-term plan. It was something he had never mastered, unable—or unwilling—to look beyond the short term.

As the thoughts rolled through his head, one of the voices became clearer. He recognized the deep tenor as Urik, and there was a sense of irritation to his tone. The words were still muffled and unintelligible, but Endric knew something was off. A feeling at the pit of his stomach warned him that he didn't want to be there when the conversation ended.

Endric slipped carefully down the hall, keeping one eye toward the door, his curiosity aroused. Urik's rooms were near the end of a hall, and he turned down one of the intersecting corridors, intending to slip away completely. Yet he paused. He didn't know what it was that made him pause, and later wouldn't know whether to be thankful or to curse.

Peering around the corner, he saw the door open. The hall was dimly lit with a single sconce, and only a little light spilled out from the open door. A cloaked man emerged, carrying a small box. Something reflected strangely from its surface, almost writhing in the shadowed light. Endric blinked, uncertain what he was seeing, but the image passed. The man carrying it was short and lean, and his dark hair was kept long. He quickly slipped the box under his cloak, and it disappeared completely.

The man made his way down the hall, away from Endric. His eyes darted from doorway to doorway as he slipped soundlessly away, nearly fading into the shadows between the sconces. Endric watched him, and the man looked over suddenly and stared into Endric's eyes, quickly appraising and dismissing him.

The experience was unsettling. Rarely had Endric been so summarily discounted as a threat. He stood frowning as the man disappeared around a corner in the corridor and was startled by a firm hand upon his shoulder.

"Endric."

He turned, his head clearing from the lapse. This was becoming a problematic trend for him. "Who is that?" he asked without preamble.

Urik grunted in a clearing of his throat. "That is for the council to discuss."

Endric opened his mouth to reply but reconsidered and closed it. He already feared upsetting Urik and didn't want to start the conversation on the wrong foot. The questions about the box he kept to himself.

The irritation he'd heard in Urik's voice through the door was plain upon his face. His forehead was lined. His eyes, usually flat and dull, blazed with another emotion Endric was unaccustomed to seeing in Urik—anger. Again, he wondered who the visitor had been.

"Sorry Urik," Endric said, trying to sound contrite. He wasn't sure he succeeded.

Urik's face softened and his mouth turned in a half smile. The irritation lining his forehead faded and he snorted as he shook his head. "What do you want?" Urik asked as the en'raen put his hand under Endric's elbow and guided him down the hall back toward his office.

Once inside, Endric's strange unease began to fade. It was as if the closing of the door closed the emotion Urik's visitor had evoked. Until it was gone, he had not been aware of what he had felt. Now it was like an irritant suddenly relieved, an itch that had been scratched. Endric looked at the door as if he could see through it, wondering what about the man had left him feeling as he did.

"Endric?" Urik said.

"I was to have found you after three days," he answered.

Urik narrowed his eyes briefly. "It has been five."

Endric nodded, forcing himself to keep his attention on Urik.

"What did you do the last two?"

"Patrol," he answered, hoping to keep the annoyance he felt from his tone. Urik arched an eyebrow and Endric shrugged. "I couldn't find you, so figured I would continue with my assignment until I did."

Urik nodded slowly. "Uneventful, I hope."

"For the most part," he answered. He had not decided how much to tell Urik of what he had seen, fearing that he would get additional patrol assignment for abandoning patrol for his own curiosity.

"Only most?"

Endric blinked slowly, cursing himself. "We patrolled Stahline," he said carefully.

A strange flicker of emotion crossed Urik's eyes. "What happened?"

Endric inhaled deeply, deciding to keep to the truth. At least part of it. For now, he would leave out the fact that he had followed someone he thought Denraen. "We saw one of the Magi while patrolling in Stahline."

Urik grunted and turned away, taking his seat behind his desk. "The Magi do live in the city, Endric." There was a hint of annoyance to his tone.

"I was surprised that I would find one of the Magi in that part of the city. At night," he finished.

Urik paused from shuffling through some of his papers and stared at one for a moment. "We do not keep tabs on the Magi," he said without looking up. "Is that all?"

The en'raen continued his deliberate sorting of papers, and Endric worried that he'd caught the man at the wrong time. More patrol, then. Pendin wouldn't be pleased.

"It appeared as if he was meeting with someone," he continued.

Urik looked up slowly and frowned. "The Magi may meet with whomever they please, Endric. Careful that you do not offend them."

Endric shook his head. This was not going well at all. "I wouldn't do that," he started. At least not intentionally. "I know the Denraen serve the Magi."

"Serve the Magi?" Urik asked, setting aside his papers and fixing Endric with his full attention. "Is that what you think?"

Endric shrugged nervously. All he cared about now was getting his next assignment. Somehow, he had already upset Urik, and each comment only made it worse.

Urik leaned forward. "The Denraen do not serve the Magi. We serve the same ideals." A hint of annoyance edged his hard tone. "There are many things we share with the Magi. According to tradition, the council must even approve the selection of general, though there has never been a dispute. But we do not *serve* them. It's a shame you of all people feel that way, though I am unsurprised." He paused a moment, considering. "Let me phrase it in a way you might appreciate. We are like two soldiers advancing in different regiments. Same objective. Different trajectory."

Endric felt a moment of surprise. If they didn't serve the Magi, then nothing was done to change that perception. Perhaps there was another reason for that. He hesitated to say anything more but knew Urik wouldn't accept silence. "What objective, then?"

Urik grunted, then glanced down as he spoke, thumbing through his papers absently. He settled back in his chair and rubbed his temple, scrubbing at his close-cropped hair for a moment before putting his hand over his mouth while he thought, as if debating how much to say. "The answer to that question requires that you remember the origins of the Magi."

"The Magi settled in the city nearly one thousand years ago," Endric answered. "The thirteen founders were the first priests of the Urmahne."

Urik nodded slightly. "Spoken like someone raised within the city walls."

Endric sensed a hidden insult but was uncertain what it meant.

"You speak the old tongue?" Urik asked.

Endric nodded carefully.

"Then you know the meaning of the word *Urmahne*." He said the word with a strange inflection.

"Most take it to mean peace," Endric answered.

"Most?"

Endric shrugged, feeling uncertain. "The old tongue is complex. A single word can mean many things," he said. "I only know one translation for *Urmahne* though."

Urik tilted his head. "As far as most know, there is but one translation."

Endric spoke without thinking. "Is there another meaning?"

Urik smiled then, barely a flash of teeth. "The true meaning has been lost with time. Most assume *Urmahne* translates like other, similar words, but there are those who wonder if its original definition wasn't something different." His eyes were bright as he spoke. They reflected the light from the brightly burning lamp sitting upon his desk, but there was something more as well. An intensity that surprised Endric. "None can say with certainty, though there are scholars who still debate this."

"Who but the Magi study the ancient language?"

Urik narrowed his eyes as a flicker of darkness crossed through them. "The Magi are not the only scholars, Endric. Pursuing knowledge is man's obligation, our duty, to the gods. Know that there are many seekers of knowledge, and not all are as benevolent as the Magi or the guild."

He shook his head, fearing upsetting Urik but not following. "The guild?"

"The Guild of Historians."

"Most historians I've met use their studies as an excuse for free passage," he said. A few had even been smart enough to hide that fact. "None seemed particularly interested in study."

Urik blinked. "Too many claim membership to the guild where none has been granted. That has weakened what was once a powerful alliance of scholars."

His words seemed to come out with a little more venom than he had intended. Urik leaned back and inhaled deeply. "Once, the historians were respected, wise. Kings sought the council of the greatest historians. Some historians even traveled here." Endric frowned. "Yes, to this city. The historians and the Magi scholars often worked together, poring over some of the oldest texts. The Magi trusted the historians with some of their greatest works, and the reverse was often true as well."

Urik hesitated, a distant expression clouding his face. "That was the respect the guild wielded. There has not been a historian in the city since before you were born." He shook his head. "When I was young, we used to look forward to their visits, knowing we would be regaled with their stories. The historians were travelers and saw and heard much. For that, they stayed for free. And I never once saw one pay for his food. So that much of their reputation is earned. But so too are other aspects."

Endric waited for him to elaborate, but he didn't.

"But we were speaking of the Magi, not the historians. That is a different story, though in some respects no less interesting."

"Why?" he asked, wondering suddenly about Urik's life before the Denraen.

"The Guild of Historians has nearly as interesting a history as the Magi. And nearly as much mystery. Few are granted access to the guild or its resources. Many have tried and failed. Now most simply claim membership where none has been granted." He narrowed his eyes again, a hint of anger edging his tone. "They are little more than simple thieves, taking shelter and food from those who don't know better."

"If those posing as guild members have weakened the guild, why do they not take action? Have some sort of marker of membership?"

Urik sighed. "That is not their way. The guild is comprised of scholars. Historians. Seekers of knowledge. Any sort of action is viewed as unnecessary and beneath them."

"Does this not cause them to lose respect? Since I have never seen a historian in the city, it implies the Magi feel the same."

"There are other reasons the historians haven't traveled to the city that have little to do with the respect the Magi have for them."

He didn't elaborate and Endric didn't press. "How do you know so much about them?" he asked, fearing it sounded like an accusation.

Urik considered the question for a moment before answering. "I lived for many years in Voiga. During that time, historians traveled through those lands."

"Why?"

"For many reasons, though there was only one primary purpose."

When Urik said nothing more, Endric pressed. "What was that?"

"The same reason your father sent Andril south," Urik said. He had been looking down at his desk as he spoke, but looked up with the words, his eyes suddenly hard. He studied Endric's face, watching his expression, before glancing back down.

Endric knew little of why his brother had been sent south. Olin had mentioned some kind of warrior priests, but he saw little reason historians would be interested in that. Cults cropped up periodically, and a few gathered significant followers. None had ever threatened the Urmahne. And certainly none had ever threatened the Denraen.

"Andril didn't mention any reason for his mission," Endric said.

"Why should he?"

That the comment was true made it sting no less.

Urik looked up again, closing his eyes a moment. "We were speaking of the Magi, the first of which were the founders. All that we know of the Magi today comes from them. Creators of the Urmahne. Gifted with abilities that no man could claim. A claim to the ability to speak with the gods." He glanced at one of the sculptures on his shelf before continuing. "This lends authority to the Urmahne tenets they taught, that are said to be handed down from the gods themselves."

Urik turned, staring at the wall behind him, as if he could see through it and all the way to the palace. "The Magi taught man about the Urmahne, and the Council of the Magi has always led them, serving as a guidepost for the rest of the Magi. They are among the most powerful and influential Magi, and chosen for this reason."

"How are they chosen?"

Urik shook his head. "Few outside the Magi could answer that, and I am not among them." He shrugged. "Most among the council have lived their entire lives within the city walls. Few venture out and see the world the rest of us live in, preferring to hear secondhand reports."

"Most?"

A small smile threatened Urik's lips. "There is one on the council now who once lived in Voiga. Even served as the teacher in the city." From his tone, it was clear that Urik found it both odd and impressive. "He is known now as Tresten."

"What was he known as?" he asked, finding Urik's phrasing odd.

Urik met his eyes. "He has gone by many names during his time. I have known him as Tresten for as long as I can remember."

"Do you know him well?" Endric asked, wondering if it had been Urik meeting with Tresten that he and Pendin had come across. "You said you once lived in Voiga."

Urik shook his head. "Few can make that claim. He is old, nearly the eldest. Once, he was among the few Magi who traveled. Now he stays within the palace." He paused to look down to the parchment he had grabbed before setting it aside. "Though I have lived in Voiga, we were not there at the same time."

"What brought you to the Denraen?" Something at the back of Endric's mind warned him to be careful. Instinct. Though he didn't understand why he should feel the warning, he trusted it.

Urik looked up and frowned. "I saw injustice. In my previous position, there was little I could do. Serving the Denraen changed that. The Denraen serve the greater good, foster the same peace the Urmahne teach. That is what we share with the Magi. That is why I joined."

"You weren't a soldier before you joined?" he asked, struggling to keep the surprise out of his voice.

Urik nodded. "I had been a soldier. Once. I had served my nation for the required term but left." He frowned. "When I was young, I thought differently than I do now, thought there were other avenues than violence. I understand now that sometimes the threat of force is the best deterrent."

Endric stared for a moment, taken aback. He had known Urik had been chosen years ago and had worked his way up through the Denraen ranks quickly, but had assumed he had been a lifelong soldier. How else to explain such a rapid ascent?

"What did you do before joining the Denraen? How were you chosen?"

Urik shrugged and remained silent for a dozen heartbeats, leaving Endric wondering if he would answer at all. Finally he did, answering only the second question.

"There was a choosing. They are not closed to outsiders—that, too, is tradition. I had not really expected to be chosen, yet Tordal saw something and now..." He shrugged again. "Now here I am. Nearly fifteen years later." His expression turned distant again. "Not where I thought I would be when I was your age."

Endric glanced around the office again and noticed a small bowl in the far corner. He didn't need to inspect it to see that it was made of unadorned stone. A simple wall carving was nearly obscured by a bulging shelf, and he suspected it depicted one of the huge trefoil leaves found at the heart of the Great Forest. The vague painting of clouds over mountaintops that hung on the inside of his office door took on new meaning.

What did it mean that Urik was a devout Urmahne?

He caught Endric looking and stood slowly. "I think I have said enough for today." He started toward his office door, pushing Endric in front of him. "And it seems from your question about the Magi that we still must work on the ideals of the Denraen."

At the door, Endric paused, waiting for his next assignment, feeling dread building.

"It seems patrol has served you well," Urik continued, "forcing you to ask some of the most basic questions one of the Denraen should ask." A hint of a smile darkened his face. "Find Calnin. He will be expecting you for patrol this evening."

CHAPTER 7

"What did you do to upset Calnin?" Pendin asked as they stood outside the barracks.

The hazy gray daylight common to the mountain city didn't make this part of the city any more welcoming. Strange shadows still shifted and slid across the street, almost as if intentionally keeping the area darkened. The inky oil lamps hanging along the street did little more than thicken the haze, creating a wispy veil of malodorous smoke.

Pendin continued, "He seemed quite pleased with your assignment."

Endric looked over at his friend. "You mean you're not?" He tried to keep the question light but couldn't keep the strain from his voice.

Pendin frowned and didn't look over. "More patrol in Stahline. I'm beginning to think I'm being punished for knowing you."

Endric sighed. "I'm sorry, Pendin."

Pendin shrugged, the movement a slight heave of his broad shoulders. "At least it's daytime."

They walked in silence, their boots clomping along the stone. They rarely saw another person, and those they did see quickly turned and ran. Probably to warn any others that a Denraen patrol neared.

"Did you know the Magi confirmed the selection of general?" Endric asked, breaking the silence.

Pendin glanced over at him and frowned. "They do? I thought the council chose the general."

Endric shrugged. "They do, but the Magi approve it. Urik mentioned it yesterday."

Pendin narrowed his eyes. "Before or after he gave you this plum assignment?"

"Before, I think. And it was Calnin who gave us this assignment."

"But Urik that assigned patrol."

Endric nodded once, not wanting to argue. "That means my father was confirmed by the Magi."

Pendin grunted. "If you two could ever remember you're father and son, you might have learned that. Maybe we wouldn't have to be on patrol. And maybe you could have served under Andril. And maybe—"

"Maybe I could have done many things differently. I don't think it would have mattered to him. He blames me for my mother leaving. Probably Andril does as well." Endric blinked slowly, telling himself it was the smoky air that bothered his eyes. "At least Andril is more like him. Even looks like him." He shook his head. "I'm not like my father at all. Just a constant reminder of her absence."

Pendin slowed and turned to him. "Endric..."

Endric took a deep breath, pushing the dark thoughts away. "I'm sure Andril knows all about my father's promotion," he said softly. "But I do not."

Pendin watched him for a moment before they started off again. "I just don't know what it's like to have family and not even speak to them."

"And you're still so close to yours?" Endric asked.

Pendin nodded. "I still see them," he said quietly.

Endric fell silent. The admission was more than he usually got from Pendin. "How do they feel about you serving the Denraen?" he finally asked.

Pendin shrugged and said nothing. For a while, Endric figured that was all the response he would get.

"My parents pushed me to leave Stahline," he said. "For a time, I worked the mines. In Stahline, everyone works the mines. That wasn't the life my parents wanted for me. Or my sister." His voice fell off toward the end. "I got out. She didn't."

"She's a miner?" Endric asked. He didn't think many women worked the mines.

"Not anymore," he said, his words soft and laced with a hint of pride. "Seamstress now. Doesn't pay much, but enough."

"What did she do in the mines?"

Pendin looked over and frowned. "Women can only work cart or candles in the mine. Laboring is left to the men." He paused, shaking his head. "Teralin mining is dangerous work. Not just the heat of the ore, though scorchers have killed many a miner. Air will sometimes suck from the caverns, suffocating you. And sometimes mines just collapse suddenly."

Endric shivered, thinking about the different dangers of the mines and suddenly thankful for the relative safety of the Denraen.

Pendin shook his head. "Now I don't think I could even go back in. Once, I thought nothing of it."

"Why would you have to go back in?" Endric asked.

Pendin didn't answer and Endric didn't press.

They turned a corner where the shadows deepened. Their boots echoed strangely, and after only a few steps, Endric heard a sound behind him. He stopped and turned quickly, hand falling to the hilt of his sword. Pendin took a few more steps before he realized Endric had stopped.

The street was empty. Most of them had been, but he *had* heard something.

Endric took a few steps in the direction they had come, sliding carefully and with all the silence he could manage. The shadows seemed to deepen and the air around him seemed darker. Thicker and almost inky.

A sense of nausea in the pit of his stomach returned. Unsheathing his sword as quietly as possible, he swiveled his head as he searched for movement. Anything that would explain what he'd heard.

"Endric?" Pendin asked but saw the naked steel in Endric's hand and unsheathed his own sword.

Endric answered with a single shake of his head. Pendin understood and fell silent. They moved carefully, their steps muted, until they reached a small alley. Endric paused and cocked his head, listening. Something was off, though he couldn't yet put his finger on it.

Then he heard it. Soft. More like a hiss than anything. He turned to face the sound with his sword held steadily in front of him.

"Show yourself," he demanded. He put all the authority of the Denraen into his voice, and even Pendin glanced over at him.

There was nothing for long moments. Finally he heard a quiet laugh that sounded like stone squealing across stone. A dark figure stepped from the shadows of the alley. A long cloak covered his face and was pulled tight around his waist. Another figure followed, shorter and thinner. Neither appeared armed.

"What business do you have here?" Endric challenged. Seeing a cloaked figure a second time on patrol seemed a strange coincidence. At least this one didn't appear to be Denraen. Or Magi.

The figure in the cloak pulled back the hood, and Endric frowned as recognition dawned on him. It was the miner who had attacked him in the tavern. Though the man was unarmed, Endric still tensed a bit when he realized who it was.

"You."

The man nodded and his mouth opened in a sneer.

"What business do you have here?" he repeated.

The miner snorted. "I need no business."

His voice was rougher than Endric remembered and sounded as if he had been screaming for days. "Are you following us?"

"Why would I follow Denraen?" He spat the last word.

"We're tasked with keeping peace along these streets," Pendin said.

"And we are here peacefully."

"I doubt that," Pendin suggested, his tone hard and edged with a hint of anger.

The miner leaned back and pushed up the sleeves of his robe, revealing the strange tattoos once more. Again they appeared to swirl as if alive, though Endric was sure it was just the way the light filtered through the streetlamp smoke. They were more extensive than the last time he had seen the man, nearly blackening his arms. His neck appeared tattooed as well, though he couldn't be certain.

"Did you enjoy your night in jail, Denraen?" he asked, again spitting the last word. Then he smiled, his yellowed and pointed teeth making it look like the snarl of a wild boar. He turned away from Pendin, ignoring him completely, and focused on Endric, who blinked and tried hard to keep emotion off his face.

Somehow, this miner knew what had happened after their fight. It was a fight that should not have gone on nearly as long as it had. No miner should be able to move the way this man had.

"Did you enjoy your beating?" the miner asked softly.

With that question, Endric knew who had ambushed him when he tried to leave the tavern. "At least I wasn't beaten in a fair fight."

The miner's dark eyes fell on him with a nearly palpable weight. "It will not happen again," he said. The hoarseness in his voice turned it into a growl.

"No. It won't," Endric agreed, resisting the urge to thrash the man again. There was no doubting what his punishment would be for fighting with the miner again.

The miner narrowed his eyes a moment and then laughed a low and harsh laugh. "No? Then perhaps you're afraid."

"And why should he fear you?" Pendin asked.

The miner slid his gaze over to Pendin and a dark smile crossed his face. "Answers will come soon enough, traitor," he promised.

"Whatever you think you will accomplish will fail," Pendin said as he took a step forward. For a moment, Endric feared he would attack.

The miner laughed again, the harsh sound grating. "You know nothing of what will be accomplished." The man smiled, his pointed teeth bared like a snarl.

Pendin started forward and Endric put an arm up to restrain him. "Go," he said to the miner. "Or I will have every right to detain you. Forcibly."

The miner sneered. "You can try."

"Go!" Endric said and raised his sword.

The miner glared at the blade a moment. "Another time, Denraen," he spat. Then he turned back down the alley.

The smaller person with him had remained silent but had lowered the hood of their cloak at some point. Endric glanced over and recognized them as the other person from the tavern, the thin one who'd left immediately. He had taken the person for a boy but realized from the full lips and slightly rounded frame that it was a girl. Thin and plain-looking, she wore her short-cropped hair tangled and unkempt. Only her dark eyes were remarkable, staring intently at him for a long moment before she turned and followed the other miner.

Endric inhaled deeply and shook his head. Sheathing his sword, he asked, "Did he come only to taunt me?"

Pendin stared after the miner for a moment. "I'm not sure that was all there was to it."

Endric flicked his gaze back to the alley. He saw nothing but darkness and hazy smoke. "What else is there? Does it have to do with him calling you a traitor?"

Pendin shook his head but didn't meet his eyes. "I'm not sure," he admitted. "My family won't speak of it. Especially to me."

Endric narrowed his eyes. "What does that mean?"

Pendin shrugged. "I didn't think much of it until…" He motioned after the departed miner. "With his comments, I'm forced to believe the miners are up to something."

"Your family won't speak of it?"

Pendin shook his head. "I can't ask them to. The miners can be a closed community. Sharing something like I've heard is a sure path to retribution."

"What have you heard?" Endric asked, not wanting to know what sort of retribution the miners would exact.

Pendin hesitated. "Rumors—probably nothing to them—suggest some of the miners are organizing. Threatening some kind of revolt."

Endric looked at his stout friend. The light cast strange shadows across his face, leaving the long scar along his cheek looking more pronounced. "What would a revolt achieve? Couldn't the Magi just find replacements?"

"Not without effort. Teralin is not easily mined and takes a certain skill to extract."

He believed that, especially after what Pendin had said of the dangers of mining. "What do they want?"

Pendin shook his head. "Don't know. Better wages? Shorter days? It's dangerous work, Endric."

He paused and grunted, careful he didn't say anything that would upset Pendin. "What could they do anyway?"

"Withhold the teralin."

Endric met Pendin's eyes and knew his friend was serious. He knew the man well enough not to ask how he had heard these rumors. Not from his family, but Pendin's hesitation to speak told him enough. "Why would that work?"

"You know that teralin is found in only a few places. We sit atop the home to one of the largest known deposits. Probably *the* largest. The ore can be found elsewhere, but never in the quantities found in the city, and never as pure."

The ore was important to the Magi. They claimed it necessary to help them speak to the gods. None but the Magi knew whether that was true.

But if it was withheld?

A thin smile pulled at his lips. "Clever."

Pendin looked at him and shook his head. "Not clever. Dangerous."

"Why? Because the Magi will have to go without?" He shrugged. "The strategy might work."

Pendin's eyes narrowed and hardened, and he held Endric in his gaze. "The Magi won't stand for a disruption in the teralin."

"Then what?"

"Who do you think will be asked to solve it?"

Endric didn't have to think long. The Denraen would be asked to step in. If that happened, a confrontation and outright fighting was likely to result. Miners would be hurt or killed.

He couldn't help but remember that the tattooed miner had a strange arrogance. Was there more to this than Pendin knew? More than he was letting on?

"It won't come to that," Endric said.

Pendin looked down the alley. There was no movement. Nothing but shadows and darkness. "I had not thought so," he said, then shook his head. His broad face was drawn and tight with worry. "Now I'm not so sure."

CHAPTER 8

They finished their patrol without any further excitement.

Pendin became more withdrawn and quiet, and Endric didn't bother him. Pendin was already disturbed by the encounter with the miner, enough so that his brow remained furrowed and the scar on his cheek contorted. Whatever role his family would play in the planned revolt clearly worried him.

The conversation with the miner had soured Endric's mood as well. Patrol alone was punishment enough, but patrolling Stahline was more than degrading. Then to have Pendin drawn into it…

Endric didn't know what Urik intended him to learn on patrol or what his intent was in forcing his friend to accompany him. As bad as Listain would have been, this seemed somehow worse, more devious.

And there was nothing he could do about it.

They were near the barracks when the rain came, making him even more angry. The sky darkened quickly and distant peals of thunder rolled toward the mountain like a drum signaling an attack. Sharp needles of cold rain struck in a sudden torrent. A violent shiver overcame him. The rain seemed to awaken Pendin, and he shrugged. Endric frowned at him a moment, then ran toward the entrance to the Denraen great hall.

Inside, he shook off the rain. An uneasy feeling gnawed at his stomach, made all the worse by the strange energy emanating from inside the barracks great room.

Usually it was full of noise and chatter from men just off patrol. Tonight was different. Conversation was muted. Many were silent. Most among the Denraen disliked the frequent rains of the city, but this silence was more than he could explain by the weather. All looked up when he came in and stared at him for long moments.

"What happened?" he wondered aloud, looking for a familiar face to ask.

It took a few moments, but he saw Senda sitting in a corner near the door. She held a book, but she didn't appear to be actually reading it, and she stood as soon as she saw them. Almost as if she had been waiting for them, though Endric had never known Senda to wait for any man. She hurried over to them, leaving her staff leaning against the wall.

Endric frowned as she approached. "What's wrong?" he asked without preamble.

She shook her head with barely more than a slight twitch. "See Dendril, Endric."

He narrowed his eyes. "What is it? What did I do?" Andril had said the miner was the son of a Mage. Endric wouldn't put it past him to claim insult. Dendril had little reason to believe Endric's innocence.

She shook her head more emphatically. "Please." A pleading note entered her voice.

Endric's pulse quickened. Senda never pleaded. Something was very wrong. "Senda?"

"Don't make me be the one to tell you. See your father."

He watched her for a moment more before turning and leaving the great hall. He said nothing to her or Pendin. His heart had started to hammer in his chest, and a cold sweat erupted on his brow. He brought an arm across his forehead and wiped a mix of rain and sweat away. The walk down the hall to his father's office seemed to take forever. He resisted the urge to run. Or turn away.

Endric didn't know what could have happened. A new worry struck him as he considered Senda's words, her tone. What else could there be? Could something have happened to his father? He'd served as general for years and was still a relatively young man, but still…

By the time he reached the heavy door to the general's office, his heart was pounding so loudly, he could hear it. The man posted at the door frowned at him for a moment, then nodded to the door. It was uncommon to see someone standing guard, though not unheard of. He knocked once.

"Enter."

The voice behind the door sounded weary and tight. Endric was not sure it was his father until he pushed open the door and saw the man was alone. His face was more wrinkled than he remembered. His normally bright and piercing eyes were dull. He stood behind his desk, staring at a brown sack upon it. Otherwise, he didn't move.

Dendril flicked his gaze up when Endric entered. "Endric," he said, then looked back down to the sack sitting on his desk. He closed his eyes and inhaled deeply. When he opened them, he was suddenly the same cold general he had always been. "Endric," he said again.

Endric walked carefully into the room, fearful of what brought him here. His father looked otherwise well, answering at least one of his questions.

That didn't stop his heart from pounding. Nearing the desk, he said, "General. I was told to report. What is it?"

He trailed off as he noticed what was in the sack on the desk. He saw hair matted with old, congealed blood. A head.

He looked up at his father, swallowing hard. "Who is it?"

His father shook his head once. "Endric," he repeated, as if unable to say anything else.

"Who is it?" he asked again. The intensity in his voice was unintentional.

He suddenly knew why Senda had met him at the door and why the men in the great hall had been so quiet. And his heart pounded so hard, it threatened to leap out of his chest. Nausea began building in the pit of his stomach. Everything around him grew muted and distant.

"Father?" he asked. His voice was no more than a whisper.

His father closed his eyes. "I am sorry, Endric. It's Andril."

CHAPTER 9

Endric fought back the tears that threatened to well up. The general wouldn't see weakness from him. Not this man who had rarely been more than the Denraen general to him. Nevertheless, he struggled to hide the tide of emotion threatening to sweep through him as he felt the last remnants of his true family stolen from him.

The brown sack pulled his attention, and bile rose in his stomach. Somehow he averted his gaze from the horror the sack held. He fixed his gaze instead on the sword Trill mounted on the far wall. Strangely, Endric suddenly wondered when the sword had last been taken out of its decorative holder. As far as he knew, his father had not seen battle in many years. He now sat comfortably behind his desk and sent his soldiers out to die. Like his brother.

Unintentionally, his hand reached his sword and he squeezed the hilt.

Andril.

His brother was gone. Only his head remained. His throat swelled with the thought.

A sense of hopelessness seeped into him. All that he was, he attributed to his brother. He had been the steady influence Endric's entire life. His mentor. Teaching him much more than how to wield a sword. Endric had brushed so many lessons off, not wanting to be the clone of their father that Andril often threatened to become. Still, there had been differences between them. Slight, but important.

How could something have happened to Andril?

"What happened?" Endric demanded. His voice was hoarse and he coughed. It kept him from breaking down. He took a deep breath and noticed a musty odor. It was a distraction from thinking about Andril.

Dendril looked at him carefully. His eyes flashed with cold fury for a moment before it faded and they became dull again. His cheeks fell slack and even his beard seemed to sag. The change was brief. A moment later, he took a deep breath and frowned, his face firming and his eyes narrowing.

"He's gone."

Endric squeezed the hilt of his sword. "I can see that, Father!" Tears streamed now. He didn't want to look at the sack but couldn't take his eyes away. He made no effort to wipe his tears. Let his father know that he hurt. "What happened?" The last was nearly a scream.

The door to the general's office opened slightly, and the Denraen standing guard peeked inside and was waved away by his father. Dendril didn't meet Endric's gaze and said nothing. Instead, he carefully picked up the sack—what was left of Andril—and set it on a nearby table. Endric watched, unable to speak. His hand hurt from clutching his sword. Distantly he felt a strange sense of relief that his father had not set Andril on the floor.

"Father." Rage was still in Endric's voice, but he spoke in a whisper. Anger surged through him, hot and steady, such that he nearly shook with it. Endric's breath quickened as he forced it back, struggling to clear his mind. He would learn what happened. He would learn who was responsible.

And they would suffer.

Dendril moved back to the desk and sat. The papers atop the desk were smeared with blood that had seeped from the sack. Dendril moved them carefully to the side. Then, with his desk in order, he met Endric's eyes.

"I'm sorry, Endric. He's gone." He sighed. His face again softened for a moment.

"I need to know what happened."

Dendril shook his head. "Need?"

He glared at his father. "Who did this?"

Dendril turned away and inhaled deeply, resting his large arms on the desk. "Does it matter? Your brother is gone, Endric. Mourn him."

"Of course it matters!" he screamed. "He was my brother! I will know what happened!"

"Why should you know what only the council has been told?"

The question hurt more than any sword could, the implication clear.

Endric's gaze was pulled back to Andril's head. Hollow eyes stared lifelessly from his head. Even in death, Andril seemed to admonish him for arguing with their father.

"He was my brother," he said with a little less venom.

"And my son. You think I do not hurt as well?" he asked, his voice rising slightly before he composed himself and closed the sack, covering Andril's head. "But he was Denraen. Mourn him as a soldier. It is what he would want. What he would expect."

Endric looked over at his father and hesitated. Dendril admitted his pain. Suddenly, the rage in him began to slip. His father was right. Andril was Denraen. He would want to be mourned like any other. The Denraen would continue without him.

He slumped into a chair across from the desk, putting him closer to Andril's severed head. Moments passed. His father said nothing and Endric didn't hide the tears.

As the anger started to disperse, turning into tears and sorrow, he began thinking more clearly. "Why send you his head?"

Dendril sat back in his chair and closed his eyes for a long moment. "He was your brother. Maybe it's right that you should know." He paused and glanced over to the table where Andril's head sat.

"This was a message," Endric said as the realization hit him.

Dendril nodded once, staring past Endric. "Andril was sent south. It was to be intelligence gathering only. He should not have met resistance."

"The warrior priests," Endric said, remembering what Olin had said. Even Andril had seemed hesitant before he left, and Endric wondered if he had known.

Dendril blinked. "Yes. They call themselves Deshmahne."

Endric frowned, translating the word from the ancient language. The name itself was a mockery to the Urmahne priests. Perhaps that was the point. "Deshmahne?" he repeated. "That is what Andril was sent to investigate?" How could his brother be killed investigating priests?

Dendril nodded and considered Endric for a long moment. "What I will tell you now is known only to the council. It is only because of Andril that you will hear these words." He paused, letting the words hang in the air. "It will not pass beyond you."

Endric nodded, afraid to say anything that would change his father's mind.

"What we have is mostly conjecture." The words were clipped. "Andril was led to intervene on behalf of the Deshmahne priests. Last we heard from his men, he had neared the southern border of Gomald. They were to cross Coamdon and into Voiga, where the priests have built their temple. Sometime before they could reach Coamdon, they were killed."

"All of them?" Endric couldn't help but be shocked. The idea that Andril was dead was hard enough to fathom, but losing two hundred Denraen was harder still.

A single nod was his response.

"Was it Gomald?" The king had caused trouble for the Denraen in the past but had never been openly confrontational. And Endric doubted Gomald would kill a Denraen squad.

"Not Gomald."

"How certain are you?"

Dendril turned back to him and stared. "Quite."

Listain then. The spymaster had ears everywhere and certainly had infiltrated the local militia. What more did Senda know?

"Then who did this?"

Dendril shook his head. "We do not know. It is unusual to hear so little."

That meant even Listain couldn't glean information. If that was true, it was certainly worrisome. He didn't know what that meant. "There are suspicions."

Dendril nodded. "Rumors point in only one direction. The Deshmahne."

"The priests. That is not possible."

"It is entirely possible."

Endric's mind raced. That priests would dare attack the Denraen shocked him. That his father sat here so calmly shocked him more. "When do we attack?"

He needed to be part of that mission. Would Urik allow him to go or would he be held back, stuck on patrol, trying to learn the ideals of the Denraen?

Dendril looked at Andril's head again before answering. "Action will be taken, but first we must learn more."

"But this was an act of war!" he said, surprised by his father's comments. Surely he wanted vengeance as well!

He shook his head. "It is not that simple," Dendril said, as if explaining to a child. "Over two hundred Denraen lost. We need to know how and why before we plan any counterattack. There may be powers at play we do not fully understand."

"They are priests, not Magi." Endric felt the anger that had faded begin to return.

"Priests have their own type of power. They use influence and manipulation." He paused, as if considering whether to share the next. "There are rumors that these Deshmahne are more than just a simple cult. We cannot plan our next move without knowing more."

"But this was Andril!"

Dendril stood. Fury raged across his face. Endric barely looked at him before backing down. His father leaned on his desk, and his thick arms tightened.

"The Denraen are about more than Andril," Dendril said. He didn't raise his voice, and it made the words all the more menacing. He shook his head. "You still do not understand."

Dendril inhaled deeply and glanced again at the sack that held Andril's head. He stared silently for a long moment, frowning. When he turned back to face Endric, his eyes were drawn. He shook his head. "I was mistaken in telling you."

Endric saw the conviction in his eyes. There was disgust written there as well. Other emotions warred deeper behind his flat gaze, but Endric didn't know the man well enough to read them.

"Go. Mourn your brother as you would any of your Denraen brothers. Then report to Urik." He let out a controlled breath. "I believe he has you on patrol. That will continue for now." He sat down at his desk and pulled a stack of papers in front of him. As he started to thumb through them, he said, "Dismissed." He didn't look up again.

Endric said nothing, knowing he would get little more from his father. Andril was gone. Killed investigating priests that called themselves Deshmahne. His head had been sent as some kind of message to Dendril.

He would learn the truth behind the attack.

He swallowed hard, then walked over and looked at the plain brown sack. Closing his eyes, he took a deep breath and peeled back the fabric to look one last time upon his brother's face. Decay had already begun to set in, but there was no doubting that this was Andril. His firm jaw was marred now by several small gashes and his nose was broken, but it was otherwise his brother.

Endric leaned down and kissed his forehead. "Goodbye, Andril," he whispered. His throat tightened and he could say no more. Tears streamed again.

He set the sack down and turned away. Dendril watched him with an unreadable expression on his face. Endric said nothing as he left the room, but his hand moved to find the hilt of his sword and he squeezed.

Though he didn't know what he would do next, he knew one thing. He wouldn't rest until Andril was avenged.

CHAPTER 10

As he opened the door to his father's office to leave, he saw Urik down the hall. His face looked pained. Of course Urik knew. The entire Denraen Council likely knew. All the men in the great hall had seemed to know.

Andril was beloved by more than just Endric. His death would affect everyone more than simply losing another soldier, and it would be hard to mourn him as he would have wanted. He was Dendril's son. More than that, he was Andril, one of the en'raen. The man who would be general.

No longer.

Endric didn't know who would be groomed for Dendril's seat and realized that only part of him cared. It wouldn't be Andril.

He blinked with the thought and pushed away the tears threatening to well in his eyes again. Urik paused in front of Dendril's door, staring at Endric as if waiting for him to say something. He didn't want to talk to the en'raen. His throat wouldn't have allowed it anyway.

Endric walked quickly down the hall. No one met his gaze. He was not sure how he would have reacted had anyone tried. He didn't stop until he reached his quarters.

The room was as he had left it. Plain. The simple narrow bed pushed against the wall. A beaten trunk sat near the foot of the bed. A small, chipped basin rested in one corner. Standard soldier quarters in the city.

Except for the stack of books.

They were stacked along the wall near the head of his bed. Not neatly aligned as his father would like, but not as disorderly as in Urik's office. Mostly, they were gifts from Andril.

He froze when he saw them and didn't stop the tears then.

It was Senda who found him. For that, he was forever thankful. Her soft-soled shoes scuffed the stone floor—no doubt on purpose—and he turned to see her standing in the doorway. He nodded once and she stepped across the threshold before closing the door silently behind her. She said nothing. Instead, she just stood there. Waiting for him. Her face was statement enough.

He turned to her and fell into her embrace. Endric sobbed into her shoulder for longer than he cared to admit. When he stood, he turned away from her to dry his cheeks though he knew it unnecessary. She waited for him as she always had.

"Andril is gone," he said finally. The statement was unnecessary, but he felt better for having said it.

Senda nodded. She understood. He knew that she would. Her own father had been Denraen and had died when she was still young. That loss had driven her. Still drove her, he suspected. Now she was Denraen as well, serving under Listain. Though she was skilled with the staff, her true calling was as a strategist, making her highly regarded by the spymaster. Her one fault was her tie to Endric.

"I know."

He blinked slowly and turned to sink onto his bed. He rested his head in his hands. Senda sat next to him. Waiting.

"I could have been with him," Endric said.

That thought had troubled him the most. Not death. He had been Denraen long enough to know that death was inevitable. There was an unknown quality to death, but he had a sense of something in the beyond. Probably not the same as what the Urmahne believed, yet he felt that there was something after this life.

Rather, what bothered him was the idea that he could have helped Andril in some way. It was folly to think like that. He knew that if his brother and his extraordinary skill with the sword had not been enough to survive, there was likely little that he could have done to help. Still, he couldn't shake the thought.

"You could have," Senda agreed.

"I should have been with him," he told her. He felt the angry bile that rose in his voice and swallowed it back down.

"Then we would be mourning you both."

He knew she spoke the truth. It didn't change how he felt. Not the regret at how things were left between him and Andril, nor the anger at his loss. Worse was the growing sense of guilt that he could have done something to help his brother and had not been there for him. As Andril had always been for him.

He swallowed hard and sighed. "His head was sent back."

She nodded.

"It was a message." He worded it as a question and looked up. His eyes searched her face for an answer.

"It was," she agreed.

She reached out and rested a hand on his leg. Her touch was warm through his pants, which were still wet from the rain. He didn't pull away.

He met her eyes. She didn't look away, though he didn't expect her to. The silence didn't mask his request.

"What did Dendril tell you?" she finally asked. Letting go of his leg, she brushed her black hair from her forehead as she spoke. It was a decidedly delicate motion for someone who fought to hide her femininity.

"He said they know nothing concrete."

"That is mostly true."

"That it was likely these warrior priests that call themselves Deshmahne."

"Also true."

He met her crystalline blue eyes. "How?"

She shrugged. "Not sure. Little is known about the Deshmahne. There are rumors. Little fact."

"Could they really do this?"

"If even some of the rumors are true, then yes."

"What do you know?"

She shook her head. "If your father didn't tell you, then you know I cannot either."

"Senda—" He stopped himself. He wouldn't push her. Not Senda. It would do no good anyway. He changed tactics. "Dendril says there will be no response."

Senda frowned and straightened her back. "None?"

"Says we must gather information first."

She nodded slowly. "The entire regiment was lost. The Deshmahne are suspected, but it's unknown how. That is the prudent course."

Endric felt himself tense. "Not prudent. Afraid."

"You know better than that. Dendril fears nothing," she said, her respect for the general clear. "More Denraen could be needlessly lost if he rushed into action."

She looked at him for a moment, appraising him, her eyes narrowed to slits and her forehead wrinkled. He always felt a little uneasy when he saw that expression on her face, uncertain what was taking place inside her head. Senda had an analytical mind, and he knew her intelligence was nearly unrivaled.

"What are you going to do?" she finally asked.

He closed his eyes and inhaled deeply through his nose. Andril couldn't go unavenged. If the Denraen did nothing, then that just might happen. That meant that he would have to go against the Denraen. Or the wishes of his father.

"I don't know," he answered slowly. "Probably wait to see what Dendril does." He couched his words with a sense of caution. Best that Senda believed he would obey the Denraen. She narrowed her eyes again and finally frowned. Endric suppressed a shiver. It was as if she read his mind.

"Don't do anything rash." The words were firm. A warning.

"Senda—"

"I know how you think, Endric." Her voice softened as she said his name. "Mourn your brother. See what Dendril does. Let the Denraen settle this." The last came as a request.

The advice was the same as what his father had given, though more gentle. Senda held a soft spot for him, but their friendship was too valuable for him to act upon it. His dalliances never lasted, and he couldn't lose Senda when it inevitably was over.

It was the reason she warned him. She might indulge him a little now, grant him some leeway, but he knew if he started working against the Denraen, Senda would have little choice. She would exploit her knowledge of him to protect the Denraen. There was little doubt that Listain would enjoy that moment.

He didn't answer her request. Rather than make a promise he was unsure he could keep, he chose to change topics. "There are rumors of a miner rebellion," he offered. Giving her information might lead her to reciprocate.

"What do you know?"

Endric sniffed as the question was reflected back onto him and he shook his head. "They may withhold the teralin."

He watched her face and realized she had not known. Did that mean Listain didn't know either? She quickly worked through the implications and frowned.

"Where did you hear this?" she asked, sliding forward on his bed to hover on the edge. Her arms were locked at her sides as if she readied to launch from her seat.

Should he reveal Pendin? He was a friend to Senda as well, but the intense look on her face gave Endric pause. There was something more to her expression as well. If he didn't know her as well as he did, he might not have seen it. A hint of nervousness. Why would that information make her nervous?

"What does it mean, Senda?"

"I'm not sure. Perhaps nothing." She paused, thinking about something before continuing. "Maybe more than I know. I must—"

A knock on the door cut her off.

They both looked to the doorway quickly, and Senda pushed herself off the bed. Endric stayed where he was. Olin stood in the doorway, looking between the two of them. A mix of amusement passed across his face and was replaced with a more solemn expression. It was little different than his norm.

"Endric," he said, hesitating. "I just heard about Andril." There was concern in his words and an offer of support. Olin didn't need to speak it for him to know. The man rarely said much, but what he did say held layers of meaning.

Endric only nodded and fought back tears again. Senda had kept him from dwelling on his loss, but with Olin's arrival, the feelings surged anew. He glanced at Senda. She stood near the open door, biting her lip. Olin looked over at her as well.

In another time, Endric would have laughed at the pining look upon Olin's face. Senda ignored it as if she couldn't see his expression.

"Endric. I am so sorry," Senda said. "You know I will do anything I can." His eyes widened a moment at the unexpected offer. "For now, I must find Listain."

As she left, he wondered again what more she knew but didn't tell him.

Olin looked from Endric toward Senda as she departed. "I came only to offer condolences," he said and turned to follow Senda out the door, pulling it closed as he left.

And so it was that he was alone, staring again at the stack of books Andril had given him. The tears fell freely then and didn't stop for a long time.

CHAPTER 11

Endric stared at the palace, his mind blank and unable to concentrate on anything. Clouds wrapped the upper spires like a cloak, shrouding the peaks from view. The pale stone seemed duller than usual, as if it, too, mourned, and rain ran in rivulets down its side.

Endric blinked slowly, sighing. Rain soaked the edge of the street, but he didn't move. It had taken all the energy he could muster to simply leave the barracks. His feet carried him here, to look upon the home of the Magi. Now all he could do was stare.

How could the gods have allowed Andril to die?

A chill wind whistled from the north and he shivered, but even that was half-hearted and did little to warm him.

A week had passed and he still struggled with Andril's passing. Patrol had been abandoned. He had not bothered to seek Urik's approval and distantly wondered what the en'raen would say when he next saw him. Endric had spent his time confined to his room and rarely even came out to eat.

Pendin saw that he had food and drink. His friend simply sat with him the first night, saying nothing, but there was something comforting in his presence. After that, he had seen that Endric had privacy. If nothing else, Andril's death eased some of the tension that had grown between them. Pendin said nothing of their assigned patrol, and Endric mostly forgot about the miners and the possible rebellion.

He suspected Senda and Olin had stopped to check on him as well. Though he had not seen them, he would often awaken to the pleasant scent of Senda's soap and know she had been there. A part of him missed her presence, but he would never tell her that.

"It's been a week."

Endric turned slowly to see Urik standing in the street, dark cloak keeping the rain off. The en'raen left his hood down.

"How are you?" Urik asked. Endric was surprised to hear a measure of concern to the words.

"I'll be fine," he said. He had spoken rarely since learning of Andril, and his voice sounded foreign.

Urik furrowed his brow and huffed out a breath. "Eventually that will be true enough. But it will take time."

Endric only shook his head in response. There was no other answer. On top of his sadness, the feelings of guilt remained nearly overwhelming.

He constantly replayed each interaction he'd had with Andril in the days leading up to his departure. Each memory was painful and left him with a hollowness deep inside, but a particular memory made him feel even worse.

Andril had shown a certain uncharacteristic hesitation before leaving. Endric had thought he intended to ask him to join his regiment, but Andril had done nothing other than rebuke him. Even then, he could probably have pushed Andril to let him join him. When his brother had needed him most, he had not been there for him.

Endric felt a growing sense that Andril had known his mission was anything but straightforward. Had he learned something more about these Deshmahne? Wondering what his brother might have known drove him crazy.

"Nothing can change the fact that Andril is gone," Urik said when Endric remained silent.

The words startled him and he shook his head again. "I should have been with him." The words sounded bitter, even to him.

"And your father would be mourning two sons now."

"My father wouldn't mourn my loss." He remembered how flat his father's eyes had looked after learning Andril's fate. His death wouldn't cause the same distress.

"You think your father cares so little about you?"

He only shrugged.

"Any other soldier would have been kicked from the Denraen for half the offenses you have. Still, here you are. Not because you are a skilled soldier—which you are—but there are dozens of men your equal with the sword. Your father knows why you rebel." Urik paused and took a step forward. "Knows. And understands. It is this reason you remain Denraen.

"You would push away your father rather than understand him. Andril's loss has hurt him. Yours would hurt as much. If you think otherwise, you are more misguided then I was led to believe." A moment passed as Urik stared at the palace before he looked back at Endric. "Or perhaps this is simply your anger at losing your brother. That, I can understand."

The comment pushed through the sadness. "You've lost someone close to you too," Endric realized.

Anger briefly flashed across Urik's face and was just as quickly crushed, leaving his usual flat expression. Slowly, the en'raen nodded. "I have," he admitted.

Endric sighed but didn't say anything. If Urik wanted to tell him, he would.

"I lost a son once," Urik said. The words seemed to stick in his throat, as if even saying it pained him. "And my wife. Years ago, and before I lived in Voiga."

He turned away, but not before Endric saw the grief still evident in his eyes.

"I grieved a long time. For months, I was inconsolable. Eventually the pain faded and passed." The tone of his voice gave lie to those words. "As it will with you. My only advice to you is to hold his memory close. Over time, it too will fade."

A distant peal of thunder accented the statement and the rain fell heavier, water pooling along the street.

Urik sighed and looked Endric in the eyes. "I am sorry for your loss. Andril was a good Denraen. He was a better man. Now," Urik said, his voice firming. He'd moved on and expected Endric to as well. That was the Denraen way. Mourn and move on. "You have neglected your assignment."

"I would have been useless on patrol."

Urik shrugged. "It's time you return to your duties."

"To learn the ideals of the Denraen," he quoted.

Urik nodded and watched Endric's face.

"When?"

"Find Calnin for your assignment. He will expect you tonight."

Endric could only nod. Calnin meant more patrol, and likely Stahline again. Did Urik intentionally assign him to Calnin because of their history, or was it coincidental? Either way, the result would be unpleasant.

"Yes, sir," he said, thumping his fist to his chest in a lazy salute.

Urik considered him for a moment before turning, heading away from the palace. Endric watched the rain slide down his cloak and considered asking what he really wanted to know. "Urik!" he hollered, deciding.

Urik stopped and turned slightly.

Endric hurried over to him, splashing through puddles as he did. Rain soaked through his boots unpleasantly. "How did he die?"

Urik cocked his head and stared for a moment. "You know that information is restricted to the council," he said, speaking quietly.

Endric nodded. "I have to know."

"Some would say you honor your brother best by obeying the Denraen."

He said nothing, uncertain how to respond.

Urik watched him for a long moment, then shook his head. "It is for you to decide. A man must choose his own path." He said the last quietly and with a hint of sadness. He inhaled deeply, and his eyes hardened. "Know that I will deny telling you this." He waited a moment for Endric to nod his acknowledgement. "Very well. First some background. Reports tell us the Deshmahne claim the gods do not exist. We know that they celebrate power and the destruction of that which the Urmahne would protect." A wave of darkness swept across his face. "In this, they openly bastardize the lessons of the Urmahne. Humility gives way to coveting strength. Peace gives way to bloodshed." Urik stopped, catching himself. Anger seemed to surge through him and he visibly suppressed it.

"Why Andril?" Endric asked.

Urik shook his head. "Who can say? Wrong place? He was sent to investigate the reports, to learn about the Deshmahne and their role in the growing conflicts in the south. He was not expected to meet resistance, at least not where he died. He had not even reached the southern continent."

"Where did he die?" His father had not given him details. For some reason, he found them necessary.

Urik scratched at his arm, ignoring the rain running down his face. "They were waiting for the tides to reveal the land bridge so they could cross. They were to go into Coamdon and meet with the Deshmahne, hope to learn more about their intent." Urik's mouth turned briefly in a frown, and a fleeting expression crossed his eyes. "Instead, they were ambushed as they waited. Apparently slaughtered."

"By how many?"

The en'raen shook his head. "We do not know."

"But you have an idea." Listain was very good at gathering information and making educated guesses. He was certain his father would want to know all he could and would have asked Listain to investigate. The council would have been informed. That would be how Urik knew as much as he did.

"Some," he agreed.

"How many?" He repeated the question. He needed to know how many men it had taken to kill his brother.

Urik sighed. "Probably no more than fifty."

Endric frowned. Fifty men against the Denraen? And priests at that? "How is that possible? Fifty priests destroyed an entire regiment of Denraen?" Endric shook his head. "Including Andril. There is more to it than that."

"Possibly," Urik agreed. "As I said, they were ambushed."

Endric immediately turned over what he knew about everything from the geography of the crossing to how Andril ran his regiment. There was no way that all those men were lost in a simple ambush. Urik watched him and said nothing. The en'raen knew more but didn't elaborate. What could explain this?

That was not the question he had asked. He wanted to know how the Deshmahne had managed to kill the Denraen. He needed to know why.

"Why now? What reason did they have in attacking the Denraen?"

"You begin to ask the right questions," Urik said. The rain fell heavier and he glanced at the blackening sky. "A better question is what message did they send your father by killing your brother. What message did they send by annihilating a regiment?"

Endric thought about the question for a long moment before answering. There could only be one intention in a message of that sort, and it was one that the Denraen were unaccustomed to receiving. It reflected a lack of concern about the Denraen response, no fear for the consequences.

Attacking the Denraen was a demonstration of strength. A declaration of power.

"I see from your face that you have come to the same conclusion as the council," Urik said.

"They don't fear the Denraen."

Urik shook his head. "If they did, they do not any longer."

"And what is our response?"

The en'raen sighed. "For now, we acquire intelligence. We must know how the Deshmahne destroyed an entire regiment. We cannot risk another such loss."

There was a certain inflection to his words, almost distaste. Endric realized that not all of the council agreed with the plan. "Waiting allows the Deshmahne to grow stronger. Gain influence."

Urik nodded. "This show of strength was perhaps not for our benefit. Others have seen and now know of the Deshmahne. Many people respect strength, regardless of who wields it."

"Was this the first such demonstration?"

Urik shrugged slightly and rain sluiced down his arms. "Not if you believe the rumors."

"Then it will not be the last."

The en'raen's eyes hardened and a dark flicker of emotion passed across his face. He shook his head slightly.

"Will waiting improve our response?"

"I fear the Denraen cannot simply wait for the Deshmahne to grow stronger. The longer we wait, the stronger the Deshmahne could become. Eventually, it may take an act of war to stop them."

He didn't need to say it was unlikely the Denraen would openly engage in such a war. That, more than anything, went against the core tenets of the Denraen. The Magi would also oppose anything of the sort.

"There is more to these priests, isn't there?" Endric asked. Senda had mentioned rumors, but they seemed impossible to believe.

Urik met Endric's eyes. "Do you need me to spell it out?" he asked. "For the Deshmahne to defeat a regiment of Denraen, there must be more to them. Simple soldiers wouldn't defeat a regiment of Denraen, even in ambush." He frowned and scrubbed a hand across his head, sending splatters of rain from his hair. "If not soldiers, then what? Are they somehow endowed with special strength or speed? Or worse—are they gifted like the Magi?" He grunted and shrugged, folding his arms across his chest. "Nothing is truly known. They celebrate power and violence. They decry the gods the Urmahne celebrate. And their influence spreads." He took a deep breath. "That is the mystery the council and your father fears. That is why I fear delay."

The idea that these priests had access to some dark ability had a disturbing logic to it. Endric shivered again, unable to help himself. Urik saw it and nodded, as if understanding.

"Now that you know," Urik continued, "you will say nothing until the council acts." He turned and started off before pausing. "That is not a suggestion, Endric. Report to Calnin tonight. Your time of mourning is over."

Urik marched away, ignoring the rain and the increasingly bitter wind as he headed down the street, back toward the barracks. Endric watched for a moment, struggling with his order, knowing Urik was right. He had grieved for a week. More than Andril would have wanted. Duty called.

The loss of Andril somehow made suffering patrol even more difficult. Calnin relished the assignment, and Endric couldn't really blame him; were their places reversed, he would likely do much the same. If Pendin were again assigned patrol with him, the tension between them would return. He didn't know if he could handle alienating Pendin now.

Endric sighed and turned back toward the palace. Clouds hovered even lower, obscuring much of the towers, leaving only the main, broad portion of the palace visible. Sighing, he turned to return to the barracks when something caught his attention and he froze.

A figure shuffled around the palace grounds. Obviously Magi, and with his back stooped by age. The Mage followed the outer stone wall separating the grounds from the rest of the city, standing tall enough that Endric could see the tops of his shoulders over the wall. At each teralin gate, he paused and placed a hand upon the metal. He held the teralin gate until a deep thud, like a heavy bell tolling, almost shook his hand free. By the third gate, Endric saw that he closed his eyes as he touched the metal, his lips moving as if speaking to himself.

Endric watched him complete a circle of the grounds before stopping and surveying the garden. Through the nearest gate, Endric saw him start forward, a slight hitch to his step making him seem to limp, stopping along the pathway leading to the palace entrance. There he sat and crossed his legs, eyes closed but his face looking out into the city.

Rain fell on his tired face and he smiled.

CHAPTER 12

Only the pale moon lit the night sky. In the distance, thunder rumbled and Endric could almost imagine the clouds rolling toward him. Occasionally, a dark cloud passed over the full moon, throwing the night briefly into darkness. Rain fell endlessly and the city stank of dampness and mold for it.

He paused, unable to ignore the feeling that something followed him, but he heard nothing other than distant thunder and the incessant rain. There came a burst of far-off lightning, and strange shadows flickered with it before everything once more fell still.

Endric moved carefully, slipping into the rocky Lashiin ruins on the edge of town. He should have reported to Calnin by now, but he was just not ready for more patrol. Part of him wondered whether Pendin would be disappointed or annoyed. Probably a bit of both, if Endric knew him as he thought he did. Urik was a different matter.

A shiver overcame him as he passed through the remnants of a stone doorway that arched high overhead. He scrambled up the loose rock until he reached a relatively flat area where a half wall remained. There he sat, leaning out and looking into the night.

Hearing a soft cascade of loose gravel, he turned. Even without seeing her, he knew it was Senda, recognizing the flowery scent she wore.

"Did you follow me?" he asked, turning away and looking over the wall.

At least he knew now what it was he'd sensed, surprised she had followed him here. Few enough dared enter the ruins in the daytime.

She sniffed but didn't answer. Instead, she moved to crouch next to him, laying her staff on the ground and hugging her knees to her chest.

"Pendin worries," she finally said.

He glanced over. She looked up at him; her eyes glowed softly with reflected light. A hint of nervousness was evident in her tense arms and shoulders. Even her eyes darted slightly.

"You are assigned patrol tonight."

He sighed and blinked slowly, turning away. "My friends shouldn't suffer because of me," he said softly.

Senda didn't answer at first. "Talk to Urik," she suggested.

"I already did."

"Then find a way to move on." Her voice was not harsh, and the gaze she fixed upon him was worried but no less uncomfortable.

"I'm trying," he admitted.

Senda took a soft breath, and Endric waited for her next admonishment. What she said next surprised him, though he knew it shouldn't.

"How can I help?"

She stepped closer and touched his arm. He expected her to pull him away from the wall but she didn't, only standing there, the warmth of her hand seeping through his shirt. He didn't pull away.

"I don't know. Everything is..." He hesitated, not knowing what he wanted to say. "Wrong," he finished.

"Hiding doesn't help." She moved closer and their bodies touched slightly. She fixed him with an open expression. He was aware of the heat between them and tried to ignore it.

Endric shook his head. "What else can I do?"

"What do you want to do?"

Endric looked away. "Honestly?" he asked, his voice strained. "I want vengeance." He closed his eyes, pushing back the tide of emotion that threated to overwhelm him. "Andril is gone. Killed by these Deshmahne priests. And the Denraen do nothing."

"What you want would put countless others in danger."

He remained silent. That she spoke the truth didn't make it any easier to hear. Andril wouldn't have put additional Denraen in danger without understanding the risks.

Inhaling deeply, Endric opened his eyes and stared out at the night, letting the palace draw his attention. The huge structure swallowed everything else, towering over the rest of the city, and the view from the ruins only magnified it.

"Why did you come here?" she asked. He felt the warmth of her breath as she spoke.

"The solitude," he answered.

She tried to laugh but it came out as mostly a cough. "There are better places."

"Are there?" he asked, turning back to her.

"This place is…"

"Old," Endric suggested. "Some say the ruins were ancient when the Magi first settled the city."

Senda frowned at him, some of her confidence returning. "This is not a place for idle conversation."

Endric waited for her to elaborate, but she didn't. He understood her reservations about the ruins. Many felt the same superstitions when it came to the old religion. He had not expected that from Senda. "Why did you come here?"

"You were to return to patrol tonight. I worried that you would…"

He shook his head. "I will not do anything foolish, if that's what you fear."

"No?" she asked, cocking her head slightly. "You think taunting the gods is not foolish?" Her gaze skipped across the stone before settling once again on Endric. "You sit in the Lashiin ruins and stare upon the palace of the Magi, the first of the Urmahne. How is that not foolish?"

Endric surprised himself and smiled. "You give the gods too much credit. Or too little." He shrugged, holding out his hands to keep her from interrupting him. "To the gods, I'm a rather small drop in a large storm."

Thunder sounded in the distance, as if emphasizing his point.

"Still," Senda said. "This place is not meant for nighttime contemplation."

Endric glanced at the broken stone around him, the low wall seeming to hold back the night, and at the other scattered remnants of structure. "I think it is a *peaceful* place for contemplation."

Senda frowned again but said nothing, and Endric let the silence between them grow. He had known some women who couldn't let simple silence rest, uncomfortable in the absence of noise. With Senda, there was no tension, nothing awkward to the silence, and Endric realized he enjoyed feeling Senda's warmth as she stood next to him.

There was not absolute silence. Wind whipped through the ruins, stirring stone and whistling through strange corners. Distant thunder, so common to the city, promised the coming rain. A few insects even called quietly, adding their sound to the others of the night.

Through it all, he heard the rhythmic sound of Senda's breathing and found it soothing.

Silence was not the only reason he enjoyed the ruins. The view here allowed him to stare at the entirety of the palace without any of the neighboring buildings obstructing his sight. During the day, the palace had an almost austere aura, and he saw it as somewhat oppressive. Night was different. Especially when the moon was bright. At night, the white stone walls were nearly luminescent and he felt a sense of peace. He needed that now.

"They speak of your father differently now," Senda said finally, easing into the silence between them.

Endric glanced over and waited.

"There was another attack in Brohstin. Much was similar to how Andril and his regiment were attacked."

"Deshmahne then?"

Senda nodded slightly. "Some think so."

Endric didn't need to ask for clarification. "What does Listain know?"

She met his eyes and he saw a decision made. "Very little," she said and sighed. He knew it cost her to break her confidence with Listain. "Rumors mostly."

"I have heard some of the rumors," he admitted.

Senda tilted her head. "Urik?" she asked but didn't wait for his response. "You are one of only a few that even know what they call themselves. The other rumors are more frightening."

Endric held her gaze, feeling a surge of anger. "You mean that fifty of these Deshmahne killed a regiment of Denraen."

She nodded. "Unfortunately, that is more than rumor."

"Urik thinks they are endowed with abilities," he said, wondering if Listain had shared the same with her.

Her eyes widened briefly and she nodded.

"Like the Magi?" he asked, thinking of what Urik had mentioned. What would happen if even one of the Magi joined the Deshmahne and attacked?

Senda shook her head slowly. "From what we know, it is not the same." Endric felt a hint of relief. "The Magi are born to it. The Deshmahne are rumored to come upon it differently. That is part of the appeal. Any man can gain powers akin to the Magi."

"At what cost?"

She shook her head, leaving her dark hair flickering behind her and flowing in the gentle breeze. "That is not known."

"How is that even possible?" He turned back to stare at the palace of the Magi as he asked the question. There was no doubting the appeal. The idea was frightening if true and explained how Andril and his regiment had been so easily ambushed. Endric couldn't imagine facing an army of men with such endowments.

"We don't know how it's possible. Or even if it is. These are only rumors still."

Rumors. With enough evidence to make them believable. Andril's death was proof of that.

"Endric." She said his name softly.

He closed his eyes, unable to keep his thoughts straight.

"You know this is bigger than Andril," she said. Her words almost begged his understanding.

Endric opened his eyes, blinking back the sudden pain. Every conversation turned his thoughts back to his brother, a reminder of how he had failed him. "I know."

There was nothing else for him to say, and Senda didn't force him. They let the silence fall between them once more as both turned to stare at the palace, his thoughts turning over.

Had he missed something? The meeting he and Pendin had observed in Stahline. The miners. The Deshmahne. Andril's death. Could they all be tied together?

He turned to Senda, thinking to ask her, and saw movement near the palace.

Dark shapes moved through the night, visible only as a contrast to the white stone, and seemed to shimmer as they crossed the open lawn stretching in front of the palace. He wouldn't have seen it if not for his vantage.

At least three shapes moved across the lawn and turned toward the back of the palace. The way they moved was unnatural and coordinated, unlike any creature he had ever encountered. He stared, trying to determine what it was that he saw, but the clouds that had been gathering in the distance began to move over the moon, casting everything into a deeper darkness.

"What was that?" He spoke aloud without really intending to.

"Not sure," Senda answered in a hush. "But I saw what you did."

He looked over and saw a nervous expression upon her face. There was something she wasn't sharing. Endric waited, thinking she would say something more. When she didn't, he started down the small rocky embankment, moving quietly and carefully so as not to disrupt any of the crumbled stone.

"What are you doing?" she whispered.

He paused, his eyes lingering on the strange movements on the palace lawn. "Investigating."

Senda hesitated, then followed as silently as she could.

CHAPTER 13

"You know we're not to enter the palace grounds," Senda hissed at Endric.

He glanced back at her. There was reticence in her steps. "You don't have to follow. This will fall only on me."

The words had the expected response and she glared at him.

"You know something," he said, watching her for a moment before continuing. Gates occasionally interrupted the low wall encircling the palace, and Endric suddenly remembered the Magi walking from gate to gate in the rain and wondered if they were locked.

"Endric."

He heard the message as she said his name. There was something she couldn't reveal.

As he reached the nearest gate, he hesitated before pulling at the small carved handle. Tradition held that the teralin gates would remain unlocked, but Endric didn't know that any had ever tested tradition. Tradition also held that none other than the Magi—or their servants—would enter the palace grounds. Now he intended to test one and violate the other.

He took a deep breath and glanced at Senda. Her dark eyes were drawn and worry mixed with fear across her face. Then he pulled.

The gate swung open easily and without sound. The metal, like all things teralin, was warm to the touch, not quite hot. It was slippery, almost as if covered in grease, and he feared burning himself by leaving his hand upon it. Men had been scalded by the touch of teralin. According to Pendin, that was only part of the reason why mining was so dangerous.

Endric slipped through the open gate. He glanced at Senda to see if she followed. She watched him for a moment, then clenched her jaw as she stepped onto the palace grounds, eyeing the teralin like someone might watch a dangerous animal. She didn't take her eyes off it until she was well past.

Within the palace grounds, everything was still. Small shrubs lined the pathway, neatly groomed. Some taller shrubs were sculpted into shapes resembling birds, wolves, or other creatures. Huge pots with flowers in bloom interrupted the line of shrubs, their colors subdued in the darkness. Only the mingling of their fragrant aromas announced the variety within the planters. How did they coax these plants to grow well here, this high on the mountain?

As they made their way along the path, eyes open for movement, Endric saw a few intersecting pathways. Small, carved benches marked each crossing. Endric didn't need to sit to know they were made of teralin as well. He could almost imagine the Magi sitting upon the benches, staring at their lush garden. Sculptures of the gods were placed carefully along the path, their features long since worn away. Fitting for the nameless gods.

Nearer the palace, a few trees stretched like shadow figures, only the upper branches and their leaves moving in the wind. The thirteen trees on the grounds were the only trees in the city, each planted in memory of the original thirteen founders. The constant rain and lack of predictable sunlight stunted their growth so that they were twisted and deformed, looking nothing like Goldenwren trees anymore. Even their trefoil leaves had changed, distorted and crumpled so that they were more olive and brown rather than the gold, wide flowing leaves of their namesake.

A gust of wind sent the branches fluttering again as it whistled through the garden, sounding every bit like a far-off moan. Otherwise, nothing moved.

He crept toward the nearest tree and hovered in the deeper shadows it offered. Senda sidled next to him. The palace loomed larger here, and the white stone seemed to glow with its own light, part of the mystique of the palace. Andril had long ago taught him that it was little more than retained light, absorbed and reflected at night. This light allowed him to make out the movement along the far northern wall.

Cloaked in blackness that seemed deeper than night, it was only the contrast with the palace that made the creatures visible. There were three of them, and they flickered as they moved. Watching them was dizzying.

"We should get help," Senda suggested, the nervous edge still clear in her voice.

"I don't think there's time," Endric said. For some reason, he suspected that whatever moved wouldn't be there long.

He slid to the next tree, now closer to the palace. Up close, the rough bark had a pungent odor, and he had to take shallow breaths to keep from feeling light-headed. Peering around the trunk, he spied the figures stepping in a strange pattern. Endric stared for a moment, trying to figure out how best to approach without being seen. No nearer trees or shrubs stood between him and the figures.

Coming up with nothing better, he crouched low and slid through the soft palace lawn, only darkness and shadows between him and the figures.

As he neared, the shapes became clearer. And less clear.

He couldn't explain what he saw. Part of him didn't trust what his eyes revealed. Cloaked figures, standing nearly as tall as he, stepped in a sort of rhythmic movement. Each step was jerky, a staccato dance, and the shape seemed to flash briefly into shadows darker than night as it moved, disappearing then quickly reappearing as a smudge of darkness. The effect was disorienting.

Endric would say they were men, but he had never seen men move as these figures did. Suddenly their steps ceased and they stood, fully upright. The pale moonlight illuminated them, and even then he found it difficult to penetrate the darkness and shadows swirling around them. Endric froze, thinking they saw him, cursing silently before rushing forward, praying the noise of his movements didn't betray him.

When they flung off their cloaks as one, revealing bodies covered by paint or ink, he nearly stumbled, barely catching himself in time. They wore nothing else and stood otherwise naked to the night. The markings swirled and moved on their own, as if the very skin beneath them was alive. Even then, shadows clung to their skin.

They were men, but unlike anything he had ever seen. Painted in such a fearsome fashion and performing some sort of ritual on the palace grounds, Endric knew he didn't want to wait to find out why.

Each man then raised his hands toward the night sky and wordlessly chanted. Sliding closer together, slithering toward the center of the circle, they made no other sound. The night itself seemed to hold its breath. Their fingers touched, twisting into a knot. The muscles in their bodies were taut.

Then the markings upon their flesh started swirling faster, a furious energy begging for release. Deep blackness seeped from them, darkening the night. Even the soft glow of the palace stone could no longer penetrate the shadows.

Endric harbored no illusions that he wanted to witness the culmination of this ceremony.

He had been unable to take his eyes off them but now, as he watched and realized *something* was about to happen, his mind suddenly lurched forward as if unfrozen. He grabbed his sword and unsheathed as silently as possible. He heard Senda suck in a breath behind him but paid her no attention.

He had to stop this.

There was no reason to the feeling, but it was nearly overpowering nonetheless. A tension had built in the air, and he felt a rolling nausea in the pit of his stomach, a warning that something must be done. Now.

Endric glanced quickly over at Senda. Her mouth was drawn and a look of horror crossed her face. Not even willing to meet his eyes, he knew she wouldn't help. Part of him hoped the Magi would sense what was happening and interrupt, but all the windows on this side of the palace were darkened and there was no time for a warning. The same was true for summoning the Denraen, though with the palpable power building, he doubted there was much they could do anyway.

That left him.

Endric closed his eyes, struggling to think of what he could do, unsure what it was he witnessed but certain it needed to be stopped.

His eyes snapped open. Then he flung his sword toward the figures.

There was no intention of actually hitting them; a sword was not meant to be thrown like he just had. Still, it flew true, end over end, slicing the air, almost parting the darkness as it whistled toward the figures. When it neared the circle formed by them, it bounced back, as if hitting some physical barrier.

The nearest figure snapped his gaze toward Endric. A dark snarl crossed his face and he took an almost unintentional step forward. With the movement, the tension in the air suddenly snapped away. A loud *crack* thundered through the air. If Endric had not known otherwise, he would have thought it from a lightning strike. The darkness lifted and the sense of swirling movement to the markings on their skin disappeared.

The nausea in his stomach was gone. Now another feeling filled him. Fear.

"What are they?" he whispered. Senda touched his shoulder. He didn't dare look back, didn't dare take his eyes off the figures.

"I have no idea," she said. Her voice quavered more than his had.

The figures glared at him, malevolence in their dark eyes. Their gaze pierced the night, almost as physical as daggers. Endric resisted the urge to step back. The strange markings on their flesh worked onto their faces as well, black lines forming a pattern. The markings occasionally seemed to slide and slither across their bodies, though with less intensity than before. There was something familiar about the markings that he couldn't place.

Hatred and malice radiated from them. Endric shuddered, recognizing nothing natural about the horrible emotion rolling over him. Like a presence, it couldn't be denied. The sense washed over him, pressing into him and overwhelming everything else. His body had slumped as if sapped of strength and will, and his knees buckled.

Loss filled him.

Andril was gone. Endric knew he should have been with him. Perhaps then his brother would live. Dead, and his last memories were of arguments he knew he never should have started.

His father hated him. Endric couldn't blame him for wanting more from him. Even now, with Andril gone, he antagonized his father. Now, even hope for reconciliation was gone.

Then there was his mother. The woman he never knew. She left when he was only a child, too young to remember her. Somehow, he had managed to offend her as well, chasing her away from their family. Andril and their father had been right to blame him.

"Endric?"

He heard Senda's voice as a distant sound, as if speaking through a thick door or from far off.

"Endric." She spoke again, closer now, uncertainty to her voice.

He thought of his friends. Surely they would be better off without him? Pendin would no longer be forced onto patrol. Olin could find his place in the Denraen, no longer held back by their friendship. Even Senda would be freed from his taint.

"Endric!" Senda spoke with urgency now.

Endric shook his head, feeling his mind clear slightly as he did, a haze lifting. Slow recognition dawned on him and he breathed deeply, inhaling the cool night air, feeling his head clearing with each breath.

He glanced over at Senda. Fear crossed her face, but recognition as well.

"Endric?" The question was clear in her voice.

He nodded. "I think I'm fine." Whatever had happened was gone now.

He turned his attention back to the figures, the nearest man tensing. Endric wished he still had his sword, but at least Senda had her staff. She was exquisitely skilled with it, and her presence gave him some measure of comfort, but without his sword he might as well be naked. He could protect himself in normal unarmed circumstances, but there was nothing normal about this.

"Be ready," Endric whispered, not daring to turn his attention away from the men.

He heard Senda raise her staff, the air whistling as she started spinning the long length of hardwood.

Then there was a folding of shadows, like night covering night, and the tension built again. He felt helpless before it, uncertain what these men even were and even more uncertain how to stop them. His skin started tingling, almost burning, and the hair on his arms and the back of his neck stood on end. The nausea in the pit of his stomach returned, building as the tension in the air became almost unbearable.

Then it snapped out of existence with another *crack*.

With it, the figures were gone.

The night sky lightened and the outline of the palace was again visible. No one else stood on the lawn. Nothing moved. It was as if what they had witnessed had never happened. only his sword remained as a testament to whoever they had been and whatever they had been trying to do.

CHAPTER 14

Endric stared at the open ground and then hurried forward after his sword. It rested on the lawn not far from where the nearest man had stood. The wrappings on the hilt were singed. The blade was hot to the touch as well.

It was not the only oddity he discovered. The ground around the palace was unmarked, as if it had not even been stepped upon. The grass, which should have been tamped down, stood tall.

How? He had seen how the strange figures had moved, stepping through a rigid dance. There should be some evidence they had been here.

Turning to Senda, he opened his mouth to speak but froze as two tall shapes emerged from a nearby door. For a moment, he feared the strange men had returned, but these were too tall. That left only one other answer. Magi.

"Get away," he whispered to Senda.

She shook her head. "There's nowhere for me to go."

"I'll cover for you. We both can't be seen here."

"You will not suffer for this alone," Senda said.

Endric shook his head. If Senda was implicated with him in this, she could lose her position with Listain. He didn't want to be responsible for the continued suffering of his friends.

The approaching Magi wore long, billowy cloaks. One was bearded and his back stooped slightly. His hair was shorn close and gray, and a bald patch reflected what little moonlight filtered through the clouds. The dark fabric of his cloak was more heavily embroidered. Everything about him called attention to his age; even his fingers were twisted with arthritis. A wide band of black encircled the fifth finger on his right hand.

Even so, there was a presence about him, a certain pull of authority. This was the Mage he had seen in Stahline.

The other Mage appeared youthful by comparison. Long hair was peppered, though mostly gray, and pulled back behind his head. His cloak was a lighter color than the older Mage's, and less embroidered. He stood tall and his eyes were serious. His chin was sharp and angular and his nose long and hawkish.

The Mage caught Endric staring and turned his intense gaze upon him. Though the impulse was there, he didn't shy away. The Mage glanced with a clear disdain at the sword still held out in his hand.

"You are Dendril's son." It was the older Mage who had spoken.

Endric nodded and sheathed his sword. The blade had cooled but was still hot, and he felt it through the sheath.

"Why are you on the palace grounds?" the other Mage asked.

He glanced at both Magi. How truthful should he be? He was certain that the older Mage was the same one he and Pendin had seen in Stahline meeting with one of the Denraen. A sudden worry struck him—could he trust these Magi?

"I saw something moving across the palace grounds. It was late to be one of the Magi," he said, deciding to start with the truth.

The elder Mage frowned. "And you both decided to investigate?" His aged voice was thin and warbly.

He shook his head. "Not both. Me. Senda tried to stop me." He hoped she wouldn't say anything. Let the blame fall only upon him.

Several moments passed. At least in this, she complied.

"Hmm." The elder Mage turned away from Endric and looked over at the ground where the strange figures had performed the ceremony. "Why here?" he asked without taking his eyes off the tall grass of the lawn.

Endric inhaled. He would be direct. The Magi might know if he weren't.

"There were three figures. They crossed the lawn from there." He pointed to the gate he'd seen them come through. "I interrupted them as they performed some sort of ritual."

The elder Mage had turned to watch him as he spoke and widened his eyes briefly.

The other Mage glanced down at the lawn. He took a few steps before looking back up at Endric. "There is nothing here other than Denraen bootprints."

"They were here," Endric said. "I can't explain why there are no markings. And I don't know where they went. They disappeared." Even to him, the explanation sounded hollow, and he had seen it with his own eyes.

"I saw it too, Magi," Senda said. Her tone was deferential. More of what his should have been.

"Hmm," the elder Mage said again.

The other Mage stared at Endric for a long moment, then turned to face the elder Mage. "I see nothing here, Tresten."

Endric's ears perked at that name. Urik had mentioned the name Tresten, speaking of him with a certain reverence and referring to him as the only one on the Magi Council to have left the city. What did it mean that he was here?

"Are you certain, Alriyn?" Tresten looked up and blinked, but not before Endric saw that his eyes had taken on a milky haze, as if a film covered them. They cleared as he opened his eyes, now bright and piercing.

"What do you see, Elder?" Mage Alriyn moved to stand near Tresten and looked where the elder Mage had been staring.

Mage Tresten walked over to Endric, smelling of roses and fresh rain. The scent took him off guard and he frowned. Mage Tresten moved slowly, as if each step pained him. As he stood before Endric, his back stooped and bent, it was almost as if the weight of walking was too much for him to bear. And still he was tall. Nearly a hand taller than the other Magi, he would have towered over Endric at his full height. An aura of authority radiated from him. More than that, he exuded a sense of peace.

Endric suddenly felt an overwhelming sense of awe. It was unlike anything he had ever experienced.

"Son of Dendril," he began, then smiled. A wave of relaxation radiated from him and blanketed Endric. Muscles he had not known were tense loosened and relaxed. "Your father speaks highly of you."

He shook his head, uncertain whether to be surprised by the fact that Dendril spoke with the Magi councilor or embarrassed by the confusion. "You must mean Andril. I am Endric."

The Mage tilted his head. "Hmm." He stared at Endric for a long moment, and he felt exposed, almost as if the Magi knew what he thought. "Andril?" he repeated and shook his head. "I am sorry that he has passed. Your father spoke highly of him as well."

Endric swallowed hard at the sudden memories flooding him. He looked away, trying to avoid Tresten's eyes, unsure what to make of him. The Mage seemed different than any other he had ever encountered. There was no arrogance. Not like the other Magi, Alriyn, appeared to possess. Though old, he didn't appear frail. Rather, he appeared to have a distinct strength.

"I'm sorry I entered the grounds and approached the palace. I will report my actions to my father and accept the consequences for violating tradition," he said without looking up.

Tresten raised his eyebrows. "Less violation than you think," he said. Alriyn looked at him curiously. "I would know what the figures you saw looked like."

Endric took a deep breath, knowing how foolish it would sound. He pressed on anyway. "They were men, though they didn't move like any man I have ever faced. They were cloaked and covered at first. During their ritual, they tossed their cloaks off and their bodies were covered with dark paintings."

As he spoke, he realized where he had seen similar markings. The miner, related to the Magi and quicker than any miner had a right to be, had similar tattoos. With the realization, he wondered at the connection and if the Magi were in some way involved.

Tresten watched him intently for long moments. When he spoke, the words were quiet, almost as if he didn't intend to speak aloud. "As I feared."

"What were they?" Endric asked.

Alriyn looked at him sharply for daring to speak, but Tresten didn't take any offense to the question. "Theirs is a dark art, arcane, and one that should have been lost thousands of years ago but still somehow exists."

Alriyn looked over at Tresten and frowned. "Elder? Are you certain you should—"

Tresten nodded, cutting Alriyn off. "Endric should know what it is he did for us this evening. Had they succeeded..." He looked back toward the space used for the strange ritual. Almost as if he could see it, though no markings existed.

Slowly, Tresten turned his attention back to Endric. His eyes nearly glowed. "What you came upon was a Deshviili, a ceremony of destruction. I can only speculate at the target." He glanced at the palace, then around the lawn, frowning as his eyes passed over the nearest gate. "Performing such a ceremony takes great strength in the dark art. Few are thought to have the necessary power. If interrupted, it cannot easily be repeated. Too much is spent in building the needed energy. The fact that you live gives evidence of that."

Endric shivered.

"I do not know how you managed to interrupt a Deshviili. It should not be easy. For that, you have the thanks of the Magi."

"Elder?" A worried frown plastered Alriyn's face.

Tresten shook his head. "They should not have been able to gain access to the palace lawn, Alriyn." His tone was angry.

Alriyn nodded. His face was tight. Endric recognized the emotions there as the same ones he had felt. Fear. Worry. What could unnerve the Magi?

"What are they?" Endric asked again, needing to hear from the Magi what he suspected.

Tresten closed his eyes and sighed. "You know who they are, Endric. I see it in your face." Endric nodded and said nothing. "They are the celebrants of destruction. They would deny the gods. They are the Deshmahne."

Behind him, Senda gasped.

CHAPTER 15

The night hung heavy and still after the proclamation.

Tresten had said nothing more after naming the Deshmahne, simply dismissing Endric and Senda to return to the Denraen. He turned and headed back toward the palace, his back seemingly more hunched, as if the weight of the discussion weighed upon his shoulders. The power he exuded was unchanged.

The other Mage paused and stared at them. He frowned for a moment, then opened his mouth as if he wanted to say something before shaking his head and turning away. Endric watched him follow Tresten, returning to the small side door they had come from. Had Tresten been the Mage he saw in Stahline? The importance of that meeting remained as much a mystery as the identity of the Denraen the Mage had met with. Endric couldn't shake the idea that something important had taken place.

He sighed. Everything about this night had him unsettled, and his heart still fluttered in his chest. Even attempting to slow his breathing didn't help.

"Endric."

Senda's soft voice startled him and he turned. The moon had crept out from beneath the clouds, now brightly lighting their path. Her dark hair trailed behind her, billowing off her Denraen grays. She wore the same uniform as the men.

There were few women among the Denraen, but most were like her. Strong. Fierce. Proud.

There was a different set to her jaw tonight. Senda's normally soft face was tight, and her hand squeezed her staff, almost afraid to let it go. It wasn't only him who was unsettled.

"Rumors are true," he said.

She frowned and narrowed her eyes before making the connection. Then she nodded. "There were too many stories of strange abilities for there not to be a shred of truth," she began, trying to keep her tone confident. Endric knew her well enough to recognize the hitch for what it was as she spoke. "There was immense power here tonight, Endric. Even I felt it."

He nodded. He had felt it as well. Tresten had even commented upon it, and for that Mage to make note of power meant something.

"We should report to Dendril," Senda said. Nervousness crept back into her voice.

"I will. You find Listain. Add this to what is known of the Deshmahne. Maybe this will persuade the Denraen to act."

"Endric, I—"

"You saw what happened here tonight. Regardless of what happens to me, the Denraen need you."

"Just the Denraen?"

He sighed. "I don't know what I am going to do," he admitted. "But I may need you too. Tresten may not have been offended that I violated tradition, but the other Mage certainly was. There will be repercussions."

"I saw what happened. We had reason for entering the grounds."

"I had reason," he corrected. "You know it doesn't matter. Not when I'm involved."

She opened her mouth and he raised his hand, silencing her. Her eyes narrowed and she frowned, but she didn't say anything more. They knew each other too well.

The walk back through the city was silent. There were the sounds of the night—the occasional chirp of a creakerbug, a lonely hoot from a mountain owl, and their footsteps along the cobbles—but otherwise the city was quiet.

It was late, and he didn't expect anything else. Most in the city were asleep. As he should be. Somehow, he had managed to find trouble again. This time, he was not sure of the consequences.

There was little doubt that he had stopped something. Even Tresten appeared worried about the Deshviili. There was another worry Endric had noted. The Mage had seemed surprised the Deshmahne had been able to enter the palace grounds, almost angry. Was there something that kept the dark priests away from the palace? If so, what had changed?

A growing sense of nausea began burning in his stomach. This was the mystery he needed to help solve. It might even be the key to steering his father toward attacking the Deshmahne. Now that he had seen them, he had a better understanding of how his brother had been killed. With the power the priests obviously wielded, the unimaginable dark art, any doubt he had harbored that they had been behind the attack on Andril and his regiment vanished.

More than ever, he knew they must be stopped. Not for vengeance, though he couldn't deny such desire remained. Rather, after witnessing how helpless he had felt, the tide of hopelessness radiating from them, he truly understood the danger of the Deshmahne.

The challenge would be convincing his father.

The massive council table was empty. It didn't make him any more comfortable sitting there, knowing his brother had once sat along the same table, only for different reasons. Endric sat there for questioning. Andril had sat there for council.

Dendril stood behind him. Pacing. Occasionally he would grunt.

As he'd promised, Endric had reported to his father. The general was not pleased to learn they had violated tradition and entered the palace lawn. He wondered what sort of interrogation Senda faced. There was little doubt in his mind that she had reported to Listain. He hoped she stuck with the planned story.

"You do not understand the consequences of your action," Dendril said.

Endric sat quietly. He understood them well enough but feared more the consequences of inaction.

Dendril took the silence for guilt. "Maybe you do understand. That doesn't explain what you were thinking. Do you want me to expel you from the Denraen?" He shook his head. "I had thought that Urik could help—"

"You have not let me explain."

"Then tell me, Endric. Convince me why you continue to defy me." His father came to sit at the head of the table and rested his large arms atop it. His face was weary and his shoulders sagged. His eyes were clearer than when he had last seen him, but more troubled.

Endric glanced around. Again his gaze settled on the huge sword hanging on the wall. Trill had been given to his father long before he joined the Denraen. Endric didn't know anything of his father then, and Dendril never spoke of it. At least not to him.

The sword was an amazing piece, from the carvings along the hilt to the detail on the bladeguard. The blade itself was a work of art, the steel folded in such a way to make it nigh unbreakable. Trill was created by bladesmiths more skilled than any still alive. And his father hung it in his office. A sword like that begged to be carried, to be used.

"Endric!" Dendril said his name with a snarl, grabbing his attention. "Is there anything you wish to say? Do you even care to remain Denraen?"

"Father, I—"

He was interrupted as the door to his father's office opened and a familiar figure entered. He had to duck underneath the doorframe, leading with his balding head and close-cropped hair, though his stooped posture likely made that easier. His cloak was darker than Endric remembered, blacker than night, and the embroidery worked upon the front and sleeves had a nearly recognizable pattern.

Mage Tresten swung the door closed behind him.

As he crossed the distance from the door to the table, he drew himself up. The stoop to his back disappeared completely. Years melted from his face. He flexed fingers no longer deformed by arthritis. Still old, he no longer appeared frail. Quite the contrary: He suddenly appeared a powerful Mage in his prime.

"Your son served the Denraen well this evening, Dendril," he said without preamble. Even his voice was stronger. Less reedy and deeper. "You should praise, not punish. They seek access, and perhaps something more, though I would not know how they have discovered that."

Dendril stood and nodded slightly to Tresten as he entered. A question pulled his mouth into a frown. "Tresten." He turned to Endric and narrowed his eyes. "Explain."

Endric was surprised to hear Dendril commanding one of the Magi, let alone a councilor, but Tresten was unfazed. "Deshmahne have entered the city. By accounts," he said, nodding to Endric, "three attempted a Deshviili. They were unsuccessful."

"Deshviili?"

"A summoning of sorts. Perhaps more, though I do not know with certainty."

"What would they summon?"

Tresten's gaze shifted to Endric, and his father nodded as if that were answer enough.

"How?" Dendril asked.

"I believe your son interrupted the ceremony."

Dendril turned to Endric, a mask of darkness plastered to his face. "You saw this?"

Endric nodded.

"This is why you entered the grounds?"

He nodded again.

"Did you see where the Deshmahne entered?"

"No, I—"

"How did you see the Deshmahne on the grounds?"

Endric closed his eyes. Would his father even allow him to explain? Now that he knew about the Deshmahne, his anger over Endric's breaking the rules and entering the palace grounds had disappeared. Only now it would be replaced by anger over abandoning his patrol. "I was in the Lashiin ruins," he answered. Nothing other than the truth would explain how he had seen the Deshmahne near the palace.

Dendril considered the comment for a moment, then grunted. "Senda was with you?"

"No." His father's implication was clear. He wouldn't sully her reputation with rumors of that sort. "She followed me to the ruins."

His father grunted again. Tresten watched them with a bemused expression and let the conversation play out. It wasn't until they were finished that the Mage decided to speak.

"If I may?" he said, looking at Dendril. "Whatever reason he had for being among the ruins"—he glanced at Endric, and a sly smile crossed his thin lips—"his presence served a purpose. The Deshmahne are gone, but there remains a concern."

"I will learn where they entered."

"Where is not as interesting as how."

Dendril nodded. "I don't know, Tresten. Gods! I don't know how they crossed the barrier. They should not have been able to do so. They will not have access again."

Tresten snorted softly at Dendril's choice of words. Some among the Urmahne frowned at such comments. Tresten didn't seem the type. "This is not their first show of strength." The implication was heavy. "Nor the first barrier they managed to breach. Many felt to be impenetrable have fallen before their art." He hesitated, lowering his eyes, dropping his voice as he did. "There was great power at work tonight, Dendril. If they had succeeded…"

The general nodded slowly. "I know. Much would have been lost." Dendril pursed his lips, scratching at his beard for a moment. "And their target?"

Tresten shook his head. "The Deshvilii was near the north tower," he said. "I assume they intended to claim its contents. Perhaps they did not know I moved them long ago."

Dendril's eyes widened momentarily. "They have details of the palace."

"They must."

"How?"

Tresten shook his head and shrugged. "The palace is over one thousand years old. How is no longer important. It was good that I made preparations, else tonight might have been worse. Regardless, it cannot happen again."

Dendril sighed and his shoulders sagged again. Endric saw a strange expression flit across his face and then it was gone. He suspected the thought that lingered, though. His father wished Andril still lived.

"What preparations?" Dendril asked.

"The gates have been neutralized. As much of the city as I could find as well. The items of power within the palace moved to a safer location. It was all I could do. I no longer have the strength I once had at such things."

Dendril nodded carefully. "It should have been done long ago."

Tresten fixed him with a dark expression, his eyes suddenly hard. Dendril met his gaze for only a moment. "You know that such a thing has consequences."

Dendril nodded again. "I only meant—"

"I know what you meant. And what you also have neglected. There are few enough within the conclave that we cannot lose even one."

"I continue to serve," Dendril protested.

"Do you? Then why must I remain within the city?"

Dendril shook his head but had no answer. Endric looked from his father to the Mage, completely lost in their conversation. The look upon Tresten's face said more than his words ever could. The words had seemed harsh, but his face wrinkled with concern and he leaned forward, as if wanting to reassure Dendril, before catching himself.

Finally, his father looked up. "I will do what must be done, Tresten."

Tresten blinked. "I know that you will. Know that *I* will do what I must." The words seemed laced with a threat. "Tonight was very nearly a disaster. You must work with the conclave to ensure the Deshmahne do not acquire what they seek. The throne would allow them to steal from even me."

Endric felt lost by the conversation, but Dendril obviously followed. "They could not do that—"

"How do you think they've gained the power they have?"

"Not that way."

"I think we will find he has perfected the arts he long has sought."

"Who?" Endric asked.

They both turned to him, as if acknowledging his presence for the first time. They stared for a long moment before Dendril shook his head. "There is much we still do not know of their abilities. Andril was evidence of that," he said to Tresten, his voice catching as he spoke Andril's name. "Now is not the time to attack."

Tresten tilted his head. "Perhaps not directly, though there are those that oppose them even now. But if you do not plan an attack, then at least ensure our defenses are capable."

"It will be done," his father repeated.

Tresten considered his father a moment and then nodded. Before he turned to the door, he hesitated and placed a firm hand upon Endric's shoulder. A wave of cold seeped into his skin as he squeezed, then as quickly was gone. Tresten smiled solemnly, then nodded again, saying nothing more as he glided across the floor. His posture slowly resumed his stoop as he neared the door, and by the time he had it open, he was the image of the frail elder Mage once more.

When the door closed behind Tresten, Endric swiveled in his seat to face his father. Dendril was standing and leaning with one hand on the table and looking toward the door to his office. His eyes were distant and unfocused. His mouth was drawn tight. Slowly he inhaled, then blinked, shifting his focus to Endric.

"What was your assignment tonight?"

Endric blinked, considering his response before answering. "I was assigned patrol," he said, swallowing as he did.

Dendril cocked his head. "Were you assigned to patrol the ruins?"

"No."

"Then why were you there?"

"I like the view," he answered simply.

Dendril grunted. "Or you were hoping to romp with your friend."

"Senda?" Endric frowned, feeling a surge of anger in his belly. "She followed me. Yes. She is a friend. No, not one I have bedded." He shook his head again and leaned forward. "She is concerned about me." The accusation in his tone hung in the air for a long moment.

"And you think I am not?"

Endric closed his eyes and looked away from his father. "Not like Andril."

"I know you grieve your brother. I do as well. But we must move on. Surely you see that. You are Denraen. You can't continue to defy your responsibilities."

Endric nodded slowly. His father was right. Now was the time for him to move beyond his grief. Andril would want that for him. "I will follow my orders."

"That is not what I mean, and you know it."

"After everything, you still want me to lead?"

Dendril leaned back and sighed. "No. I do not."

The comment should not have surprised him, yet it did. "You think I can't lead?"

"I think you can lead. That is the problem."

"Why?"

"You don't understand consequences. Simply action. I have no doubt that men would follow you. Your skill alone would endear you to many. Your name would to others. Yet you are not prepared to lead."

"You're disappointed I am not like Andril."

"Is that what you think?" Dendril asked. "Andril was a fine soldier and an excellent commander. Skilled, intelligent, and levelheaded." He grunted. "You are skilled. And intelligent. Levelheaded you are not. When you can master your emotions, you will not only be a better soldier, you will be a better man." Dendril's eyes narrowed. "Then you may be ready to lead."

Endric opened his mouth but hesitated, knowing his father was right. Emotion often got the best of him. That was the reason he had been assigned to Urik in the first place. From a young age, Andril had mastered his emotions, able to control his anger and push it aside to the point that Endric once thought his brother never got angry.

"What will you do about the Deshmahne?" Endric asked. After seeing them tonight, he understood the danger they posed.

Dendril frowned at him and leaned back. Then he shook his head. "Tresten is right. You served well tonight. Stopping the Deshviili..." As his father's words trailed off, Endric absorbed the rare praise. "I do not know what would have happened had they been successful."

"Why attack the palace?"

Dendril shook his head. "The palace holds something the Deshmahne consider extremely valuable. With it, they would gain great power."

"What is it?"

The general shook his head. His mouth tightened into a serious frown. "The fewer that know, the safer we are."

"But you know." Dendril nodded and Endric didn't press for more. "You still have not said what you will do about the Deshmahne."

"No. I have not. You will get your orders."

Though he didn't say it, Endric heard the unspoken words. Like the rest of the Denraen. Dendril wouldn't make an exception for him.

"May I be dismissed?"

Dendril nodded. He opened his mouth to say something more, but Endric had already turned and started toward the door. He did, however, risk a glance back. His father sat at the table, leaning on his heavy arms, and stared at him. Strangely, it was not a look of disappointment on his face. Rather, it was a curious expression, as if he wasn't quite sure what to make of him.

CHAPTER 16

Endric found Pendin in the great hall. It was late and mostly empty, but a few men lingered. Food was always available—they had to feed hungry soldiers—but late at night, the selection was poor. Usually cold, too.

Pendin sat at a table near the door. A small leather-bound book lay open on the table and he fingered the pages but didn't turn one in the few moments Endric watched. The corners of his mouth wrinkled, and he would occasionally scrub his hand over his head. He was worried.

He looked up as Endric approached. The worry on his face turned to something different, almost relief. "Where have you been? I know you weren't on patrol tonight," he said quietly.

"I didn't realize I had to report to you as well. I thought Urik alone was enough." He closed his eyes, frustrated at letting his annoyance with his father creep into his conversation with Pendin.

"That's not what I meant," Pendin said. As he stared at Endric's face a moment, he hesitated. "What happened?"

Endric sank onto the bench. The great hall was lined with tables and benches, and countless soldiers sitting down to eat had long ago worn the wood smooth. There was a certain comfort to the room, a coziness belied by its size. His friend knew him well and recognized the signs. "I know the name of the Mage you followed from Stahline."

He pitched his words so they wouldn't carry. Others in the Denraen wouldn't understand their following one of the Magi. It might get reported and lead to questions he didn't want to answer. Especially not if his father was asking.

Pendin widened his eyes. "How?"

"I met him." When Pendin frowned, he went on. "I followed three figures I later learned were Deshmahne onto the palace grounds. After chasing them away, two Magi came from the palace. One was the Mage we followed. Name of Tresten."

He didn't know whether to laugh or press on as he spoke. Pendin's face was a mixture of shock and disbelief. Had Endric not lived through it, he would have felt the same.

"You did what?" Pendin finally sputtered a little too loudly. The few others in the room glanced their way. Lowering his voice, he asked, "You went onto the grounds uninvited? *And* were seen by Magi?"

He nodded. "There was also a Mage named Alriyn. Do you recognize their names?"

Pendin blinked. "Yes. They're on the council. They're both Elders."

Endric frowned. The Mage seemed youthful compared to Tresten. "The other is the eldest? Tresten?"

Pendin shook his head. "No. Tresten only returned to the city in the past ten years. From what I can gather, he has declined the high seat on the council."

"What would one of the elders be doing in Stahline? That's even stranger than we thought."

"There's something else you should know."

"What?"

"The miners chose tonight to begin their strike."

"The same night as the Deshmahne attack?" he asked. "That can't be coincidence."

Pendin shrugged. "I don't know why it would be anything else."

Endric closed his eyes and thought. The miners were striking. The Deshmahne attack. The Magi—Tresten—were concerned about how the

Deshmahne were even able to enter the city. This was not coincidence. There was some sort of connection.

It hit him hard, like a punch in the stomach. "The mines," he whispered.

"What?"

"The Magi said the Deshmahne should not be able to enter the city. Tresten didn't know how it was possible. If the miners were striking tonight, the mines were empty. The Deshmahne came into the city through the mines."

"That's not possible. Only an urmiiln—a senior miner—would be able to navigate the mines."

"Who organized the strike?"

"Not sure," Pendin said with a shake of his head. "Though Giyoln is rumored to lead the rebellion."

"Do you know him?"

"Of him. I think few know him. As urmiiln, he no longer serves as an active miner."

"Then one of the urmiiln *could* have helped the Deshmahne."

"Not Giyoln. He was seen among the striking miners. Even if he didn't lead them, he was there. Is there."

Endric leaned back, the sudden flutter in his chest leaving a knot in his throat. The connection was there. He knew it—but he would need proof. Especially if there were miners involved. The Urmahne priests had taken on the role of protector to the miners. Not surprising, since the miners served the priests. Now those workers were nearly untouchable for fear of raising an alarm. Even with the miners striking, the Urmahne priests would need more than the circumstantial evidence he had to allow the Denraen to investigate. There had been too many conflicts between the miners and the Denraen over the years. More often than not, the miners had instigated something the Denraen felt compelled to squelch before it got out of hand.

The miners had the ear of the priests. The priests had the ear of the Magi. The Magi should listen to the Denraen, yet they didn't. At least, it seemed that way to Endric. They would need evidence—and someone willing to listen—if he intended to take on the miners. He suspected they had one among the Magi who would listen: Tresten. But they still needed proof.

"We need to get into the mines."

Pendin snorted. He met Endric's eyes and then laughed. "You're kidding?"

"The miners are striking."

"Doesn't mean the mines are empty."

Endric frowned. "Why not?"

"Teralin is difficult to mine. Does strange things. You shouldn't leave an active mine unsupervised or there will be problems. Caves collapse. Some simply get too hot. No one knows why; men who have mined other ores say it is unlike anything else. Almost as if it moves."

Endric sniffed and narrowed his eyes in disbelief. "You sound like you believe what the priests say about the ore."

Pendin shrugged. "I've worked in the mines, Endric. Hard to explain to those who haven't. There is something… different about teralin." He smiled, then shrugged again. "I don't know if it is all the priests claim—I've never spoken to the gods—but teralin is unusual."

"How many will be in the mines?"

"Probably a few senior miners, though it is hard to know. There might be more. The miners have never rebelled like this." Pendin studied him. "Why bother with the mines? What do you think you'll find?"

He shook his head. He wasn't sure. He needed proof. But did he expect to catch the Deshmahne in the mines? Not after what he had seen near the palace. Even if the dark priests had been weakened by the Deshviili, was there was anything he could do if he came across them? The answer was easy.

"Nothing," he said, trying to keep the annoyance out of his voice. "Only I'm sure they used the mines. Tresten said they should not have been able to get into the city. As if it were warded. The mines are the only way. We need to be able to prove it, close the mines to the Deshmahne."

"That may not be possible. The mines are extensive and twist deep into the mountain's core. I suspect there are few who know exactly how extensive. Maps are useless; there are hundreds, maybe thousands, of mines that have been abandoned as the teralin is mined. For every active and known abandoned mine, there are likely dozens that would be left unaccounted."

"Do the Denraen know this?" he asked. This was the first he had heard how extensive the mines were. He found it hard to believe the Denraen would leave the city so unprotected.

Pendin shrugged. "Probably not the full extent."

Endric sniffed and shook his head, closing his eyes. "I need to find Urik," he decided. "Maybe he can help. If Andril were here, he'd know what to do. This is beyond me."

Pendin shot him a hard glare. "You always compare yourself to Andril so negatively. If you saw what the rest of us see, you would know that you didn't always come out so far behind. Ahead in many ways."

Endric smiled at his friend. "That is nice of you to say. Untrue. But still nice."

Pendin sighed. "Endric—"

Whatever he was going to say was cut off as the ground beneath them rumbled. It was as if the room shuddered. The rumbling lasted nearly a dozen heartbeats, a heavy shaking that lifted dust and mortar out of the cracks in the wall and even toppled a few benches. Then it slowed to a stop.

Around them, dust hung in the air. He coughed and tasted the chalky particles. Pendin stared at him nervously, then looked around. The others in the great hall had jumped to their feet, and more than one ran toward the door.

"We should get outside," Pendin said.

Endric frowned. "What was that?"

Pendin shook his head. "I don't know. Felt like a rockslide. Or a cave collapse. Whatever it was had enough energy to shake the barracks." He looked above him at the huge beams framing the ceiling. "I don't want to be here if this collapses."

"The barracks?" As far as Endric knew, the barracks had been in place for several hundred years. Modifications had been made over time and additions had been added, but the main structure—the great hall included—had stood for centuries. Some areas, especially some of the older parts, were crafted much like the palace. As if cut from the stone of the mountain. They could even be as old as the palace. The senior officers occupied those spaces. His father. Urik. Andril's old office.

"Come on!" Pendin urged, pulling on Endric's arm.

He stood reluctantly. The hall had emptied and the ground had not moved again, but he decided to trust Pendin in this. The man *was* descended from miners. They hurried through the barracks, following a stream of like-minded soldiers out into the open night air. The cool air triggered another cough.

It was dark. Heavy clouds covered the moon, hanging fat and low, like inky smears on the night. The lighted windows within the barracks provided barely enough illumination to see their way. He still coughed, and his breath puffed out in a mist.

Endric inhaled deeply, clearing the dust from his lungs. As usual, the air smelled of coming rain. Pendin steered him into the grassy practice area and then stopped just as the rain began. Around them were dozens of other Denraen. Most were dressed, though few enough had the sense to grab their weapon. Endric was thankful for the presence of his sword on his hip.

"Pendin. I need to find Urik."

"What can he do?"

"What if that was the Deshmahne's doing?"

Pendin shook his head. "You think these priests could make the entire city shake?"

Endric shrugged, his thoughts turning back to the enormous power he had sensed as they readied the Deshviili. Then he nodded, shaking with the memory. "I do."

As he spoke, the ground heaved again. A few of the men around him screamed. Some stumbled and Endric braced himself, grabbing Pendin. His muscular friend stood steadfast, rolling with the shaking like a seasoned sailor on the open ocean. Stone creaked and groaned somewhere nearby; in the dark, it was hard to tell. There came a loud crack, like a tree branch falling. Only, this level of the city had no trees.

"The walls," Pendin shouted. He need not have though. The deep rumbling suddenly stopped. The suddenness was unnerving. Though it was now quiet, a few men moaned as if injured. Pendin's voice rang out loudly but was muted in the heavy air. "That crack came from the walls," he said, his voice now hushed.

"How do you know?"

"The direction, the feel, the way it echoed." He shrugged. "I just do."

"This is no cave collapse."

"Endric—I know you saw something from the Deshmahne tonight, but what you suggest is impossible. For these dark priests to be able to do this…" He looked around. "They would have to be as powerful as the Magi once were. Maybe more so." He shook his head and turned back to Endric. "That isn't possible."

Endric blinked slowly. He knew what he had felt earlier. And Mage Tresten had been fearful of what the Deshmahne could have accomplished with a successful Deshviili. He didn't know what magics the Magi were capable of doing; few anymore saw a demonstration of their abilities. Those stories that came out were likely as much exaggeration as truth. But he knew what he had felt from the Deshmahne.

"What else then, Pendin? What could have caused this? Why did it stop so suddenly this time?"

As if in answer, he heard a quiet murmuring behind him. It began softly, building to a clear call.

"Look!" someone shouted. "The palace!"

Endric turned. A pale blue light shone from the windows of the tallest tower. It glowed steadily, unnaturally. There was no doubt in his mind what he was seeing or what generated the light. And why the heaving ground had suddenly stopped.

Somewhere in the palace, the Magi used their abilities.

CHAPTER 17

He led Pendin through the barracks yard, stepping around or over men lying on the ground, injured or simply stunned. He recognized none. A few stared up at the third terrace and toward the palace high overhead—and the pale blue light emanating from the upper windows of the tower—and barely blinked, as if transfixed.

Endric started toward the barracks again, intending to head back in and find Urik, but Pendin grabbed his arm. "Not yet. Wait until the engineers have been by."

"You said it was the wall that cracked."

Pendin shook his head once. "Probably the wall. But don't take any chances."

Endric grunted in frustration, then turned and circled the barracks. More and more lanterns appeared as they neared the main street. Someone had even bothered to relight the normally darkened streetlights. Wind gusted around him, biting cold through his shirt. The shadows that flickered down the street reminded him of his experience in the barracks. He shivered but quickly suppressed it as he grabbed the hilt of his sword and squeezed.

Then he saw his father. Urik stood nearby and they conversed quietly. Urik moved his hands as he spoke, obviously animated, while Dendril merely listened and nodded. Listain was nowhere to be seen.

Endric nodded to Pendin. His friend frowned but followed with a certain reluctance. Though never implicated by his actions, Endric knew his friend didn't relish the possibility of being near Dendril during a reprimand.

"We must speak to the Magi, Dendril," Urik said as they neared. "Perhaps you could—"

Dendril interrupted him with a single shake of his head. "No, Urik. The Magi have this well in hand. I won't question them on this."

"But after tonight—"

"I have made my decision in this."

Urik hesitated only a moment. "You could ask Tresten."

Dendril narrowed his eyes. "There will be no further discussion. Not on this." He turned as Endric neared, and his eyes were hard. They didn't soften as they would have for Andril. "Do you have something to report?" he asked, his voice gruff.

Endric tilted his head at the question. "No," he said, drawing out the answer. "Just want to know what is going on."

The corners of Dendril's mouth curled. "You know what is happening."

Urik turned from Dendril to Endric. "What does he know?"

"He interrupted the Deshviili tonight."

Urik frowned. "You didn't say it was Endric."

"That wasn't important."

"Are you certain?"

"Yes. I am. Do not test me, Urik."

Endric was no longer sure what was happening. There was tension between his father and the en'raen, and he didn't understand the source. What was Urik asking of Dendril, and why did his father not want to do it? Was it about the Deshmahne again?

"This was Deshmahne then?" Endric asked.

Dendril shook his head. "That's not certain."

"But the Magi are doing something to stop it."

Urik tilted his head at Endric and gave him a tight smile. "The boy sees it too." At Dendril's hard glare, he raised his hands. "I only intend to protect—"

"No." Dendril said the word quietly, and it knifed through the air. There would be no further challenge to his authority.

"They use the tunnels," Endric offered. If this was Deshmahne, he would find a way to motivate a Denraen response.

Dendril frowned. "They wouldn't be able to navigate the tunnels."

"Not without a guide." Endric turned and motioned toward Pendin. The sick expression on his face said enough. He didn't want to be involved. Not in this, not where his allegiance to his family could be questioned. Endric understood that. But he knew what the Deshmahne had done. He'd seen his own brother's head. In a bag. And there was no telling what they intended to do at the palace.

"The miners began their strike tonight," Dendril said. It was a question, and he looked to Urik for answer. The en'raen nodded slowly. The general pursed his lips, and his eyes were drawn.

Endric recognized the frustrated expression; he had caused it often enough. Why had Urik not told him? Endric suddenly felt uneasy and a bit on edge. The familiar warning nausea rolled in the pit of his stomach. There was something he was missing.

Dendril closed his eyes and exhaled through his nose. "Can't be a coincidence." He paused, looking around. "Where is Listain?"

Endric stared at his father a moment. The Deshmahne had attacked the city and were now somehow causing the ground to tremble. The miners were revolting. And now Listain was missing. His heart started fluttering in his chest. Was that the connection? Had the spymaster somehow organized all this?

He didn't get a chance to ask the question. A runner approached, panting and dirtied. His chest bore the three stripes of his rank, the fabric of his uniform ripped near his rank. A dried stream of blood came from a gash on his cheek. The man would prize the scar later. Endric didn't recognize him.

"General," the man said.

Dendril nodded. "What is it?"

"One of the outer buildings has collapsed."

His father narrowed his eyes. "Where?" The man gestured over his shoulder and Dendril's eyes widened slightly. "Was anyone hurt?"

"You need to come."

"What is it?" Endric demanded, interrupting.

The man turned and glanced briefly at Endric. "It's Listain, sir," he answered as if Endric were an officer. He wasn't sure what it would mean if Listain was injured or why the spymaster had been away from his office and the barracks in the middle of the night.

Endric looked over at his father. Had Senda been with Listain? She had planned on finding the Raen after they separated earlier. "Was there anyone else with him?" he asked the runner.

The man shook his head. "Unknown. Significant structural damage. We know the Raen is there, but trapped. We are unable to move the rock to reach him." He turned to Dendril. "Engineers fear there isn't enough air for long."

Dendril had his eyes closed again. When he opened them, he looked at Endric. "I need you to summon Tresten."

"The Mage? You're asking me to go onto the grounds. Again," he asked, incredulous. Did his father really expect him to summon one of the Magi? He should be helping with the rescue—even if it was Listain. Senda could be there. The thought of losing another person close to him caused his throat to swell, and he couldn't say anything more.

He didn't have to. Dendril only nodded curtly. Urik looked at Endric and frowned. His eyes narrowed, and Endric could tell the man was trying to work through what he had dealt with that evening. He knew not even Urik could imagine what he had seen.

"You've already violated the tradition once today." He shook his head, biting off another comment. "But this time, you will go on my authority. Find Tresten. Bring him to the south guard station." When Endric hesitated, he said, "Go. Now."

Endric turned away and motioned to Pendin, who followed. They jogged along the street, weaving around the men standing. Some were silent; others spoke quietly. Everything remained fairly organized. As the Denraen should.

It wasn't until they were several hundred feet from the barracks that Pendin spoke. "Why are we summoning a Mage? And why was there tension between Urik and the general?"

Endric shook his head. Pendin had sensed it as well. Of course he would. For all his physical strength, Pendin was intuitive. That was another part of the reason they had become such fast friends. "I think there is more to my father's relationship with this Mage than they let on." He paused a moment, debating whether to share his fear for Senda with Pendin. She was his friend too. "Senda may be with Listain. She was going to report to him when I saw her last."

Pendin took a deep breath and nodded once. His steps increased in speed, and Endric hurried to keep up. They followed the road to the main palace gate. Neither said anything more. Endric hoped Tresten would provide more answers. The Mage had been fairly forthcoming with him so far, so much so that he was beginning to feel deluged by everything. If he was this easily overwhelmed, how had he even considered anyone else replacing his father? Though he didn't always agree with him, the man led the Denraen well.

He paused at the gate. This, itself, was a barrier. All knew teralin held heat, and the fear of that heat had stopped more than one person from trying to sneak past the wall surrounding the palace. The metal itself was valuable, mostly to the priests though it had other uses, but he had never heard of anyone thieving the teralin gates from the Magi. Many had debated whether it was fear of repercussions from the Magi or fear of the teralin itself that stopped most men.

The gate was elaborately made here. The teralin was thick, the bars nearly a hand wide, and likely accounted for several months of mining to recover this much of the metal. A gate this size was nearly priceless. Then there were the decorations worked into the metal. Though some twisted into blurred faces—renderings of the gods—most were shaped into the other symbols of the Urmahne. Trefoil leaves, split branches, even the tower were shaped into the teralin. The effect was awe-inspiring.

Or it had been, once. Living in the city took much of the awe of the Magi out of him. There were still a few people who visited and had never seen the city. He had seen the expression on their faces as they approached the palace and the gate leading to it. To one not born of the city, it was almost a religious experience.

Endric sighed. If only he had such faith. Andril had had the required faith. That had granted him a sense of peace, a quiet strength. If only he could be like Andril in that regard. Perhaps then he could more easily serve.

His hand hovered over the gate. Heat radiated from the metal. This much of the ore would be quite hot. It wouldn't burn—shaped teralin never did—but that didn't mean it wouldn't hurt. Steeling himself, he twisted and pushed on the handle, swinging the gate slowly open. He had to suppress a scream as he did.

Pendin looked at him, a hint of amusement crossing his face. "It's worse in the mines," he said quietly.

Endric began wondering just how much experience Pendin had in the mines. He had mentioned working in them briefly, but did he have more extensive knowledge? Could he...

He pushed the thought away, inhaling deeply. He wouldn't doubt his friend. Pendin had been nothing other than a friend since they first met. There was no reason to doubt him. No. He needed Pendin now. Especially since Andril was lost to him.

"Do we just walk up to the front door?" he asked Pendin.

He shrugged. "What did you do the last time you were here?"

Endric snorted with a suppressed laugh. "Only violate centuries of tradition by entering the grounds and brandishing my sword at a pair of Magi councilors."

"We could repeat that..."

He laughed again. It felt good, as if it had been too long since he had last let himself truly feel joy. Even though he worried for his friend, he knew he couldn't hold all his emotions inside. Too often, he bottled up what he was feeling until it exploded. That was part of his problem.

He still felt the pull of tension in his shoulders, but the worst of it had eased. He looked up at the tower still lit with the unnatural blue light. There had been no more tremors since they left for the palace, and he wondered if that was the Magi's doing or simply chance. The lingering questions caused the tension that had been easing to slowly begin to build again, and with it, frustration at his impotence about what was happening.

Nodding toward the palace, he started off down the path leading toward the main entrance. His heart skipped a bit faster in his chest. He almost wished he were more devout; a prayer might help them now.

He paused as they neared. Ornately carved doors nearly twice his height curved up into an arching doorway. They looked to be made of the same pale stone as the rest of the palace, but Endric found that hard to fathom. Stone doors would be nearly impossible to open. But perhaps that was the intent.

He frowned as he looked at the carvings along the surface, detailed etchings recognizable to any of the Urmahne faith. The centermost scene depicted the Ascension—the time when the gods left their earthly home to sit among the heavens. Urmahne taught that the Magi still spoke to the gods, acting as their voice, and that they would one day return. Endric believed that the gods had once lived on earth—the tower was a testament to that—but was not sure how he felt about the rest of the religion.

Teralin handles decorated with twisting vines ending in wide trefoil leaves sank into the stone on each door. Even if he had the stomach to grasp the handle, he was not sure he could even open the door. Then he realized he wouldn't have to.

As he started to turn to ask Pendin's opinion, one of the doors slowly swung toward him. He wondered briefly what he would say to the Mage he assumed opened the door. Who else could? Instead, a small man emerged from the shadows to peer up at him. The white shirt and pants he wore flowed with each step. His gray hair was worn long and tied loosely behind his head. Not a Mage. A palace servant. Their dress and appearance stood out from the other workers in the city.

"You would be Endric, son of Dendril," the man said after considering him for a long moment. His voice was thin and creaked as he spoke. Turning to Pendin, he brought a gnarled hand to his wrinkled face and frowned. "Then you are likely Pendin Tisguid."

"How do you—" Pendin began, but Endric cut him off.

"I apologize for the lateness of our visit, but the need is urgent. We seek Mage Tresten."

The man tilted his head. "You mean Dendril seeks Elder Tresten."

Endric frowned and slowly nodded. "Is he available?"

The man glanced up and behind him, in the direction of the lighted tower. Was Tresten the source of the light? Was he the reason the tremors ceased?

"I believe he is expecting you," the man said.

With that, he turned and left Endric and Pendin standing alone on the threshold of the Magi palace, the huge stone door cracked open. They looked at each other and Endric frowned. He dared not enter the palace. Not without an express invitation. That went beyond what even he dared try. Yet he was not certain what was expected of them.

Long minutes passed. Pendin didn't speak and Endric chose not to disturb the silence. Not even insects interrupted the silence of the night. He tapped his foot silently in agitation at having to wait. Each minute mattered. Finally, the door opened again and the familiar stooped form of Mage Tresten stood before them.

He smiled. It changed his face somehow, distorting the image of the nearly invalid Mage, and Endric felt a strange kind of power emanating from him.

"Mage Tresten," he began but didn't get the chance to continue.

"No need for formalities. Dendril has need. What is it?"

Endric hesitated. How had Tresten known they were coming? He didn't seem surprised. Even the old servant had said the Mage was expecting them. Another time, he would have cried out with frustration. Everything about tonight created new questions, and there had been few answers.

"To be honest, I'm not completely sure. We are to take you to one of the guard stations. I think it is the Raen." He said nothing of his friend. Listain would matter more to the Mage.

"Listain?" Tresten murmured, then nodded. "Show me."

With a quick flick of his wrist, the huge door swung closed. Endric was not entirely certain he even touched it. Mage Tresten started down the path leading away from the palace. He didn't look back to see if they followed.

When they were a little ways from the palace, Tresten glanced over at him. "You seem troubled."

"I am." He paused, collecting his thoughts. "Were you expecting us?"

Tresten looked over at him, then at Pendin. His friend had remained silent in the presence of the Mage. That wasn't surprising. Pendin had a bit more faith in the Urmahne than he did. "Willam told you that?" Seeing Endric's nod, he continued. "He has served the Magi long and well," he said softly, then shrugged. "Perhaps he misspoke. Is that all that is bothering you?"

Endric nearly tripped with the question. Tresten seemed genuinely concerned, though the Mage could simply be pretending. Who could know the mind of a Mage? He shook his head. "That is not all," he answered honestly.

"It is what you saw? The Deshmahne are men, Endric. Endowed by their mystical arts, but men nonetheless."

Endric frowned. It was interesting that Tresten felt the need to frame it like that—as well as strangely reassuring. Had he been fearful of the Deshmahne? "They used the mines, Mage Tresten."

He smiled sadly and sniffed. "Just Tresten, Endric. And I suspected as much."

"The miners staged their rebellion tonight."

Tresten cocked his head and paused briefly midstep. Endric almost tripped again trying not to collide with him. "More layers here than I anticipated."

"Did the Deshmahne create the earthquakes?"

"I believe so."

"How?"

Tresten shook his head. "Little is known about the arts the Deshmahne use. They guard those secrets closely. But the most powerful of them, like the men you saw tonight, are able to perform destructive works that defy imagination." He shook his head again and sighed, looking over at Endric.

Endric suddenly thought of Andril and what his brother must have faced. Tresten saw his face and nodded. The Mage's shoulders stooped as if he was fatigued, but his eyes were still bright.

"Was it you that stopped them?"

Tresten nodded. "I interrupted the flow of their destructive energy. As did you earlier tonight. They were tired from their attempt at the Deshviili, else I might have been ineffective." He sighed again. "As it was, they still managed some damage."

They had reached the gate and Tresten pulled it easily open, no grimace on his face as he grasped the teralin, and they paused to stare into the city. Dust hung over the buildings like a low-lying cloud. Any other night, Endric would have thought it only mist. Tonight, he knew better.

More buildings were damaged than he had noticed before. As they followed the street, they found one after another with evidence of cracking. Some had simply collapsed. It would take years to repair all the damage he saw. The street itself bowed, as if the pressure beneath had been too much to bear. These cobbles had been in place for hundreds of years, only needing occasional replacement, and now they were completely damaged. People stood outside shops and homes—sometimes one and the same—and stared around them. Most wore the same dazed expression Endric knew he had felt when the earth first shook beneath them.

Endric looked at Tresten. The Mage had closed his eyes and was shaking his head slowly. His shoulders rolled forward and his spine curved as if the weight of the mountain pressed upon him. And perhaps it did. He looked even older than when Endric had first seen him. Weakened and tired. Endric didn't know what it had taken to stop the Deshmahne and was certain he wouldn't understand were the Mage to try to explain again. He looked as tired as he claimed the Deshmahne had been. What would have happened had the dark priests been at full strength?

"More damage than I had thought." Tresten sighed, opening his eyes. He pulled himself upright, some of the vigor returning to his step, and said, "Come. We must find Listain. And your friend Senda."

Endric blinked in surprise. "You knew?"

Tresten nodded once. "She serves Listain well. I knew she would report on tonight's events. Seeing as how she is not with you and the worried look you've worn upon your face, I can only deduce that is what you fear."

"It is."

"And Denraen Tisguid fears his parents' involvement with the miner rebellion."

Pendin said nothing, only nodding.

Tresten sighed again. "Show me this guard station."

Endric took the lead as they made their way into the city. They were forced to take a less direct path than he normally would, diverted by an occasional building toppled across the street, blocking traffic. Strange they had seen nothing this severe on their way to the palace. They encountered a few people, and at one point heard sobs and a woman wailing. Tresten stopped and looked at the woman. She was covered in dark dust—broken stone and ash—and blood smeared her forehead from an open gash.

"What is it?" he asked softly.

"My daughter," the woman sobbed. "She's trapped. My husband and son have run for help, but no one has come. Please, Magi. Ask the gods to save her!"

"I will do what I can."

Pendin stepped forward with his mouth open, ready to speak. Endric stopped him with an arm across his chest. They were pressed for time, true, but Endric wanted to see what the Mage would do. Could the Magi truly speak to the gods? Would they intervene on such a request?

The answer was more mundane than that. Still amazing to witness.

Tresten raised his arm. A swirling energy, palpable but invisible, flowed from him and into the rubble. His long face pulled tight in concentration. Suddenly his eyes narrowed and then the rock exploded outward, away from them, revealing a small child huddled beneath. Amazingly, she was unharmed.

"Mama?" she asked, opening her eyes.

"Tralia!" her mother shouted, sobbing harder. She turned briefly to Tresten. "The gods be blessed!" She climbed in to claim her daughter.

Tresten nodded, then turned away to lead them around the rubble, an opening now cleared by whatever he had done. The energy still swirled around him, though it lessened until Endric could no longer feel it.

He followed the Mage. "The gods had nothing to do with that child being saved."

Tresten glanced at him and smiled briefly. "It is all perspective," he answered. "To you, it is only a powerful Mage who worked his ability. To that woman, the gods guided my hand to save her daughter. Who is to say which is right?"

Pendin chuckled and Endric turned to him and frowned, feeling a brief surge of annoyance. Still, seeing a Mage's power was beyond what he had imagined. The thrill of it surged through him and he felt a moment of doubt. Could the Urmahne teachings be right?

The Mage looked at him again, smiling briefly as if guessing his thoughts. Endric fell speechless. They remained silent as they worked toward the guard station. The station was known as little used, old, and with an interior much in need of renovation and upkeep. Why would Listain be there? Was it his search for secrecy, or was there another reason?

Which building they were seeking became obvious as they neared. The dust and smoke were thicker around it. Endric covered his mouth with his sleeve as he moved. Massive stone fragments were strewn across the road, radiating outward as if from an explosive blast. The center of what had once been the building was completely destroyed, little more than fine debris remaining. Even the walls were barely visible. Strangely, the neighboring buildings had not suffered nearly as much. It was as if that specific one had been targeted.

Along the street stood Dendril and Urik, staring at the demolished guard station. Dendril's back was straight and he simply stared at the broken rock. Urik seemed agitated, his head swiveling, looking for movement or possibly hearing something. Dozens of other Denraen worked among the rock, searching under flickering lantern light. Overhead, the wan moonlight struggled to shine through the thick clouds. It had little hope of penetrating the dust cloud.

Dendril turned when they approached, and a flash of relief crossed his face. It was the most emotion he had seen from the man since Andril's death. "You came."

Tresten grunted, more of a huff. "I have been a little busy." He ignored Dendril's glare and looked into the rubble. "You are certain Listain was here?"

His father blinked slowly before speaking. Endric recognized the expression; his father was considering his words carefully. Why?

"Listain was here."

Tresten nodded, accepting the answer. "Anyone else?"

Endric felt his heart flutter, thankful the Mage had asked the question and suddenly wondering about his feelings for Senda.

Dendril shrugged. "There are several who work directly for him. Some may have been here as well."

Endric felt his brief hope sink. Tresten nodded again and stepped toward the demolished building. As he did, Urik whistled a distinctive two-note call—a signal to retreat—and the men searching the fallen building immediately stopped and moved back onto the street. Endric was not sure what to expect. He had seen what the Mage could do to help the woman on the street. Was it too much to hope for the same with Senda now?

He felt the buildup of pressure behind his ears first. Then the hairs on his arms stood. Even the hair upon his head twitched, as if suddenly alive. Tresten had not moved, standing still and immobile, nearly statuesque. Endric could almost imagine the energy the Mage manipulated swirling around him. As he watched, he no longer had to imagine; the dust from the debris of the collapsed building began twitching and swaying in the air, creating a slow but steady spin around them. Blue light, like he had seen radiating from the tower window, seeped into the air, though it didn't seem to come from any particular source.

Some of the men raised their hands in supplication. He understood. To one devout, seeing this was to see the gods, however indirectly.

Yet Endric didn't feel that way, knowing there was a different answer, no less impressive but not dependent upon the gods. He could no longer doubt the Magi abilities. Whether they truly spoke to the lost and nameless gods was something entirely different and not required for Tresten to do whatever feat he now performed.

The blue light and dust plunged down into the earth in a torrent, sending a blast of dirty air blowing up behind it. Men who had stepped closer to watch were thrust back, most coughing and covering their mouths to keep from breathing in the stale air. A few fell over from the force of whatever it was that Tresten did. The Mage raised his arms, and with it, the largest of the rubble simply lifted from the ground as if light as air. He twisted at the waist and nodded at the men standing in the street. Those who watched jumped and hurried out of his way. Others were pulled by their friends. When the street had emptied, Tresten lowered his arms and the rock lowered slowly with the motion, depositing onto the recently vacated space.

Tresten turned back to the collapsed building and pointed. A wave of blue light zipped around the ground, illuminating a crater in the ground. It stretched deeper than Endric had expected—much deeper than any guard station should—as if there had been several sublevels hiding beneath the basement. Fragments of lower walls remained, even some floors. In the shadowed darkness, nothing moved.

"Nothing lives here, Dendril." Tresten spoke softly, still staring at the remains of the building. "I can sense nothing of Listain. Or any of his apprentices."

Endric took a breath to steady himself. The news was not all bad. "What was this place?" he finally asked his father, keeping his tone neutral.

Dendril shook his head. "It was Listain's."

Endric blinked at that. The Raen should have his office in the barracks, near the general, like each of the en'raens. Urik. Andril. Listain had chosen to set himself apart in what appeared to be a deep underground bunker.

His heart skipped a beat with a sudden thought. "Are there tunnels here?"

He stepped closer to the edge of the new crater. Areas in the crater were darker smudges, interrupting the strange blue light Tresten had lit.

"Some."

"Where do they connect?"

Dendril hesitated. "All throughout the city."

Urik looked at him and frowned. Had the en'raen known? Was this how Listain gathered all his information so easily? The man popped up all over the city without being seen. Rumors had started. Now he understood. There was nothing mystical to Listain either.

"These Deshmahne could have come in through these tunnels." It was Pendin. He spoke softly, a slight quiver to his voice. It didn't fit with his enormous frame.

"No. They couldn't," Tresten said.

"Why not?"

"These tunnels move only through the city. There is no access outside. And they are warded."

"Are you certain?" Urik asked.

"Quite," the Mage said. "I placed them myself."

"That leaves the mines," Endric said to his father.

Dendril nodded. He looked out into the city. Endric was not clear what he stared at, though his father's eyes lost focus and grew distant. His mouth tightened into a thin line. Then he sighed, relaxing only slightly. "This miner rebellion is ill-timed."

"Or well-timed," Tresten suggested.

"More likely." Dendril looked over at the old Mage, and their eyes met. A flash of unspoken communication—a kind of understanding—passed between them. "Will the Magi support what must be done?" he asked quietly.

Tresten shook his head once. "And risk upsetting the priests?" he asked, stepping closer. His voice was barely more than a whisper and didn't carry far. Endric was not sure any others heard Tresten speak.

Dendril blinked slowly. "We run other risks if we do not pursue."

"I trust in your judgment."

The general narrowed his eyes, then nodded one time. "Thank you for coming, Tresten."

"If only I could have helped more. I wish I could have helped find Listain."

"You have done more than I could hope. Listain is not here. I pray that he found a way out before the building started to fall."

"I as well. Other scenarios are less pleasant." Tresten met Dendril's eyes once more. Again, something passed between them.

Dendril breathed out slowly, then nodded.

"I must return to the palace. If there are other needs, I may again be summoned." With that, Tresten turned and started away from the crater and the rubble. His back still stooped, though less than Endric remembered. He moved carefully, his long legs carrying him quickly away. Soon he had faded into the dust and darkness of the night.

"We must find Listain," Dendril said after Tresten had disappeared. He looked at Urik.

The en'raen shook his head. "You know how challenging that can be. If he is down there," he said, waving a hand toward the revealed tunnel system, "then he will be nigh impossible to find."

"Urik. We must know if Listain lives."

Realization dawned on Urik's face, sweeping down from his brow and drawing his mouth open. "You fear the Deshmahne may have captured Listain?" Urik asked, his voice no more than a soft whisper.

Better that the other Denraen didn't hear the question. Endric had, though, and understood Tresten's concern and what had passed between the Mage and his father.

"It's a possibility. This building was targeted. Others were damaged, but not like this. This is more than coincidental. We must know."

"Listain would say nothing."

"Not to ordinary soldiers, no."

Urik closed his eyes and nodded. Endric knew what his father meant. If the Deshmahne had captured Listain to pull information from him, it was unlikely there was much he would be able to do in the face of their dark arts. Endric had felt the power they wielded, both in the Deshviili and in the strange earth rumblings that caused most of the city to be damaged. What was one man in the face of that power?

Another thought came to him, stemming from his long-held distrust of the Raen. It was a distrust he knew his father didn't share. Still, it was there. A sudden shiver worked through him with the thought.

What if this was not an attack at all? What if Listain worked *with* the Deshmahne?

He turned to Pendin. His friend saw the expression on his face and shook his head. Endric needed to say something to his father, at least put the idea out there. As he started to, the ground rumbled again, heaving more violently than before.

Endric was tossed into the air and landed painfully, hitting his side as he did. The wind was knocked from him, and he coughed as he struggled to breathe. Nothing but darkness and spots crossed his vision.

The ground still shook, and he felt himself sliding.

Breath hitching, he scrambled for a handhold, but there was nothing to grab onto.

Then he was falling. Above him he heard his name.

"Endric!"

As he fell, he wondered briefly who worried for him.

CHAPTER 18

Around him, the darkness was overwhelming, but flashes of light at the periphery of his vision hinted at something more.

Was he dead?

No. He felt pain. His arms and legs screamed from dozens of scrapes. His sides ached as if he had been punched, and his head throbbed. He wouldn't feel that if he were dead.

Endric took a deep breath. His chest tore with pain at the effort and he coughed, spitting out a chunk of blood or phlegm. Afterward, he felt little better.

There were vague differences in the shadows. As he looked up, he saw lanterns high above him, their weak light not illuminating more than a few feet. The strange blue light Tresten had cast had disappeared with the Mage.

Endric was in the crater.

"Endric!" The voice seemed to come from a distance. Whether it was the height from which he had fallen or something wrong with his ears, he didn't know.

"I'm here!" he called back weakly. His throat was raw and he coughed again.

He heard something from above, faint. Several voices mingled, muffling the words. Did his father even worry about his fall?

Did Endric care if he didn't?

He took another deep breath, steadying himself. Denraen training took over. Gravel and loose dirt clung to his palms, which he wiped on his pants, then checked his legs, arms, and back to feel for obvious fractures. He felt the back of his scalp but found no open injuries, and no place hurt more than any others. His sword still hung from his side. That was important.

He had been lucky. He would have bruises, probably some cuts that might need stitching, but nothing obviously broken. He took another deep breath, inhaling and exhaling until it no longer hurt.

What had happened?

He remembered preparing to speak to his father, then the ground rumbling again. There had been no further trembles since long before he'd summoned Tresten. Did that mean the Deshmahne had returned? Or was this something else?

The thoughts were hard. Pounding in his head made it fuzzy.

How was he going to get out of this? The crater was much deeper than he had expected, though the depth had been hard to gauge from above. Now he realized that Listain's tunnel system must have been impressive. Still was.

"We'll send someone down!"

It was Urik's voice. Did that mean his father had left? Would he have mourned him as he mourned Andril?

He shook his head. The pain helped clear the thoughts away.

He was left to await his rescue. Looking around, he saw that he was on flat ground. One of the tunnels? Though his eyes had begun to adjust to the dark, he struggled to see through the blackness. He stood carefully, uncertain if he would feel more pain, but all he felt was a brief wave of nausea that passed quickly. Stretching his hands out, he felt for the walls.

When he found them, they were smooth but straight. Not curved as he would expect in a tunnel. Following along the wall with his hand, he reached up and eventually found part of what seemed like ceiling. Not tunnel then. A room. Or a hallway.

What was this place? How had Listain built it under everyone's noses? Dendril seemed to know, as did Tresten. Did that mean the Magi had helped?

The smooth stone seemed evidence of that.

Stepping forward, sliding his foot across the ground so as not to stumble upon anything in the darkness, he moved back and away from the center of the building. The walls continued, less damaged the farther he traveled, and eventually he came to a door. Frowning, he felt for a handle and twisted. It opened easily.

Endric gasped at what he saw on the other side.

Along the wall hung small lanterns unlike anything he had ever seen. Staggered dozens of feet apart, they glowed with a pale light, stretching impossibly far into the darkness.

What was this place?

Stepping into the tunnel, he ran his hand along the wall. It was cool and smooth as glass. The ground seemed the same, though he felt surefooted and didn't fear slipping. Different from the stone of the hall he had just left, though he was not sure how he knew.

There was no way this was crafted by men. That left the Magi. Had this been designed for their purpose? How, then, had Listain been given access?

Moving helped to clear his head. The pounding pain was still there, lessened but not as overpowering as it had been when he regained consciousness. Tresten said he'd not found anyone within the remnants of the building. Had Listain escaped before the collapse? Could Senda be with him?

Endric needed to know.

He looked behind him, toward the darkness that was the outer hall he'd come through. How much time would he have before someone came for him? Not as much as he might need. He closed the door, pulling tight on the handle and twisting. In the darkness, the door might not even be found.

He hurried down the tunnel, letting the soft light of the lanterns guide him. After a while, the tunnel split off to the left and right. Lanterns lit both ways initially, though faded to darkness on the right. Left would take him toward the barracks. Right looked as if it could lead back under the rest of the city. Endric went left. It helped that it was the one he was sure remained lit.

Endric didn't know what it was he expected to find. Likely nothing. Still, something nagged, an irritating itch that he felt compelled to follow. Not the usual nausea he felt when something was off. He had learned to trust his instincts, and they had saved him on more than one occasion. This was different.

The tunnel narrowed as it stretched onward. The soft light glowed at intervals, barely illuminating the tunnel but casting enough light for him to continue moving safely. Without that light, Endric was unsure what he would do. Would he have pressed onward? Unlikely. He was not normally scared of the dark, but getting lost within this stretch of tunnels made him more than a little nervous.

Occasionally he would see deeper shadows along the wall. Once, he stopped to investigate and realized they were branching tunnels. None were lit. Whether that was by design or for another reason, Endric didn't know, but he chose to ignore them. What were the chances he would find someone along the darkened tunnels? An encounter like that in the dark would be deadly, which would be more likely than to expect he would emerge victorious.

He continued along the main tunnel and followed the light. If anyone had come this way, they would have needed light. That left him hopeful he could find Listain, and Senda with him.

Then what?

He wondered what he was doing, why he pushed himself through the underground maze, injured and exhausted from the day. His father would be more than angry with this. Might it be enough to finally expel him from the Denraen? Probably not, but it wouldn't keep them on good terms. There were likely many reasons few knew about the tunnels. Now here he was exploring them.

The lights in the distance had seemed to stretch on indefinitely when he first started off. Now there seemed to be an end in sight. Darkness awaited him up ahead. Did the tunnel or the lanterns end? He didn't know how long he had been walking—the strange lights and his still-throbbing head from the fall made telling the passing of time difficult—but he'd gone a long way. What would the reaction be if he had to turn back?

Finally, he reached the darkness.

The tunnel simply ended. Another door, much like the one he had entered through, blocked his way. After briefly worrying that it would be locked, he twisted the handle to find that it opened easily. The other side led into a wide room. Lanterns of traditional style, not the strange lanterns of the tunnel, blazed brightly. The floor was stone and smooth, but not the glasslike smoothness the tunnel had possessed.

Endric passed through the door and closed it solidly shut behind him. Looking around the room, he noticed a familiar scent to the air. Moments passed before he recognized the still mustiness of the lower level of the barracks. Had he come so far already? Could the tunnel have led directly to the barracks?

A staircase at the far end of the room caught his attention. He hurried toward it and nearly tripped upon something lying at the bottom of the stairs.

A body.

It was dressed in Denraen grays and twisted, so it was hard to tell if it was male or female. His breath caught as he took a step back. The person was lying facedown. Endric's heart started hammering, fear for Senda sending it pounding wildly within his chest.

Kneeling before the body, he reached out carefully and felt for the person's neck, checking for a pulse. Best not to twist an injured man if he still lived. The strange contortions the person was in made that unlikely, but he would rather be certain. There was no pulse. Grasping the shirt firmly, he lifted and twisted the body over.

He had to move the shirt to see a face, then fell backward with surprise. Olin's dead eyes stared up at him. His head lolled on his neck, obviously broken. His face had a few scrapes, but nothing significant.

Why was Olin here?

He looked around the room behind him. There was no damage from the earthquakes. No cracks were obvious on the walls, and the ground beneath him was undamaged. The lanterns hung as if they had been there for years, and though recently lit, they hadn't been moved. Then what had happened?

A soft noise higher up caught his attention. Something or someone was there. Suddenly concerned that there might be another injured person on the stairs, he gently laid Olin down and stepped over him, hurrying upward. A dozen steps up, he saw another person. They lay on the stairs, feet toward him and head resting on a higher step. Long dark hair had been pulled into a braid and trailed off to her side. A few strands had pulled free.

Senda.

Endric leaned down and checked for a pulse. Faint, but it was there. She stirred beneath his touch and her eyes fluttered open, distant and unfocused, but open.

"Senda," he said, touching her cheek. It was cold. Blood had crusted dried, and he scratched it off as he stroked her cheek.

"Endric?" she asked, her voice weak.

"I'm here."

"Olin?" she asked and started to push herself up.

Endric kept a hand on her shoulder. He didn't know the extent of her injuries and didn't want to risk further injury. "He's gone. What happened?"

"Gone? Not Olin!" she whispered. Her eyes fell closed again and she took a ragged breath.

"Senda. What happened? Where is Listain?"

"Listain?" She repeated the question. Her lips were dry and cracked, and her tongue slipped out tentatively to moisten them. Her eyes snapped open again. "Listain!" she screamed.

She tried sitting up again and he held her back. He didn't know how badly she had been hurt, but Senda was strong and pushed up wildly, her legs thrashing. At least they still moved. Her back arched and her arms quivered with the effort she exerted trying to get up. Her eyes darted from side to side, unfocused. After moments of struggling, she sank back and sighed as if exhausted. Endric had barely been able to hold her back as she struggled.

"He's gone," she whispered, chest heaving with the effort of speaking.

"Where did he go?" he asked.

She shook her head. "With them."

A cold shiver passed up his spine. Them. Did she mean Deshmahne? "Senda. Did Listain go with the Deshmahne?"

Her body tensed as he spoke, then she hissed. It was a feral sound.

"Senda?" he said, touching her forehead to soothe her. Her injuries must be more than what were visible.

She relaxed at his touch but didn't reopen her eyes. Her breathing slowed and became rhythmic and steady. Endric kept stroking her hair, finding it softer than he had expected. Nothing about Senda was soft; no woman could be soft in the Denraen. Yet here she was, helpless. She snuggled into him as he sat there. Endric found that he didn't mind.

What had happened here? Olin was dead, Senda barely able to speak. And Listain missing. Could the Deshmahne have reached these tunnels? Tresten said they were warded—that the Deshmahne should not be able to access them. What if Listain helped? Could the Raen be involved somehow?

He closed his eyes, letting his mind work. Urik worried about Listain. That was clear. His warning for Andril was also clear, and now Andril was gone and Listain's position was safe. Yet Dendril trusted Listain. His father didn't trust easily, so his faith in Listain meant something. It must.

The Raen's thin face floated across his mind. He saw how much the man enjoyed taunting him. There had been definite satisfaction when he had been imprisoned, but it was more than that. He and Listain had never seen eye to eye. Still, did Listain taunt him because he disliked him or because of the way he perceived Endric treated his father?

He had no answer. The man was a skilled soldier and a brilliant tactician. And he had control over his entire spy network. His absence left a huge hole in the Denraen. If he had been only captured, he was at risk to share vital intelligence. But if he had gone willingly...

Senda knew the answers. He needed to get her to a healer so she could wake and tell them what had happened, and he needed to get out of the tunnels to talk to his father. Scooping Senda up carefully, he started up the stairs. Though she was lighter than he had expected, his legs felt the strain of each step. She was not frail—not Senda—but not as solid as she always appeared in her Denraen grays.

The stairs were not lit and curved gently around, leaving the flickering lantern light of the hall behind him. Soon he was cast into complete darkness.

He didn't know where the stairs let out, though he suspected somewhere in the barracks. As far as he could tell, there were no doors. Or light. The stairs kept climbing. How far underground was he?

Carrying Senda caused his arms to start burning, even as light as she was, but Endric didn't want to set her down. Not that he feared being able to lift her. No, Senda had been through too much to be laid down upon the cold stone stairs in the dark. Better that he suffered than she.

He continued up. The steps were narrow, more so than they had been in the wide hall at the bottom of the stairs, and became shallower as well, taking some of the strain off his legs. He kept an arm out in front of him, supporting Senda but careful that he didn't crash her into some unseen wall, until he discovered something blocking his way.

He shifted Senda and felt along the surface, praying it was a door rather than a wall, else he would be forced to turn around and return to the tunnels and all the way back to the crater.

The rough texture of wood greeted his questioning hand. A door. Were he more pious, he would have offered a prayer to the gods. As it was, he searched for a handle by running his hand along the door. A splinter caught his palm and dug in painfully, but he ignored it.

As he leaned against the door, something warm pressed on his hip.

He tentatively reached toward what he had felt and found soft heat radiating from what seemed to be a handle made of teralin. Frowning, he steeled himself and grasped it firmly and pushed.

The door opened slowly, but it opened.

The other side of the door was a room he had never seen but knew existed. A small space had been carved out around the door, just enough for it to swing open. Wooden crates were stacked to the ceiling around it, creating a barricade that extended into the room. A small amount of light trickled back through the slats in the crates—enough to see clearly after the darkness of the staircase, though he didn't know the source. Endric stepped out and closed the door behind him, noting the absence of a handle on this side.

The room was an old storeroom that, for as long as he knew, had been barely used. Most knew it as the box room. Crates were recycled through here, but there were so many that the Denraen would almost certainly never run out. The Denraen used the boxes for various things, most often as packing for deployments. Some made sport of it and decorated them with markings of their regiment or other things dear to them. The crates this far back had never been decorated.

Endric could follow a weaving trail through the boxes. Senda barely moved, only crying out occasionally as he bumped into the stacks. Otherwise, she was silent. As far as he could tell, there was little physically wrong with her, which frightened him more. There might be little the healers could do.

He pushed the thought from his mind. He needed to focus on what it was he could change. Pressing along the narrow path, he slowly made his way forward. If someone didn't know the door was back there, it was unlikely to be found. Just how Listain would want it. It just didn't make it any quicker to access.

As he neared the front of the box room, the stacks weren't as tall. Denraen had painted most at some point. In the flickering lantern light, it was difficult to tell what was painted upon most of them, but a few stood out. As he stared at the markings, he began to wonder why the lantern would be lit. Most men brought their own light when grabbing boxes. Those assigned to return the crates came in pairs and were known to light the lanterns.

Endric paused, listening for anything that might tell him there were others in the room. He heard nothing. That was good. It would be best if others didn't discover the secret of the tunnels. He wasn't sure how his father would manage to keep them completely secret, especially after seeing the remnants of the guard station, but he wouldn't be the one to spoil that mystery. Besides, it could be useful to him as well. There would be time later for him to explore the extent of the tunnels.

He smiled, realizing how much that would upset Listain.

After waiting a few moments, he moved forward. At the front of the room, several stacks of boxes had fallen, tipped over. Legs stuck out of one end of the pile. His breath caught until he saw the dark gray uniform and realized the men were fallen Denraen. He struggled for a moment with what to do before deciding to get Senda out first and then come back for the men. His father needed to know whatever information Senda could provide.

The other side of the door to the box room was chaos.

Dead men lined the hall like a trail. Nearly a dozen.

What had happened here? Endric's heart quickened and he hurried past the bodies, not bothering to look at faces. There would be time to mourn later. Most carried a weapon, though a few were unarmed. None wore any armor. Whatever had happened had come quickly.

He quickly shifted Senda to his shoulder—she moaned something inaudible—and unsheathed his sword. There was a quickening of his pulse as he did, and his senses seemed on edge. As he listened for anything moving, he noticed a stench in the hall, like rotten fruit. It was faint but unexpected. Suppressing a shiver, he couldn't be slowed by his uncertainty.

Still, he paused. He heard nothing and finally moved forward, stepping quietly and carefully around the fallen men.

The hall was in the lower barracks. Storerooms occupied much of this level. The rest of this sublevel were the cells, though they were separated from his current position by a thick wall at one end. A separate stair led to them. Unfortunately, he was all too familiar with that area. He was less familiar with the storerooms. Doors led off the hall, most shut tight. He paused at each one, careful not to overlook something on the other side.

As he neared the far end of the hall, the stairs now visible, the bodies began to space out. None had visible injuries. He held his sword steady in his hand, leading with it. Muscles were tense throughout his body, and his eyes flickered with each shifting change in the shadows. Part of him feared the strange dark attack he had experienced recently, dreading the sudden weakening and nausea. That it never came didn't ease his nerves.

The stairs were dark. The lanterns that normally lit them were either broken or, as he soon came to realize, missing. Endric inhaled deeply, then started up. It was likely that whatever had killed the Denraen had already moved through. Most likely to the tunnels. There had been many branches to the main path, none of them lit, and he realized he *had* been lucky not to encounter anything there.

The stairs were silent. He moved as quietly as possible, pausing occasionally to listen for sounds of someone else. Breathing or movement. He heard nothing other than his own paranoia and continued upward.

The next level was deserted. More storerooms. He pressed upward.

The next floor was at ground level. Light began filtering into the stairs, enough for him to see that he was alone. The lanterns along here were neither damaged nor missing. Just unlit. That was odd. Steeling himself for what he might see, he hurried up the last few steps.

And froze.

The hall was wide here, and the stairs opened near the great hall. Men moved around normally, as if unaware that below them, nearly a dozen men had been killed. Engineers examined walls in the hall, jotting notes and speaking to themselves in hushed voices. Others returned from outside, streaming back in. Many went to the great hall to gather.

Endric hurried down the hall to the barracks entrance. Outside, the night was quiet and the air cool. A few men gave him an uneasy look as he passed. Whether it was the still-unsheathed sword or Senda draped over his shoulder, he didn't bother to ask. Most gave him a wide berth.

He paused, looking down the street toward the crumbled guard station building he had started from. A group of men made their way down the street, steps confident and backs tall. Even from this distance, he recognized his father's broad form. The man remained powerfully built even as he aged. Urik walked alongside him, average height and build, but his steps were no less confident. Other Denraen trailed behind, Pendin probably with them.

As they neared, Dendril stopped short. Endric quickly sheathed his sword and shifted Senda back to his arms, cradling her softly. She was warm but motionless. She needed help that he couldn't provide, and he hated that.

"Endric?" Dendril asked, unable to hide the surprise in his voice.

Endric nodded.

"They couldn't find you in the crater."

"I found the tunnels."

Dendril stepped closer and raised his hand. "That is not for you to discuss. Not here."

Endric noted the lack of questions about any injuries and snorted. "Too late. Nearly a dozen men are dead near the storeroom. I found Senda on the stairs, Olin dead in the hall outside the tunnel."

"Dead?" Dendril repeated. "How?" He scanned the outside of the barracks, fearful of another collapse.

"Probably tossed down the stairs."

Dendril glanced over at Urik before looking back to his son. "Did you see Listain?"

"Not Listain. Senda said he is with the Deshmahne."

"Taken?"

He shook his head. "Something has happened to her. I can't find obvious injuries, but she will barely wake. We need a healer. She knows what happened to Listain."

Dendril sighed. "What is happening tonight?" he said quietly to no one in particular. He sounded almost as if he expected an answer. He touched a hand to his chest and closed his eyes, breathing softly. No one else spoke. When he opened his eyes, they were clearer—more focused—and he turned to Senda. "Get her to the healers."

"Father—the healers can't help with this. Summon Tresten again!"

Dendril shook his head. "Not for this, Endric. Take her to the healers. They will see that she gets well."

"But she may know something about Listain!"

"I know you worry for your friend," he said, nearly insinuating at a relationship. "But it's likely she knows nothing of Listain."

"I saw the hall—"

"Enough!" Dendril spoke more loudly than was necessary. Such an outburst was unusual for the general, and the few men around them looked away. Urik didn't. Something flickered across his eyes, a sort of sadness, that Endric didn't understand. "You will obey me in this."

"Father?" he asked and then glanced back to the barracks. Men still streamed in. Most appeared wary. The night was otherwise clearing, the dust that had been hanging in the air now settling. The clouds overhead even began to thin, letting the light of the nearly full moon remove some of the mystery of the night.

His father was essentially dismissing what had happened. The Deshmahne had attacked the Magi palace tonight, and then the city itself. Tresten had gone so far as to ask Dendril to pursue them. Now his father seemed to brush away the overall threat. Regardless of what Listain's allegiances were, the man was missing!

"The Deshmahne have attacked the city, Father." He spoke softly but couldn't keep the anger from his voice. "They have attacked the Magi." He took a small step forward. His father was taller than him and wider. Endric ignored their size difference. "They killed Andril. And now you will let them have Listain?" he said, unable to keep the sneer off his face or the disdain from his voice.

"You know not what you speak of. Take Senda to the healers and return to your quarters." It was a command.

"I understand why you fear them. But let us take our forces and destroy them. We need to protect the city. The Magi."

"You think I hesitate out of fear? You are still a child, son. Someday you may understand." With those words, he started to turn away.

Anger at his father seethed through him. The man refused to give him even a hint of the respect he had given Andril. Endric had earned some little measure today by stopping the Deshviili and discovering the attack in the tunnels, enough that his requests should not be taken lightly. And yet Dendril brushed him off.

Endric glanced at Senda, lying motionless in his arms. He was barely aware of her weight. She had not moved for a long time, and he wasn't certain what that might mean, but he was afraid. After what he had seen of the Deshmahne, he worried what type of unseen injuries she might have. What had she witnessed?

Senda had often encouraged him to grow up, to become the person she had always seen in him. That was the reason she was often disappointed with him. She saw him as Andril saw him. He had played that off as he had played off his brother, ignoring their heartfelt requests. What had happened with his brother couldn't be changed. But he could change how Senda looked at him.

His father was another issue that needed to be dealt with. He didn't know exactly what he intended, but could no longer stand being treated as anything other than the lowest of the Denraen. Something much bigger than all of them was taking place, and he knew he couldn't stand on the sidelines any longer. Inhaling deeply, he felt Senda briefly stir in his arms. He didn't look down at her.

"Look at me!" Endric demanded.

Dendril turned back warily. Pendin stepped toward him, but Endric shook his head. His friend ignored it, standing just behind Dendril. Closer to the general than Pendin would normally like.

"Let me be a part of this. Don't push me away. I need to be a part of this."

"Need to be?" Dendril repeated. "You think you are ready to command?"

Endric took another deep breath. Was he ready to accept the responsibility his father had always wanted him to take? Was there another choice? Part of him knew what was at stake. More than just the attack on his brother. More than the attack on the city. The Deshmahne were unlike any threat the Denraen had faced. He would be a part of their response.

Pulling himself up, he stared his father in the eyes and didn't turn away from the steely glare he found in return. "I am."

Dendril snorted, then shook his head. "I do not." The judgment was spoken softly and hung in the air.

"You have been trying to get me to accept responsibility for years. Now I'm ready and you refuse me?" His father truly must hate him. Or hate the fact that he was not Andril. He could never replace Andril and didn't want to, but he *was* ready to take the commission once offered.

"You seek retribution. That's not the trait of a leader, not the quality I want in the men who command my Denraen. I will not have someone with vengeance on their mind leading my men to their deaths. The ideals of the Denraen are greater than that." He lowered his voice. "You think I fear the Deshmahne, and that guides my response. Yet there is much you do not know and are not ready to know. Now. You have your orders. Dismissed."

Endric looked to Pendin, who only shook his head. It was as if his friend knew what he was thinking, knew the storm that was brewing in the back of his mind. And perhaps he did. Pendin had always known him well. Would he support him still?

Urik stared at him, a tight frown upon his face. Even the en'raen had wanted more of a response. If the en'raen didn't know why the Denraen didn't attack, could there really be any reason other than his father's fear? What didn't Endric know? And why would his father not share with him— or at least Urik?

And where was Listain? The fact that Dendril barely worried about the missing Raen weighed on him with surprising force. Though he despised the man, Listain was the spymaster. His absence, however it had come about, was dangerous to the entirety of the Denraen.

Someone had to do something about it.

His heart started pounding and a rushing sound beat in his ears. Nausea ate at his stomach. Could he do what he was thinking? Did he dare try?

"You don't even know what the men are saying, do you?" he asked, decided. Nervous sweat broke on his forehead. "Calling you weak."

Dendril turned slowly. "Careful, Endric." The warning was spoken without inflection, devoid of feeling.

"You've been acting strange since his death. People notice. And speak about it. Now even some of your officers think a different course should be taken." He was careful to keep his gaze steady. He wouldn't give away his conversation with Urik. Still, he couldn't help but see the worried look on Pendin's face.

Dendril narrowed his eyes. "You were dismissed. This is your last warning."

"What would Andril say?" he asked, knowing how to hurt him.

Rather than say anything, Dendril's expression hardened. The heat in his eyes left and his frown disappeared.

"Would he say that someone else should lead the Denraen if you were unwilling?"

A frightening calm overtook his father. "You are still a child who thinks he knows everything. You have much growing up to do before you can understand." He laughed. It was a dark and joyless sound. "And now you think you could lead the Denraen?"

"Better than you have lately. First Andril. Then Brohstin. Now the Deshmahne attack. Still you hesitate to lead." He grunted and shook his head.

"Action must be taken. If not by you, then someone who will."

"Wait to challenge me until you have become a man."

"You fear that I will win?"

Dendril shook his head. There was a hint of sadness in his face that nearly froze Endric. It passed, and Dendril's face became unreadable. "I fear that you will lose."

Endric stared and said nothing.

Dendril slowly nodded once. "Is this a challenge then?"

Endric's heart was hammering. Could he go through with it? Was he ready to lead if he succeeded? Was he ready to die? That was what he risked if he failed.

He flicked his gaze to Pendin. His friend was shaking his head, fearful of what would happen. He looked over at Urik. The en'raen was worried, his eyes darting from Dendril to Endric. The other Denraen had respectfully stepped out of earshot. Then Senda moaned and stirred in his arms, as if struggling to wake, before finally settling into silence. He looked at her—the sharp jaw, the defined chin, lean nose—and knew he couldn't let her be hurt further. Too many had been hurt already.

His father's inaction had led to this. Now there was no other choice.

"Father, I—"

His father shook his head once. His eyes were dark. Angry.

There was no choice.

Endric took a deep breath. "I challenge you, Dendril, General of the Denraen, for command of the Denraen."

CHAPTER 19

"Why are you doing this?"

Endric looked at Pendin across Senda's sleeping body. She had barely woken since she was brought to the healers, though whether that was her injury or some concoction she had been given was unclear to him. The narrow cot was one of many in the small room. Walls pressed in oppressively and every time he moved, it felt as though the ceiling hovered barely overhead. He couldn't help but think the healers needed more space.

Others lay on cots like the one Senda slept upon: men who had been hurt in the earthquakes or by falling debris. Some had been hurt in the cleanup. None of the men in the lower barracks hall had survived. The two healers now on duty wandered between beds, checking on their patients, applying compresses or foul-smelling salves. Occasionally they eyed him with stern, disapproving expressions, yet he had stayed with Senda as much as possible.

Endric looked down at her, ignoring Pendin's question for now, as well as the annoyed healers. Asleep like this, she seemed smaller and Endric felt a strangely protective urge. The feelings surprised him and were why he had stayed by her so much. He had always cared for Senda, but fearing for her safety and then seeing her hurt had cast a different light on his true feelings. If only she would awaken so he could tell her what he had done.

"Action needs to be taken." He spoke without looking up. Pendin had tried to talk him out of this already and nearly succeeded.

"It will be. You don't give him enough time."

Endric closed his eyes and suddenly couldn't get the image of his brother's head out of his mind. He no longer felt the overwhelming urge for vengeance. It was still there, only now it was mixed with the need to stop the Deshmahne before they gained more strength. Then they might be impossible to stop, and too many others would get hurt. Now it was only Denraen, but others were not as able to defend themselves.

"There has been more than enough time, Pendin." He shook his head, rubbing a hand through his close-cropped hair. "You weren't there. You didn't see the Deshmahne attacking the palace. The Denraen can't allow them to continue their attacks."

"We don't even know that there have been other attacks!"

"Brohstin was one of them."

Pendin sighed. "This is not you," he said, changing tack.

"I know you fear for me, but you don't need to worry. My father won't kill me."

"And you?"

He shrugged. "What else is there?" he asked. "Persuade me! I can think of nothing to do differently. My father's council fears to challenge him, and Listain is still missing. Andril would have been able to force my father onto the right path, but he doesn't listen to me like that. And I have no one to blame but myself."

The last was somehow the most painful.

Had he not antagonized his father all these years, pushing him away, he might be in a different position. It seemed so long ago that he had been offered a commission. A last attempt. And he had refused again.

"What happened with the miners?" he asked. He knew Pendin would have investigated. Endric still wasn't sure how much family Pendin still had in the mines, but knew his father at least still worked them.

"They have locked down the mines."

Endric frowned. "How?"

"The entrance to the active mines has been barricaded. None may enter or leave."

"How long can they sustain that?"

Pendin shrugged. "No one knows how many supplies they have. Or if there are other ways of obtaining more."

"The Deshmahne are behind this."

"Those who aren't in the mines aren't speaking. No one can confirm anything."

Endric closed his eyes. How could all this have happened so quickly? Why couldn't Andril be here to help? His brother was much better suited for what was needed. He felt tears well up with the thought; it was not the first time.

"Why must this be you, Endric?" Pendin asked softly.

"No one else will," he said, opening his eyes.

"Does that make it the right course of action?"

He had asked himself the same question and still hadn't come up with an answer. Urik had told him that others on the council argued for action his father refused to take. The men of the Denraen grew restless, waiting for clear leadership, answers, and nothing had been given to them. Now they could wait no longer.

"Not right," he finally said. "Just less wrong."

"Senda wouldn't want you to do this."

"She already knows."

"And she approves?" Pendin asked.

"No. But I think she understands." She always understood, or at least tried to.

"If you lose—"

"I won't," he said, thinking of his father. Trill hadn't been taken off the wall in over a decade. There was no rust on the sword, but that didn't mean there would be none on Dendril. Endric never even saw him practicing anymore. Once, he had been a fixture in the yard, training the men, demonstrating his skill. There was leadership in simply doing that. Men saw and respected the demonstrations. Most were bettered by the experience. Now he left those demonstrations to others. Andril had been one of those others.

Endric could only sigh. The thought of beating his father didn't make him happy, but he knew of little else to do. He had a real chance. Though he had never faced his father in practice, those who had compared his skill to his father's. Andril had been better still.

"If you lose," Pendin repeated, breaking into his reverie, "you'll either be dead or expelled from the Denraen."

"I know." That was the risk he took, and he was slowly resigning himself to that fate. "But if I win…"

"Endric—I love you like a brother, but even I don't think you are ready for that."

Endric snorted but said nothing. Pendin was probably right, but that didn't change what he had to do. What he would do. He looked over at his friend, his gaze pausing as it crossed over Senda's still form, and met his eyes.

Pendin softened his expression immediately. "If I can't change your mind, what can I do?"

He smiled and felt the first moment of relief he had felt in days. "I don't know. I know that I may not win. Maybe that's not the point. Facing Dendril may convince others to push forward with what they feel is necessary. I know Urik at least feels we should attack. There are others on the council who feel the same."

"Endric—"

"The idea of actually winning is frightening. I've never even led a division, let alone the entirety of the Denraen. And now I think to do this?"

"Endric!"

He looked over at Pendin, flashing annoyance. His friend glared at him and pointed to Senda. Her eyes had fluttered open and she stared up at him, fixing on his face. He hadn't realized he was holding her hand, but he was suddenly aware of her squeezing him back, holding tightly.

"Senda?"

"Endric." She spoke his name as a whisper.

He grabbed one of the nearby stools and lowered himself onto it, pulling himself up even with her face and staring into her pale blue eyes. They stared at each other for long moments, neither speaking. Finally a tear streamed from the corner of her eye, streaking down toward the blanket. Endric softly wiped it away.

"Glad to see you awake, Senda," Pendin said. "Now talk some sense into him." He patted her shoulder and turned to leave, but not before winking at Endric.

They both watched him leave, then turned to look at each other again. "How much do you remember?" His hand had lingered on her cheek, and she nestled into it.

"We were in Listain's office when the first quake hit. Olin and I weren't sure what was happening, but Listain was terrified. We wanted to get up to the street, but he led us down toward the…" She trailed off, a hesitant look on her face.

"I know about the tunnels, Senda. That's how I found you."

She closed her eyes and slowly nodded. "Of course. We went toward the tunnels, taking the barracks route. There was something he needed." She paused, the effort of speaking so much making her chest heave with each breath, taxing her. She looked up at him and smiled. After a few slow breaths, she continued, "I don't know what it was. We were underground when another quake came. By then, we were nearly to the barracks. That's when we were attacked."

She closed her eyes again and her breathing slowed. Endric wondered if she was drifting back to sleep.

He wasn't sure he could let her; there were still questions he had. "Senda, where were you attacked?"

Opening her eyes slowly, she hesitated as if trying to remember it clearly. "So much is a blur for me. I remember the attack coming at us. Listain holding them off, then Olin." She paused suddenly and tried to sit up, her eyes wide. "Olin?"

Endric helped to lay her back down, unsure how much stress she could take. "He's gone," he said softly. "Why was he even there?"

"He saved me. It was my fault he was there. I recruited him for Listain."

"A spy?" Endric asked, his voice louder than he had intended. One of the nearby healers looked over at him and placed a pudgy finger to his lips. Endric ignored him. Olin had been a spy. How had he not known? Yet it made sense. The man was quiet and bright. Little escaped his observing eyes. He would have made an excellent spy.

"Yes. For nearly a year. He was giving a report when the quake hit. Otherwise, he wouldn't have been there." She sighed deeply. "What of Listain?"

"You don't know?"

She shook her head. "I can't remember. Bits and pieces are clear. I remember fighting with something. Olin too. Listain doing something to help us get past the attack, toward the barracks." She paused, narrowing her eyes, then smiled. "Then you. You brought me out."

"I did. When I thought you were dead…"

She fixed him with a serious gaze. "You worried?"

He snorted. "More than I expected to. Senda, I—"

She brought her free hand up and shushed him. "Don't say anything now. Let's talk more when I wake." With that, she leaned back and drifted off to sleep. Her rest was brief, then her eyes snapped open again. "Why am I to talk sense into you?"

He swallowed hard. Sitting so close to her, feeling the skin of her cheek on his hand, he wasn't sure what he was doing anymore. Yet what he did was bigger than him. Than Senda. "I challenged my father."

She said nothing for a dozen long heartbeats. "Oh, Endric."

They sat quietly for long moments until she drifted back to sleep. Endric watched her until he was content that she was fully out, and then he slowly and regrettably pulled his hand away.

He looked back at her as he left the room. His throat felt tight as he watched her lying there, looking tiny on the narrow cot, breaths coming slow and regular, each with a soft rise of her chest. He had to force himself to turn away.

Endric wanted to be alone, but the halls were full of men. Some wanted to stop and talk to him, many offering support. Others simply wanted to steer clear of him, like he carried some sort of disease. He understood that; he had long worried his friends suffered from their association with him. Soon that would change, regardless of the outcome of the challenge.

It was the men offering their support that bolstered him the most. There was something reassuring about knowing he wasn't the only one who felt Dendril's approach with the Deshmahne was wrong. Most were simple soldiers, frontline men. None of the officers said anything to him. Not that he expected them to. The risk was too great. They would support Dendril publicly until such time that he was no longer general. Occasionally, he caught a wayward glance, an approving nod, but he wasn't sure how much to read into such expressions.

Senda remained in his thoughts. Dangerous, he knew. He needed focus now, not the distractions of a woman. Still, he couldn't shake his concern for her. She had said little when he told her of what he had done. Likely she would have figured it out anyway. Senda was nearly Listain's match in plotting and, as far as Endric was concerned, her intelligence exceeded Listain's. It was not those thoughts that weighed on him. Rather, it was the image of her small form lying on the cot. Helpless.

If he lost, would she suffer? Would Pendin?

He worried about the impact his actions would have on his friends. Always before, they had been shielded, as had he. Now they would be exposed. Loyalty might be questioned. There needed to be a way to protect them from repercussions.

He found himself in the officer's wing and heading toward Urik's office. That had not been his intent, but fear for his friends had directed his feet. The halls here were darker, the stone walls different. This part of the barracks was old. Even the air smelled of it. Whereas in other parts of the barracks there was evidence of the earthquake in lanterns broken or wall hangings damaged, if not in outright cracking of the walls, this section had been completely unharmed.

Not for the first time, he wondered when this building was constructed. And why. Few buildings in the city were built like this, but enough had been that he wondered at their original intent. Surely this had not always been the

154

barracks. Or the smithy nearby, built in the same manner, had not always been intended for its purpose. Now it was little more than rubble. Could it be that the tunnels he only recently learned about connected all the ancient buildings?

Questions for another time. Urik's door was cracked open and he knocked briskly. The door swung open. The en'raen stood with his back to Endric, near one of his shelves. His body blocked whatever it was he was working on. He turned and nodded at Endric before turning back to what he was doing and hurriedly finishing. When he stepped away from the shelf, Endric saw only stacks of books.

"I didn't expect to see you here; figured that you would be preparing for your challenge. What is it that you need, Endric?"

Endric shook away the questions turning over in his head to look at Urik. The man was crisply dressed in his uniform though, as was his custom, he didn't wear his sword. Most of the officers kept their swords strapped to their hip at all times. Many of the enlisted men as well. His head was bare, exposing his close-cropped gray hair. His usually neutral face held a hint of worry, carrying it as mostly a tightening of his eyes.

"Have I made the right decision?" he asked, surprising himself with the question.

Urik motioned him in and Endric stepped across the threshold, closing the door behind him before taking a seat at Urik's desk. The en'raen sat on the opposite side and leaned forward on his elbows, fixing him with a steady gaze.

"I don't know," he answered slowly before sighing. "Nearly a third of the city has taken some damage. The third terrace has none, a few shattered windows. The second terrace suffered more, with the guard station you saw and the attack on the barracks, but it was the first terrace with more significant damage. It will take years to rebuild. The people are scared, uncertain why or how this could happen. There are even rumblings from the Magi that more needs to be done."

He turned and looked toward the back of his office, as if looking through an unseen window. Endric followed the direction of his gaze and saw that

Urik stared at a painting hung in the recess between bookshelves at the back of his office. The painting was of two streams merging into one. On the shores of the streams were small green shrubs with distinctive leaves. He didn't need to look closely to know what type they were. In the distance, as if on the horizon, was a dark shape with a shadow that loomed over the entire painting. Within the shadow were hazy faces, indistinct, but there if you looked at it the right way. It depicted the Urmahne faith, though he had never seen a painting quite like it.

"And now you have challenged the general. You and I spoke briefly about the challenge, and now that it has been made, I am uncertain how I feel about it." He shook his head and then turned back to look at Endric. "We cannot let them grow stronger. To do so invites the possibility of more destruction. That I am certain of." He hesitated a moment. "If they have Listain, there is much they could learn of our defenses, of the city."

Endric nodded. Listain's absence put everything in a different perspective. He was still not clear what had happened. No one was until Senda shared what she remembered. As much as he hated Listain, he doubted the man was working with the Deshmahne. Such deception to the Denraen, and his father, wasn't something he saw in Listain.

Then there was the tie to the miners. Could the miners be working with the Deshmahne, or was something else behind that? Someone had coordinated the attacks. Listain seemed the likely one to do that as well. But why would Senda make it seem like they had been fighting the Deshmahne if Listain was involved?

So many questions. And none made the decisions he had made any easier. "What comes next?"

He had been so worried about Senda that he hadn't bothered to learn what he needed to do to satisfy the challenge now that it had been offered. If any would know, it would be Urik.

"Next, you and your father will meet for combat. Tradition dictates that it be open to the public, though either of you may request otherwise. I would suggest the barracks yard. This satisfies tradition by being open, but the walls grant a semblance of privacy to this spectacle." He shook his head slightly. He really was unsure what to think of this. "The challenge must be observed by members of the Denraen Council and the Magi Council. Beyond that, any may watch who wishes to do so. The weapons are of your own choosing. Most prefer the sword." He spoke matter-of-factly and without emotion. He watched Endric as he said the last.

Endric only nodded. Of course he would choose the sword. Would his father? Trill had sat, unmoved, on its decorative holder for so many years. Could his father prefer a different weapon?

Urik nodded. "The challenge is complete when either combatant yields. Or dies. Either satisfies the challenge. The last piece is perhaps the most important. The winner must then be affirmed by the council."

"Denraen?" he asked, though thought he knew the answer.

The en'raen shook his head. "Magi. That is why they must be present at the challenge. The council affirms all ascending generals, regardless of how they are promoted."

"Has anyone ever not been affirmed by the council?"

"Once. That was long ago." Urik's mouth turned into a tight frown. His eyes narrowed and his brow furrowed in concentration. "The challenge has been so rarely used. The Denraen are peacekeepers, and holding combat for leadership is the opposite of that. Only in extreme cases has it been justified."

"Do you feel it is justified now?"

"I cannot deny that this is an extreme case. Never before in this city's history has it been attacked like this. Never have the Magi been so openly defied. No longer are the Deshmahne some distant threat. And no longer can we claim they are but a cult." He shook his head, and his words grew more heated as he spoke. "The Denraen have already been called upon to protect the city. There is little doubt that we will be called to protect others as well. We must be ready to answer that call."

Urik paused, collecting himself, and Endric waited for him to continue, but he didn't. Urik had not answered his question, not really, but the passion that he spoke with was answer enough. "When will the challenge take place?"

Urik frowned. "Has no one told you?"

Endric shook his head. He had been sitting with Senda waiting for her to wake since that night. It had been nearly two full days. Now that she had woken, a sense of relief filled him, as well as a tinge of regret. Their relationship would change whether he won or lost. Just when he had come to the realization that he wanted a relationship with her.

"Once offered, the challenge must be satisfied within three days, else you forfeit."

"Three days?" he asked. "That means—"

"You must meet your father in combat tomorrow."

CHAPTER 20

Endric was standing with his hand on the door when he heard the knock. He had been expecting it, but was still startled. Squeezing the hilt of his sword briefly, shifting the scabbard as he did, he pulled the door open. Pendin stood dressed in his formal gray uniform. Crisp and clean. Endric wore similar gray clothes, typical Denraen attire, though his were looser fitting. He didn't want to be restrained by his uniform.

His friend didn't wait for an invitation before pushing past him and into the room. "You don't have to do this," he said without preamble. "There is no shame in withdrawing the challenge. I have checked; it can be done. It will be up to your father if there are any consequences, but he has been lenient with you for so long—"

"I will not withdraw the challenge." He spoke softly but firmly.

"Endric—"

"You know I cannot." He frowned at Pendin, who closed his eyes and shook his head while he sighed. "You know me. You know this is not about me."

"I thought I knew you."

Endric narrowed his eyes. "What does that mean?"

"The problem I have with this is that none of this is you. Since you first saw the Mage in Stahline, you've been acting strangely. And that was before

Andril's death. Since then, you have been acting more like him than yourself!"

"That may be true. He was a better man than I will ever be. I can't change the way things were left between us, but I can stop being the selfish boor I had been. That was one of the last things he asked of me."

"Andril wouldn't have done this. He wouldn't have wanted you to do this, either."

"He wouldn't have had to. My father listened to Andril. If only he listened to me."

"Then make him!"

"I tried. And failed. This is the only way."

Pendin sank onto his bed. His face was forlorn. "There is always another way, Endric. You didn't even bother to look."

"Pendin—"

He leaned forward and shook his head, saying nothing for a moment. When he looked back up, his eyes were tight and reddened. "I had to try. One last time. I knew it wouldn't matter." He sighed again and then stood. "Let me stand with you at least."

Endric smiled sadly at his friend. "It would be better for you if you didn't. I don't want to give him any reason to expel you if I lose."

"You're my friend. I won't let you face this alone. I can accept whatever consequences may come of it."

Pendin reached out his arm and Endric grabbed it, pulling him into a hug.

"Thank you. You're more than a friend, Pendin—you're my brother," he said. Separating from Pendin, Endric swept his gaze around his room and turned, walking quickly into the corridor.

The hall was quiet, almost eerily so. A few doors were open as they made their way through the barracks, but Endric didn't look into the rooms. Most were curious if Endric would actually go through with the challenge. Some stood in their doorways and nodded as he passed. He didn't offer any response, trying to keep his mind focused.

They hurried down the stairs leading to the main hall. More men were congregated here. Most seemed to be idling, but he knew better. They waited. Watched. He swept his gaze over them, not letting it linger, trying to avoid anyone he might recognize. As he did, he realized the mistake he was making.

The Deshmahne attacks hurt all the Denraen. The challenge had been offered because the voices and needs of these soldiers had not been met. Endric suddenly stopped and looked over the men standing around the corridor.

The faces of many were neutral. Their lives would be changed somewhat if Endric were to assume command, but not enough that this mattered much to them. The challenge was more a curiosity. Some, though, smiled as he looked at them. A few of these nodded. He recognized men he had trained with, fought alongside. Men who had shared with him the worst assignments the Denraen could ask. These were men who would fight at his side because he was Denraen.

Slowly, he nodded in return. These were the men he fought for. These were his soldiers. With a sudden flash of insight, he suppressed a laugh. For so many years he had fought the leadership offered to him, yet all along a part of him had never fought, instead having claimed men as his own. Now he stood for them.

Pendin touched his shoulder and he turned. A smile split his mouth and Pendin frowned. "What is it?"

Endric shook his head. "Doesn't matter. Come."

The hall grew more filled with men as they made their way. Despite the crowd, a path opened for them and the Denraen stood back. He made a point of looking at each as he passed. Pendin hurried him from behind, a gentle hand on his shoulder pressing him forward. And then they reached to door to the barracks yard.

Propped open, it let hazy gray light filter into the hall. The day was overcast, then. Not that he expected anything else. Rare was the sunny day. "It will probably rain too," he mumbled.

"What was that?" Pendin asked.

Endric shook his head. "Nothing."

He stepped past the doorway and into the grassy yard. There were more Denraen here, though most lingered along the walls, keeping the ground otherwise clear. He saw more men that he recognized here. Many were higher-ranking soldiers and likely to be on his father's side, though that wasn't a given. Urik flashed a tight smile. The en'raen stood at the center of the lawn near a taller figure. As he neared, Endric recognized Mage Alriyn from the night of the attack.

"That's Alriyn," he whispered to Pendin.

"I know."

"Must be the council representative."

"Will that be a problem?"

Endric shrugged slightly. "Only if I win," he said and continued forward. The Mage watched him as he approached, his face unreadable. Just like every other Mage face he had seen. He towered over Urik, who was only average height, and was noticeably taller than Dendril. His father stood with his back to him, speaking to Rold, one of the fen'raen. He had wondered what weapon his father would choose and was mildly surprised to see the greatsword Trill sheathed at his side. The pommel was unmistakable.

A few other men of the Denraen Council stood speaking to Dendril, but they didn't command his attention. Standing next to Urik, hands entwined and a nervous expression upon her face, stood Senda.

He stopped when he saw her, pausing briefly before continuing forward. He had not expected to see her out of the healing ward so soon. She hurried over to him and placed a hand on his arm. For her, it was an extreme show of emotion before others in the Denraen.

"Please do not try to talk me out of this, Senda."

She smiled. There was an edge of sadness to her face as she did. "That was never my intent."

Endric hesitated. "Then why are you here? You should be recovering with the healers."

She glared at him. "There is little more they can offer me at this point. And I am here for the same reason as Pendin."

Pendin laughed lightly. "Probably not *quite* the same reason," he said, trailing off as she turned her glare upon him. He shrugged and stepped away, giving them a small bubble of privacy.

"Are you ready for this?" she asked.

She stood close to him, her smell clean. As she looked up at him, her dark eyes held his. The lines around them told him everything about the worry she felt. Still, she managed to keep her fears out of her voice. The question she asked him could hold so many meanings, but the most direct was her intent.

"I'm not sure that I can be truly ready," he said.

"You wish to proceed?"

He nodded slowly. "It must be done."

She watched him as he spoke, and hesitated to say anything. Finally: "Regardless of what happens, I will be—"

He cut her off by touching her cheek.

She turned into his hand, closing her eyes, and nodded. "Good luck then."

He took his hand away reluctantly and turned back toward Pendin. A wry smile lit his face and he only shook his head as he rejoined Endric's side. They strode forward together and reached Urik. Senda stood to his left, Pendin his right. If Olin lived, he would have been with them as well.

Urik looked at him a moment, his flat eyes unreadable, then nodded. "Endric, son of Dendril. Do you present yourself for the challenge?"

"I do," Endric answered.

Urik tilted his head briefly to Endric, then turned to Dendril. "Dendril, commander of the Denraen. The challenger presents himself."

With those words, Urik stepped away. The other Denraen standing nearby followed suit. Senda and Pendin each waited a moment before they stepped back, leaving only Dendril and Endric. Mage Alriyn stood apart from the soldiers, watching with a strange expression on his face.

Dendril stepped forward but didn't unsheathe his sword. Endric had expected more formality, but there appeared to be none. His heart hammered and his hand hovered over the hilt of his sword. He didn't squeeze it though.

His father was dressed simply. A gray shirt. Dark pants. The sword Trill.

Endric had dressed comfortably, but more formally. His father had not afforded him that honor.

"You still press forward with this folly?"

Endric shook his head at his father's choice of words. "You have left me with no other choice."

Dendril grunted and started slowly pacing in front of him. "Still a child who thinks fighting is the only option. There is always a choice."

Endric frowned at his father's words, feeling a brief moment of panic. Pendin had said something similar as he tried to talk him out of the challenge.

He forced it down, needing to maintain his focus. "There comes a time when fighting is the only remaining option." He threw his father's words back at him, an explanation once given for the role of the Denraen in a world of Urmahne.

"You know half of what you think you do, son." The words were almost sad. Dendril shook his head, still pacing. "You could have made a fine leader in time. Like your brother in so many ways."

"But different in all the ones that count. At least to you."

His father shook his head again. "Still a child," he said quietly.

"How much longer do you intend to insult me?"

Dendril sighed, closing his eyes for a long moment. When they reopened, his expression had hardened. "I am not insulting you. Just stating facts. Were you not so blinded by your anger and desire for revenge, you would be open to doing the same." He suddenly stopped pacing. "If this must continue, then come. See if you can best me, my son."

With that, he unsheathed Trill.

The sound rang across the barracks yard, a pure note unlike any Endric had ever heard. He felt another moment of uncertainty but pressed it down as he unsheathed his own sword. "I will not go easy on you."

"Nor I on you," Dendril answered.

Endric narrowed his eyes as his father stepped back into a defensive stance. Waiting. He would let Endric begin the challenge. Fine. With a slight nod, Endric leapt forward. He had worked with the sword long enough that attacking was something he did easily. He didn't attack recklessly. Or carelessly. Not against a swordmaster like his father.

Dendril blocked easily with a few fluid swipes of Trill, each time stepping back into a defensive posture. And waiting.

Endric wasn't sure what his father was playing at by not attacking, and it forced him to step back and circle. He kept his sword tip up in a ready pose as Andril had taught him, though he tried not to think about that. His father kept him in view and maintained a slight distance. He had the advantage of the longer reach, but Endric had speed on his side.

Endric attacked again, sweeping his sword rapidly through several forms. Dendril blocked each attack methodically, barely exerting himself. Each time, he returned to his defensive stance. Though Trill was a greatsword, his father didn't seem to struggle with its weight, moving it fluidly.

Endric pressed forward, slicing quickly in an upward attack toward Dendril's face, moving the sword down at the last second toward his arms. His blade slid down Trill and Endric flicked it forward, biting Dendril's forearm. Dark blood seeped through his shirt. Endric bounced back and out of the reach of Trill. Moving warily, he watched his father.

A slight murmur from the Denraen watching came at the sight of Dendril's blood. Endric knew most had not given him much of a chance. Not against his father—Dendril had once been the most feared swordsman in the Denraen—but Endric knew that years had passed since he had held a sword. Those years would have taken off speed and reaction. Andril had almost beaten Dendril the last time they had practiced, and that had been nearly five years ago. He was not his brother's equal, but he counted on the fact that Dendril wouldn't be anymore, either.

Still, dueling with his father was harder than he had expected. Not physically. Endric practiced nearly daily. The stakes were higher, but he was no more fatigued than he would be working with Pendin. Emotionally, however... Regardless of what had happened, Dendril *was* his father.

If only that made everything better.

Staring at his stern face, the ease with which he blocked his attacks, it was hard to forget that this was the man who had taught him his first sword forms. That was so long ago, back before he had tasked Andril with his training. Memories of how helpless he'd felt when he was first learning how to swing a sword came flooding back. He remembered how easily his father had blocked his attacks. Even as he gained skill, he had never been much of a match for his father. Now he fought for something greater than his pride.

His father toyed with him, still not respecting him. Shoving the memories away, clearing his mind, Endric slashed forward with rapid movements. Trill blocked each attack easily. Dendril stepped back into a defensive stance once more.

Endric struck again, a flurry of movement, as fast as he had ever attacked. Each blow was blocked. His father's movements were easy, as if Endric never threatened to harm him.

A surge of anger flooded him.

It was unwise to fight angry. That was a lesson Andril had tried to hammer home time and again. He couldn't help it. His father's face was wrapped in a condescending frown. The same expression had adorned his face during every one of their practice sessions.

Endric leapt forward, swinging angrily, pressing through one form after another. Trill met his sword, clanging loudly, and each impact shuddered up his arm. Endric stepped back, watching his father. His face remained unreadable.

He was not fast enough. Not good enough. His father knew it.

That's when Dendril chose to attack.

It was almost casual. His sword whistled through the air so quickly it was almost a dream. Endric barely blocked it in time. The attack was followed by another. Then another. And another. Each in rapid succession, cascading atop each other. He felt the sharp sting of Trill's bite across his arm but didn't bother to look. There was no time.

Endric danced out of range, buying seconds. He had expected his father to be slowed by age and lack of practice. There was no sign of it. Instead, he seemed even faster than Endric ever remembered. It was obvious that Dendril had been simply playing with him from the start.

That thought more than any other brought the rage back to the forefront of his mind. Endric stepped in, slipping under Trill's streaking blade, and slashed quickly through two quick forms. Dendril grunted, and he knew one must have hit.

Endric slid back, out of Trill's reach. He was breathing heavily and sweat ran from his brow. His arm stung from where he had been hit, but he dared not look at the injury. He watched his father, keeping his sword at the ready.

Dendril's left arm was stained with blood. A small splotch grew across his right chest—the second hit he had felt. Other than that, he stood almost casually in his defensive stance again. He breathed easily. It was as if he barely exerted himself.

It was then that Endric truly knew doubt.

His face must have shown it. His father chose that moment to attack. Shifting from his defensive stance to his attack in less than a heartbeat, he slid forward, darting like a snake. Trill sliced out, an angry fang.

Endric stepped to the side, bringing his sword up, but was too late. He felt the collision of blades as the force bounced up his arm. Trill glanced off, then pierced his left shoulder.

Endric cried out. There was a sound behind him. A scream. He briefly wondered who worried for him. Maybe Senda. There was much emotion in that scream.

He shifted his sword, taking a quick, deep breath to silence the pain in his shoulder. He skittered back, trying to keep space between him and his father and the incredible reach of Trill. His shoulder cried out in agony. He pushed away awareness of it, clearing his mind as much as he could.

The speed of his father's attack had overwhelmed him. Endric had known he was fast with the blade. But Dendril—and his sword Trill—had been a blur. He wouldn't last long this way. Dendril knew it.

So he attacked. He threw himself forward. It was reckless, but there was no other way he could hope to win. Throw his father off-balance. Maybe he could slow the man and gain the upper hand. It was his only option.

Endric ducked under another slice from the greatsword. He felt it whistle over his head, barely missing him. Stabbing forward, he thought to press through a gap in his father's defenses, thinking to pierce his thigh. Somehow Trill appeared, blocking his blow and turning it away.

Rather than backing up, he pressed closer. Kicking up, he hoped to catch his father off guard. Dendril caught his heel easily and threw him back with surprising force. Endric landed on his back and rolled, coming to his feet quickly. His breath had been knocked from him, but he couldn't lie still, else his father could finish him. He held his sword unsteadily in front of him.

Dendril watched the bobbing tip of the sword. "You should never have challenged me." He didn't breathe heavily. "You are not yet ready."

Hot anger surged in Endric with the words and he lunged. His father's face twisted briefly from a look of sadness to one of resignation. Endric swung his sword, spinning and bringing the blade around. He found nothing but air.

His father had not been where he expected. Suddenly Trill appeared, slicing toward him. Endric felt hot pain and wetness on his legs. He stumbled and swung his sword up wildly. Dendril knocked it away, and the force of the motion knocked Endric's own sword into his chest. He felt the blade bite into his flesh and screamed again. Hot blood streamed across his chest, creeping with unpleasant warmth.

And he fell. Overhead, the gray sky suddenly thundered. Taunting him. Hated rain would come on the day he died.

A dark shadow fell over him. Through eyes blurred by pain and sweat—maybe some blood—he saw Dendril move to stand over him.

He had been critically hurt. The agony running through the entirety of his body spoke to that. Would his father taunt him again?

"You are still a child," he said. There was no emotion in his voice.

Then another shadow streaked toward his face. Not Trill's blade, he realized. The hilt of his father's sword slammed into his forehead.

Then there was blackness.

CHAPTER 21

He awoke to the warm taste of blood in his mouth, metallic and oozing over his cracked lips. Working his dry tongue to moisten them, he found a shallow pool of sticky and drying blood. Attempts to open his mouth, however carefully, were met with nothing but more pain. Endric was aware of the rest of his body, but it was a distant sort of sensation, one filled with nothing but agony. He couldn't remember how he had come to be this way.

He managed to open his eyes. Bright sunlight shot a new torture to the back of his skull, causing him to close them just as quickly. Sunlight, so rare in the city, still pressed through his closed lids and a burned afterimage sent stars across everything.

Slowly he tried again, this time filtering the light carefully through squinted eyes. Long moments passed as his eyes adjusted before he was gradually able to open them completely. There was nothing but blue sky above him. Cloudless and without a hint of gray. It was a sky too beautiful for the city, too beautiful to see while he was feeling the way he did.

Endric turned his head slowly. Tense muscles fought him with the movement. His neck screamed as he moved, and he fought the urge to cry out, though he was not sure he even could, were there the need. He managed to raise his head, turning it the barest amount to each side, and saw nothing but tall grasslands. The ground around him had been patted down, the tall grasses bent and broken, and streaks of blood covered much. Looking farther in the distance, he saw mountains, their peaks obscured in the clouds, and memories came back to him in a flood.

He had challenged his father. He had lost.

And now he was no longer even in the city.

Settling back into the grass, he closed his eyes once more. Taking slow breaths to steady his thudding heart, he considered what had happened. He remembered the challenge, remembered the way his father had toyed with him before defeating him easily and quickly. Had Endric known the level of his skill, he might have…

He sighed deeply. There was nothing he could have done differently. His father did nothing about the threat the Deshmahne posed. Not just to the Denraen, but to people not equipped to face them. What kind of pressure would these dark priests place on unsuspecting nations? Who would protect them if not for the Denraen? Wasn't that their purpose?

He coughed, feeling stabbing pains across his chest as he did, and pushed the questions from his mind. They were no longer his concern. He had been expelled from the Denraen. Left to die on this grassy plain, staring up at the mountains he had once called home.

He closed his eyes again. He lost track of time as he tried to move something other than his neck. Moments or hours could have passed as he slowly learned that he could move his sword arm again. Amazingly, it felt the least injured. Endric no longer felt throbbing throughout his entire body—it was now a constant ache.

The sun beat down on him with unrelenting heat. He felt his body baking in it, wondered when night would fall. How long had he lain here? Hours? Days? His eyes were closed, but still, light slipped through his lids. No longer fading in and out of consciousness, he was now bombarded with painful questions. He tried to stop them but couldn't shut his mind down now that it had started up.

How much longer could he last like this? Another cough racked his body, freeing congealed phlegm from his lungs. He tried to spit but didn't have the strength. He didn't know how badly he had been injured. The pain in his thighs reminded him he had been hurt there, but he remembered still being able to stand after that injury. The pain across his chest was sharper. He was reminded of it with each breath. He should laugh, if he could, at how he had sustained that injury. His own had blade defied him, crashing into his chest under the weighty attack of the sword Trill. That he still lived told him the injury was not too deep. At least not deep enough to puncture lung or heart. And still, he could barely move.

His injuries might not be life-threatening, but exposure to the sun and heat just might be.

How had he gotten here? Was this final punishment for years spent arguing with his father? To be tortured and burned up by the sun, unable even to crawl toward protection? Cruel and beyond what he thought his father capable of, though truly he no longer knew what his father might do. His easy defeat was testament to that. Now he would pay for not knowing the man.

Another cough rolled through him, this time forcing him to surge forward. He still couldn't work his legs and his left arm was dead to him, but he was upright. His head swam for long moments and dark spots danced across his vision before finally clearing. The change in position did little to change his perspective.

Around him was nothing but open plains. The mountains were far in the distance, far enough that he knew it would be a day's ride or more to reach the lowest foothills. From there, it would be another day. More, in his current condition. And of course, that depended on finding a horse.

He coughed again and fell backward. Unable to stop the movement, he hit his head on the hard dirt, cushioned only by the trampled grass around him. Spots swam across his vision again, and his head pounded. Closing his eyes, he questioned why he even considered returning to the city. There was nothing there other than his friends.

He worried about what would happen to Pendin. Senda should be fine; her ties to Listain kept her secure. The spymaster's absence probably made her role even more important, though Endric had no idea how many people worked with Listain the way Senda did. Still, he worried for her and hoped his father was decent enough to leave his friends out of their dispute. They had suffered enough for their friendship with him over the years. Maybe they were even better off with him gone.

Overhead, a hawk circled, cawing harshly each time it made a tentative dive before pulling up and circling again. It was only time before it dove for real. There was little he could do to fend it off if it attacked. His arms didn't have strength enough to shoo the flies pestering him, let alone something larger. The gods protect him if anything larger than the hawk prowled nearby. Thankfully, the wolves that hunted the mountains rarely came this far down in the plains. Too hot for them.

He let his eyes close. Time passed. He might have slipped in and out of consciousness or simply slept. He no longer cared. The sun crawled across the sky, though it grew no cooler for it. He had no more sweat in his body, and his lips had cracked while he was unconscious. His tongue was sticky and he couldn't manage to moisten his mouth, let alone his lips. Breaths came slowly and raggedly, the pain across his chest still sharp. It was the only pain that still bothered him much. That should have worried him, but it didn't.

Visions affected him. He saw his brother's face. Once so vibrant and full of life, he instead saw it as he had the last time—caked in blood and with huge chunks of flesh missing. In the vision, the mouth worked as if trying to speak, but nothing came out. A sense of sorrow surrounded Andril, not the anger Endric expected. Andril had rarely been one to become angry—not like Endric, who so easily grew enraged—and even in death he had not found rage. Dull eyes haunted Endric, almost an accusation, condemning him for daring to challenge their father. Endric couldn't make his own mouth work to speak, and the vision passed.

He saw Olin, his quiet friend, now gone, killed by the same bastards who'd taken his brother from him. Endric hadn't taken the time to mourn him as he should have, and now didn't have the energy to do so.

He saw Pendin. Sadness haunted him. His friend, so physically strong, had weathered much in his life. Endric didn't know all the details of what he had been through. The miner rebellion had challenged him. There had been a hint of understanding as he had explained the motivation behind the revolt. Endric felt a pang of regret for not being more supportive when his friend needed him and hoped again that he was not punished for their friendship. Pendin was a skilled soldier and could accomplish much. In the vision, his face wore nothing but a frown, his eyes soft and troubled.

The vision passed and was replaced by Senda. Endric moaned as her face swam into view, almost as if she were right above him. Her hair flowed free in waves down her back though she rarely wore it that way. She carried a look of concern. Her dark eyes were penetrating, as if she could actually see him. Hers was the hardest face to see. He had been surprised at his feelings for her. Always they had been friends, never more, but the past week had shown him how much he cared for her. Now she was lost to him. Perhaps it was better for her that he was.

Endric forced his eyes open and used the bright sunlight to burn away the remnants of the visions. He couldn't shake the sadness he felt at seeing his brother, Olin, Pendin, and Senda. In spite of the sunlight, the image of his father's disappointed face threatened to swim forward and join the other visions, but he focused on his pain, the heat, his surroundings, and ignored it.

Time continued to pass. He was aware of it as a vague thing—a shifting of shadows, the changing gusts of wind, and the steady throbbing pain in his chest, pounding rhythmically like a drum. The pain pounded, out of sync with his heartbeat, an annoying staccato pulsing. Focusing on that kept his mind off the visions that still swam in his mind.

Sensation slowly returned to his leg, first as a twitch, but gradually as something more. He was able to flex his leg. Strength had not returned to his arms. He could raise them—and that for only a moment—but little else. Coughing fits came and went. None were as strong as the one that sat him up. He wondered whether that was important.

The daytime had been punctuated by the calling of the hawk circling overhead. There had been other sounds—buzzing of insects, a strange humming he had not been able to locate, the rustling of the grass in the wind—but little else other than the hawk. He watched it periodically, its pattern a slow spiral that swooped low every so often. He couldn't help but flinch as it did. It had finally given up as it watched him regain movement, flying off to stalk different prey. Only part of him had been thankful, knowing he didn't wish to be picked to death by a hungry predator bird. Another part simply sought release. He could rejoin his brother in the afterlife. It was strange that he felt closer to the gods as he lay dying, his hazy mind seeking the reassurance of a faith he had not thought he had. Prayers came easier to him than they had since he was a child, and he offered a silent one to the gods for peace.

After the hawk left, he heard a faint scratching nearby. The sound was, likely as not, an animal scurrying across the plains. Hopefully something small. A mouse or rabbit. The sound grew more frequent and he looked around, struggling to see if there was anything nearby. The long grass hid everything. So instead he watched for movement.

He saw the grasses bend at the corner of his vision and turned slowly to watch. A dark ear was the only thing visible through the grass. The rest of the creature was hidden. Endric didn't need to see more. He recognized the laca by the dark striping on its ear, typical of its kind. The wild, predatory dogs were common on the plains but typically hunted small game. Unless they were hungry. Or ill. Then they were known to scavenge.

The laca moved slowly through the grass, stalking him. He barely had enough strength to move his arms, let alone fend off a starving animal. Lacas were fierce fighters and had been known to bring down prey as large as deer, though that was, likely as not, the work of a pack. Only, lacas were never seen in packs. They were rarely seen at all, their movements stealthy.

Endric imagined the dog's sharp teeth tearing into his flesh and shuddered. That was not the end he wanted. He could do nothing to appear threatening—he was barely able to sit upright—and had no weapon nearby. All he could do was hope the laca would grow bored and think he was too large to be easy prey. That he had not moved more than his arms or his head made that unlikely.

The laca continued to circle. The only way Endric knew it was still there was by the sound it made moving through the grass. Even that was hard to hear. He saw a flash of brown fur at one point, but then it was gone. Moments later, he heard movement from the opposite side. There was no way the laca moved that quickly. Was there another?

The heat of the day finally eased as the sun settled into the horizon. Endric's heart beat rapidly as he strained to listen for sounds of the laca. He had not seen the beast in nearly an hour. Occasional gusts of wind kicked up, stronger than they had throughout the day, stinging his flesh and making it difficult to hear the sounds of the predator. With the fading light, he knew it unlikely he would see signs of the animal before an attack. The chill air made his cracked skin burn. His flesh pimpled, but he didn't know whether that was the cool air or fear.

During the day, he'd cursed the warm clothing he wore. Now he realized he didn't wear enough. Not that it mattered. He wouldn't last long in his current condition. His mind was clouding, thinking of things that were unimportant, but he couldn't shake the thought that perhaps more clothing would have better hidden him from the laca.

It was still out there. Circling. Waiting.

What other predators hunted the plains? There were worse things than the laca.

Dying was bad enough, but the slow death that would come by teeth and claws might be worse.

The moon had come up, first as a pale crescent barely peaking above the mountains, but it grew steadier as it rose higher in the sky. Darkness came but was not absolute because of the bright moon, so different here than in the mountain city. Clouds dotted the sky but seemed wispier and not the thick blankets that so often smothered the city. The sound of the swishing of grass—the slow movement of the laca—continued into the night. After a while, he could hear its breathing as a slow panting. A soft whine whispered into the night, and Endric shivered again.

What was the damn laca waiting for?

Different sounds broke the night silence. Insects chirped a rhythmic song, steady though with cycling intensity. He heard the hoot of an owl, the sound quiet and somehow reassuring. The distant howl of wolves reached him this far in the plains, its plaintive sound familiar. A few answering calls followed, even farther away. Too bad they weren't nearer. Then his end would be quick. They went for the throat, killing quickly. Not like the laca. The wind whistled over all of it.

Through the wind came another sound. At first, he thought it just the distant cry of wolves, but the tone was different. Harsher, deeper. Almost a braying. The laca nearby whined again, louder this time. When the sound drifted closer, the laca suddenly stood, ears upright and hackles raised. He stared at Endric with dark eyes that reflected the moonlight. The braying repeated, nearer, and the laca darted off, quickly disappearing into the grasses.

Endric breathed deeply, relaxing. Tension flooded from him. It was a brief respite.

The braying sound came closer, and a nauseating realization hit him: he might be the prey.

Endric closed his eyes and let the wind whisper around him, washing over him with cold fingers. Was he ready to die?

Inhaling deeply of the crisp air, his body still thrumming with pain, he pressed the visions of his fallen brother and friends now lost to him out of his mind. Instead, he offered a silent prayer once more, surprising himself at how easily it formed in his mind. He didn't pray for his life; rather, he asked the gods to grant his father the help he needed to stop the Deshmahne.

Endric still didn't have the strength to do more than lie still. He could move his arms and legs, but there was no power there. He wouldn't even have been able sit up were it not for the coughing fit. The wind gusted again, carrying the sound of the braying closer. The sound was purer as it neared, not as harsh, almost as if the message the creature announced with its call had changed. Long moments passed. His heart thumped quickly, and as he listened to the braying, he was able to ignore the pain throughout his body. He lifted his head—barely more than fist high off the ground—and peered into the night. Nothing moved.

The creatures were closer, now near enough that he counted at least three distinct voices, each with a different call. Always, they stayed out of view. His heart hammered wildly and a cold sweat had pimpled his skin. Distantly, he was surprised his body still had the moisture to sweat. Still, they didn't attack. Endric began to wonder why, feeling a faint hope that maybe they were afraid. Or worse: They toyed with him.

He felt the next sound before he heard it as a distant rumbling. Like the thunder so common in the city, but instead as a deep pounding of the earth. The sound started faintly, growing more prominent until he heard it atop the call of the creatures. The sound was easily recognizable, and he felt a different fear slide through him. Galloping horses.

With a dawning terror, he realized the braying beasts belonged to whomever was coming on horseback. No man kept such creatures. And he knew the gods had denied him as he had once denied them, leaving him to a fate worse than death.

CHAPTER 22

The horses continued toward him, their hooves thudding a steady drumbeat that pounded through his body. The braying creatures remained out of view though he heard them clearly. Hints of shadow were all he saw. Even that was more likely imagined. The strange calls, so like voices, changed and moved as they circled him. There was no doubting they had found him. And were waiting.

Then the horses neared. He felt it as much as heard it. They, too, stayed out of sight. A soft whistle pierced the night, undulating gently and barely more than the sound of the wind. The braying ceased suddenly. In the sudden stillness, only the faint sound of creaking leather interrupted the night.

Another soft whistle—two soft beats—disturbed the silence, and suddenly the animals stalked into view. Three of them, as he had heard. They were tall, taller than any dog or wolf he had ever seen, yet moved with a catlike grace. They advanced toward him, sharp teeth evident in the moonlight, before stopping and sitting in a circle.

Endric had never seen their like. He stared at them, and a deep intelligence stared intently back at him.

His heart still hammered and he almost didn't notice the riders' approach. When he did, he blinked in sudden shock. Six tall stallions carried riders dressed strangely in painted leathers. The horses didn't seem afraid of the creatures that now rested around him, stepping comfortably next to them before halting. One of the riders dismounted, a leisurely jump from the saddle, and came toward him. He was wide—at least as wide as Dendril—and nearly as tall. As the man neared, Endric realized his face was painted in reds and blacks to match his leathers. A long, curved sword hung from his waist.

Antrilii warriors.

He knew little of the Antrilii. Few did, save for their reputation as fierce warriors. None had marched against them in centuries and survived. Few now tried. Even the Denraen left them alone. They roamed an area in the far northwest that was unpopulated except for their people. Yet here they were. Surrounding him.

"Can you move?" The man's voice was thick with an accent, and his face was deeply scarred beneath the painting. Long dark hair was tied back into a tail and braided below the knot.

Despite his training as a Denraen, Endric felt a shiver race down his spine. He could barely shake his head. Sweat ran down the side of his face and mixed with the drying blood. Again, he was surprised he still had the moisture to make sweat. The Antrilii pulled out a long knife, its tip curved wickedly and the blade shining dully in the moonlight. Endric steeled himself, almost thankful the end was near. A curse to the gods formed on his lips, but he couldn't bring himself to speak it.

He managed a nod and was surprised when the Antrilii laughed. "I will not kill you." Dark eyes met his for a moment before he continued. "I cannot say what the gods might choose." Strange how the words reflected his thoughts. The curse disappeared from his mind.

The man cut the remnants of Endric's shirt and pulled it away. The movement was agony and he cried out, the first sound he had made in a long time. One of the other riders neared him with a waterskin, and the two men began to wash his wounds. There came a pungent odor, one of spice and herbs, and Endric knew another pain as a medicated poultice began to settle into his flesh. He didn't cry out again.

They held him as they washed, cleansing his chest. The wound was the worst of his injuries, and he wondered how it looked. The Denraen in him would prize the scar.

The leg wounds came next. Pain shot through him, nauseating him in waves. When the Antrilii finished washing the cuts, Endric knew what they next intended but was not sure he would have the stomach for it.

They gave him little choice as they began to stitch the wounds. There were few tortures like the one he had already endured, but this brought another edge to it. Each stab of the needle was another insult, and he could feel the coarse thread as it was pulled through him. Gritting his teeth, he willed himself to numbness, fixating on anesthesia. He was only partially successful.

As they finished suturing, the Antrilii ran their hands over his arms, legs, and head. Other injuries were found and cleansed with the same sharp pain, but there were no others to stitch. Endric knew the damage he had sustained, could remember each blow vividly. The entire battle was etched in his mind, forcing him to relive it as the memories flooded over him. The first, and most minor, had come when he thought he had a chance against his father. The more serious injuries were sustained as he learned the fallacy of that belief.

Water was dribbled into his mouth, and he coughed again before swallowing it. Parched mouth and lips rejoiced at the water. Cool and with an unusual mineral tang, it tasted sweet. He tried drinking more, but the waterskin was pulled away. Endric left his eyes closed. He felt helpless. Barely able to move, and now he had been found and stitched by Antrilii warriors. The stories of the Antrilii were infrequent, and he feared the men's intent. Their fiercely painted faces and their dark leathers didn't give him hope for a benevolent purpose, but the fact that they'd helped him did.

Then there were the creatures with them. He didn't know what to make of them but realized they hunted with the Antrilii. That meant domestication. Who could tame animals like that? How had others not heard of them?

They sat him up and the world spun, taking away all thoughts and questions.

He struggled to keep his head up while at the same time trying not to vomit, managing only the first of his goals. Ragged heaves racked him, sending new pains throughout, pulling at the stitching on his chest. Long moments passed before the retching eased. The waterskin was placed back in his mouth and more drops of the pleasantly tinged water dripped down his throat, barely what he needed. At least the nausea didn't return.

Endric sat supported for long moments. One of the creatures whined briefly before being hushed by another of the riders. Endric attempted to open his eyes. The spinning had stopped, though dizziness remained. A small victory.

He cast a curious glance at the animal; a cat that behaved like a trained dog. Each of the creatures had tall ears that twitched in the night air, obviously hearing imperceptible sounds, and their dark eyes blinked quickly as glances were cast about the clearing, resting often on him. They seemed to be weighing him. He pulled his gaze away from their intelligent eyes.

"They are merahl," the nearest Antrilii said, anticipating his question. "They are the descendants of a greater race."

Endric managed to *humph* in response, surprising himself again that he was able to make any sound at all. He peeled his eyes from the merahl and looked up at the strangely dressed Antrilii. The red paint smeared across his wide face looked like blood, and the maroon upon his leather matched, making the Antrilii appear as if he just came from a slaughter. A braided beard adorned his chin and his eyes wore an intensity that reminded Endric of his father.

He looked away to watch the other Antrilii. He knelt nearby, watching him. His face was striped black with paint, making him appear feral. His leathers were a deep black and would blend into the darkest night. The other Antrilii remained mounted. Endric couldn't see them, though the occasional whinny of horses told him they were still out there.

"We will ask later what happened," the nearest Antrilii announced. "For now, you will come with us."

Endric shook his head. Patched, he felt no different than he had hours before; he would prefer to be left to die.

The Antrilii laughed. It was harsh and mirthless. "It was not a question."

With that, he heaved Endric easily to his feet. The man lifted him into a saddle and deft hands tied him to it. He was to be their prisoner.

Endric suppressed a laugh. They were sorely mistaken if they thought he would bring some sort of reward. Still, though he was tied to the saddle, the Antrilii had kept him comfortable. Knots had been pulled tight but didn't chafe. They were practiced at this sort of thing.

Endric quickly realized there was little he could do to fight, so he weakly gripped the pommel to give himself the semblance of freedom. The Antrilii grabbed the harness and began to lead them south out of the clearing.

A whistle was followed by, *"Merahl, groeli!"*

With it, the merahl stood and trotted from the clearing; a low growl sounded in each animal's throat as the cats passed the horses and continued away from them, blending quickly into the night. The sound was directed at the horses, more like a call of sorts, almost like they were speaking to them. Endric found the idea that these merahl communicated with the horses to be nearly impossible to fathom.

"They hunt for us," the Antrilii explained.

Endric managed a nod. What else was there to say? The Antrilii seemed to take the merahl as nothing out of the ordinary. Their sheer size was exceptional. The way they had watched him was barely short of unsettling. And nearly tame, like a family dog.

He was a prisoner to the Antrilii—tied to a saddle, injured near to the point of death, and being led away from the only home he had ever known. He should feel more fear than he did but couldn't muster the energy for it. Too much had happened and too much was still at risk, yet he need not care any longer. It was not his responsibility to understand what he had observed over the past month. Not that it ever was. Nor was it his responsibility to worry about the Deshmahne. He would be glad to leave that to his father.

Except Dendril did nothing.

Endric closed his eyes as helplessness washed over him. He suppressed a sigh and focused on the slow trotting of the horse, wondering where the Antrilii led him. Gradually, he felt his strength beginning to return and realized he was using his legs somewhat to keep him atop the horse. His arms remained weak, though there was a growing strength to them as well. Licking his cracking lips, trying to moisten them, all he tasted was his dried blood.

His jaw ached as he worked it, and he wondered why he hadn't felt it before.

"What?" he finally croaked.

The Antrilii leading him looked over at him and frowned. His shadowed face was like a nightmare. But not his eyes. There was a passing moment of compassion.

"Why heal?" he asked. The words were stiff and harsh as they passed through his raw throat, yet there was no denying that was what they had done. He didn't know what medicines they used, only that they were unlike anything the Denraen had for injuries.

The Antrilii grunted. "Why let you suffer?" he asked. They went a few more steps before he spoke again. "I said that later you would tell me what happened."

The man's accented words were hard to understand and Endric found he was leaning forward as he strained to comprehend. He nodded as he realized what the Antrilii had said.

The man smiled with a flash of teeth. "Good. Then tell me."

The threat was barely veiled, and Endric felt a shiver run up his spine at the command. So similar to his father, with the same expectation of an order being followed. Still, he hesitated. What would the Antrilii do if he explained? He was their prisoner. It would help him for them to know that he was Denraen, only giving more fodder for demands that he was certain would go unmet.

"A mistake. One that I will not make again."

The Antrilii turned to him and stared. "Seems like you angered someone. That cannot be simply a mistake."

Endric closed his eyes and coughed. "Angering him was not the mistake."

The Antrilii surprised him then and laughed. It was a hearty sound and rumbled into the night. "I see now."

He opened his eyes and looked at the Antrilii. "Do you?" Could the man know he was Denraen? Would it matter?

"You underestimated someone." He laughed a moment longer before it died off. "That is a mistake that can only be made once. You were lucky to live through it."

"I didn't think my father would actually try to kill me."

The huge Antrilii narrowed his eyes at him. "Were you willing to kill him?"

The question cut to the heart of the matter quickly. Endric had gone into the challenge knowing what the possible outcome might be but had not really thought his father could best him. He had figured the man too old, too slow, leaving Endric able to carefully end the fight without harming him seriously. Deep down, he hadn't thought he could lose. That had been his real mistake. He remembered distinctly the time in the fight when he'd realized how wrong he was.

"Not at first."

The Antrilii raised an eyebrow.

"I lost control of the fight."

The Antrilii snorted and nodded. A knowing look crossed his face and he turned away, saying nothing more. They went a while longer in silence. The merahl called occasionally, each voice distinct, howling across the plain. It was as if they spoke to each other while they hunted.

"What do they hunt?" For what creature would the Antrilii feel motivated to leave their northern home to hunt so far to the south? The distance was not insignificant. Endric had traveled much of the southern part of the continent as part of the Denraen but rarely even reached Rondalin, let alone the mountain ranges of the north that the Antrilii called home. Still, he knew how far they had traveled to reach this far into the plains. Strange that the Denraen had not heard of their travels.

The Antrilii looked back at him. "They hunt groeliin." He watched Endric for a moment before turning away and said nothing more.

Endric wasn't certain he even heard the man right. The thick accent made his words sound almost like he spoke through a mouthful of mud. Groeliin? Endric had never heard of the creature, though in truth he had never heard of a merahl before tonight. What other creatures did the Antrilii know about that Endric had no knowledge of? Yet if they hunted these creatures on the plains, then he should have known something about them. The Denraen routinely patrolled the area.

He shook his head. The answer was likely much simpler. Either he'd misunderstood the Antrilii or the word was from the Antrilii native tongue. He wondered which it was and decided to ask later.

They traveled south for what must have been hours. The night grew cooler and a light fog settled across the plains, dampening the long blades of grass they traveled through. The Antrilii leading his horse didn't seem to mind the cool air or the wetness, holding casually to the reins. Endric had tried to steer the horse with his knees, but the animal ignored him, trusting the Antrilii leading it. Even the horses were well trained.

Endric didn't know what time it was when they stopped. The moon had shifted in the sky and hid behind a bank of clouds. Only thin light filtered through, and he had trouble seeing clearly. The Antrilii seemed to have no such trouble, navigating confidently. The constant calling from the merahl led them south and a little east. After crossing a small stream, the Antrilii leading his horse whistled again, a low, haunting sound. It was answered by a quick bark from the merahl.

The other Antrilii stopped and dismounted. They worked quickly, making camp with practiced hands. The horses were left to graze, and Endric was surprised no one bothered to tie them up. They didn't wander far. One of the Antrilii disappeared, returning a short time afterward with a bundle of branches. A small, smoky fire blazed only moments later, seeming to erupt of its own accord from the gathered branches. One of the Antrilii sprinkled something atop the fire and the smoke quickly dissipated.

The Antrilii leading him untied him from the saddle and carried him near the fire. A small flask of water was set into his hands. He looked up briefly at the man who gave it to him and saw an expressionless face beneath the dark paint.

Endric drank slowly, carefully letting the cool water slide down his throat. He coughed once, but even the coughing fits seemed to be easing. Strength had returned somewhat to his arms, and he found he could move them with only minimal pain. His legs remained weak but better than they had been before the Antrilii lifted him into the saddle. Even the worst of his injuries—the deep gash on his chest—only throbbed. The sharp, stabbing pain was no longer a companion. Whatever medicines they had used on his wounds appeared to be working.

Eventually the merahl returned and stalked into the clearing, curling up near the fire. One was missing, and Endric looked around and saw it prowling just at the edge of his vision. Almost as if on patrol. He shook his head, amazed by these creatures. The two lying by the fire seemed like large house cats curled up by a fireplace, basking in the heat. Dangerous house cats.

After a while, the Antrilii roasted something atop the fire. The smell was enticing, and he was handed a hunk of meat a short time later. Endric eyed it carefully before taking a cautious bite. The meat was juicy and flavorful, and he savored the taste. One of the Antrilii sat nearby, eating quietly.

"What is it?" he asked the man.

The Antrilii looked over at him. His face was smeared with orange and red paint, dashes of black mixed within. His hollow eyes wore a hot intensity. "You have never had hare?" His accent was even thicker than the other's.

"Never like this." It was true. The meat was seasoned unlike anything he had ever tasted, yet still had a hint of familiarity about it.

The Antrilii grunted. "Most flatlanders do not like Antrilii cooking."

Endric shrugged. "Who caught it?" He had not seen anyone disappear to hunt. Since it wasn't salted, he figured it was a fresh kill.

"Merahl."

Endric raised his eyebrows.

"They don't only hunt groeliin for us."

Endric was sure he heard the word correctly this time. "What is a groeliin?"

The man shook his head. "Groeliin can't be explained. Must be seen." He offered no further discussion, turning back to his food.

When finished, Endric sat back and looked over at the merahl sitting before the fire. Their tails were curled around them and they lay still. As he watched, he realized that was not quite right. Their ears twitched, swiveling in response to sounds Endric couldn't hear. Though they rested and another of the merahl still prowled around the edge of the camp, these merahl remained on guard. They made a formidable defense.

He looked up at the night. Cool air blew across his face. The moon had emerged from the hovering clouds and had traveled across the sky. Morning was close now. He should sleep, but he couldn't shut down his mind. Too many thoughts raced through his head, tormenting him. Lying back, he decided to try, unsure how long they would be stopped and when he might next have the opportunity for rest. He didn't know when it was that he fell asleep.

Endric was jostled awake by a rough hand on his shoulder. Blinking his eyes open, he saw one of the Antrilii kneeling before him. His face was painted with swirls of dark paint, brown and dark red, and he wore deep black leathers. A long sword hung from his waist and he pushed it back as he knelt. A thick beard covered his chin, braided like the others.

"Up. Time to ride."

He looked around. He still lay where he had sat the night before. The fire had been extinguished and buried, leaving little evidence there had ever been a fire in the first place. The other Antrilii prepared their mounts. Endric was only slightly surprised they had not run off. The merahl were gone, but he heard their distinct call in the distance.

Most of the day had passed while he slept. The sun was up but slipping toward the horizon. How had he managed to sleep through the daylight? He shook his head, feeling groggy like he would after a night of hard drinking. How injured had he been?

The same Antrilii from the day before led his horse over to him. "Can you ride?"

Endric had barely been able to use his arms yesterday; his legs had been useless. Pain still throbbed across his thighs at the spot where Trill had cut into him. He stretched his legs and found he could move them. There was only one way to determine whether they would bear his weight. Endric stood slowly, stretching tight muscles that screamed in protest. "I think so."

The Antrilii watched him with an unreadable expression before helping him into the saddle. Endric gripped the pommel and locked his feet into the stirrups. The saddle was shaped differently than those the Denraen used, but was comfortable nonetheless. The horse didn't make a sound as he situated himself, keeping itself rigid. What Endric had taken to be reins the night before had been little more than a line tied to the saddle. Without reins, Endric wouldn't be able to guide the horse on his own.

Not that he expected the animal to respond to him anyway, especially not after seeing how they had not even bothered to tie the horses up the night before. The horses of Coamdon were oft considered the best of breed, their breeders and trainers unparalleled. Seeing the way the horses worked with the Antrilii—and not for them—Endric wondered if that were true.

The Antrilii led the horse south, following the others. The occasional call of the merahl led them forward. Endric loosely gripped the saddle as he rode, feeling strength slowly return to his arms and legs. He tried again to steer the horse with his legs but was unsuccessful. The Antrilii looked back at him as he did, almost as if he knew what he was doing, yet he said nothing. The horse simply ignored Endric, swishing its long tail up and whipping his arm. Maybe he was not ignored entirely.

They moved steadily, never hurrying. The man walking never appeared to grow tired, and his steps didn't slow. The others rode at an easy pace, breaking a path in the grass. An occasional copse of tree dotted the plain; otherwise there was nothing but rolling grassland. In the growing darkness, a stillness hovered over everything.

They had ridden for several hours without stopping when the periodic call from the merahl turned into something different. Harsher than the braying he had heard the night before, this sound was like an angry snarl. The sound was continuous and grew quieter. The merahl hunted and had found a scent.

The Antrilii on horse looked back at the man leading him. He nodded, and four of the men suddenly lunged forward. The remaining mounted man rode off but not far, unsheathing his sword and riding in a slow circle around them. Endric frowned at the tactics. The mounted Antrilii seemed as if he patrolled, but the merahl sounded as if they hunted far in the distance.

"They have found the trail," the Antrilii leading him said.

"Whose?"

"That of the groeliin." He looked into the distance as he spoke.

"I still don't know what they are."

The Antrilii grunted and turned to him, eyes intense. "Be glad you do not."

They rode in silence for a while longer. Endric waited for the man to say something more, anything, but he didn't. After a while, the merahl called a new sound. A continuous cry echoed in the air, haunting. Endric shivered. Knowing what made the eerie sound didn't make it easier to hear. The merahl howled like that for nearly an hour before it suddenly ceased.

He was led steadily south. Toward the merahl.

When they finally fell quiet, it was like a blanket had fallen over his ears. Day had turned to a night that was completely silent. Not even the insects disturbed the silence. Endric shivered again.

"What happened?" he finally asked.

The Antrilii looked back at him with an unreadable expression. "The fight is over."

Endric frowned. "The fight?" The Antrilii didn't respond. "That's it? You're done hunting?"

The man laughed. The mirth didn't reach his eyes; they remained shadowed by the dark paint upon his face. "For tonight, probably. More remain."

"More hunts?" Endric was confused. He didn't think it was the Antrilii accent that confused him. Rather, it was the idea that there was much more to what was taking place than he understood.

The Antrilii nodded. "More hunts. More groeliin."

"Then you will return home?"

The Antrilii shrugged. "Depends."

"On what?"

"Depends on what the merahl find."

As he spoke, the merahl called out again with the distinctive braying they had been following all day. The sound seemed to get farther away, and Endric realized they were on the trail of these groeliin again.

"I guess the hunt is not over," Endric said.

The Antrilii looked back at him and smiled with a flash of teeth. "You understand the merahl?" Seeing Endric's puzzled expression, he shook his head. "No. The hunt never really ends." He smiled, a wolfish smile, again.

After battling his father, Endric had learned the man was dangerous. He had heard stories of his father while growing up. Most seemed exaggerations, tales of his exploits with Trill, battles won. Fighting with him—even an older version—he realized that those stories must have been true. Dendril *was* a dangerous man. Something about this Antrilii's smile told Endric he was just as dangerous as Dendril. Maybe more so.

Endric shivered again, looking over at the Antrilii as he did.

As they made their way south, he wondered again why they held him. They could have left him to die. Likely as not, without the merahl scaring off the laca, he would have been torn apart by the wild hound. Yet they had treated and stitched him. Now he would live, but for what?

The merahl barked into the night. Another hour or so passed until the other Antrilii suddenly rejoined them. One of the men had a cut on his arm. A band of cloth was tied around his upper arm in a tourniquet. The others looked unharmed. A small bag was tied to the saddle of one of the men, darkness staining it. Blood. Painful memories of his brother came back to him at the sight.

They rode only a little longer. The Antrilii were silent; only the occasional sound of the merahl broke the night. After a while, they stopped near a copse of trees to make camp. One of the men whistled softly. The Antrilii leading his horse helped him from the saddle, then left him alone. Saddles were stripped from the horses and they were left to forage. One of the Antrilii lit a small fire. Others worked at their own tasks. The merahl eventually returned, looking no worse than they had the last time he saw them.

Endric sat. Even surrounded by the half dozen Antrilii, he was lonely. He looked up at the open sky where the moon glowed brightly. A few clouds dotted the blackness. Around him stretched open grasslands, but it was an illusion. His legs ached and he was exhausted from the ride. His chest hurt and he still had a dry cough.

Shackles might not bind him, but he was no less a prisoner. There was no place for him to go and no way to escape. He looked at the Antrilii and their expressionless, painted faces. Hopelessness flooded through him, and he wondered why the gods had spared him.

He should have died upon the plain.

CHAPTER 23

Endric awoke the next day feeling much stronger.

The camp had been cleared and the fire buried by the time he stirred, though he woke sooner than he had the day before. Fatigue still limited him and he still was tired. Part of the healing, he supposed. He stood and stretched, working the tight muscles in his shoulder.

As he did, he watched the Antrilii. Two of the men wrangled the horses, though the chore was not challenging. The horses came to them and waited patiently while saddled. Another man knelt in front of the merahl. Endric watched awhile, thinking it strange that the man murmured quietly to them. They looked back at the Antrilii with an attention that almost made Endric think they understood him. He was still uncertain how he felt about the strange creatures. Uneasy, mostly. The other Antrilii stood, talking quietly.

Endric frowned. It was as if they waited for him. That was not how he expected a prisoner would be treated. They had healed him as well, to the point that he was beginning to feel almost normal. He was surprised that he felt as well as he did, especially knowing how close to death he had come.

A nagging worry at the back of his mind pulled at him. Now that he was feeling better, he should be trying to escape, only he didn't feel like escaping. A sense of curiosity plagued him.

He wondered about the merahl, about the Antrilii, but mostly about these strange creatures the Antrilii hunted. Watching the Antrilii in their leathers and the fearsome paintings upon their face, he decided that the groeliin must be some prize for them to hunt so far from their lands.

What were they? The Antrilii had returned from the hunt with a bloodstained bag but little else. No other evidence of a victorious hunt. Nothing like the hunts he was accustomed to.

Then there was the simple fact that nothing was left for him in the city. Pendin and Senda were likely better off without his presence. Now that he had been expelled from the Denraen, there was little else in Vasha for him. That fact left a hollow feeling in his chest. A lifetime in the city—born and raised within the mountain city's walls—and now there was nothing.

Endric swallowed hard, forcing down the lump in his throat.

An Antrilii approached. He was the same one who had been leading the horse, the one who had healed him. Endric watched him warily. The man wore his dark blood-red leathers, and his face was painted differently than the day before. No less frightening though.

"Can you ride?" His gruff voice matched his wide frame.

Endric stared at him for a moment before nodding. "What's your name?"

The Antrilii narrowed his eyes. Endric worried for a moment that he had insulted the man. Perhaps the Antrilii were not free with names. There were some who still clung to the ancient belief that names gave power. Even the Urmahne still held on to part of that belief; it was the reason the gods were not named.

"I am Dentoun," he finally answered.

"Endric," he said, offering his hand. Though he was trapped with them, he wouldn't behave as if he were a prisoner.

Dentoun gripped his hand with his own wide hand, squeezing just enough that Endric sensed the strength in the man, and shook once before releasing. "Endric. We hunt."

He whistled softly, a different sound than he made for the merahl, and his horse trotted over. Dentoun helped him into the saddle with less help than he'd needed the day before but still more than Endric preferred. He was not used to needing help with anything.

Once Endric was in the saddle and Dentoun had tied his line to the pommel, he whistled again. This time it was for the merahl. The animals responded quickly, standing with ears alert. The Antrilii who had been kneeling in front of them was now mounted and he leaned over, whispering something softly to them. A low, deep-throated growl came from them and they each bared their teeth, almost as if they were smiling. Then they loped away.

Endric watched them, still amazed. The merahl were unlike any creature he had ever encountered, and he began to wonder if they were as sentient as the Antrilii they worked with. Not served though. Something told him that the merahl didn't serve. The strange creatures disappeared into the rolling hills of the grassland, only their occasional call still marking their location.

Dentoun led him after the others. The sun still hung brightly in the sky but was now sinking toward the horizon. The Antrilii rode without talking, and the persistent silence became unsettling.

"Why do you hunt the groeliin?" he asked. For a while, Endric didn't think he would answer.

"Why do the wolves of your mountains hunt?" Dentoun asked in answer. His accented voice was difficult to understand at times, but he was clear as he spoke those words. "They are wolves. That is what they do." Dentoun shook his head, and his braided beard swung from side to side. "We are Antrilii. We hunt groeliin."

Endric frowned. Had Dentoun known he was from Vasha, or was it simply an observation? "I've never heard of these creatures before."

Dentoun grunted. It came out more like a growl and reminded Endric of the merahl. "There are few that remember."

It was a strange choice of words. "Are they common?"

The Antrilii looked back at him with hot fire in his eyes. Endric was almost forced to look away.

"Not here. Be thankful of that."

"But in your homelands…"

Dentoun nodded. "The groeliin are why we roam the north."

"Why are they here now?" Endric still had no idea what these creatures were, but the Antrilii seemed to fear them. At least, as much as the Antrilii seemed to fear anything, which was not much.

Dentoun grunted again, another growl. "They have escaped."

"Escaped what?"

"Antrilii."

Endric felt his eyes widen. "You had captured them?"

The Antrilii shook his head again. "The groeliin occasionally try to push to the south." He shrugged. "Usually they fail. Sometimes not."

"What happens then?"

He shrugged again. "We chase."

Endric shook his head in puzzlement. "Why not let someone else deal with them?"

Dentoun considered him for a moment. "Who could do this?"

Endric hesitated, unwilling to reveal his affiliation with the Denraen. "There must be some soldiers able to help."

The Antrilii sniffed, then answered with a single shake of his head. "This is something we must do."

"I don't understand."

"If you would face groeliin, you would understand." He fell silent for a few moments. "We are Antrilii. This is our task."

Endric felt no clearer on the issue, but at least he knew Dentoun's name and some little about why they had appeared in the southern lands.

The Denraen knew of the Antrilii, knew them as skilled warriors, but nomads who wandered the near-deserted north, not settling in one place for long. Few knew how many Antrilii actually lived in the northern lands. That was the extent of Endric's knowledge. Now, at least, he knew they hunted groeliin. Whatever they were.

They rode on in relative silence. The merahl called, keeping a steady pace in front of them. The moon lit the night with a gentle glow, and no clouds marred the sky. In other circumstances, it would be a peaceful night, made all the more relaxing by the wind whispering softly through the long grasses.

As they topped a gentle rise, Endric saw the landscape laid out before him in a familiar pattern and recognized where they were.

They rode nearly straight south, cutting through the grasses. The horses had no difficulty with footing, and Dentoun didn't seem to fatigue as he walked alongside the horse, leading Endric. If they continued this direction, they would reach Ilowan.

"There is a town not far from here," he said to Dentoun.

The Antrilii didn't look back as he answered. "Aye. We will pass through tonight."

Endric considered the response. He had not expected that the Antrilii would pass through Ilowan, instead thinking they would avoid the small town if possible. The Antrilii continued down the gentle hillside, following the rolling landscape. Hours passed as they rode, the moon again sinking down in the sky. The night grew quieter and even the call of the merahl grew less frequent. Still there, though, and reassuring for its presence.

He was surprised at that. Having creatures as powerful and as obviously intelligent on his side provided a certain comfort in the deepness of the night, even if they didn't follow at their side. Knowing they roamed the rolling grasslands, scaring away other predators as they had the laca only a few nights before, was heartening.

Eventually they topped another rise and followed it down to a darkened valley. Fog circled around the horses' hooves as they descended, growing thicker the farther they went. Morning mist, a marker in the valleys for the time just preceding dawn, had significance to some in this area. This fog was thicker than he remembered, covering them like a blanket, eventually even muting the sounds of the horses' hooves and the occasional call from the merahl. Were it not for the line tied to his saddle, he would have felt increasingly isolated. The stars still shone overhead, faintly twinkling, and only increased his sense of desolation.

So it was that they reached the low wall surrounding Ilowan without additional warning. The wall, made of pale stone likely quarried from the beds of the near half-dozen rivers running through this part of the land, reached the chest of the horse. More of a boundary than true protection, though it was likely enough to keep nocturnal predators away. A call from the merahl erupted from nearby, within the town, putting lie to that thought.

Ilowan was a simple town. Its people were farmers mostly, though some skill with woolens came from them as well. Endric had stayed within its walls at least twice while on patrol with the Denraen. It was similar to the other small villages that dotted the land. The people had been generally friendly, appreciative of the Denraen, and had provided for their needs without question, happily accepting their coin. He wondered how they would react to the half dozen Antrilii, dressed in dark leathers and carrying an assortment of weapons.

Probably with fear, he decided, looking over at Dentoun. It wouldn't be the vicious curved sword he carried, though admittedly that was intimidating. More likely his painted face, glistening in the moonlight, a fearsome expression upon it, would send dread through them.

A low growl penetrated the fog and the night, piercing like a sword through flesh. The merahl had found something. The sound was nearby. Definitely within the city. He wasn't sure when the merahl had slowed or if he had missed one of the Antrilii whistles communicating with them.

The Antrilii dismounted and followed the stone wall as it circled the town. Endric climbed clumsily from his saddle to follow. His legs were still stiff, and his arm throbbed. Less than it should have, he knew. He gave thanks again for the medicines the Antrilii had used. They reached the gateway to the town. The wooden gate hung open, one side tied back, the other swinging slowly in the light breeze flowing over the hilltop, as if moved by an unseen hand. Endric shivered.

The town was quiet. The fog lifted somewhat as they passed into town, and he could see the small houses protected behind the wall. Something was wrong.

He couldn't put a finger on what it was. As he looked around, he saw nothing moving and no lights flickering in any of the windows. He didn't know what time it was, but much of the night had already passed. There should be some townsfolk awake at this time, he realized, some activity. Endric had never known a baker who slept past midnight. Yet there was no smell of rising bread. Another thought troubled him. Ilowan was a farming town. The farmers, at least, should be readying for the day.

There was absolute stillness.

Something else troubled him. An odor tickled his nose unpleasantly. He couldn't place the scent or its location; it seemed to come from the entire town. "There is something not right here," he said to no one in particular.

Dentoun walked near him and grunted. "Groeliin."

Endric looked around, suddenly feeling more uneasy. "They're here?" He saw nothing else—just the small houses, a small grass plaza, and the town wall.

Dentoun shook his head. "Not here now." His voice was pitched low and carried only to Endric's ears. He didn't look over to him; his eyes were searching the shadows for signs of movement. His body was otherwise relaxed, though his hand hovered near his sword. Endric understood, feeling naked without his own sword.

One of the merahl appeared out of the mists, sliding into view from behind a distant house. The merahl moved gracefully, silent in the night, hackles raised and ears upright and alert. The creatures stalked over to Dentoun and whined. The sound was barely more than a whisper of wind.

Dentoun leaned forward and whispered something in response, and the merahl loped off, disappearing into darkness. A quiet call interrupting the night was answered by two other voices on the other side of the town.

He was startled into movement as Dentoun led them deeper into the town. A darker shadow blotted the roadway not far from the town gate. As he neared, his nose told him as much about what it was as his eyes.

A body.

It lay sprawled upon the road, its legs spread in a grotesque split. When he realized the body was missing its head, he looked away, sickened. The memory of his brother's head sitting atop his father's desk made the sight too difficult to look upon. His eyes fell upon another body in a similar condition.

It was then that he recognized the odor. Rotting flesh.

"This is groeliin?" he asked, finding the idea hard to believe.

Dentoun nodded.

The creatures attacked men in town? Few animals would even dare approach a town, let alone enter. If these creatures had, what exactly were these groeliin?

"Are you certain? The Deshmahne beheaded my brother in a similar manner."
This seemed more like the kind of attack the dark priests would make.

Dentoun looked over at him. His mouth tightened, and the shadows
around his intense eyes deepened. "Perhaps they are the same."

Endric shook his head. "Deshmahne are men," he answered firmly. They
might have abilities he didn't understand, but they were still men. They could
be killed.

"Then not the same."

"Why do you think this is the groeliin?" he asked.

Dentoun looked back down at the splayed bodies, and Endric followed
his gaze. The remaining clothing writhed eerily. Endric didn't need to
examine the corpses to know maggots had made their home. Another wave of
nausea threatened him.

"Come with me," Dentoun said quietly.

The Antrilii led him house to house, torches suddenly in hand, casting a
horrible light upon everything. Even in the weak torchlight, the horror was
unmistakable.

There were no survivors.

The street was littered with dead men. The first bodies they had found
had been in the best condition. Others had bite marks and some looked as if
they had been chewed by animals. A deep scent of rot hung over everything.
At first, he wondered why they had only found men, and when he learned the
answer, he nearly vomited again. They found the remains of women and
children behind barricaded doors. Oftentimes there was nothing but scraps
of clothing remaining.

Endric had seen much in his years with the Denraen, had known battle,
bloodshed, and death, and so was surprised by how this massacre disturbed
him. There was something different to this attack, something almost evil.

As the Antrilii led the search of the town, he realized he was the only one
having difficulty. The faces of the Antrilii were firm, fixed with their painted
masks. They moved in businesslike fashion in their search of the town, very
professional, and he realized this was not the first time they had seen
something like this.

"How can this be?" His voice was hoarse, and the darkness of the night swallowed it. Fog seemed thicker the farther into the town they went, and the torches almost sputtered, as if the darkness itself tried to extinguish their light.

There was no answer; the Antrilii continued their search.

Occasionally the dark-furred merahl would return, hackles raised as they stalked protectively around the Antrilii. At times they would growl suddenly and then quiet again. They, at least, seemed to sense the inhuman destruction of the town.

When they reached the other side of Ilowan, Endric found Dentoun and limped over to him. Grabbing him roughly by the sleeve, he turned the Antrilii to face him. The broad man didn't try to shake Endric off, watching him carefully from beneath his painted face.

"Where are the groeliin? This entire town is slaughtered. These men had to have injured some of them." Endric had seen many of the slain men with swords or clubs lying next to them, under them. They had not been unarmed.

Dentoun shook his head. "These men would do nothing."

Endric looked back at the town with a surge of anger. "These men died defending their families! They were not cowards!"

"No. Not cowards," Dentoun agreed. He did not raise his voice to match Endric's anger. "There was little they could do against this enemy."

Endric stared at him incredulously for a moment, then looked at the other Antrilii standing nearby. "These groeliin killed this entire town, and you hunt them with your small band?" One of the merahl growled then, as if it understood the comment.

Dentoun whispered something unintelligible and the growl ceased. Turning back to Endric, he motioned for him to follow. They walked over to the town wall and Dentoun knelt.

Endric copied the posture, the stiffness in his legs making it more difficult than it should be, so he leaned against the wall for support, feeling the cool stone penetrate his shirt.

When Dentoun spoke, his accented voice was soft. "Listen carefully to what I tell you now. You have seen the destruction wrought by the groeliin." He swept an arm toward the town. "We do not hunt the groeliin for sport.

We do it because these men could do nothing against the groeliin. Few can. These men died because they couldn't see the groeliin." He paused, watching Endric as the words sank in. "Groeliin have a dark magic, something in their blood that hides them from man." He shook his head and grunted, a mixture of anger and frustration. "You cannot fight what you cannot see."

Endric laughed without a hint of mirth. "If men can't see them, how do you expect to fight them?"

"Because there is something in our blood which reveals them. The Antrilii have long stood as the barrier to the groeliin; we have battled them because we must, because we are of the few who can. The gods have chosen us for this, and we will not fail."

There was an urgency and a fierce pride to Dentoun's words, such that Endric couldn't doubt the man. He leaned back against the wall, thinking about what it was the Antrilii was telling him. He no longer doubted the veracity of Dentoun's claim; what he had seen in the city was truth enough. He struggled with understanding how such fearsome creatures could be otherwise unknown and the idea of trusting their fate to the nomadic, warlike Antrilii.

"You said the groeliin have moved south before?"

"They try every season."

Endric frowned. "What season?"

"Breeding season. Sometimes a brood will break free. We chase."

"Like you are now."

Dentoun nodded. "This is not a large brood."

Endric looked back toward the remains of Ilowan, wondering how much damage a large brood of groeliin could do.

"They usually do not get this far. I am not sure why they press this time."

"Have they ever come south in large numbers?" Endric asked, feeling it was somehow important.

Dentoun nodded gravely. "Once. It was over a thousand years ago."

"What happened then?" he asked, though he was beginning to suspect. He wasn't as well versed in the histories as he should have been, but he knew Vasha was over one thousand years old and founded by the Magi. The timing was too close to be coincidental.

Dentoun frowned at him. "You do not know?" he asked, watching Endric's face. Seeing him shake his head, he continued, "No. I see that you do not."

"Know what?"

Dentoun sighed before answering, his features softening. "Much was lost. Cities destroyed." He looked over at the remains of Ilowan and shrugged. "Men were forced to start anew."

"And the Magi?" he asked. "What role did they play?"

A wry smile curved the Antrilii's lips, contorting the painting upon his face. "Most have forgotten their role. Intentional or not, the result is the same." A hint of sadness entered his voice. "Before there were Antrilii, the Magi fought the groeliin. Once, they were all that stood between mankind and complete destruction. Of course, they were not known as Magi then."

"What were they called?" Endric was surprised to be interested, but hearing that the Magi had not always been the peace-loving Urmahne was more than a little fascinating. The idea that the Magi would fight anything, let alone creatures that could destroy an entire town, was laughable. The Antrilii at least looked the part. Dressed in leathers, faces painted garishly, they carried swords that seemed a part of them. He believed the Antrilii could battle these groeliin.

"They were men, gifted by the gods. They fought the groeliin, pushing them back. It was only by the grace of the gods that the groeliin were defeated. Our records are vague, but the gods must have performed some miracle to help, else mankind was lost."

Endric suppressed a smile, not wanting to upset the Antrilii. Dentoun spoke about the gods nearly as reverently as the Magi. The gods performed a miracle? More likely it was less profound. The gods had never interfered in the lives of men, if they even existed at all. He shook his head, pushing away that line of thinking.

"I can see you do not believe," Dentoun said. The expected anger was not present in his voice. "Few understand the destruction even a single groeliin can manage. None have seen the effort of all the broods attacking at once; not for a thousand years has that been seen. Not even the Antrilii can make that claim. Luck or the gods will keep the groeliin broods from working together. If that happened, even Antrilii wouldn't be enough." The emotion in his voice made it clear that Dentoun believed what he said.

A tingle worked its way down Endric's spine. "How have I not heard of this before?" The Denraen patrolled these lands and traveled to the north.

The Antrilii nodded. "Most have forgotten."

"Most?"

Dentoun shrugged. "There are those who still remember."

Endric leaned back again the wall again, settling his head against the stone. The Denraen *did* patrol the north, but not often. It was mostly unsettled save for Rondalin—little was in the Antrilii range other than small mining towns. The northern ranges were not as flush with ore as those in the south. The people who lived there were isolated. Endric had never questioned why the Denraen didn't patrol more often into the northern ranges. Perhaps only to minimize contact and conflict with the Antrilii; Endric sensed the Antrilii would be a formidable foe even for trained soldiers. But perhaps there was another reason.

Could his father know about the groeliin? Did the Magi?

"Do the Magi still know?" he asked. The answer to that question would be easier to stomach, but he knew he would need to learn the other. Dentoun nodded carefully, as if considering how much to share. Endric wondered why the Antrilii had shared this much, though the destruction in Ilowan needed answers.

"It's possible. Most choose to forget."

"Why? If the groeliin are capable of destroying a town the size of Ilowan, what stops them from attacking a larger city?"

Dentoun smiled then, flashing his teeth. "Antrilii stop them. The Magi do not want to know the truth."

Endric frowned. "What truth?"

"The truth of their origin. The Magi were soldiers once, warriors. Like the Antrilii. When they laid down their swords, the Antrilii didn't. We remember."

Dentoun stood as he said that last, sad and proud at the same time. Endric wondered what it cost this man, his people, to constantly battle these groeliin, to stand between men and this destruction. He watched as Dentoun walked away. A whistle, low and solemn, was followed by the merahl standing and loping off. Their calls followed, piercing the night.

The Antrilii mounted quietly and rode away from Ilowan to continue their hunt.

CHAPTER 24

Endric spent the rest of the night in silence. They stayed on the road leading south from Ilowan, the horses moving swiftly. None of the Antrilii spoke, although that was not unusual. There was still a somber sense casting a pall over the ride. Endric was certain the Antrilii felt it even though he couldn't read them. The merahl ranged ahead, lost in the long grasses and the night, always making their presence known with their calls.

Images from Ilowan kept creeping into his mind. Bodies mangled and broken. Children missing arms, legs, and chunks of flesh. The scent of rot that hung over the town as they passed through it. He couldn't imagine what kind of creature could do something like that.

It was not just the imagery that troubled him. He had thought the Deshmahne posed the greatest threat; perhaps they still did, but whatever the Antrilii faced was as much or more of a threat. How could the Antrilii wage such an ongoing war without anyone else knowing? Dentoun didn't seem to want recognition. He spoke with a sense of duty that Endric suspected stemmed from a deeply held belief in the gods. He truly believed.

If only it were so simple.

He was shaken from his thoughts as his horse pulled to a stop. The night was late, full darkness upon them and likely only a few hours until morning. The thin light of the moon, which had been with them until they left Ilowan, had disappeared behind clouds, stealing their only illumination. The air was crisp and smelled of the coming dew; the stench from Ilowan hung in his nose as a malodorous memory. Would they camp sooner tonight?

The merahl called in the distance, farther than they usually ranged when stopping for the day. Camping wasn't the reason for the stop.

Endric looked up and toward Dentoun. The Antrilii had released his hold on the reins; it was the first time Endric had been put in the saddle without the Antrilii holding the other end of the lead. For a moment, the temptation to kick the horse to a gallop and escape nearly overwhelmed him, but he quickly came to his senses.

Where would he go? He had nothing. No home. No family. Only his friends, who were better off with him gone. Though he might be their prisoner, the Antrilii had shown him no ill will, treating him instead with courtesy. He wondered if they would even stop him if he tried to escape.

Dentoun walked ahead, following the road. Little more than hard-packed dirt, it sloped up the hillside. A few small trees dotted the plain. A larger copse nearby was little more than a darker smear in the night. It was toward this that Dentoun walked. A distinctive *snick* echoed back to him as the Antrilii unsheathed. His steps slowed and became cautious.

Endric narrowed his eyes, gazing into the distance, trying to see what had caught the attention of the Antrilii, and saw nothing but darkness and shadows. One of the merahl barked twice, its voicing distinct, like it was speaking, and close now. There came a snap, like that from breaking branches or dried grasses, and a merahl burst into the open. Even from a distance, Endric could see its body was tense, its narrow tail pointed, alert. Another merahl called, barking three times, on the far side of the trees.

Without thinking, he reached for his sword, feeling a sinking sensation in his stomach when he remembered he was unarmed.

Could the groeliin be close? Endric had thought the merahl would give more warning if they were, but they had only made noise about the same time that Dentoun had walked ahead. Was this some kind of trap? Looking over at the other Antrilii, they appeared alert, tense, but not worried and not readied for attack. No trap then.

"You can show yourself." Dentoun's accented voice boomed into the night. "We have you surrounded."

The three merahl called, their voices arranged like the points on a triangle around the thicket of trees.

"Your merahl certainly do," a steady voice answered from the darkness. The voice carried easily. There was a hint of an accent to it as well, one Endric couldn't place. Most spoke the common tongue, but some regions were more accented than others. Even among the Denraen there were accents.

Dentoun quickly sheathed his sword. Endric saw him shaking his head as he did. "None possess the merahl." Strangely, he laughed.

A shadow emerged from the line of trees. A man, head covered by the hood of his cloak, carrying a long staff. "That is true enough," the man said. His voice was melodious, not as deep as Dentoun or his father's, but still rumbling gently in the night. With the words, he whistled softly, the sound very similar to what Dentoun made, and the nearest merahl suddenly relaxed. It started forward, sniffing the newcomer before wagging its tail once and calling quietly to the others.

"Novan," Dentoun said, his voice familiar. "I should say I am surprised to see you."

"Are you?" the man asked.

Dentoun laughed again, a deep sound that rumbled from his chest easily. "The gods know I would be lying if I did."

The man pulled back his hood, laughing as he walked toward the road and Dentoun. A sliver of moon emerged from behind the clouds, its sudden light enough to see the man's shorn head and features. His eyes were bright and more intense than Dentoun's, if that were possible. They seemed to take in everything, noting him sitting atop the horse with barely more than a pause before glancing at the other Antrilii. "A hunting party," he said and then nodded. "Though small."

Dentoun grunted. "You think a larger group necessary?"

The man shrugged. "I have seen Ilowan."

"I have seen worse from only a few groeliin."

"As have I, old friend," Novan said. "But this is more than a few groeliin."

207

Dentoun nodded carefully. "Aye."

"I wonder why."

Dentoun sniffed. "There is no why with groeliin."

"I know you of all men do not believe that, Dentoun," he said, saying the Antrilii's name with the same inflection that Dentoun had.

Who was this man? By his dress, he was not Antrilii, though he was obviously familiar with them. He seemed to have an understanding of the groeliin, knowing the destruction they could cause. And he had obviously seen Ilowan.

Dentoun tilted his head and said nothing, his lips tightening into a frown. With the painting upon his face, he looked frightening. Novan simply smiled.

"Come," Novan suggested. "The night is long and it is time to camp."

Dentoun snorted. "I suppose you already have a camp."

Novan nodded, tipping his head and staff. "Near the Vinriin ruins."

The Antrilii considered Novan for a moment, then laughed again, the irritation he had shown only moments ago completely gone. "You were waiting for us?"

Novan flashed a quick smile. "I felt it safest for you to find me," he answered simply.

"Historian. One day you may outlive your welcome."

"That day is not today," Novan answered, turning his back to Dentoun and starting off across through the tall grasses and away from the road. He whistled once and the merahl loped off as if following his command.

Dentoun grunted, shaking his head, and returned to grab the rein he had dropped before following after the man. Endric watched as Novan disappeared into the grass.

A historian. Not what Endric would have guessed. The historians he had met during his travels had been mostly freeloaders, hoping for a free drink or night's rest. This man was different. Urik had spoken of the historian guild, his tone almost respectful, near reverent, and the en'raen had obviously held a deep resentment toward those only pretending at membership. Something told him that Novan, unlike the other historians he had met, belonged to the guild.

They followed Novan into the grasses. They were taller here but dry and made a strange swishing sound as the horse trampled through. The dry scent of the broken blades was pungent, though not unpleasant. Nothing like he had smelled in Ilowan. Endric wouldn't soon forget that stench. In the distance, Novan stood silhouetted against the hilltop near a pile of broken rock.

The Vinriin ruins were like the Lashiin ruins of Vasha, only on a larger scale, the remains of an ancient settlement. Whereas the Lashiin ruins were likely remnants from the founders of the mountain city, perhaps even the earliest Magi, the Vinriin ruins were thought to be much older. The ruins nestled into the back of a hillside, mostly hidden from view and overgrown with grasses and weeds. Endric had never seen them up close, passing by only from a distance. Ruins like it were scattered over the northern continent. For the most part, they were left alone. Many held a superstition about the ruins, a fear of disturbing the long departed. Only the ruins of Thealon had been incorporated into a modern city, and then only because the tower was there.

Reaching the ruins, Endric felt a prickling on his skin as he passed into the outermost pile of rock, which marked a boundary of sorts. A low mound of rubble seemed to stretch out in a circle from that point, like a fallen wall. The stone was mostly fragmented, though some larger boulders remained. The horse stepped across, kicking up a bit of dust. Endric saw Dentoun mutter something to himself as they entered the ruins but didn't hear what the Antrilii said.

The prickling on his skin faded but didn't disappear. Perhaps nothing more than a chill.

They followed Novan into the ruins. As they went farther in, the stones were stacked, and though fallen, he could almost imagine the shape of buildings once standing. Some stacks were huge. Grasses grew up in clear spaces, almost leading them in a path through the rubble. Occasionally, low walls remained intact. He imagined faint tracings in the stone, like there were in the Lashiin ruins and others, unreadable and interpretable.

There was no record of what had been here, and the people had long since been gone. Only the broken remains of their city remained. Some buildings held. These were smaller, more shelter than anything, and weathered by rain and time so that their original shapes could no longer be seen. Others were simply the outer walls, nothing of the interior of the building remaining. Nothing taller than a single story still stood. Weeds and grasses poked through, and occasionally small, white-blossomed flowers, a contrast to the night. The air was clean and fresh, almost fragrant from flowers both seen and unseen.

It was near a tilted stack of stone that Novan camped. A horse was tied near his campsite. That alone was enough to tell Endric the man was not Antrilii; their horses were trained not to wander. If he needed more confirmation of that fact, Novan had removed his black cloak, revealing a plain dark shirt and pants beneath. No hint of leathers and no weapon other than the staff he held casually in his hand. Endric knew not to take the weapon lightly; he had seen Senda, a master of the staff, disarm men twice her size. Something told him that Novan was at least as capable with the staff.

The Antrilii dismounted. Their horses wandered into the ruins—not far, but away from Novan's mount—and began grazing. As far as Endric could tell, the merahl had not entered the Vinriin ruins. He heard them calling, still barking the occasional sound, but it was distant.

Was there something about the ruins that unsettled them, or were they simply continuing their usual patrol? The ruins were eerie but he didn't feel uncomfortable, just as he was never uncomfortable in the Lashiin ruins. Rather, he felt a sense of age and sadness, of wisdom lost.

The Antrilii quickly fell into their typical camping pattern. Soon a fire was lit and the smell of some animal roasting wafted over to him. Endric had stood apart as Dentoun and the other Antrilii spoke to Novan. He heard nothing of their conversation, not even bothering to listen. Instead, he looked around the ruins, making out the lost details in the stone, the piles of rubble he imagined had once been grand buildings, the smattering of weeds along what had likely once been roads. About him was a sense of stillness, like the night waited with its breath held. The strange tingling still prickled his skin, like goose pimples in the cold, though not as acutely as when they had first passed into the ruins. There were no other sounds in the night.

One of the Antrilii motioned him toward the fire, gesturing with a steaming hunk of meat. Endric felt his stomach roll, aware of the pangs of hunger assaulting his stomach. Finding Ilowan had distracted from eating.

He approached quietly, seeing the historian still speaking in low tones to Dentoun. The Antrilii shook his head as they spoke, irritation plain on his painted face.

"Eat. Take your mind off what we have seen," the Antrilii who had called him over said. He was a large man, nearly as wide as Dentoun, though his face was not lined with the years of the other man. His paintings were mostly black, as were his leathers, turning him into a shadow against the fallen stone of Vinriin. Endric wondered if that meant anything.

He nodded, accepting the meat and then biting carefully, enjoying the savory taste. "Why is he upset?" He didn't expect an answer.

The Antrilii grunted. "Novan thinks it more than groeliin in that town. Dentoun thinks the result is the same. The town is destroyed."

Endric turned and watched Dentoun speaking to Novan as he ate. The historian spoke quietly, gesturing with his hands as he did. A dark ring circled the middle finger on his right hand. There was something familiar about it, but he couldn't place why. Dentoun had sunk into a frown, not responding to the other. Finally he spoke a brusque word and turned to the fire. As he walked away from Novan, a tight smile crossed Dentoun's face, nearly amusement. It was the most emotion Endric had seen from the Antrilii.

"Nahrsin, come," he said as he passed. The dark Antrilii raised his eyebrows and sniffed but didn't say anything, following Dentoun as commanded.

"Novan thinks there were other men in Ilowan," Dentoun said as he walked away.

"There were many men in that town," Nahrsin commented.

Dentoun grunted. "He thinks these were gone before the groeliin came. Thinks many were dead before the groeliin."

"What kind of men would do this?" Nahrsin asked. They neared the fire and Endric didn't hear the reply.

The historian startled him with a cough. Endric spun, surprised he hadn't heard the man approaching.

"You're not Antrilii."

Endric looked down at his clothing. Dressed in dark pants stained with his blood and a shirt borrowed from the Antrilii, he wasn't sure how he looked. Certainly not like a Denraen. "I am not." He licked the last of the grease from his fingers, wiping them on his pants. His stomach still rolled with hunger.

"How did you come to travel with them?"

Endric looked over at the man, meeting his eyes. There was a question written clearly in them, but also wisdom. This was not a man he could lie to. "They found me upon the Tolsii Plains."

Novan raised a brow and said nothing for a moment. "Do they know *why* you were upon the plain?"

What did this man know? The question itself was probing, leading, as if Novan already knew the answer. Endric would need to be cautious. "Some."

The historian smiled. The expression was disarming and Endric relaxed, realizing too late that had been Novan's intent. Like a predator before an attack. "When will you tell them you are Denraen?" The question was spoken quietly but seemed to thunder into the night.

Endric considered his next words carefully. "I am not Denraen." Losing to his father had left him expelled. He didn't know what would become of him, but he was no longer Denraen. Strangely, he felt a hollow sensation in his chest with the thought.

"Perhaps no longer, then," Novan said.

Endric narrowed his eyes, then shook his head. "Why would you think that of me?" Attempting to make the question casual failed; he was certain the stress in his voice gave him away. He suppressed the urge to reach for his sword, regretting again that he was unarmed. He couldn't grow accustomed to that fact.

Novan smiled again. "You carry yourself as a soldier, with your back straight and gait confident. And you reach for your sword for reassurance." Novan flicked his eyes from Endric's hand up to his face. "There are other tells. The boots you wear appear Denraen issue. Your hair is cut in the style of the soldiers. And I hear no accent to your voice." He lifted his eyebrows as he finished.

Endric sniffed. "As you can see, I carry no sword. Reassurance or no, any man would reach for a weapon after seeing Ilowan," he answered. "As to the others, many men dress the same in Thealon."

Novan shrugged slightly. "Yet those aren't really the reasons I think you are Denraen."

"Oh?"

Another smile, barely a parting of his lips. "You were found upon the plains, near the base of Isalain Peak. From the looks of you, seriously injured. Near death, I would venture to guess. There are few reasons a man would be found in such a state." He gave Endric a searching look. "Should I continue?" he asked, the question probing but gentle.

Endric closed his eyes. "You have made your point."

Snapping his eyes open again, he looked at the historian. The man wore a neutral expression. Except for the hand holding his staff, his posture was relaxed. That hand wasn't tense, but Endric saw a readiness to the way he held his weapon. He was prepared to defend himself if necessary. Endric snorted, shaking his head. He carried himself in much the same way. At least he did when he was armed.

"What is it that you want?" he asked, resignation flooding through him. So many failings lately. Endric was uncertain he could tolerate more. Sighing, he wondered if it would have been better had the laca taken him back on the plain.

Novan smiled broadly. "What does any historian want? Only your story."

"Not much of a tale there," he muttered and turned away.

The historian stopped him with a hand on his arm. His grip was surprisingly strong. "It need not be tonight," he said, "but sometime I will hear that story." He released Endric and walked over to the Antrilii, his voice a rumbling undercurrent as he spoke to them.

Endric stood apart, lost in thought. Novan had reminded him of how he had failed the Denraen. Days had passed since the Antrilii had found him, and he had allowed himself to forget. Now it all flooded him with painful memories, each stabbing sharper than the next. Boot steps crunched across the stone, and Endric looked up to see the black-clad Antrilii approach.

"You keep yourself apart when the gods have brought us together," Nahrsin said.

Endric blinked slowly. The words were unexpected. "The gods?" he asked. "I have trouble believing our meeting the work of the gods."

Nahrsin shrugged, shadows from the fire playing strangely across his painted face. "No man can know their plan. We can only work in their honor."

Endric shook his head. He had prayed to the gods while lying near death upon the Tolsii Plains, and the Antrilii had come. Who was he to think it was not part of some grand plan? Still, there remained the nagging doubt, the questions he long had felt, and he knew he couldn't believe. The gods, if they existed, didn't intervene for one man. His prayers had been selfish and had changed nothing.

"Do you honor the gods when you fight?" Endric asked.

Nahrsin laughed. The sound was carefree and surprising coming from the imposing warrior. "How would you suggest we honor them otherwise?"

"The Urmahne teach that the gods demand peace. That is how the gods are honored."

Nahrsin shrugged. "I know little of the Urmahne," he admitted. "But then, I am Antrilii. The gods gave us the *bneiin* to protect." He shrugged again. "When you see groeliin, you will understand. In this, we honor the gods."

Endric frowned. "What is *bneiin*?" The word sounded familiar, like a twisting of the ancient language, but Endric couldn't place its meaning.

"That is our home. The north. Mountains." His face slackened and his eyes lost a bit of focus as he spoke. Nahrsin obviously missed his home. "We are here now," he said, his gaze gaining intensity. "The groeliin will not escape our hunt. This is the gods' will," he finished with a quiet ferocity.

Endric realized the Antrilii sacrificed much by traveling south, hunting the groeliin, but to them it was a simple matter. They acted because they believed. How must it feel to have such faith? He looked at Nahrsin, watching the faint firelight flicker over his painted features. These were not simple warriors.

"Come. Sit by the fire. Tonight is not a night for solitude," Nahrsin said. He turned and walked away from Endric, leaving him standing alone, considering whether to follow and staring at the man's broad back.

Endric looked over at the other Antrilii. Dentoun still spoke to Novan, though the conversation appeared more relaxed. A few of the other Antrilii sat nearby, listening. The rest sat near the fire, eating and talking quietly. The smoke from the crackling fire wafted over to him, a welcoming scent, and Endric was drawn to them. Dentoun looked up as he approached, narrowing his eyes briefly before looking back at Novan. The other Antrilii ignored him. Only Nahrsin had seemed welcoming.

He was growing to realize that whatever else he was, he was not a prisoner. Not really. And yet there was no place else for him to go.

What was he now? So much of his identity had been tied to being a soldier. That was all he had known. Now he could no longer even claim that.

Endric blinked slowly, telling himself it was the smoke from the fire that burned his eyes. He took a seat atop a small boulder. The stone was mostly smooth, though there were deep lines still present, grooves in the surface, and he wondered what the rock had once been. The flames from the fire licked the night, and the crackling as the green branches burned pushed back the darkness nearly as much as the light. In the distance, the merahl still called.

Nahrsin brought him a steaming mug. "This is *jor*. We drink on nights such as this."

He took it, enjoying the warmth from the cup. "Such as what?"

"On nights when we are reminded why we must hunt." Nahrsin took a seat next to Endric, a cup in his hands, and took a long drink, sighing deeply as he did. He said nothing and stared into the flames.

Endric sniffed the steaming liquid, uncertain what to expect. Hesitantly, he put the mug to his lips and took a sip. It was surprisingly sweet. And good. Taking a long draw, he felt an immediate flushing in his head and found himself mimicking Nahrsin, sighing as he stared at the flames. Long moments passed. Only the murmuring of nearby voices and the steady crackle of the fire counted time.

"I was a soldier," Endric said. He took another long drink from the mug, savoring the flavor. He had never tasted anything like the *jor* before.

"You do not stop being a soldier," Nahrsin said, nodding. He had not turned from the flames, staring into the fire as if finding an answer to some unasked question.

Endric closed his eyes. "After what I have done, I must."

Nahrsin tore his eyes away from the fire and looked over at Endric. "The gods will always forgive." He spoke solemnly and with a reverent tone. Endric recognized the inflection, having heard it before; Andril had spoken with a similar tone. Nahrsin believed.

Endric sniffed. "I don't know if the gods will forgive, but I know my father will not."

Nahrsin laughed, startling him. "That is all you fear? Your father?" He laughed again, deep and hearty. A few of the other Antrilii looked over, and even Novan paused in his conversation with Dentoun to watch. "Fathers want us to grow. Make mistakes. Become our own man. Missteps are necessary on this journey." His laughter had died off and his painted face took on a neutral expression. "There is never a need for forgiveness if you learn from your mistakes."

Endric shook his head. "You don't know my father."

Nahrsin chuckled. "He cannot be any worse than my own."

Endric cocked his head and narrowed his eyes, following Nahrsin's gaze. "Dentoun is your father?" he asked, making the connection. The Antrilii nodded, and Endric saw the similarities. The same width to their build, the same angular cut of the jaw, and the same dark hair. "I can see how that would have been challenging."

He knew very little about the Antrilii culture but had seen enough of Dentoun to know that he reminded Endric of his own father. It was easy to imagine what Nahrsin must have experienced. Both were sons of soldiers, warriors. Both were driven, Dendril by the Denraen and Dentoun by the groeliin.

"He pushed me, as was needed. I couldn't lead my people if he had not." Nahrsin spoke softly, obvious warmth entering his voice. Endric wished he could feel the same for his father.

"My father couldn't be bothered to participate in my training," he said quietly. It should not still hurt, but he couldn't shake the knot of emotion he felt at saying the words. Dendril had trained Andril, but his own father had not wanted to assist in his training. Even after all these years, he still hated his father for that.

"Perhaps he knew he was not the best instructor for you."

Endric shook his head slowly and said nothing. His father was the best swordsman the Denraen had. His quick defeat was testament to that. What could he have been had he access to that knowledge?

"You think Dendril was not interested in how you were raised?"

Endric spun at the comment and was surprised to see Novan standing behind him. The historian sat on a nearby rock, not waiting for an invitation. He still grasped his staff.

"How do you—"

Novan's eyes seemed to flash for a moment. "I am a historian," he answered, as if that was enough. And maybe it was. "I am a seeker of truth, of knowledge. Perhaps we were brought together for a reason. You seem to carry a fallacy with you that must be corrected."

"You think you know all about me?" Endric asked, biting back the surge of anger he felt. He could do nothing anyway. He was trapped. Weaponless. Surrounded by strangers with nowhere to go.

Novan was not baited by his comment, speaking evenly when he did. "You are Endric, son of Dendril, Lord General of the Denraen army. You are his second son, Andril the first, and from the condition you were found in on the Tolsii Plains, I must presume that you challenged your father for leadership. And lost."

Endric looked away, unable to meet his eyes. He felt Nahrsin staring at him from the other side. He kept his gaze locked on the fire. A dark shadow moved in front of his field of vision. Dentoun didn't say anything to announce his presence. He didn't need to.

Blinking slowly, he looked up at the large Antrilii. The man stood, frowning, a look of concern etched upon his face. The shadows seemed to flicker upon him, slipping strangely over and off the paintings on his face. The effect was disturbing.

"Son of Dendril, it is time that you tell your story," Dentoun said.

CHAPTER 25

"You have not said why you felt compelled to challenge your father," Novan said, twisting the dark ring on his finger as he spoke. His breath misted the cool air and in the distance, one of the merahl cried out as if punctuating what the historian said.

The sky had lightened a bit by the time Endric finished speaking, no longer the inky black of deep night, yet still dark. The fire crackling nearby cast everything in flickering shadows, and a fragrant smoke whispered out in a thin haze. Endric had not spoken long, keeping the story brief and focused only on his disagreement with his father. He left out the reason why. Some details just were not his to share; he would protect the Denraen in that.

"That is Denraen business," he answered. Should he tell them about the Deshmahne—how they had killed his brother, attacked the town, and still his father was unwilling to respond, unwilling to even consider that his son told the truth?

Blinking slowly, he knew he couldn't, so he pushed the thought away. He was no longer Denraen, yet it was still hard to let go of the anger he felt at the dark priests. They *had* killed Andril. Olin. And nearly Senda. They had attacked the Magi and destroyed part of the city. As much as he wanted to let go of that anger, he couldn't.

Shaking his head slightly, he recognized the irony. After years of his father trying to get him to care about something other than himself, when he finally did, he was thrown from the city.

Dentoun grunted and nodded as if satisfied by the answer. The man was a warrior—a soldier of sorts—and it didn't surprise him that he understood.

Novan, on the other hand, was not placated. "You have said nothing of your brother." The hood of his cloak pooled around his neck, menacing shadows flickering upon his face.

Endric closed his eyes and took a deep breath of the cool night air, trying to push away images threating to overwhelm him.

"What happened to him?" Novan asked, his voice softening, though no less intent. He leaned back, and the fire lit his face. Concern etched into the wrinkles around his eyes.

Endric shook his head, exhaling. "Andril is gone. Lost during a mission."

"This is Deshmahne then." Novan's face was flat, but his eyes had tightened. His voice carried the heat of anger as he spoke of the Deshmahne.

"What do you know of them?" His hands clenched unconsciously at his side as he thought of the dark priests. He had to consciously relax them and still felt the itch to reach for a wished-for sword.

"So the rumors are true."

"What rumors?"

"I had thought the stories spread by the Deshmahne. Still could be, I suppose. They claim great strength, stating there had been a demonstration of their prowess. When the rumors spread of the destruction of a regiment of Denraen, I had thought it idle boasting." Novan shook his head. "That, unfortunately, was wrong."

"What are these Deshmahne?" Dentoun asked. His face had deepened into a frown as Endric told his story. He sat, his back rigid, upon the stone as he listened. Somehow the painting on his face had lost its mystique, leaving the man looking fierce but not frightening. Still not someone to take lightly.

Novan glanced at Dentoun and nodded. "They are dark cultists. Nobody knows when they were truly founded, though the guild speculates they have been around for hundreds of years."

"How is that possible?" Endric asked.

Novan shrugged. "The fact remains that they have existed for many years. It is an intricate religion, one that seems to have evolved over time. They are led by a high priest, made powerful by his dark magics."

Dentoun scowled as the historian spoke but Novan ignored it, simply raising his eyebrows as if shrugging. There was a strange rapport between the two men. Endric wondered if the Antrilii distrusted magical abilities. So little was known about the Antrilii and their beliefs that he couldn't know, but the man had made comments about the Magi that left him wondering.

"Though we know of the high priest, none has ever seen him. For many years, they have remained secretive and gained membership slowly. Lately, this has changed. Men seek them out now, wishing to learn the secret of their power, and they have grown quickly in numbers. And boldness." He sniffed, spitting the last out as if it were distasteful.

"You say these priests are powerful?" Dentoun asked, leaning slightly forward. Nahrsin sat across from him, silent, taking in the conversation.

Novan nodded. "They practice an ancient and arcane art tied to markings upon their bodies." He looked to Dentoun as he said that.

The Antrilii's eyes widened a moment before he frowned.

Novan nodded again, as if answering an unasked question. "These marking imbue them with unnatural abilities. Many have tried to study the extent of their powers. All have failed. Or died." Novan sighed, fixing each with a firm stare. "Never has there been open confrontation with the Deshmahne. They have gained influence by moving in the background, through manipulation and small demonstrations of their strength. Outright defiance of the Denraen would imply a different tactic has evolved. I worry what it means."

Endric knew what it meant, having seen the attempt upon the Magi. He still didn't understand the purpose. "I saw an attack firsthand. They infiltrated Vasha and tried to attack the palace. One of the Magi named it a Deshviili."

Novan's frown deepened. "You say it was tried?"

Endric nodded. "It was unsuccessful."

The historian considered him for a moment, his eyes focusing as if seeing something visible only to him. "This does not bode well," he finally said. His voice was soft, edged with a hint of worry.

"What do they seek, Novan?" Dentoun asked.

The historian shook his head. "I am uncertain."

Dentoun laughed, startling them. "It pleases me to see you this way."

Novan narrowed his eyes at him, irritation plain upon his face.

Dentoun didn't mask his emotions but did seem to hide them better than the historian. "But you are more than uncertain. You are worried. If you worry, then others should as well. You may not know what they seek, but I think that you have an idea."

Novan nodded slowly. "Some."

"Hmm."

The Antrilii's comments and the way he questioned Novan surprised Endric. Dentoun obviously held the historian in high regard. It was clear the men had met before, and he was beginning to wonder how much history they shared.

Novan blinked slowly, taking a deep breath. As he exhaled, the air misting around him, his dark eyes sparkled with intensity. "The palace was not the only recent target."

Endric shook his head. "Why do you say that?"

"There have been other attacks in the past few months. With each attack, the Deshmahne grow bolder. In Coamdon, only a few men were injured. The Deshmahne attacked quickly, more like thieves in the night, and disappeared. At first it was not clear who had attacked. Few believe it was the Deshmahne." He grunted with irritation. Clearly, there was more to that story than he shared.

"Voiga was different. The attack seemed as well planned as in Coamdon, though the intent hazier. Dozens dead. Almost as if that was the purpose of the attack. Most think it *was* the intended purpose." He shook his head and then scratched at his scalp. "There was another aim in that attack, I think. Diversion."

Endric tried to think of what could connect the two other attacks to the attack on the Magi but wasn't able to come up with an answer. The historian didn't say where in Coamdon the attack occurred; the southern nation was large—nearly as large as Thealon—and stretched from the forests of Voiga to the hot desert of Siinan. The nation was known for several valuable exports, each reflective of its different regions. From the iron and silver of the mountain mines to cloth and wool of the plains, each was valuable, but nothing he could imagine the Deshmahne wanting. That was what Novan implied.

Voiga was stranger still. The forested nation was known for its lumber and fishing. Novan implied the attack masked an ulterior motive, but Endric couldn't think of what that could be. Yet the historian tied these attacks to the one on the Magi. There must be some connection.

"Coamdon, Voiga, and now the Magi." Dentoun looked at Novan as he spoke. Endric realized the Antrilii saw the connection. Nahrsin, at least, looked as lost as he felt.

Novan nodded carefully, his fingers still fidgeting with the dark stone ring on his finger. "If I am right, I fear you must hurry, old friend," Novan said quietly. "Hunt the groeliin, but return to your home."

Dentoun nodded and then stood, turning and walking away from the fire. Endric watched the man leave. His heart fluttered as he wondered about the connection between the attacks. Did Novan think the Antrilii homeland was at risk for attack? He had not realized there was a true Antrilii settlement, thinking that they roamed the north.

"What is this, Novan?" he asked. "What do you think the Deshmahne are after?"

The historian didn't have a chance to answer. At that moment, there was a sharp howl in the night, different than anything he had heard before. There was no questioning its source. One of the merahl.

"*Ishi?*" Nahrsin said softly, standing suddenly. He turned and stared into the darkness, his body suddenly tense. The Antrilii's hand reached for his sword instinctively. When no other sound followed, Nahrsin turned, looking to Dentoun. The large man shook his head once before tilting it in the direction of the sound.

Around the camp, the other Antrilii had frozen. Each looked out into the night, waiting. Another howl came, similar to the last. It was not the sound of the merahl hunting. That was an eager sound, one demanding to be followed, the sound of a challenge offered. This was much different. There was pain to it, a sharp edge, ripping at the night. Endric felt his heart beat fast as the echoes faded.

"Is it groeliin?" he asked. The question was directed to no one in particular. He knew the answer even as he spoke.

Novan shook his head. "This is not groeliin," he said, his voice soft. The historian was on edge, his hands tense. Like Nahrsin. "Something has happened."

They waited a few more moments, but no other sounds came. Endric realized they had been expecting the voices of the other two merahl. Nothing else disturbed the night.

"Shinron. Graime," Dentoun said, nodding to two of the Antrilii. He whistled low and the horses came galloping into the clearing. The Antrilii responded immediately, leaping atop the horses. Dentoun climbed atop his own, patting the sleek horse as he did.

"Dentoun. That was not the call to attack. Use caution," Novan said.

The Antrilii leader cocked his head, considering what the historian said, then nodded. "We all ride."

The other Antrilii quickly mounted. Even Novan's horse was saddled without much delay. Endric stood among the others, unarmed and feeling conflicted. Part of him longed to see what had happened to the merahl. Another hoped for an opportunity to slip away.

"You will ride with me," Novan said, settling his internal debate. He reached out to help Endric into the saddle, his grip surprisingly strong. He pulled something out from beneath his cloak and handed it to Endric. "I suspect you know how to use this."

Endric barely had time to grab the item as they surged forward. He clung to Novan with one hand. His other held a leather-sheathed sword. Strangely, a hollow sensation in his chest seemed suddenly filled. The hilt was solid and the weight reassuring in his hand. His injuries had mostly healed; only a little stiffness remained across his chest.

They rode quickly. The horses' hooves made a low rumble. Dentoun took the lead. Endric was wondering how the man knew which way to travel when another pained howl erupted, guiding them forward. Dentoun had one hand on his saddle and his curved sword unsheathed in the other. The other Antrilii followed suit. They made no other sound as they rode. Each man's face was tight and grim.

Topping a rise, Dentoun halted them as the pale moonlight revealed the cause for the merahl's distress.

Nearly a dozen men, each armed with dark-bladed swords, circled another man. He held his own sword spinning in front of him. He was skilled—it was obvious even from a distance—but no match for a dozen opponents. The merahl, Ishi he presumed, stood by the man's side. The creature was obviously injured, favoring one leg, yet the two of them still managed to hold back the attackers.

Novan swore under his breath as he surveyed the scene.

"What is it?" Endric asked.

"Deshmahne," he spat.

"Here? Why?" Then a different question came to him. "How can you tell?" A seething anger at the dark priests began to rise from deep in his gut.

Novan shook his head slightly, ignoring the first two questions. "The swords." He sniffed derisively. "Only the Deshmahne carry such blades."

Endric stared at the swords, wondering what it was that offended Novan. From the distance, he saw nothing other than the dark blades. The man they attacked continued to sweep his sword in a quick circle, faster than Endric could have imagined. And he had thought his father a skilled swordsman. The merahl protected his back, snapping and snarling at the other attackers. Endric knew they couldn't hold out much longer.

Dentoun apparently realized the same thing and suddenly surged forward. The other Antrilii followed. A deep battle cry erupted from Dentoun as he rode down the slope. The sound startled a few of the attackers, giving enough pause that the man managed to drop one of them in a dark spray of blood. As the Antrilii streamed down the hillside, the Deshmahne spread out, their movements coordinated, and turned to face them. Four Deshmahne still surrounded the lone swordsman, pressing forward with renewed fury.

And then they were upon them. Endric had thought the cavalry charge would scatter the Deshmahne, but they managed to slide out and away from the horses, streaking in as the horses passed and attacking their flanks. One of the horses screamed and stumbled, throwing its rider. Shinron, Endric thought. The man stood slowly, shaking himself.

He was too slow.

The Deshmahne reached him before the other horses had turned. They were impossibly quick, attacking with precise ferocity, and though the Antrilii was skilled with his blade, he couldn't counter the number the Deshmahne threw at him. He fell, a bloody snarl on his lips. With the last of his life, he cried out and slammed his sword forward, catching one of the Deshmahne in the stomach and pinning him down.

"Dismount!" Dentoun commanded.

Endric recognized the wisdom of the decision. The Deshmahne were too fast; whatever dark arts they possessed, speed was among them. The horses would be a detriment. Endric wondered how they hoped to counter the speed of the Deshmahne. The dark priests moved so fast as to be nearly impossible to stop. It was a wonder the other man had survived.

Dentoun whistled twice. The sound was shrill, urgent, and suddenly the other two merahl appeared out of the darkness. Dentoun leapt forward, using the distraction to launch his attack, his sword swinging in a whistling arc. At the same time, the merahl attacked, fangs bared and snarls erupting from their throats. Endric leaned forward instinctively, as if to attack.

The Deshmahne had killed his brother. Attacked his city. Injured Senda. They were the reason he'd argued with his father. Now the focus of his anger stood before him.

He wanted to fight them. Needed to fight them. Hatred burned through him with a force unlike anything he had ever felt.

Novan held him back. Endric tried to shrug his hand off his shoulder but couldn't shake the man's grip. He turned away from the historian and glared at the Deshmahne, watching in awe as Dentoun attacked.

The man was a blur with his sword, moving so quickly that Endric could barely keep up. Two Deshmahne dropped before they realized the attack was on, both beheaded. He was not bothered that he felt a hint of pleasure.

Nahrsin followed his father only a moment later, sliding into attack, his sword moving as quickly as his father's. Whereas Dentoun attacked with a combination of strength and speed, Nahrsin moved with a lithe grace, twisting and thrusting. Both men were astounding swordsmen. Endric recognized a few of the forms Nahrsin used. Only a few. Instinctively, he compared his skill to that of the Antrilii and knew he would last barely a few heartbeats against them.

Still, the Deshmahne were faster. Their black blades nearly sizzled in the night. They collided with the Antrilii swords in a dull clang, the sound nearly as unnatural as the movements of their wielders. Endric was not sure how the Antrilii saw where they were attacking; the swords became nearly invisible as they moved, seeming to suck in the darkness around them and covering the Deshmahne with a deeper blanket of shadows, as if the night itself strove to hide them.

Nahrsin and Dentoun were pressed back. Only their speed and skill kept them upright. Endric struggled even to follow the course of the fight. He heard an angry scream, nearly human. One of the attacking merahl had snarled in pain as it must have been struck. The sound unsettled Endric.

Then the other Antrilii reached the fight, their battle cries mingling with that of the merahl. Novan stayed back, watching, and let the Antrilii lead the attack. Five Deshmahne remained, facing five of the Antrilii. As Endric watched, he realized they were evenly matched. The Deshmahne moved with more speed, but the incredible skill of the Antrilii evened the fight. The merahl tipped the scales, surrounding the Deshmahne, their angry roars pushing the Deshmahne toward the Antrilii.

A sharp tug on his shirt startled him, nearly tossing him to his back as he spun. Stumbling, he barely caught himself when he heard the loud crack of the historian's staff striking something nearby.

He looked up to see Novan facing one of the Deshmahne, having thrown him out of the way.

The historian spun his staff in a blur, snapping out in quick attacks that were stopped by the strange dark blade. Novan tired quickly, but his attacker didn't slow, pressing him steadily back and away from help. A dangerous smile plastered the face of the Deshmahne.

A flickering shadow was all the warning he had that he had not been left alone. Endric dove to his left, rolling and coming up as quickly as he could manage. The injury to his legs stiffened them, though there was not much pain, so he moved more slowly than he would have liked. He unsheathed the borrowed sword, spinning into a defensive stance as he faced his attacker.

The Deshmahne before him was slight of build. A dark cloak covered his thin frame but didn't hide the bony figure. Dark markings streaked up the exposed skin of his neck and onto the edges of his face. Endric frowned; there was something familiar about the markings that he couldn't quite place. There was no time to consider as the dark blade flashed toward him.

He reacted. The sword he held was similar enough to his own and he was able to move quickly, blocking the attack a mere hand width from his face. Endric pushed him off, turning to put his back toward Novan. He was not sure what had happened to the man the Deshmahne initially were attacking, but there were at least two of the dark priests not accounted for.

Endric whipped the blade through his sword drills, the familiarity of the forms quickly returning. His body was still stiff from the injuries he had sustained when facing his father, his left shoulder nearly creaking, making every movement a little jerkier than it should have been. Not nearly as fluid as he was accustomed to being. Still, that was not the reason for his difficulty.

The Deshmahne was quick. Too quick. Endric felt hot pain on his arm as the dark blade slipped through his defenses. He leapt back and the Deshmahne smiled again. Endric felt his heart hammer as an uncomfortable realization overcame him.

The man knew he had Endric beat. Endric knew it too.

The Deshmahne darted forward, the strange blade slicing toward him. The movement was a bit lazier than his previous attacks, but even it was barely stopped, deflected away at the last possible moment. As the dark blade neared him, heat radiated from it.

Stepping back, Endric quickly thought through his options. Around him, the sounds of the struggle raged, barely registering in his mind. He heard screamed challenges from Antrilii mixing with low growls from the merahl. The Deshmahne made occasional grunts. There was the sharp smacking of Novan's staff as he swung it, the air whistling, though even that sounded as if it were slower. Atop it all was the unnatural clanging of the Deshmahne swords.

Still, all that was a hollow sound. His heartbeat thudded urgently in his ears, overpowering the other sounds. His chest heaved and he struggled to catch his breath as he inhaled deeply of the crisp air. And his mind raced.

He was not as fast as the Deshmahne. And, unlike the Antrilii, he might not even be as skilled as the Deshmahne. That bothered him. He was unaccustomed to being so overmatched, having only truly experienced it when his father had simply dominated him. This Deshmahne was handling him easily. He had little doubt the others would as well. Not to mention the fact that each of the Antrilii would best him if he were forced to face them. He might well be the least skilled swordsman fighting.

The realization was jarring, nearly pulling him out of the fight.

He had no choice but to shake the thought out of his mind. Something to consider later. If he survived. There must be an advantage he could find, some edge he could use, but his panicking mind struggled to find one, holding on to the fact that he simply was not good enough.

And he would die for it.

The Deshmahne smiled again, whispering something Endric couldn't hear. The dark markings on his neck seemed to swirl, moving as if alive, but he knew that to be simply a trick of the shadows. The dark priest watched him, almost enjoying the realization that had overcome him. Relishing in Endric's anguish.

Distantly he began to wonder why he had even thought himself capable of challenging his father. He didn't have the skill to lead the Denraen, yet he had thought himself ready. Truly, he was still a child, as his father had said.

Another mistake made. One of many in his life. There were so many things he couldn't take back, mistakes that couldn't be forgiven. The fact that he had never gotten to apologize to his brother was the most agonizing.

The Deshmahne feinted but didn't attack, remaining just out of reach. A dark excitement clouded his face, parting his lips into a twisted smile. He was enjoying watching Endric, almost as if aware of what he was thinking. Like he was feeding off it.

He wondered if that was what Andril had faced in the moments before he had died. The ease with which the Deshmahne attacked made clear how so many Denraen had died.

Still, he was not sure the Deshmahne had even attacked the Denraen. They might not have needed to. Endric had seen the power of the Deshviili. Even abbreviated, there was no doubting the potential destruction the Deshmahne were capable of creating. And he had seen the effects of the attack on the city.

The Denraen could have died without even seeing their attackers. Andril might have died without knowing what it was he faced. That, as much as anything, hurt him.

Endric didn't know why these thoughts troubled him. He was losing focus on the fight in front of him, though he knew it only a matter of time before he succumbed to the Deshmahne attack. The sounds around him grew ever more faint, leaving him lost with nothing but his dark memories. Shame and sadness overwhelmed him.

It would be these emotions he felt as he died. And there was no doubting that he would die here and now. He felt his sword lowering as if his arm grew weak.

Strangely, a lesson from his past drifted into the forefront of his mind. Not one from Andril's lessons, which surprised him. This was something his father had actually taught him. He heard his deep voice in his memory, almost as if speaking to him.

Speed can slow. Skill can fade. But if you lose your mind, the battle is lost.

Endric took a deep breath, slowing his breathing. The dark thoughts moved to the background. Like a mist clearing, he realized what had almost happened. He had nearly given the Deshmahne exactly what he wanted.

The dark priest sneered and attacked with a frenzy. Endric was forced to deflect a few quick thrusts and found it easier to do the more he cleared his thoughts. Always, he fought on instinct; it was one of the flaws his father had found in him. Rightfully so, it would seem, seeing as how easily he had beaten him. Yet his instinct had carried him far. Perhaps it was more than a flaw. Could he intentionally use his instinct to guide him?

As he parried with the Deshmahne, he realized a pattern to the attack. He couldn't quite see what the pattern was; instead, he sensed it at the edge of his awareness. There was a coordination to the cacophony of the battle.

As he became aware of it, he found it easier to block the Deshmahne attack, almost as if anticipating what he would do. When the dark blade thrust forward, Endric parried, knowing where it would be. Another thrust, another block. Then another. And another. Each somehow blocked as he anticipated where the dark blade would be rather than reacting.

And yet he couldn't keep this up. His recent injuries made his joints tight, and he grew tired.

So he surged forward as he felt another quick thrust coming, turning where he didn't think the Deshmahne would be. He stabbed upward with the sword, sliding it suddenly into the dark priest's gut before spinning and pulling the sword free. Hot blood spilled onto his hands, dripping from the wound. The Deshmahne stood, his mouth agape for a moment, and then fell to the ground in a heap.

Endric stumbled, fatigue overwhelming him. As he steadied himself, he realized the din of the battle had ended. The Deshmahne were all down, dead or dying.

The Antrilii stood. A few looked bloodied and one of the men, Graime, limped, leaning on his sword for support. Dentoun kneeled before a headless Deshmahne, staring at him with a curious expression. He reached out tentatively and touched dark markings on the priest's arm, pulling up a sleeve to reveal extensive tattoos. Suddenly he spat and stood, kicking the dark-bladed sword away from him as he did.

Two of the dark-furred merahl sat off on the side, licking wounds, looking like enormous house cats as they did. Blood stained their fur, and Endric wondered just how much of it was their own. Now that he had seen them fight, he felt even more impressed by them. The other merahl prowled around the Antrilii, circling them, ears alert and flicking at sounds too low for Endric to hear. A low growl occasional erupted from its throat like a quiet warning.

Novan stood off to the side. His chest heaved visibly and he leaned on his staff. Otherwise, he was uninjured. One of the Deshmahne lay near him, an arm bent awkwardly and his spine twisted beneath him. He still breathed but wouldn't be attacking anyone soon. His dark-bladed sword lay gripped in his hand. The ground around the sword burned, the long grasses trampled during the battle and singed by an unseen fire.

Finally he turned to the man the Deshmahne had attacked. He felt a hint of surprise that the man still lived. Attacked by a dozen Deshmahne, only the aid of Ishi had kept him alive. When the Antrilii joined the fight, the man had still had four Deshmahne to contend with. Each of the dark priests lay dead, three of the four beheaded. The fourth was mauled to a bloody mess. That would be the merahl. That meant the man had killed three Deshmahne on his own. Even remembering the speed with which the man moved, that was surprising.

The man caught him staring and nodded. Dressed simply in a brown shirt and breeches, he wore his gray hair long, pulled back behind him with a leather thong. He still gripped his long sword, though the blade had been wiped clean. A couple of days' growth peppered his youthful face. As he nodded, he considered Endric with a long gaze. His eyes carried the knowing look of a man who had seen many more years than his face would admit.

"You fight well," the man said. His voice was rough and smoky, like a man twice his age. It was a tone he had heard from a half-dozen aged soldiers. Veterans with years of training and experience behind them. Combined with his obvious youth, the effect was surprising.

"Almost not well enough," he admitted, finding it hard to take his eyes off the Deshmahne lying dead around the man. Even the Antrilii had struggled against them.

The man grunted. "The Deshmahne are never easy opponents."

Endric frowned and tilted his head as he thought. "You've fought them before?"

The man nodded and then sheathed his sword. "More often than I would like."

"Why were they attacking you?"

The man grunted but said nothing. Endric frowned again. Could it be the man had attacked *them*? After what Endric had just experienced, the idea seemed to be suicide. If not for the merahl helping and the Antrilii riding to his aid, the man might have been dead.

Novan walked over, standing in front of the man as he shook his head. After a moment, he laughed and then pulled him into a hug. "Brohmin!" he said, familiarity clear in his voice. "You should be dead."

The man shrugged, running a hand down his pants and flicking his gaze at the Antrilii before looking at Novan again. "Probably."

"What happened?" Novan asked.

Brohmin shook his head. "There were twenty of them, perhaps more. I ambushed half near the Ralstol Gorge. Couple escaped. The rest chased me here."

He spoke simply, his tone matter-of-fact, but the idea of attacking ten Deshmahne alone—even in an ambush—seemed more than a little far-fetched. Yet Novan nodded, accepting the tale without question.

"The gorge is a day or more from here," Novan commented.

The man tipped his head. "More. I'm on foot."

Novan laughed and shook his head again. "Of course you are. Come. We're camped in the ruins."

"Good place," Brohmin agreed. "Need to collect the swords first. They need to be destroyed."

Endric looked at one of the black-bladed swords lying on the ground near the stranger and saw that the grasses and ground near this blade were charred as well, just like they had been near Novan. As he looked, he saw that each place the blades touched the ground was the same.

"What are they?" he asked.

Brohmin looked at him a moment before flicking his eyes to Novan in an unspoken question. Endric was again unsettled by the age and wisdom written in his eyes, belying the rest of his features. The historian nodded once in assent.

"They are as dark as the Deshmahne who wield them. And as tainted. They should never have been forged."

Endric knelt before one of the swords. He found it hard to believe there was something inherently wrong with a sword. Even one used by the Deshmahne. Reaching forward, he felt a firm grip on his shoulder. Novan held him back from grasping the hilt. Heat radiated from the sword, and a nauseating realization overcame him.

Looking back at the historian, he blinked slowly. "What reason could they have for teralin-forged blades?"

CHAPTER 26

His question hung in the air unanswered. Everything around him was still. Even the breeze, the cool northern wind ever present since he began on his days on the plain, was unusually absent. He didn't remember when it had died. The night itself was otherwise silent, the merahl nursing wounds near the Antrilii. He had grown accustomed to their constant calls and found the quiet unsettling.

Endric turned to Novan. The historian slowly blinked at him as he considered what to say, his gray eyes seeming to weigh him. The Antrilii clustered nearby, Dentoun inspecting the dead Deshmahne, picking carefully over the bodies, examining the markings upon each man. The frown upon his face deepened the longer he looked.

"The Magi are not the only ones who have found a use for the metal," Novan said.

Endric narrowed his eyes, not understanding. "What use could there be?"

The historian shrugged. "Why do the Magi use teralin?"

"To speak with the gods," Endric answered, the words coming quickly. All who studied Urmahne learned the power of teralin and that the Magi were the only ones able to utilize it. That made it both valuable and useless at the same time.

Novan smiled, barely a twisting of his thin lips. "Is that all it is used for?"

Endric shook his head. Teralin decorations were said to dot the palace. Not that he could claim to have seen them. Few outside the palace staff and the Magi were allowed within its walls. Much of the metalwork surrounding the palace was wrought from teralin, but that was more decorative than useful barricade. Other than ornamentation, he didn't know what else it could be used for.

"I cannot say if it truly helps them speak to the gods," Novan said. "None but the Magi can answer that question. I can tell you that teralin has long been known to have very curious properties. Long ago, it was valued for a different reason than it currently is." He sighed. "The world would be better had the Deshmahne not discovered this."

He turned and moved to speak with Dentoun, leaving Endric, with more questions than answers, staring at the teralin swords. Brohmin grunted nearby and silently moved to begin collecting the dark-bladed swords, not trusting Novan or the Antrilii with the task. Dentoun pushed the Antrilii away from the swords in any case, giving them a wide berth as he continued his examination of the Deshmahne.

Brohmin wrapped the swords with a bright metal cable that he pulled from a pocket, binding them together, and then stuffed them into a deep sack he had worn strapped to his back. The still-living grasses seemed to push away from the burned areas. Teralin was strangely warm and had been known to burn, but not that fast, not like that.

Novan offered to help, but Brohmin shooed the historian away with a firm shake of his head. Novan didn't argue, instead turning away and moving to speak with the Antrilii. Brohmin handled the swords delicately, his hand practiced but covered, careful not to touch any part of the sword, as if even that would taint him. Endric watched for a moment and then turned to Novan but didn't follow, occasionally squeezing the hilt of his borrowed sword. He was thankful to have the familiarity, even if it was not his own blade. He regretted that he had lost his grandfather's sword, though likely his father still had it. While not as impressive as his father's sword Trill, it was nevertheless a well-forged blade and had been in his family for centuries.

They remained in the clearing only long enough for the teralin swords to be collected and bound, leaving the Deshmahne dead or dying upon the ground. The Antrilii had lined up the bodies, turning faces to the ground. He speculated at the significance of the positioning and then wondered briefly what the Deshmahne custom was for their dead, knowing this gesture to be an insult to the Urmahne, who were taught to bury the dead face up, looking toward the heavens and the ascended gods.

Eventually Dentoun led them back to the ruins, riding at a steady pace. Endric rode with Novan again, and Brohmin doubled with Nahrsin. Shinron's body was lashed to his horse to return with the Antrilii. Endric had not questioned as they reverently lifted him and tied him to his horse. The Antrilii didn't speak as they worked, instead humming softly, barely audibly. The merahl picked it up as well, their voices a faint howl, mixing their sound with that of the Antrilii. The overall effect was haunting.

As they rode back, the merahl did something Endric had not seen from them during his time with the Antrilii—they ran alongside the horses, never straying far. One had sustained a more serious injury, limping as it loped along, but didn't have any difficulty maintaining speed with them.

Nahrsin had attended to the merahl's injuries as diligently as to the injured men, rubbing a poultice into the wounds and bandaging the worst of them. The merahl simply sat as that was done, not making a sound, only flattening its ears in obvious pain. The other injured merahl had more superficial cuts, the blood now cleaned from its fur, care taken by one of the Antrilii in seeing there was nothing more serious. Ishi had been unharmed and now ran ahead like a scout, returning periodically to growl in a low whine that Dentoun seemed to understand. Endric wondered if he did.

They passed into the ruins in silence. The prickling upon his skin returned, almost something palpable. He relaxed, not realizing until now that the muscles in his arms and back were tense. He clenched the borrowed sword in his hand and inhaled deeply. Even still, he couldn't shake the edge of nervousness. The sky lightened as they neared the campsite, a hint of orange rimming the horizon. The air, still cool, weighed heavily on him, a hint of rain to it as it swept in with the gentle breeze from the west.

Endric was exhausted. Whether it was the long night or the effect of the battle, he didn't know. Or care. From the silence of their ride, he was certain he was not the only one who felt that way.

They reached the camp and dismounted. The merahl sat as if waiting. The Antrilii moved over to Shinron's body and pulled it from the horse, quickly carrying it out of sight. The merahl flanked the Antrilii, one on each side and Ishi in the rear. They remained uncharacteristically silent. Even the merahl understood the solemn mood.

Endric hesitated. He considered following after them but decided to leave them to their grief. Part of him was curious about the Antrilii tradition, but he decided he wouldn't have wanted a stranger bothering him as he grieved Andril.

As he turned, he realized Novan had been watching him. The historian nodded slowly, as if acknowledging the decision Endric had made. He realized Novan probably did understand; his curiosity as a historian probably drove him to want to observe as well. With the obvious comfort between him and Dentoun, he may well have been welcome, yet he refrained.

The small fire only smoldered now. The newcomer, Brohmin, tended to it, adding a few dry branches before sprinkling a dark powder overtop. Flames sprang suddenly to life, heat piercing the cool of the night. Much of the remaining tension Endric had been holding eased in a near-instant relaxation.

"Sit, Endric," Novan said. Even his voice soothed.

Endric nodded as he took a seat atop one of the stones ringing the fire. Could it have been the same evening that he'd sat around the fire, explaining his troubles with his father? After the battle with the Deshmahne, it felt more like a week ago rather than mere hours. In that time, his perception of many things had changed. Especially of himself.

He had thought himself a skilled swordsman. So much of his identity had been tied to that. Even after losing to his father, that had remained; Dendril was known as one of the finest swordsmen alive. After what Endric had seen tonight, he no longer could claim similar skill.

There was no question in his mind that every one of the Antrilii warriors would best him. Brohmin too. Perhaps even Novan could beat him with his staff. It was a humbling experience to suddenly be the least skilled with the sword again; he had not felt that in many years, yet there was no denying that truth. And that was before he counted the Deshmahne. He had been lucky to survive his fight with one of them.

"You are wondering what happened back there," Novan suggested, shaking him from his quiet reverie.

Endric nodded, turning to look at Brohmin. The man sat apart from them, staring at the fire with quiet contemplation.

"I cannot promise that it can be easily explained," he continued.

"Brohmin hunts the Deshmahne?" Endric asked, putting words to the question that had been troubling him.

"He is the Hunter." Novan spoke the title casually, but a bit of awe entered as he spoke.

"What would have happened had we not arrived to help?"

Novan glanced over at Brohmin. The man had not moved and his eyes still held an unfocused look as he stared into the fire. One hand rested on his hip, brushing the hilt of his sword as if expecting an attack. The other curled into a tight ball, only his thumb working, rubbing in and out of his palm. Endric realized that he twisted a dark ring on his middle finger. He stared at it, frowning in recognition before looking over to Novan and seeing a similar ring upon his finger.

The historian saw him looking and smiled slightly. He turned to glance at Brohmin, shrugging. "I have learned not to doubt that one." He sniffed softly. "He sets his mind on what must be done and does not look back." Respect edged Novan's voice.

"I don't understand. What is it that needs to be done?"

Novan turned back to him and frowned. "You have seen the Deshmahne, Endric. Tonight was not the first time, if what you told me is true. I doubt that it will be the last."

He leaned forward, his gray eyes reflecting the firelight. The waning shadows of night were pushed away by the bright fire, which cast a faint glow about him. His mouth pulled tight into a thin line, his lips nearly disappearing. Novan pushed the sleeves of his cloak up, exposing long, thin arms. Endric glanced at them briefly, realizing as he did that he searched for markings of some kind before shaking his head at the foolish thought.

Novan was watching him carefully, his face unreadable.

"I'm sorry," Endric said, feeling his face flush with embarrassment. Now he was jumping at shadows, thinking the historian could be Deshmahne. The unfamiliar sense of inadequacy made him question more than he should have.

"There is no reason to apologize. Caution is imperative when dealing with the Deshmahne." He sighed, closing his eyes and leaning away from the fire. The dispelled shadows didn't immediately return. "I offered an explanation, and after what you saw tonight, you certainly deserve one," he said, his eyes still closed. "The Deshmahne are destruction. Not only do they seek it out, causing it, they wish to embody it." He shook his head and opened his eyes, fixing Endric with an intense stare.

He could only nod, remembering what Urik had once said. "They celebrate destroying that which the Urmahne would protect," he quoted. The Urmahne cherished peace, claiming that through peace, man could learn to understand the gods. That ideal was the reason Endric had long struggled with the religion.

Novan frowned and nodded, considering Endric for a moment. "Spoken like one of the guild."

Endric shook his head. "I only repeat what I have heard."

"Hmm." Novan said nothing for a moment. "You mentioned the Deshviili. There are few known Deshmahne ceremonies. The Deshviili is one. Those who know of the Deshviili fear it. It is their most destructive celebration. The earth shakes. Buildings collapse. Entire towns have been leveled in a Deshviili. You are lucky the one you witnessed failed. None, save the Deshmahne themselves, have ever seen the Deshviili. Sometime, you will have to describe for me what it is that you saw. And how it was foiled."

Endric squeezed the sword he was holding as Novan spoke, thinking of his city and the effects of the earthquake. He had thought the Deshviili had failed. That was what he had told the Magi, thinking that whatever he had done had disrupted their ceremony. Only now he was not so sure. Could the damage to the city be the true purpose of the Deshviili? Or had he only redirected it? Had *he* caused Senda's injury?

Novan studied him, his face slowly softening in response to what Endric was feeling. "You are no longer certain it failed, are you?" he asked, his voice taking on a somber tone.

Endric closed his eyes as he took a deep breath. He had thought the attack on the palace the primary target. Mage Tresten had even agreed, but what if it was not? "I came upon three Deshmahne on the palace lawn. They were performing some sort of ritual." He shook his head, remembering how the shadows seemed deeper, darker than they should have been, and the jerky movements of the men he now knew to be Deshmahne. Everything about them was cloudy—even the memories seemed shrouded in darkness. "I can't fully explain what I saw. The markings on their body seemed to move with a life of their own, writhing as the power built." He felt foolish for what he said, but he could think of no other way to explain the ceremony. "I could *feel* it building and feared it. I knew it needed to be stopped." He looked at Novan as he struggled to find the right words.

"How did you stop it?"

"I threw my sword at them."

A deep laugh erupted from Brohmin. Endric looked over and the man still stared at the fire, an amused smile crossing his lips.

"Did it work?" Brohmin asked without looking up.

"I thought it did," he answered. "The sword hit something—not one of the Deshmahne—and bounced away. And then there was a loud cracking sound before they disappeared."

Novan was shaking his head, the amusement Brohmin displayed not evident. Rather, a look of concern contorted his mouth into a worried frown. "No," he said. "I do not think it worked. Only displaced the focus. There was other damage then?"

Endric nodded. "The city. I felt it first in the barracks, after we thought the Deshmahne had gone. Nearly an hour had passed since they disappeared. The shaking soon spread to much of the city. Some thought it an earthquake. Others thought it related to the miner rebellion, some sort of staged explosions. Few would believe it was Deshmahne."

"The miners staged a rebellion?" Novan asked. When Endric nodded, his frown deepened. "That is worrisome." He turned to Brohmin. "Have you not wondered how so many of these swords have suddenly appeared?" he asked the man, motioning to the sack by his feet.

"As often as I've wondered why there have been so many Deshmahne," Brohmin answered. "And wondered why they built their palace in Shinvi in the first place."

Novan nodded. "Shinvi first. Then Coamdon and Voiga. Now the Magi," he said. Worry crept into his voice as he spoke, though from the tightness to his words it was obvious that the historian tried to keep it out.

Endric frowned, furrowing his brow. Shinvi. Coamdon. Voiga. There was a connection, he was certain. Novan obviously saw it, leading Brohmin to make it as well. The man glanced over at the wrinkled sack near his feet.

"This is about teralin?" Endric asked.

Novan closed his eyes as he nodded.

Brohmin narrowed his gaze, pursed his lips for a moment, and then reached down to finger the sack. "How long have you known?"

Novan shook his head. "Not long. It was what Endric said that clarified it for me."

Brohmin glanced at him and nodded thoughtfully. "There is more to this than teralin."

"I fear there might be," Novan agreed.

A deep frown marred Brohmin's youthful face and he turned back to the fire, staring into the flames and falling silent.

"What do you know?" Endric finally asked Novan, leaving Brohmin to his thoughts. He felt a certain uneasiness about the man, fearing to disturb him. Something more than the man's sword prowess could explain it, but a strange darkness seemed to circle about him, nearly an aura that Endric could sense. "You said there were other properties to the metal. What is it the Deshmahne know?"

"The answer to your question is too complex for me to explain. And I am not convinced the knowledge should be so readily available." He tapped a finger on his upper lip for a moment, shaking his head. "Long ago, teralin was valued for different reasons. Today it is not common, but more so than it once was. Fewer mines were known, and what existed was nearly priceless. Many studied it, trying to understand its properties." He sighed. "And wars were fought over it. Over time, knowledge of teralin was lost. That is until the Magi revived it, using it in their ceremonies. To them, it was an interesting ore found in their mountain home. I don't think they even know the full history of the metal."

"And you do?" Endric asked.

Novan shook his head, his eyebrows lifting as he did. "None in the guild can claim to fully understand that history. Too much has been lost. But there are those who study it still, seeking to understand what made it sought after so long ago. I had not thought the Deshmahne were among them." His eyes darkened for a moment, his face twisting in brief irritation, nearly anger. "Now it seems that teralin has started another war."

The historian looked over at Brohmin. "Make no mistake, son of Dendril, a war has begun. Some have waged it longer than you know, fighting the Deshmahne from their very beginnings. Others are just now joining the fight. The Deshmahne grow stronger. More bold. And they seem to have gained the ancient knowledge of teralin." Turning back to Endric, he fixed him with an intense stare. "This is a fight that must be won."

The historian fell silent, glancing at Brohmin and the sack of swords before standing and walking away. Only the quiet crackling of the flames disturbed the waning night. The sky was nearly gray, light enough to see Novan's worried face as he left. Brohmin still stared, slack-jawed, looking into the flames. Even then, the darkness around him persisted.

In the distance, a mournful howl pierced the quiet dawn, echoed by two more voices. The merahl. Their haunted sound reflected the unease he felt at the historian's words. A chill ran through him. The Deshmahne had not been stopped in the city at all. Destruction might not even have been their true intent. They were after the teralin. The mountain mines were known to hold some of the largest veins of the metal ore. Others were known, but were not as large.

Coamdon. Voiga.

Teralin mines scattered throughout those countries held small deposits.

Nothing like the Magi possessed, and not enough to attract the attention of the Magi if it were to go missing. Only the priests would be upset when it went missing.

He wondered where else teralin was found. That would be the next target, he knew. After what he saw tonight, it would take skilled soldiers to even slow the Deshmahne. Stopping them might be nearly impossible.

There was a presence at his side and he jumped as he looked over. Brohmin stood near him, staring after Novan, an unreadable expression plastered on his dark face. One hand hovered near his sword, his finger anxiously working back and forth.

"What happens if they're not stopped?" Endric asked Brohmin.

The man didn't look over at him as he answered. When he spoke, his voice was hushed and coarse. "Peace will fail. Many will die."

"The priests will not let the Urmahne fail."

Brohmin turned to him then. "You think that is their only goal?"

Endric looked into the man's blue eyes. A mixture of anger and hopelessness hid in his gaze, and Endric wondered what drove him to fight the Deshmahne. He wondered what else the Deshmahne could want and had opened his mouth to ask when he was interrupted by a sharp sound piercing the night.

The merahl suddenly howled. Their voices were angry, biting. Endric found that he recognized them and shivered involuntarily.

They had found groeliin.

CHAPTER 27

Endric looked over at Brohmin, but he was already moving, grabbing the sack of teralin-forged swords and the saddle for Novan's horse. Within moments, he was mounted. One hand gripped the reins of the tall stallion, the other squeezed the hilt of his long sword. Darkness framed his face, his furrowed brow twisted in fury.

Novan stopped him, grabbing the reins before the man could leave the ruins. "This is their fight, Brohmin."

Brohmin shook his head and shot a heated glance at the historian. "This must end quickly, Novan. I can help."

He turned and glanced toward the south as if hearing something. The furrow to his brow deepened. His hand clutched the hilt of the sword at his side. Darkness seemed to swirl around him. When he looked back at the historian, his eyes were troubled and nearly black.

Novan closed his eyes and nodded slowly. "You're right. Of course you are." He sighed, releasing his grip on the horse. "I fear for you, Brohmin. Fear what this does to you."

Brohmin shook his head. "I do what is necessary."

"There are none who doubt that. Only the consequences."

The man grunted. "The alternatives are worse. You made sure I understood that." He paused, checking to see that the bundle of swords was secured to the horse. "Now it is your turn to be reminded."

Novan narrowed his eyes and pursed his lips, biting back his first response. Then he sighed again. "I still do not like it. But it cannot be helped." He inhaled, pulling himself up, touching Brohmin on the arm. Some of the darkness around the man faded. When he spoke again, his tone softened. "Be prepared for the questions this brings."

Brohmin answered with a single nod, pausing for a moment and cocking his head as if listening, then kicking the horse forward. He disappeared from the ruins quickly, darkness trailing after him like a cloud.

"I could go with him," Endric offered when the sound of his leaving faded. "I can fight." He had strapped the borrowed sword to his waist and found that his hand moved toward it, much like Brohmin's. For some reason, the idea made him shiver.

"Not this time," Novan said. His words were hushed and he stared after Brohmin. He turned to the fire and used a long branch to move the logs within the fire, stirring up the flames. The morning was cool, but Endric suspected it was not the heat the historian desired.

Long moments passed. They both stared into the flames. He couldn't help but think of the Deshmahne. They had killed Andril. Attacked his home. And nearly killed him. He shivered, unable to push back the fear the priests had instilled in him. He was unsure he would be able to face them again. Once, he had sworn vengeance.

His father was right—he was a child. He was just not skilled enough.

Even Andril had not been skilled enough. What had made Endric think he was different?

Endric tried to ignore the memories of his brother and the feelings they brought forth. It still twisted his stomach like a knot that wouldn't loosen, pressing at the pit of his gut. He swallowed again.

The historian stared into the flames, much like Brohmin had earlier. His face was lined and wrinkled, and his long finger scratched at his chin. Endric wondered briefly what he thought about.

"What do you fear?" Endric finally asked. With the way he fidgeted, looking after Brohmin as if waiting for the man to return, the historian's anxiety was clear.

Novan stood and leaned on his staff. His face appeared more wrinkled than earlier in the evening. Then, it had been firm, full of purpose. Now, he seemed aged. Even his eyes, which had been clear and bright, seemed dull. The man's fatigue was evident. Endric wondered how much the fight with the Deshmahne had taken from him. Or was there something more to it?

"I fear for him," Novan admitted, closing his eyes.

"Why? Who is he?"

"He is the Hunter," he said, repeating the title he had given him earlier. "There is a toll to what he does. We had thought the price must be paid." He shook his head. "I am no longer certain."

Endric frowned at the comment. "What price does he pay?"

Novan didn't answer that question, saying instead, "He cannot be lost. Not yet. Too much depends upon him."

Before Endric could ask what he meant, there came a thunder of hooves as a rider approached. Nahrsin rode in on his tall horse, leading another with him. Endric frowned, recognizing it as Shinron's mount, its dappled hair still stained with its rider's blood.

"Historian. Come. It's not safe here."

Novan frowned but climbed quickly into Shinron's saddle. He reached toward Endric, who hesitated only a moment before grabbing the historian's arm and sitting behind him. "What is it?" Novan asked.

Nahrsin shook his head as he turned the horses, leading them quickly out of the ruins. As they passed the outermost rocks, Endric felt a slight chill upon his arms, like a breeze across wet skin, which passed quickly. He glanced back at the Vinriin ruins as they curled around the hillside, the dark stone seeming more jumbled the farther they rode from it and not the orderly piles of rock he had seen within the ruins, and wondered again what that place had been. Nearing the peak of the hillside the ruins settled into, Nahrsin slowed the horses, pointing into the distance.

Endric saw nothing but shadows. Even the growing dawn, pale sunlight fighting through clouds, couldn't penetrate the darkness. A dense fog rose from the ground as well, further obscuring what he saw. He frowned, trying to understand what it was that Nahrsin saw that had him worried.

Novan recognized it, though. His jaw tensed and his broad forehead twitched, almost involuntarily. "How many?"

Nahrsin shook his head, kicking his horse forward. "Your man didn't know. He saw them as he rode to join the fight. He thinks a couple dozen."

Novan followed, quickly catching the Antrilii. "And you were sent?"

Nahrsin looked over at him. A curious smile curved his mouth. "Your man fights well."

Novan nodded. "He does."

Nahrsin responded with a slight lift of his brow and sniffed with a hint of a laugh. "The stories you could tell," the Antrilii said, shaking his head and scratching at his braided beard. In the early morning light, the smeared paint on his face was more puzzling than intimidating.

Novan looked over his shoulder, but the hillside would now obscure his view. He closed his eyes a moment, holding his breath as he did, and Endric felt another prickling on his skin as the cool breeze picked up suddenly. Finally Novan sighed and shook his head once, turning back toward Nahrsin and leaning forward slightly in the saddle.

"What is it?" Endric asked. His heart thumped heavily in his chest and he found his hands had clenched on their own. The historian's edginess was spreading to him. Nahrsin rode ahead, seemingly immune, his posture relaxed. Only the tight grip on his sword gave him away.

"Nahrsin was right to get us," the historian answered.

He said nothing more. The horses galloped forward, winding down the hillside toward the small valley below. In the distance, he suddenly heard the sharp cry from the merahl and wondered why he had not heard it before now. Their voices pierced the noise of the ride, anger and violence clear in the snarling tone of the howl. Endric felt a growing unease as they rode toward the sound.

Once in the valley, Novan glanced back. The historian's eyes narrowed and a deep frown crossed his face before he turned back.

"Nahrsin. We must ride swiftly now," Novan said. His voice was calm, but Endric saw Novan's back stiffen.

Nahrsin glanced back, flicking his eyes up the slope before nodding and tapping the horse on its flank with his hand. With that, he burst forward. Novan kicked their horse after and they surged forward, galloping now, faster than before, practically flying across the ground. The Antrilii horses were graceful, fast, yet still powerful as they plunged through the tall grass, leaping over as much as they trampled. Endric clung to Novan, afraid that if he let go, the speed would throw him from the horse and he would be left behind.

Finally, Endric dared to turn and look. What he saw nearly stopped his heart. Unconsciously, he leaned forward, gripping Novan harder than he intended. The historian grunted and their horse surged faster.

Atop the hill, ringing the ruins—but strangely not entering—were nearly a dozen black-cloaked riders. Endric had no misperception as to what he saw. His heart thumped painfully in his chest as a cold sweat washed over him. He felt a hint of shame in the sudden fear he felt.

Deshmahne.

As he watched, more crested the hill and joined the others. Soon the hillside seemed covered with them. Endric didn't count but knew that Brohmin's estimate had been accurate. It was hard to tell how many were truly near the ruins; the pale morning light didn't seem to reach the Deshmahne, almost as if avoiding them. Thick fog swirled around the riders and darkness blurred their features.

Still, one stood out. He sat, waiting and staring down at them, separate from the others. Light seemed to bend around him so that he was little more than a black smear on the hillside. Darkness and malice radiated from him; Endric felt it even at their distance.

He shivered and looked away, unable to shake the sense of hopelessness he had felt as he stared at the Deshmahne. It was the same sense he'd had while battling the Deshmahne, only magnified. There was little doubt that he was powerful. He wondered what Andril had felt before dying. Had he known the hopelessness and fear Endric did now? How could he not?

And if Andril couldn't withstand the Deshmahne, how could he hope to?

He shivered again with the thought.

Nahrsin led them down the shallow valley. The fog was heavier here, but he knew that in the distance, the earth flattened before rising again. A few trees scattered around them, some in clumps nearly big enough to call a grove.

Ahead, a larger cluster blocked their path as well, the start of the Trestal Forest marking the upper border of Thealon and Gomald. There was comfort in recognizing some of the surroundings.

Reaching the spot where the ground flattened, Nahrsin turned them north and they were soon nearly out of view of the Deshmahne. Endric glanced back again. The Deshmahne still sat upon the hillside as if waiting. Cloaked in shadows and fog, they made him more afraid than the fearsome, painted Antrilii ever had.

His anxiety lessened when they were out of sight. It didn't completely disappear. "Why so many?" he asked Novan.

"I don't know," the historian said, his words clipped.

Endric shook his head at the response. The historian seemed to say that when he didn't want to guess. "But you have an idea."

Novan nodded carefully. "That many can have only one purpose."

Endric's gaze drifted up the nearby mountains. They couldn't be more than a week out from the lower slopes of Vasha.

Novan glanced back at him but said nothing.

"Even with the Denraen, that many Deshmahne could tear through the city."

Novan nodded.

"Someone must warn them."

Novan glanced back and nodded again. His eyes held a question Endric was not prepared to answer.

The growing snarls from the merahl told them they were near. Distantly, he heard the sound of swords smacking into something—like an axe to a tree—and the furious shouts of the Antrilii. Another gentle slope blocked their view. Nahrsin slowed the horses, raising his hand for them to wait as he rode ahead. Novan nodded and pulled the horse to a stop.

As they did, Endric unsheathed his sword. Novan glanced at him, his mouth turned in a curious expression, but said nothing. Moments passed while waiting for the Antrilii to return, leaving him and Novan in silence. Neither spoke. Endric suspected that their thoughts were the same.

The approaching Deshmahne were a nearly palpable threat. There was little chance the seven of them—ten with the merahl, and they were injured—could stand against that many Deshmahne. They had barely survived when the numbers were evenly matched.

Endric didn't want to think about what would happen if the Deshmahne reached Vasha. The Denraen were skilled—many were excellent swordsmen—but none save his father were as skilled as each of the Antrilii was with the sword. And the Magi wouldn't fight; the idea went against the core of the Urmahne. He didn't know if they would resist even in self-interest. Or would they simply turn and run?

If they did, many would die. Senda. Pendin. His father.

That last bothered him more than he expected. There was much unsettled between them. He had not considered before now that he had expected their differences to be worked out. Eventually. If the Deshmahne overran the city, that might not be possible.

The destruction to the Denraen would be much greater than what had happened with his brother. Even the effects of the Deshviili, as destructive as that had been, might pale before what would happen if fifty of the dark priests reached the city. All for access to teralin.

Endric had never before really liked the metal, his feelings something deep and instinctual. If the Deshmahne somehow used it to gain strength and powers, he liked it even less. And if it had been one of the teralin-forged blades that had taken his brother's head?

Hot anger suddenly surged through him with the thought. He felt it like the heat from a forge and struggled to push it back. No one should experience such horror. And if the Denraen didn't stop the Deshmahne, many more would suffer. Was that not the role of the Denraen—to serve the people, offering protection to those who couldn't protect themselves? To preserve the peace?

If the Deshmahne succeeded, few would know peace again.

His jaw clenched as he looked back in the direction of the Deshmahne. As he took a deep breath, he felt an overwhelming need consume him and a decision was made suddenly. He would no longer fear the Deshmahne.

He would see them destroyed.

The desire came from his very core, raging through him and nearly shaking him from the saddle. Not for simple, selfish reasons, though he knew that was a part of it. He wanted to destroy them for what they would do if they gained even more power.

He had spoken with Urik about the meaning of the word *Deshmahne*. The translation of the ancient language spiting the peace that the Urmahne believed in. As he thought about the translation, he recognized something he had not considered. There was more to it. The ancient language was layered, and this was no exception. A deeper meaning could be gleaned from the word.

Urik had translated it as "power to know the gods." So similar to *Urmahne*, or "peace to know the gods." But even that translation had faults. The ancient language was complex, and few knew it well. He was no scholar, but Andril had seen to it that he was well versed in the language.

Another meaning, one just as likely, was "power of the gods."

With a flash of insight, he realized the Deshmahne were not priests at all. They didn't celebrate the same gods the Urmahne worshipped. There would be no prayers for their return.

He thought he knew what it was the Deshmahne wanted.

They sought to gain strength to throw down the gods. To replace them or for another reason, he didn't care. The effect would be the same. Death. Destruction. Devastation.

Novan had said that a war had been waged with the Deshmahne. Now he thought he understood why. And he would join.

He inhaled deeply, sensing a shifting of his mindset, and suddenly knew a different kind of peace.

Novan turned to Endric as if sensing the change that had come over him. His gray eyes glimmered with a question plain upon them. The question went unanswered as Nahrsin returned. Though he had only been gone a few moments, Endric felt as if hours had passed.

The Antrilii stared at them for a moment, a flash of curiosity crossing his face. He grunted once, shaking his head slightly. "Come," Nahrsin said, turning his horse quickly away and trotting over the hillside.

Endric chanced a glance behind him. There was no movement. The air was silent and still. That didn't change the itching he felt along his shoulders, the dark, nervous sensation he felt.

"They're close," he said.

The comment was not really directed at Novan, but the historian answered nonetheless. "They are. Can you feel them?"

The question was strange, but Endric nodded, suddenly aware that was what he sensed. It was an irritant, almost like an unpleasant burning of his skin. "What am I feeling?"

Novan shook his head, not looking back as he tapped the horse. The motion was similar to what Nahrsin had done to signal the horse and nothing like the traditional signals with reins. This was not the first time Novan had ridden an Antrilii mount. "Some are attuned to it."

With the comment, they crested the small rise. The Antrilii circled the darkened forms of the fallen creatures. Endric couldn't make out any details from his vantage, the wide Antrilii blocking his view. One of them, Dentoun it appeared, knelt before the creatures. As Endric watched, he stood, tucking something into a small pouch. He couldn't be sure, but it looked like a bloody hunk of flesh.

He frowned, wondering if the Antrilii collected prizes from their dead. That would fit with the rumors. The Antrilii were called savages, yet that didn't feel right to Endric. Although he had not ridden with them long, he knew there was more to them than that. They lived with a purpose, feeling that the gods directed their fate. They cared deeply about their animals—horse and merahl—as well as their dead. Endric shook his head; they were not savages.

The opportunity to question passed. Suddenly the bodies of the dead groeliin burst into flame. The Antrilii stepped back, most watching. Only Dentoun turned away, a satisfied expression on his face. In the flames, Endric couldn't make out much of the groeliin, seeing only masses of flesh. He couldn't help but wonder about the creatures the Antrilii hunted. And feared.

The merahl stayed away from the fire. Each appeared unharmed, though Ishi licked at a small gash on her foreleg. The others lay resting, long ears twitching. He still didn't know their names and wondered if the Antrilii kept them secret for a reason.

Each of the creatures turned to look as they rode toward the Antrilii before dismissing them. Endric was still amazed at the intelligence behind their eyes. They quickly decided the newcomers were no threat, but still their ears continued to twitch, swiveling to listen to sounds too low for any other ears. One the merahl bared its teeth briefly, hackles raised along its back and only relaxing as Nahrsin broke away and knelt nearby. He seemed to whisper softly as the merahl calmed.

Brohmin stood apart, barely breathing hard. He carefully cleaned his sword, wiping blood from the blade upon the ground before cleaning it with a strip of cloth. He looked up at Novan as they approached, nodding once, a searching question in his eyes.

"They are behind us," Novan answered.

Brohmin grunted.

"Your estimate was accurate."

Brohmin turned and looked out toward the Deshmahne, as if he could see through the hillside. "That is what I feared." He turned and looked at Novan. "You must reach Ur and warn Dendril. If this is truly about teralin, then he must be told."

Endric shook his head. "Dendril doesn't want to believe the Deshmahne are a real threat."

Brohmin turned to him, darkness ringing his eyes, almost swirling about him. His youthful face twisted in fury. "You think you know the mind of the Denraen general?"

Novan reached out and put a hand on Brohmin's shoulders. The Hunter turned his angry expression to the historian. His hand crept to the sword at his waist. Novan squeezed, restraining Brohmin. "He should," he said gently. "Endric is his son."

Brohmin blinked slowly and took a calming breath. "I'm sorry. These swords…" He shook his head and pointed toward the bundle of teralin-forged swords strapped to Novan's horse, as if that was an explanation.

Novan nodded. "I know."

"Dendril must be warned," Brohmin repeated.

Novan sighed. "He has been too long from the conclave."

Brohmin narrowed his eyes. "If anyone can bring him back, it is you."

Novan considered the comment and then nodded. "I may need help."

The man shook his head. "I am needed here," he said, looking out again through the hillside. "Besides. You have the help you will need."

Endric shook his head. "I can't return," he said. "Not like this. Not so soon." He followed Brohmin's gaze. "Let me stay. I'll fight the Deshmahne."

Brohmin snorted. "You will fight them," he agreed. "But you *will* go."

"You can't fight fifty Deshmahne on your own!" Endric countered.

"Do not presume to tell me what I can do," Brohmin said. His voice went soft but no less dangerous. Darkness seemed to swirl around him, nearly a palpable heat.

"Brohmin!" Novan said sharply.

The man flicked his gaze to Novan. In that predatory gaze, Endric understood his title. The man was the Hunter.

"Our time is short, old friend," Brohmin said quietly. "You know as well as I that they cannot be allowed access to the teralin. You must raise the alarm. I will do what I can to delay them."

Novan tilted his head as he considered, then closed his eyes and nodded slowly. "Peace of the Maker."

"Peace," he agreed.

Novan pulled Endric away and started toward Shinron's horse, quickly climbing into the saddle. He reached out a hand, motioning to Endric to join him. After considering for a moment, he did. His stomach twisted, a sense of nausea flittering through it. He felt more afraid of returning to the city than he would have facing the Deshmahne.

Dentoun stepped up to them. His face was unreadable. The paint, like that on Nahrsin, had become badly smeared.

"I would borrow this mount," Novan said.

Dentoun laid a hand on the horse, patting its side. He leaned in and whispered something to the horse before nodding. "You will take care of her."

"I will." He glanced at Brohmin before facing Dentoun again. "We ride to Vasha."

The Antrilii nodded. "That is wise."

"You should send a rider to your home as well."

Dentoun smiled. "My son prepares."

"The rest of you?"

Dentoun grunted and turned to Brohmin. He smiled, flashing his teeth. "Your man fought well," he said, as if in answer.

Novan nodded slowly. "That is the task given to him."

Dentoun seemed to hesitate. "It seems the gods brought us here for another reason."

"Dentoun—"

The Antrilii shook his head. "This must be done." His voice was resolute. "I have seen what these Deshmahne do with their dark magics." He glanced at the fire where the groeliin burned, shaking his head slowly before sighing and turning back to Novan. "Your man is skilled, but it will not be enough. We can help, though I think all we can pray for is strength to slow them. Nahrsin will bring warning. You will warn Vasha." He nodded, his jaw clenched and steely determination in his eyes. "We will give you time."

Novan looked away, unable to hide the moisture that suddenly appeared. "May the gods bring you peace, friend."

CHAPTER 28

Endric couldn't take his eyes off the Antrilii as Novan turned the horse from Dentoun. Nahrsin approached his father, speaking to him quietly. More emotion washed over his painted face than he had seen from the Antrilii before. The younger man nodded, his jaw clenched and breath held, before grasping his father in a tight embrace, lingering for long moments. The affection between father and son was clear—a sharp contrast to Endric's relationship with his own father—making him wish things could have been different.

Nahrsin took the time to stop and speak quietly with the other Antrilii. Each man grasped his arm in a firm shake and Graime, like Dentoun, pulled him in for a quick embrace. There was resemblance between them, he suddenly recognized. Could Graime be a brother?

"Are they—"

Novan nodded. "Brothers. Nahrsin is the eldest and will lead his people when Dentoun is gone."

Their departure had a formal air to it. After speaking with Nahrsin, each man turned away, unsheathing swords and staring into the distance.

The young Antrilii looked at his friends before turning away. He walked quickly over to Endric and Novan, nodding once to the historian. "May the gods grant you strength and speed."

Novan tipped his head toward Nahrsin. "And to you as well. You must warn your people. I fear you will soon face more than groeliin."

Nahrsin sniffed and nodded, clenching his jaw again as he pushed away emotion. When he spoke, his voice was flat. "We will be ever vigilant. If these Deshmahne seek to attack, they will find the Antrilii a different foe than any they have faced."

"There is no doubt in my mind." Novan searched the Antrilii's face. "Trust in your father's wisdom and you will do well."

Nahrsin closed his eyes. His painted face twisted in a flurry of emotions before he opened them again, calm acceptance written across his flinty features. "You are always welcome among us, historian."

Novan smiled. "The Antrilii are always welcoming."

Nahrsin looked at Novan for a moment more before turning his attention to Endric. "The gods brought us together for a reason, so I feel I must say something. Do not let past mistakes define you. Use them. Learn. No man is without fault." He smiled then, his face softening. The tone of his words, so brotherly, reminded him briefly of Andril. "Out of failure can come great success. Out of weakness can come strength. But only if you choose to learn and grow. Or so says my father," he added, laughing.

Endric laughed with him and wished he could have known Nahrsin better. "Thank you."

Nahrsin nodded. "Perhaps one day the gods will bring us together again."

Endric nodded as well. "I hope so."

"For now, may you also find strength and speed."

"And you."

With that, Nahrsin turned and ran to his horse. He rode quickly away from the clearing, moving north. The merahl Ishi went with him, loping alongside rather than ranging ahead. Nahrsin didn't look back as he disappeared from view.

Brohmin stalked over to them, carrying the bundle of teralin-forged swords. Stopping before Novan, he paused and pulled two of the dark blades from the bundle before holding it up and offering it to Novan. "You must take this. Protect it. They cannot reclaim these blades."

Novan nodded, carefully taking the sack of teralin swords. "You should not—"

"I have no other choice," Brohmin said softly. Even then, his words held an ominous inflection. "If I survive this, you can see that I am healed."

Novan blinked slowly and nodded. "This will not be the first time you have used them."

Brohmin smiled. It was the first time Endric had seen that expression on the man. Even his smile was dark, twisted. "How do you think I have survived this long?"

Novan closed his eyes. "I had suspected." He sighed, his eyes opening, and tied the bundle of swords to the saddle. "Do not let them—"

"They will not turn me, Novan." His voice surged with anger, and the darkness threatened to shroud him.

Novan stared at Brohmin for a moment before nodding once. "Then fight well and know that you will be remembered."

Brohmin smiled again, and a little of the darkness receded. "I am not dead yet."

"No. You are not." Novan turned, glancing briefly toward Dentoun and the Antrilii before looking back at Brohmin. "Peace," he said, tapping the dappled horse and starting off.

Brohmin tilted his head in acknowledgement but said nothing. He turned, the two dark blades clutched in his hands. He spun them and shadows coursed around him, enveloping him. Soon he was barely visible, a smear of shadows.

They rode swiftly and left Brohmin and the Antrilii behind. As they disappeared from view, Endric glanced back and saw a convergence of shadows and knew the attack had begun. He didn't know how Brohmin and the Antrilii hoped to slow the Deshmahne but had a growing suspicion that they would be little more than a delay.

Novan remained silent as they cantered onward. Wind whipped around Endric, whistling in his ears, flapping the sleeves of his shirt. He held tightly to the historian, squinting to protect his eyes. As they rode north, the grassy plain was increasingly dotted with trees. The heavier forests of the lower mountain slopes were still far in the distance, the huge white-capped peaks only beginning to become visible.

"The mountains in the north also contain teralin, don't they?" he asked, finally putting voice to the question troubling him since their departure. He had to yell to be heard over the horse's hooves.

Novan nodded, giving all the answer that he would. He tapped the horse twice with the flat of his hand and they slowed a bit, the rush of wind easing as they did.

"Do the Antrilii mine it?"

Novan shook his head. "They know of teralin, but no. They consider protecting the teralin part of their obligation to the gods," he said, twisting in the saddle so that Endric could hear.

"Nahrsin rides to warn his people?" he asked, and the historian nodded. "The others?"

Novan turned away. "They buy time. For Nahrsin. For us." He shook his head again. "There is little chance they will survive." He voice was soft, strained.

Endric knew the sacrifice the Antrilii made but had hoped he was wrong. Swallowing hard, he asked, "Brohmin?"

"He will pay whatever price is asked."

Endric glanced back but saw nothing. There was no movement in the distance, nothing that said they were followed. Not even shadows.

Exhaustion was starting to overwhelm him. He had no idea how long he had been awake—most of the night at least. Even, now he struggled to keep his eyes open. The wind making them water did little to help. The historian showed no signs of fatigue; his back remained straight and his head swiveled constantly as he searched the terrain as if expecting an attack. It was much like the way the Denraen were trained to ride, and Endric wondered about the historian again before pushing the questions away. He was too tired to think about them.

After a while, they slowed. Open grassland had been replaced by copses of trees. They closed in on the lower forests quickly—more quickly than he had expected. The Antrilii stallion still moved swiftly, his endurance amazing.

Endric licked lips that had grown dry from the constant beating of the wind and wondered if they had even stopped for the horse to take a drink.

Novan glanced back at him. "We can have no delays in reaching Dendril. None. Else the Deshmahne may reach the city before we can prepare its defenses, or reach us before we can make it." He considered Endric for a long moment, his body contorted so that his waist faced forward, guiding the horse with his knees, his chest and head twisted to look at Endric. "So we will take the most direct route to Vasha."

"Faster than the road?"

"There is. One the guild discovered long ago."

Endric knew what he intended. "Through the mines."

"The mountain has been mined for years. Thousands of shafts run through the mountain. Many are little more than dead ends. But centrally, there is a shaft running through the mountain like a maze. Most of the mining branches from this central shaft. If we can reach the main shaft—and stay on the right path—we have a nearly straight shot up into the city."

"How do you know this? The mines are guarded closely, the passages known only by the urmiiln," Endric said.

"As I said, the guild studied the mountain years ago."

"Even if we manage to find this central shaft, how will we keep from wandering from it?" Endric asked, thinking of what Pendin had told him.

"The central mine shaft connects the others."

He said nothing more. They rode onward, slowing occasionally to water the horse. Endric slipped into a shallow sleep once or twice more, leaning on Novan each time. The historian didn't seem to mind. Fatigue never appeared, and he rode straight-backed in the saddle. The day was sunny and overcast, the air never truly warming. As the sun neared its zenith, the trees around them thickened. Endric was surprised, thinking it would take several days to reach the forest's edge. At this rate, they would reach the lower slopes of the mountain by nightfall.

Novan would occasionally glance behind them, staring intently into the distance, even at times closing his eyes while holding his breath, as if he could sense the Deshmahne. Each time, he exhaled quietly and turned away. Endric wondered how far back the Deshmahne were. He didn't doubt they trailed behind.

Endric was no longer afraid of facing the Deshmahne. Rather, a tingle of excitement coursed through him when he thought about the opportunity. Not because he wished for death. There was still much for him to live for. He couldn't reclaim his old life, but still wanted to see Senda and Pendin. And now he had questions that needed answers. Novan. Brohmin. His father.

The Deshmahne were a threat to more than just his friends. He could see that now and wondered if Andril had known as well. Or maybe Andril's death had simply been coincidence. Either way, the threat was real. Only he and Novan stood in the way. The situation was daunting but not overwhelming. Not any longer.

It was clear what needed to happen. Not only could the Deshmahne not be allowed the teralin, they must be destroyed.

When he opened his eyes, the sky was growing dark again. A heavy mist surrounded them, covering them in a protective blanket. Shadows stretched long around them and tall pines pressed in, dark sentries in the growing eve. The air smelled of moisture and hard earth mixed with the scent of the pine; it was a familiar odor and he smiled. They were near the base of the mountain.

"You're awake," Novan said, turning back to him. His face was drawn and wrinkles lined the corners of his eyes. Fatigue finally began to weigh upon him; still he sat straight-backed in the saddle.

Endric nodded and rubbed the sleep from his eyes. He must have been asleep for hours and was surprised he had been able to do so and remain in the saddle. His back stiffened and the recent injuries to his shoulder and legs—while mostly just a memory—still ached from their time in the saddle.

"Good. You might be needed."

"Are they close?" he asked. The sense, like a burning itch along his shoulder blades, was there. Faint, but still noticeable when he turned his attention upon it.

"Not as close as before," Novan said, smiling grimly. "Brohmin and the Antrilii did as they promised. They bought us time." The historian blinked slowly, shadows surrounding his eyes, and turned away.

"How are we going to navigate through the tunnels?" Endric asked.

"The Deshmahne helped with that. They have provided a large quantity of teralin," he answered, patting the sack of teralin-forged blades.

Endric looked at the bulge strapped to the front of the saddle. He had nearly forgotten they carried the swords, but now that Novan reminded him, he saw darkness swirling around the sack. Similar to the darkness he had seen around Brohmin. He understood now why Novan knew Brohmin had used the swords; there was a taint to them, a presence different and nearly as bad as the Deshmahne who wielded them. That taint, the darkness seeming to seep from the metal itself, had contaminated Brohmin.

Endric wondered if the taint was inherent in the teralin or if it was something the Deshmahne did to it. He had never paid much attention to teralin in the city, but with the many adornments crafted from the metal around the palace, he should have seen something like that before. The fact that he had not made it likely it was something the Deshmahne did.

"You think you can use it?" he asked. He was not sure what would happen if Novan used one of the swords, but if Brohmin was any indication, he knew he didn't want to find out.

Novan smiled as if reading his thoughts. "For what I have in mind, yes. Teralin attracts teralin."

"Like a magnet?"

The historian shook his head. "Not the same. This is something different. As it attracts, it strengthens. That is why mining it has always been challenging and why those who can do so successfully are valued."

Endric frowned at that comment. The miners within the city were certainly not valued. He wondered what sort of response the average miner would have to Novan's comments.

"With the quantity of teralin we have, I think we can use it to guide us toward an active mine. From there..."

The historian fell silent, guiding the horse in a slow climb as they neared the mountain. The lower slopes rose gradually, tall, fragrant pines stretching far overhead. The ground was soft mud and made a squelching sound with each step as the Antrilii stud pulled his large hooves from the earth. The mist around them thickened as they rose, making it seem like they were ascending into the clouds, and clung to them, slowly moistening his shirt and pants. The muted call of the huge Drolin owl echoed forlornly through the fog and was the only other sound they heard.

Novan led them north before twisting around to the west, following a path or a memory only he knew. Endric couldn't see well enough to get a sense of direction, the mist and fog making anything more than ten paces away a blur. As he attempted to pierce the fog, he felt a moment of panic rise within him, fearing that the Deshmahne closed in upon them while they meandered up the mountain. Pushing it away, he focused on the sensation he felt earlier, the burning itch, which signaled to him how far back the Deshmahne rode. It was faint, little more than he had sensed earlier, but clearly growing stronger.

The Deshmahne gained on them.

"How much longer?" Endric asked.

"I search by memory of what I read."

"How long ago did you read of this?"

The historian shrugged. "Fifteen, twenty years, I suppose."

"How clear is the memory?" Endric asked, feeling a surge of worry.

Novan frowned at him, insulted. "Crystal." He turned away and said nothing more.

They rode onward. Endric wondered if the stallion tired, though he never seemed to slow. The fog thickened as they climbed, to the point where he could see little more than dark shapes around them. He wondered how Novan guided them without being able to see where he was going.

The slope steepened and the pines thinned somewhat. Endric knew they thinned even more on the road into Vasha. Eventually nothing more than bare stone hid travelers on their way into the city. More defenses. At least on a clear day. Dense fog, like tonight, was not uncommon, though less so on the upper edges of the slopes. The mountainside managed to stay mostly clear; whatever didn't come to the road seemed to often settle into the city itself.

Gradually, the night grew darker. What light remained seemed to reflect off the moisture in the fog, giving it a nearly mystic glow. They had been riding along the lower slopes of the mountain base for several hours, slowly climbing and circling the mountain. Endric wondered if they were backtracking as well. He was no longer certain where on the mountain they rode, but he knew they had long since passed the main roadway up into the city. The horse followed a path barely wide enough for them and amazingly never seemed to lose his footing. Endric's amazement with the Antrilii mount never abated.

A low howl split the night, hollow and slowly reverberating to them. For a moment, Endric was reminded of the merahl and looked up hopefully, knowing it was only the sound of one of the huge mountain wolves so common to the slopes. They rarely left the forest, hunting small prey on the hillsides. The wolves were usually not much threat to men, scared off by the horses and their weapons. At least this one sounded far enough away.

Novan suddenly tapped the horse and they stopped. Endric sat up, alert, wondering if the historian had found the cave entrance they sought. "Are we—"

Novan turned sharply and brought a finger to his mouth. "Deshmahne," he mouthed, barely whispering the word.

Endric frowned, pausing for a moment and then shaking his head. The strange itch along his shoulders had not changed. He was not exactly sure what it was that he felt—or why he could feel it—but he believed that he sensed the Deshmahne.

"I don't feel anything different," he whispered.

"I do," Novan answered, tapping the horse once.

The stallion surged forward, climbing quickly. Endric looked around, searching for the Deshmahne the historian claimed was nearby. He saw nothing. After a while, he stopped looking.

Novan guided the horse with his knees, twisting in the saddle and staring into the fog as if he saw something Endric didn't. Tension built along his shoulders and he sat straighter in the saddle than he had. One of Novan's hands drifted toward the sack holding the teralin blades, hovering over the rough brown fabric. He turned briefly and his eyes darted to the sides, his breath coming in short bursts of mist in the cool air.

Then Novan tapped the horse again and they stopped. Swinging quickly from the saddle, he hurried to a nearby wall, sliding his hands along the stone. The fog was dense but enough light was retained that Endric could see the stone rising in a sheer wall before them. He climbed from the saddle and joined Novan.

"Is it here?"

Novan shook his head once. "I'm not sure." His voice was tight, clipping his words. "From what I recall, the cave entrance should be nearby."

Endric bit off his response, wondering how the historian could see anything in the fog, and turned to help search. Long moments passed as they looked along the wall. Endric was nearly ready to give up and suggest to Novan that they search elsewhere when the historian suddenly grunted. The fog muted the sound, and Endric felt a flutter in his chest as he wondered if the sound meant Novan was pleased or surprised.

He hurried behind the huge boulder Novan had disappeared behind. There was barely room to squeeze behind the rock, but when Endric did, he saw what had generated the response. A small entrance was visible now that Novan had moved a few smaller stones. The historian crawled into the darkness, his back brushing the top of the cave.

"It is here," he said, then whistled softly. The Antrilii stallion found them quickly and Novan pulled his staff and the sack of swords from the saddle. Turning to face the horse, he paused. "Thank you for your speed. From here, we are on foot. Find Nahrsin and return to your home."

He patted the stallion on the neck, stroking it briefly. The dappled horse snorted, flipping his tail and stomping his hooves. Novan patted the horse again and he nuzzled his hand. "We must go where you cannot," Novan whispered and then rubbed the mount's forehead. The horse stomped again and finally turned, starting down the slope, quickly lost from view in the fog.

Novan started into the mouth of the cave. Endric hesitated, looking around and seeing nothing following them, then crawled after the historian. Darkness swallowed him instantly.

He crawled forward. Pausing after a long minute, he looked back. Even the mouth of the cave was obscured, everything behind him nearly as black as the teralin blades. Endric took a deep breath and turned, moving forward again, wishing for light.

After crawling barely more than a body length, he heard a faint scratching sound behind him. He froze, listening intently. The sound didn't come again. His heart hammered in his chest and a cold sweat broke on his forehead. There was no room to turn around quickly; an attack from behind would be over quickly. Hesitating, he considered moving forward again when he heard the sound return.

Endric closed his eyes; he could see nothing anyway. Breathing slowly, he waited, not daring to move. When he realized what the noise was, he suppressed a groan.

The burning itch along his shoulders was more pronounced, like a fresh sunburn. The Deshmahne was near.

He hurried forward again, not concerned with being quiet. Of greater concern was reaching a place to make a stand. He couldn't do it within the narrow cave.

Suddenly, a faint light flickered in the distance. Endric pushed faster, ignoring the scraping along his arms and back, praying quietly that it was Novan. He had not heard anything from the historian since they entered the cave, and the gods only knew how long this stretch of tunnel went.

The scraping behind him grew more prominent. Closer. Endric pressed forward, moving toward the light as quickly as possible in the confines of the narrow tunnel. The cave gradually became narrower. Would he reach Novan in time? He had no false ideas about what would happen were the Deshmahne to reach him first. An involuntary shiver went through him at the thought of the teralin-forged blade stabbing into him.

Then he reached the light. Novan grabbed him by his shirt and dragged him forward into a huge open cavern. A small globe glowed to one side, casting the pale white light he had seen. Endric had never seen anything like it but didn't stare for long. The strange lantern didn't hold his attention.

Rather, it was the dark blade held outward in Novan's hand.

"Why do you have a teralin sword?" Endric asked. His voice was breathless and his chest heaved with the effort of speaking.

"Move back," Novan said.

Endric frowned and did what the historian said, stepping away from the small opening. Novan touched the sword to the stone and muttered a quiet word. A deep rumble suddenly shook the cave, heaving Endric forward. Dust and rock sifted down from above, peppering his hair. He coughed, clearing his throat.

"Novan!" he yelled, fearing being trapped in the cavern. He had witnessed something like this shaking before and had seen what it could do.

The historian ignored him. The sword swirled around the opening to the cave, grazing along the stone. Where it touched, the rock trembled. The ground continued to heave. A faint glow surrounded the sword, more like a shifting of the darkness around the blade.

An arm reached out of the cave. The dark tattoos along the skin were clear, twisting up the pale skin. The hand clutched a sword similar to the one Novan held. The historian batted it away, grunting as he did, and then slammed the sword he held into the stone.

And then the cave collapsed.

CHAPTER 29

The pale white lantern flickered as a cloud of dust settled over the cavern. The small cave they had crawled through was gone, a crumble of stone and debris. The tattooed arm hung limp at the spot of what had once been the opening. Novan straightened himself, wiping debris from his cloak, and knelt before the arm, examining the tattoos.

"He was a sentry," Novan said, then shook his head as he stood. "They should not know of this entrance. Only the guild knew of this."

Endric frowned at the comment, pausing to make sure he didn't have any injuries. "We're trapped here now."

"Does not matter. This will only delay the Deshmahne."

"How did you do it?"

"You remember that teralin has many qualities?"

"You know how to use it?"

Novan snorted. "I am a historian. I know many things that are now forgotten. There is power in learning from the past, from gaining knowledge. The Magi have lost sight of this. The Deshmahne have not."

The historian's comments reminded Endric of what Urik had said, but he pushed thoughts of the en'raen away. He couldn't help them here. No one knew they were here, trapped beneath the earth. How long before they became lost, wandering blindly in the darkness until weakness and hunger overtook them? Or worse, the Deshmahne came upon them, overrunning them, a hot teralin-forged blade piercing his chest...

He shivered, forcibly pushing the thought away. It was a dark thought, one that was too much like what he'd felt when facing the Deshmahne. "You said the guild knew a way through?"

Novan nodded. "That is what has been written. I am hopeful it is accurate."

"And if it isn't?"

The historian exhaled slowly. "We cannot think like that. Do not let the teralin influence your thoughts," he said, stuffing the sword, and that of the now-dead Deshmahne, into the sack. Endric felt the dark thoughts begin to ease.

"Then we should move."

"Agreed. I do not know how much time we have. The Deshmahne will still follow. This will only slow them," he said, motioning toward the collapsed cave.

The historian grabbed the pale lantern and started off through the cavern, twisting to shine his light into dark recesses. Endric saw nothing other than rough walls. There was no evidence that this was anything other than a naturally occurring cavern. As they moved farther into the cavern, he heard a soft burbling sound. At least they wouldn't die of thirst.

"The Deshmahne knew of this entrance." Was that how they'd gotten into the city the first time? They could have come another way as well.

"It appears they did," Novan agreed.

"The other attacks focused on possessing the mines. The Deshmahne already had access to them. Why attack the city? The Magi?"

They walked a little farther.

"You're right," Novan said finally. "I don't know what they intend. None other than the high priest can claim they know the full extent of the plan. Previous attacks *have* been about gaining teralin." The historian shook his head. "I can't think of anything else they may seek to possess."

Endric fell silent. The Deshmahne had attacked the palace first. At least, that was what he had thought after disrupting the Deshviili. He had first assumed it was simply an attack, a way of disrupting the Magi influence, but there had to be more to the Deshviili. The attack on the city seemed mostly diversion, though an effective one.

"Their attack on the city was not simply about destruction," Endric said, thinking aloud.

Novan shook his head. "Such an attack draws too much attention."

"They had already drawn attention with their attack on the Denraen." Endric took a deep breath, pushing away the feelings of sadness that always surfaced when he thought of Andril. Especially how things had been left between them.

Blinking away the sudden moisture in his eyes, he glanced around. The cavern continued onward, stretching into the darkness, and Novan moved forward while they talked. There had been no sign of any other way out. The cavern narrowed as they walked, the walls on either side pressing closer, but overhead stretched high into the darkness above.

"They sowed fear. The Denraen will remember the losses. And how none of the Deshmahne appeared to have been killed. If that were all, it would be enough reason for the attack."

"You do not think it the only reason."

Novan turned away, staring into the darkness. The lantern only lit a small circle around them. Beyond the light's boundary, the blackness was absolute. There was nothing, no light or sound other than what they made. Even the sound of the hidden stream had faded. "No."

"Then why? Why did my brother have to die?"

Novan didn't look back as he answered. "I wish I knew. It could be something as simple as chance; misfortune that it was his regiment that went. Or it could be something more devious. Perhaps the Deshmahne knew exactly who they attacked and killed him for that reason."

"What reason?" he asked, though he thought he knew.

Novan turned back. There was sadness in his eyes. "That he is Dendril's son."

"I am Dendril's son," Endric said, more harshly than intended.

"And have faced the Deshmahne more than any man I know. Other than

Brohmin," he finished, turning away.

The historian let the silence surround them, saying nothing more. Endric didn't know what else to say. Could it be that the Deshmahne had attacked Andril as distraction to his father? The answer seemed both too simple and complex. Endric preferred the idea that he had died by chance. Wasn't it chance that he had been sent in the first place?

But he knew that it had not been. The idea and plan had been Urik's. The en'raen had said as much. Urik was to have gone, but Andril was sent in his stead. Perhaps as a simple matter of wanting to prove to their father that he was worthy of the promotion. What if there was another reason?

His heart was beating harder in his chest and he struggled to breathe. He paused, hands on his thighs, and looked up and into the darkness as he took a few slow breaths. There was nothing he could change anyway. Andril was gone. And so many questions remained. Now they would die in this cave, without food, only water burbling nearby, waiting as the Deshmahne swarmed over them...

A sudden thought broke through his sadness, his mind clearing with it.

He took a deep breath, squinting into the darkness as he looked up. "I think we are looking in the wrong direction."

"There is no other direction, Endric. It is not wide enough to look anywhere else. This cavern stretches onward and we go forward."

Endric shook his head. "Not only onward, but upward as well."

Novan looked up, following his gaze. He stared for many heartbeats, finally closing his eyes as he peered into the darkness. Slowly, the deep frown crossing his face disappeared, replaced by a tight smile. It didn't reach his eyes. "I should have felt it," he said, mostly to himself.

"Felt what?"

The historian turned and looked at him, his eyes dark, haunted. Endric nearly took a step back, recognizing it as the same expression he had seen upon Brohmin's face.

"The teralin."

Endric frowned, puzzled, and looked overhead. It was then that the realization dawned on him. Why the dark thoughts had suddenly plagued him. "Why does it affect me now?" he asked, staring into the blackness above him. He had grown up around teralin. So much in the city was forged with the metal, yet he had no memory of similar thoughts bothering him. Or maybe he simply had not known.

"Teralin in its purest form is neutral. That is how it is typically mined. The energy within the metal changes when its power is accessed, and it can never be changed back. Few have known how to access the energy in many centuries. Somehow the Deshmahne have learned." He sighed, shaking his head. "The teralin in these swords has been twisted toward destruction."

"What of the teralin in the city?" Endric asked.

"I suspect the Magi do not know how to access it."

"Meaning?"

Novan looked at him. "Meaning it would still be neutral."

Endric blinked slowly, understanding coming to him. "And primed for the Deshmahne. Extracted from the mountain all these years and yet most of it is ornamental."

Novan closed his eyes a moment, feeling along the walls, looking upward, murmuring quietly to himself. He moved away, the lantern glowing in the darkness, floating with him as he searched. Though he walked with the light, the shadows didn't leave him. Endric followed from a distance, leaving the historian to his quiet search. Novan kept his other hand up, his palm facing the dark. Occasionally he would slow before starting forward again. And then he stopped.

Novan set the lantern down and pressed his hands upon the hard rock wall. His fingers probed the rock, moving around. Then he started up.

Endric hurried over. The lantern cast a white light on the wall of the cavern. At first glance, the wall appeared smooth, but pockets of darker shadows interrupted it. Endric tentatively touched one of the areas and was surprised to find a recess. Mimicking what Novan had done, he felt along the wall and realized similar indentations were spaced regularly. A ladder.

He picked up the lantern and lashed it around his neck using the length of twine dangling from it. Then he started up the wall, after the historian. The climb was easy once he knew the cadence, and he soon rose high above the cavern floor. Endric hazarded a glance down, but the light from the lantern blinded him and he continued upward. Then he reached a ledge.

As he did, there came an explosion from behind him.

The Deshmahne.

"I thought they'd take the road up to the city," Endric said with a grunt.

Novan grabbed his arm and helped him over the stone lip. When Endric stood, he was in another cave. This was wider and not as tall. Clearly man-made. A gentle warmth radiated toward them. Teralin.

"It seems they had another plan in mind," Novan answered.

Endric looked around and then inched over to the ledge, peering down into the blackness of the cavern below. Without him sensing *something*, they wouldn't have found the hidden stairs either. But with more lighting, he wondered if this would have been easier. "We won't have long."

"No. We must hurry." Novan started forward, running a hand along the wall. "There's still teralin along this chamber. I can feel it."

Endric nodded. "I feel the warmth."

"Not just the warmth," Novan said, not looking back as he started down the mine. "This is different."

Endric touched the wall and frowned. The stone was warm with a hint of dampness to it, as if the heat pressed moisture from the surrounding rock. There was nothing else, no evidence of anything more.

"What do you feel?" he asked. The sound echoed in the cave and he worried how far his voice would carry.

Novan had continued forward, his hand trailing along the wall. Endric hurried after him, afraid to lose the historian. Novan had been acting strangely ever since they entered the cave.

He caught Novan at a split in the tunnel. The historian stood, back straight, eyes closed, breaths coming slowly. The hand holding the sack of teralin blades trembled slightly, the tightness of his grip blanching his skin. Endric said nothing as he looked around, leaving Novan in silence. One of the branching caves appeared to descend deeper into the earth while the other sloped gently upward. Soft heat wafted on gentle currents toward them from both entrances.

"We should take the way that slopes upward," Endric said. The city was still high above them, and he didn't know how long they had before the Deshmahne came upon them. There was little room for error.

Novan suddenly shivered, his body trembling violently, and his eyes snapped open.

He started forward, the sack of teralin-forged blades swinging toward the cave sloping downward. Novan disappeared quickly into darkness.

Endric paused, breathing slowly of the warm air as he stared after the historian. Could using teralin affect him that quickly? Brohmin had acted strange like this as well, surrounded by darkness and anger. Now it seemed as if the same had trapped Novan.

His hand went to the sword at his side, finding the hilt involuntarily. He squeezed it as he inhaled deeply, drawing strength from the plain steel blade. Then he started after Novan.

Several hours passed in the darkness of the old mines. Endric worried they were moving too slowly. How long would it be before the Deshmahne reached the city? Could they reach it first and warn his father? Would he even believe?

The air never grew any warmer, and they saw no signs of miners. The lantern started to flicker, its light dimming, and he wondered how much longer they would have it. Novan was useless for questions, not responding to anything Endric tried and having gone otherwise mute.

The historian paused before each branch in the tunnels, staring intently as if there was something only he could see. Each time, he would shiver and start off again. Endric had taken to waiting quietly as Novan decided which direction to take. After the first tunnel, they generally went up, sloping gradually higher through the mountain, the grade nearly the same as Endric remembered the road leading into the city itself.

The tunnel they were in now was different. Steep stairs interrupted the otherwise flat tunnel every hundred feet. Each step seemed made for a man slightly taller than him so that after only a dozen steps, his thighs burned and his lungs ached. Novan didn't slow, showing no signs of fatigue. Rather, he moved faster here, almost as if pulled forward.

After climbing for nearly an hour, Endric was nearly overwhelmed by the relentless pace. Novan pulled away, climbing as a vague shadow far ahead of him. The lantern continued to flicker, the pale light fading, so that Novan completely disappeared at times. The stairs continued upward, though in the distance the tunnel appeared to veer to the left.

What would happen if he lost the historian? Would he wander, aimless and lost, through the tunnels? He doubted that he could find the active mines, and the miners within them, on his own. Whatever drove Novan seemed to help guide him in the right direction, but what price did he pay for such guidance?

The lantern flickered one last time and finally died just as Novan turned the corner in the tunnel. Suddenly there was nothing but blackness.

Waves of panic threatened to overwhelm him. It was bad enough being trapped in the mines with no known way out and the Deshmahne behind them. But being trapped in utter darkness was another thing altogether.

His heart fluttered and he swallowed the hard knot in his throat. Never before had he thought he would be afraid of the dark. Now, standing on a huge rock stair, warm stone walls pressing in around him, he felt fear.

Endric took a deep breath and slowed his breathing through an effort of will. The knot in his throat and the nausea never completely left. There was no other choice but to go on. The Deshmahne must be stopped, and he couldn't rely on Novan in his current state. He tossed the lantern to the side and placed his hand upon the wall, letting the warmth of the rock seep into his skin. Then he started forward into the darkness.

Several times, he slammed into the next step until he began to get a feel for the distance. Staggering forward, thighs on fire, legs stinging from scraping on the rock, he hurried on. Novan had not slowed as the lantern light faded, and Endric didn't think he would wait now that it had died. If the tunnels branched again before he caught up, there was no telling how long it would take to find the historian again. If he found him.

Endric stumbled, tripping as the expected step didn't come. The hand trailing on the wall flailed into empty air. As he tried to catch himself, he fell into a wall, hitting his head against the rock. He grunted, biting back the scream welling up within him, fearing to give away his location by shouting. When the pain faded, his head still throbbing, he felt along the wall now blocking his way. For a moment, he was disoriented as he tried to find the tunnel to the left.

A quiet scraping in the distance startled him. Calming himself, he followed the sound, hoping it was Novan. Using the wall to guide him, he continued forward. No more steps blocked his way, the tunnel again sloping gently upward. Endric began to count his steps, uncertain what he would do if he took the wrong direction. After reaching his third hundred steps, he gave up.

Then the tunnel branched. He discovered that as he smacked into a divider, his breath knocked from him. He could see nothing. Moving to his right, he found the wall again and followed that branch for a dozen steps. The ground seemed to slope downward and he stopped, turning back until he reached the divider again. He took the other tunnel and moved slowly, running his hand along the inner wall, hoping it would slope upward. His tension eased when he realized that it did.

This tunnel moved upward more rapidly than the others and was narrower as well. The other wall was close enough to touch. The warmth of the teralin surrounded him, hotter than it had been. Sweat poured off him, stealing precious moisture. Endric stumbled into another step and began moving more carefully, taking the steps as quickly as was safe. His breaths came hot and ragged and his steps began to slow, dragging harshly on the rock. There was no other sound in the tunnel.

After taking a particularly large step, he moved forward onto a flat expanse, the tunnel widening again. He sensed it, unable to see the walls around him. Sweat dripped into his eyes, and for a moment he thought he saw a faint light in the distance. After rubbing the sweat out of his eyes, he saw that the light remained.

He held his breath, staring intently into the dark. The light didn't waver. As Endric started forward, it gradually brightened. He moved quickly at first, then slowed as caution got the better of him. How high had he climbed? Could he have reached the active mines?

Or had the Deshmahne circled around him?

Endric paused, taking a deep breath to slow his heart, and waited. The burning sensation he felt when the Deshmahne were near was a distant pain. This was not Deshmahne.

Then what?

He crept forward. The walls of the cave slowly resolved, becoming distinct, darker splotches now more than an arm's width away. The cave ceiling was high overhead, shadowed and indistinct. The orange light in the distance brightened with each step. As he neared, he saw that it flickered, as if a flame on a breeze.

Endric reached an intersecting corridor and stopped. The tunnel he was in continued forward, but the light came from a branching tunnel to his right. Going straight took him back into darkness, though the slope of the ground told him it led upward. The lighted tunnel remained flat.

He didn't know which way to choose. Always he had been going upward. But the light in the tunnel indicated someone was in that direction. Perhaps even Novan, though the historian could be anywhere. Endric needed to simply find his way out, not worry about the historian. Once he reached the city, he would figure out a way to warn his father.

He turned down the lighted tunnel. The light was not bright but still burned eyes that had grown accustomed to the darkness. After hundreds of steps, he reached the source of light. A large, ancient-looking oil lantern hung at another intersection of tunnels. The tunnel also continued forward past the intersection. Each direction was lighted, additional lanterns flickering far in the distance.

Endric stood, paralyzed as he struggled to decide which way to go. Standing in the intersection, he closed his eyes, hoping for the same insight that Novan had. Perhaps the teralin would pull him forward.

He stood for long moments, eyes closed, exposed at the intersection of the caves.

And felt nothing.

Feeling foolish, he opened his eyes. The caves were still and silent. Only the flickering light moved.

Suddenly he paused, watching the flickering lantern light. As he stared at it, he realized he felt occasional puffs of air, like the hint of a breeze, coming down through the tunnel. Stepping into the branching tunnels, he didn't feel the same.

He would follow the airflow.

Endric hurried through the caves, pausing at each intersection to feel for the flow of air. Each time it came down only one tunnel. Generally the ground sloped upward, often steeply. More than once, he encountered sets of stairs carved into the rock. He walked for what felt like hours. His legs ached and fatigue threatened to topple him, but he pressed onward, not wanting to be caught sleeping in the caves.

Finally he reached an intersection that was different. The caves veered off in only two directions. One side was lit more brightly, the lanterns more frequent. The other, though dimmer, had the soft breeze fluttering through it. Endric stood, his tired mind struggling with the decision.

Really, it was no decision. He moved into the dimmer tunnel, following the breeze.

The tunnel stretched far in front of him. The lanterns began to be spaced less frequently, then seemed to stop altogether. The tunnel still stretched onward. Darkness threatened to overcome him again.

Had he chosen the wrong path?

Stumbling forward, he considered turning around when he reached the end of the tunnel. The light from the last lantern was fading, but he saw no other branching. Frowning, he wondered how he had felt the pull of the breeze down a dead end. Then he saw it.

First as a deepening of shadows. Stepping over to the darker area, he saw that the tunnel didn't end as he had thought. Rather, a low opening was carved into the tunnel end. From that, a steady, warm breeze blew out. There was nothing but blackness down the narrow tunnel.

He hurried back to the last lantern and pried it off the wall, then returned to the small opening. The lantern light didn't make it any more appealing. But he was committed to this path and crawled in. The walls were warmer here, nearly hot. Teralin coursed through this part of the mine.

Endric crawled forward. The walls didn't narrow as he had feared, leaving him room to look back and see how far he had come. Eventually, even the small entrance to the tunnel was no longer visible. Still it stretched forward.

The walls were smooth. More so than the outer walls had been. The breeze didn't change, blowing toward him like a warm breath.

He didn't know how long he had crawled when his hand found an opening in the tunnel beneath him. Endric froze. Ahead, the tunnel continued forward, but the air came from the drop-off. Stretching the lantern forward, careful with the oil, he could see nothing but the rock walls.

Endric broke off a piece of the lantern and dropped it down the opening, listening carefully as he did. The hunk of wood hit with a dull thud after a little more than a second.

Not a short drop then.

He dropped the lantern next, watching the light as it fell. It flickered but stayed lit. The oil splashed out, spraying the ground, and a small fire burst from far below. Too far to safely drop.

Shifting his sword, he slipped into the opening and shimmied down, pressing his back against the rock with hands and feet. The warm stone threatened to burn his hands. Teralin was not supposed to burn, but he had seen the effect the teralin-forged blades had on the grasses of the plain. He imagined the same thing happening to his hands, his back, his feet, as he scraped along the rock, slowly easing his way downward.

As he descended, the rock became hotter, to the point where he could only rest his hand and arm for a few seconds before needing to pull away. Checking below, he realized he had only come partway down. Worry crept through him, different than fears of being stranded in the dark or being chased and found by the Deshmahne. What if the rock became unbearably hot? He could climb back up, but now that he had committed to this path, he was determined to see where the tunnel led. A foolish decision, he began to think. What if he was burned by the teralin? Any injury would make pushing forward even more difficult, and he didn't want to consider who would find him. If any did.

The heat built. His fingers and hand stung from a combination of scraping the rock and the heat; he could no longer distinguish which was worse. He feared his back was blistered and was thankful for the small barrier that his shirt provided. Endric couldn't take the pressure off his back or he'd fall straight down. He dared not look below, barely able to keep his eyes open as he gritted his jaw tight, concentrating on moving carefully.

Then he could no longer stand it. Both hands pushed away from the scalding rock at the same time, upsetting the balance he maintained with his feet. He slid, scratching his back worse, the heat of the rock seeming to eat through his shirt and into his flesh, and finally dropped. Bracing for the fall, Endric bit back a scream. The ground was closer than expected, and his breath was knocked from him as he hit the ground.

When he opened his eyes, he saw he was in another tunnel. The tunnel stretched in either direction, its walls perfectly smooth, though different than other tunnels he had been in, and wider. He wondered if it were connected in any way other than the small opening he wiggled through. The soft breeze blew through this tunnel, warmer than before and now easily noticeable.

Endric stood slowly, checking his hands for burns but finding none. His back ached and he feared for the worst, yet there was no choice other than to press onward. The lantern burned nearby, close enough that he realized his luck in not rolling in the spilled oil. He grabbed the lantern and started down the tunnel into the soft breeze, hoping the light from the remaining oil would last long enough.

He still didn't know what he expected. There was little hope that Novan had come this way; the historian likely wandered through wider and more easily traveled tunnels, yet the strange wind pulled him forward. It was the only thing he had that he could follow. For all he knew, he moved in circles, now near a tunnel he had already been through.

It was these troubling thoughts that were plaguing him when he came upon the door.

Made of solid teralin, it emanated heat like a blast furnace. The soft breeze seemed to pulsate from this heat, as if it disturbed the air enough to create a gentle wind. Endric had to take a step back in order to tolerate the temperature. He stepped away and the airflow lessened, then increased again near the door. This was where he had been pulled.

Nothing obvious adorned the sides, no carvings or sculptures like the teralin ornamentations in the city. Only a small handle, carved in intricate detail to look like the branching of a tree, disrupted its surface.

Endric sighed, glancing in either direction down the tunnel. No other lanterns lit the way. His lantern sputtered, the drop having spilled most of the oil reserves. Soon he would be back in darkness. That left the door. Of pure teralin.

Swallowing hard, he stepped forward. Heat enveloped him and sweat erupted from his face, chest, and underarms. He dared not take a breath. Another step and he stood before the door.

Endric set the lantern down carefully, feeling light-headed from the heat and lack of air. Blinking slowly, he grabbed the handle. Searing heat shot through his hand, down his arm.

He screamed, unable to contain it, and pushed.

CHAPTER 30

The door swung open slowly. The heat lessened as the massive door swung away and Endric was finally able to take a deep breath, filling his lungs with teralin-heated air, coughing raggedly as he did. Relief flooded through him as he released the handle, fearing to look at his hand and see reddened and ruined flesh. Pain receded slowly, resolving into a dull throbbing ache that seemed to ease as he opened and closed his fist. He had intentionally used his off hand, saving his sword hand for whatever defense he might need. There was no telling what lay before him.

Then he looked into the room.

When he did, he nearly fell over. The walls were lined with alcoves, and in each were stores of teralin. Some were sculpted into various shapes and forms like those in the city above. Most were not. It was a veritable treasure trove of the ore.

The room was hot from it, though less than the door, as if its massive size created a more concentrated effect. A few small lanterns were set into recesses, different than the oil lantern he had found in the caves and more like the strange lantern Novan had carried. Now that lantern lay burned out and dark, somewhere below him in the caves. He started forward into the room, staying as far from the door as possible.

The room was nearly twice his height, the long alcoves spaced evenly like shelves up the walls. Staying to the middle of the room, he avoided the teralin stores. This must be what the Deshmahne sought, the reason they attacked. So much teralin was stored here and most of it, he suspected, was still neutral. How many of the dark blades could be forged with what was in this room alone? What else could they do with it?

In spite of the heat, the thought made him shiver.

Halfway down the room, he froze. A large chair, almost a throne, was the only item on the far wall. Small lanterns hung on either side, casting a soft glowing light that still didn't clear the shadows. That alone would give him pause. What made him freeze was the realization that someone sat atop the chair.

Grabbing his sword, he unsheathed quietly and crept forward. The person didn't move and made no sound as he approached. The light resolved little as he moved closer, and he could see that a dark cloak covered wherever the light did reach. The figure didn't seem aware that anyone was in the room.

Endric slid closer, cautiously holding his sword in a defensive position. His nerves on edge, he frowned as he realized why he felt something was off. Bands of dark metal circled the figure's wrists and ankles, binding him to the chair. Heat flowed from the chair. Solid teralin, like the door.

Could anyone survive such torture? The person didn't move—no muscles twitched beneath the cloak, the chest didn't rise and fall with breath. Nothing. Whoever sat atop the chair was likely dead.

He shivered again as a new fear started through him. Endric didn't want to be caught here when whoever would do such a thing returned. And he wanted to turn away but couldn't. Locked in place, he started to turn, realizing it was past time for him to find Novan.

Then suddenly the figure coughed.

Endric took a step back before catching himself. Could Novan have been caught and tied to the chair? If it was the historian, he needed to help.

Sliding closer, he used the tip of his sword to push back the cloak. He gasped when he saw the captive's face.

"Listain?" he whispered.

A dark stubble of beard covered the haggard face and his eyes were more sunken than they should be, but there was no doubting that this was his father's Raen. Sweat slicked his hair and his cheeks were a mix of ruddy and pale. The face was more like a skeleton, the flesh thin and cheekbones prominent. Even this close to the chair, the length of the sword keeping him at a distance, the heat was nearly unbearable. How long had the man been trapped here? He couldn't fathom how Listain tolerated sitting atop the chair, only the cloak as a barrier.

"What happened?"

Listain tried to open his eyes but couldn't. "Who?" he croaked. His voice was a ragged whisper, rough and raw.

"It's Endric. What happened?"

"Endric?"

It was then that he managed to open his eyes, barely raising the lids enough to stare out, struggling as if weights hung from them. Eyes bloodshot and unfocused, he stared past Endric as if seeing something else. Fear flashed across those eyes, stark and clear, his body suddenly rigid before fading. Then Listain sagged again.

"How?" Listain said. He didn't reopen his eyes. His breathing came slow and shallow and he coughed, bringing bloody spittle to his lips.

"Who did this?" Endric asked, avoiding the question. The answer was too long, too difficult, but he realized the questions he suddenly had about Listain were nearly as difficult.

He had thought Listain was somehow involved in arranging for Andril to be out of the city and had blamed the Raen for that, thinking he wanted to usurp Dendril's authority. Had he not seen the man meeting in Stahline with one of the Magi? When he disappeared during the attack on the city, Endric had viewed it as confirmation of the Raen's involvement. Yet this was not the face of a man involved in the attacks.

Listain was a victim.

Endric almost missed it when Listain answered, distracted by his sudden questions.

"Captured," he said. "Black swords. Teralin."

Endric blinked at the answer, uncertain that he had heard correctly. "The

Deshmahne did this to you?" That meant they already had access to this room. These stores.

"Not Deshmahne," Listain said with a single shake of his head.

Endric frowned. Who else but Deshmahne would use teralin-forged swords? Brohmin had, but not by choice, and Endric was certain the man had not captured Listain. Novan had used the sword, but only once they reached the caves.

A soft click sounded off to his left, like the tumbling of a lock. Endric spun, his sword held before him, and saw an unseen door swing open. The door appeared to be made of rock and was hidden between the alcoves. A figure stepped into the room, stopping suddenly when he saw Endric, almost as startled as Endric had been. The newcomer stood in a confluence of shadows, the light from the lanterns unable to fully penetrate, but something about the person's stance was familiar.

Endric slid forward slowly, carefully, then nearly dropped his sword. "Urik?"

The en'raen stepped into the light and unsheathed his sword. The dark blade seemed to absorb the light, pulling shadows deeper around him. A teralin blade.

"You should not have returned, Endric," Urik said. His words were cool and lacked the warm familiarity the en'raen had shown him in the past.

"You?" Endric asked, flicking his gaze to Listain. "You captured Listain? What reason could you have?" A sickening sense of betrayal threatened to overwhelm him. Had this been how his father had felt when Endric had challenged him?

Urik took a step forward, jarring the thoughts from his mind, his feet nearly silent along the stone floor of the room. The dark sword was held threateningly before him. "Pray you never have to understand my reasons."

"You're Denraen!"

"And of the guild before that. And a father once." The last came out as a whisper.

The comment broke through his feelings of betrayal. Urik had been of the guild? It explained much.

"The guild sent you to survey the caves," Endric said.

Urik frowned, the comment, more than anything else, giving him pause.

"Did you let the Deshmahne into the city as well?"

Urik glared at him, nearly upon him. "Your father needed a reason to attack. He didn't believe the growing threat of the Deshmahne in the south, but *I* knew. And the Denraen have done nothing." He swung his sword and Endric danced backward, staying away from it.

"I thought I could reveal the danger, that your father learning of loss would convince him... but even that didn't. A show of force in the city didn't, either. And then you were foolish enough to challenge him." He paused, swinging his sword up to a ready position. "I would ask how you survived, but the answer does not matter."

With that, he attacked.

The teralin-forged blade swung in a quick arc. Reflexes and his readied sword saved Endric, but barely. Urik slashed a few more times, heat radiating from the sword. Each attack was blocked. Endric slid back as he defended himself, realizing almost too late Urik's plan as he felt the heat from the huge teralin throne pressing upon his back.

Endric switched to attack. His muscles were stiff with fatigue and the hours in the tunnels, but still Urik was quicker than he remembered. Nearly as quick as the Deshmahne had been, and combined with the skill of Denraen training. A near-deadly combination.

A cold chill ran up his spine. Could he have come so far only to fall short?

The city above was completely unaware of what was about to take place in the tunnels beneath it. The Magi didn't know that their precious teralin—perhaps more precious than even the Magi were aware—was about to be stolen by the Deshmahne. And if he failed, Urik could return to the Denraen. Even Dendril would be none the wiser.

A fresh surge of anger filled him, loosening tired arms, burning away the fatigue. Endric pressed the attack, knowing his time was limited if he didn't, throwing himself against Urik almost carelessly. The same way he'd attacked the Deshmahne what felt so many nights ago. Urik fell back against his onslaught, more surprised than overwhelmed, expertly blocking each thrust of his blade. The teralin-forged blade he held managed to stop each attack as Endric began to slow.

Urik smiled, recognizing that Endric grew fatigued. "You did better than I expected." It was not clear whether it was praise or a taunt.

"Face me without the Deshmahne sword!" Endric demanded. He was breathy, spitting out the last few words.

"Deshmahne? Is that what you believe?"

"I recognize the sword."

"I discovered the key to their power. Any can use it. And I will, to destroy them." He slid forward, nearly under Endric's defenses, slicing with the dark blade.

Endric felt the heat radiating off it as he skidded backward, barely avoiding injury. Sweat dripped, a heavy droplet falling into his eye that he blinked away. In that moment, Urik slashed toward his gut. Endric anticipated the attack, somehow sensing it as he had sensed the Deshmahne attack while with the Antrilii, and his plain steel blade—the one borrowed from Novan—met the teralin-forged blade.

And shattered.

He felt Urik's awful smile as he ducked, rolling away from the heat of the throne, ducking under Urik's outstretched arm. Endric kicked out as he rolled and Urik fell backward, arms spinning as he righted himself. Endric stopped, jumping into a crouch as Urik caught himself and turned back to face him.

Endric held the broken shard of the sword tightly. The sword had shattered near the blade guard, leaving no more than a few fingers of sword. Not enough to even attempt a defense. He held it out anyway, his other arm stretched out behind him, searching for something he could use. As he backed up, he felt one of the alcoves behind him, barricading him from moving farther. Left with no other choice, he reached into the alcove, quietly praying he would find something he could use.

When Urik swung the teralin blade at him, Endric's fingers found something long and solid. And warm. Closing his eyes, he gripped the teralin rod, bracing for the searing heat. There was none.

Instead, his hand tingled where it touched the teralin. Not painful or unpleasant, just warm. The sensation began creeping up his arm, oozing through him.

He swung the rod around and was surprised to find a solid shaft of teralin slightly longer than his arm. It was heavy but manageable. The rod whipped around just in time, barely blocking Urik's attack. The en'raen frowned, eyeing the length of teralin. Dropping the sword shard, Endric shifted the rod to his other hand and the warmth spread up that arm as well, seeming to slide just under his skin.

"I'd warn you to be careful with that, Endric," Urik said. "You may not like the consequences. But you would have to know how to access the teralin first."

Endric ignored him, focusing on the strange sensation now coursing through him. This was unlike his previous exposure to teralin. The swords had a darkness about them, almost innately twisted, tainting whoever carried them. Brohmin. Novan. Endric had feared the same would happen to him. But what he felt was not dark or tainted. Just warm.

There was something else about the warmth that he couldn't place. Like a tickle to his mind at the edge of his senses. An energy, almost a vibration. He felt that if he only had time, he would understand. Urik didn't give him that time.

A flurry of attacks came. Endric could only react. With each blow, he managed to move the teralin rod just in time to block. Each attack came closer, the heat of the sword nearer, pushing against the warmth flowing through him. At first, the rod simply stopped the blows. Then it seemingly repelled each attack, as if pushing the teralin-forged sword away from him.

Urik narrowed his eyes, a dark intensity filling them. Endric recognized the expression. He had seen the same on Brohmin's face. And the Deshmahne. And he wondered—was it the darkness of the sword tainting the carrier, or the other way around? Suddenly, one of Urik's thrusts slipped under Endric's defenses.

And was stopped a mere hair's breadth from his chest.

Urik pushed, straining, but couldn't advance the sword any farther, as if meeting some unseen resistance.

Endric didn't have time to think, reacting only. Swinging the rod, he struck toward Urik, hitting his arm and then back, a barrier stopping his strikes as well. The blows were enough to knock the sword from Urik's hand, and Endric spun, striking him along the legs and back once more. Urik fell in a heap, grunting with the motion.

Behind him came a gurgling sound followed by a ragged cough. Endric spun, teralin rod held in front of him, only to see Listain sagging forward, no longer able to support his own weight. Endric staggered over to the man, pushing through the thick heat radiating from the throne.

"Listain?" He reached forward but his hand burned as he neared the throne, and he was unable to tolerate moving it any closer. How could the Raen still live?

"Endric?" Listain whispered. His head tipped back, hanging weakly and lolling to the side, nearly limp on his neck. His dry mouth hung open, crusted blood on his lips. One eye opened, sunken and lifeless. The other didn't move.

"I'm here, Listain."

"Urik?" he asked.

Endric motioned toward where Urik had fallen, turning to look. The en'raen was gone. He froze, scanning the room for movement, any sign of Urik, but there was none. He kept the teralin rod held before him anyway.

"Gone," he answered, not looking back at Listain as he cursed himself for his carelessness. He should have secured the man before seeing to Listain. Now he had no idea where he had gone. Possibly back into the city. Or worse—to guide the Deshmahne to the room.

A gurgle of a moan escaped Listain's mouth, followed by a soft whine, so much like an injured dog.

Endric turned back to Listain. "How do I release the restraints?" he asked, staring at the strange bands of teralin coiled around his wrists and ankles. They were tight, pulling deep into the flesh and tearing through the sleeves of his cloak. Endric didn't want to see what the skin looked like beneath the bands, just as he still had not looked at his throbbing hand, which had opened the solid teralin door to this room.

Listain tilted his head slightly, barely able to move it. "Can't. Need to trigger the teralin."

Endric grunted in frustration. He could barely tolerate being this close to the heat of the chair, let alone figure out how to access the teralin. "Can you do it?"

Listain shook his head once, the slightest of movements. "Wrong polarity," he said, his voice little more than a croak.

Endric frowned, not completely understanding. Novan had tried to explain teralin to him, discussing freshly mined and neutral teralin. "Can you show me how to access it?"

Listain opened one eye, staring at him before flickering his gaze to the long teralin rod Endric still held. Then he shook his head again. "Wrong polarity," he answered again, then sagged into the chair, unmoving.

Endric stared at him, tempted to reach toward him and shake him awake, but didn't think he could stomach the searing pain of the chair. Instead, he tried to reach toward Listain with the length of teralin he held but couldn't push it past the haze of heat surrounding the throne. It was as if he reached a barrier and was rebuffed.

"Listain!" he shouted, but the man didn't move.

Endric walked over to the nearest alcove, searching for something, anything, which could help free Listain while there remained a chance the man might live. He needed to know what happened. The Denraen needed to know. For once, that last was the more urgent of the two.

Teralin in various shapes and lengths filled the alcove. The one next to it was much the same. Nothing was sharpened. Nothing he could use to try to cut through the restraints. Listain wouldn't survive.

He closed his eyes, taking a deep breath. There was little time, he knew. The Deshmahne were not that far behind him and would likely catch up. How long remained until they reached this room? With Urik escaping, there was probably even less time. There was nothing he would be able to do alone. He needed to reach the city and warn his father, somehow convince him of the reality of the threat. And then lead the Denraen back here.

The entire idea was overwhelming. How could he hope to reach the city in time, let alone lead the Denraen through the caves back to this room? He had overestimated his sword skill time and again. Nearly falling to his father. Getting captured by the Antrilii. Nearly losing to the Deshmahne. And now even with Urik.

Hopelessness filled him. A tinge of recognition came with it, like a warning. As it did, he pushed back the dark thoughts, feeling them give way, slipping from his mind. Almost as if they were not his own. A surge of confidence followed, strengthening him, pulling him straighter with each thought.

He had recognized the real threat of the Deshmahne. He had managed to defeat the Deshmahne in battle. And he had survived in the tunnels and found the stockpile of teralin.

As the thoughts came to him, he remembered the night he had faced the Deshmahne. The same doubts and hopelessness had come then.

He scanned the doorway, expecting the Deshmahne, the length of teralin held in front of him like a sword. What came next startled him.

Another hidden door between alcoves slammed open. A figure staggered in with hands held in front of his face. Endric flinched before frowning with recognition.

"Novan?" he asked, taking a hesitant step toward the historian.

Novan moved his hands from his face. A dark expression mixed with confusion covered his eyes. Then he blinked slowly. "Endric?" he whispered.

Endric hurried over and led him into the room. His cloak was ragged and torn and much dirtier than when Endric had seen him last. A dark teralin blade was tucked into his belt. The sack containing the rest of the swords was clutched tightly in his hand. "Are you all right?"

"I think so." He looked around, his body shaking. "I lost myself for a while."

Endric sniffed at the understatement. "How did you find me?"

"You?" Novan asked, his voice distant, then shook his head. "Not you. The teralin." He stared at the alcoves, the door, before turning and staring at the throne. Darkness passed across his eyes along with a look of longing. Novan blinked, visibly pushing the expression away.

"Can you help him?" Endric asked.

Novan stared at the chair rather than Listain and seemed surprised by the comment.

"The bands around his wrists and ankles are teralin. I can't open them."

"Who is it?" Novan's voice was still distant.

"Listain. Urik captured him and trapped him here. I do not know why."

"Urik did this?" he asked, his tone hinting at familiarity. He shook his head as he walked straight up to the chair, ignoring the heat radiating from it. Novan touched the bands circling Listain's wrists and murmured a word. The bands snapped open and fell away. He did the same to his ankles.

Novan gently lifted Listain from the chair and handed him to Endric. Listain was light and his flesh hot, like a fever ran through him, and he hung limp in Endric's arms. Novan stared at the chair for a long moment and then shivered again.

"Don't," Endric said.

Novan looked at him, a question crossing his distant eyes.

"I don't think you should sit upon it."

Novan sighed and nodded slowly. "You are right. Of course you are. I knew the sword was a mistake, but there was no other way…" He looked up suddenly.

Endric looked at him, frowning again. As he opened his mouth to ask Novan to explain, he felt a deep burning sensation suddenly across his shoulders, painful and sharp, as if sliced by a sword.

The Deshmahne had arrived.

CHAPTER 31

"Novan!" he said, urgency in his voice.

The historian glanced at him before shaking his head.

"The Deshmahne are close."

Novan closed his eyes, breathing slowly for a long moment.

The pain across Endric's shoulders intensified. Somehow, he knew they were close now. He held the teralin rod out in front of him, prepared for anything. Finally, Novan opened his eyes.

"I do not feel them," he said. He sounded worried and glanced at the teralin-bladed sword tucked into his pants. "Are you certain?" The inflection to the words implied that he believed what Endric said.

Endric nodded. "I sense them. Strongly."

He carried Listain to one of the alcoves and set him inside. The Raen still breathed, though it was shallow and irregular. He had not stirred since Novan had freed him. Endric wondered how much longer the man would live. There was little question that he would die.

He turned back to Novan, who considered him for a moment before sighing and pulling the teralin sword out from his belt. He swung it through an arc as if loosening his muscles and the sword whistled through the air, making a muffled and deadened sound. Deep shadows suddenly fell around Novan, obscuring his features.

"Are you sure that's wise?" Endric asked, frowning at the sword.

Novan snorted. "I gave up wisdom when I sought to access this teralin," he said with a laugh. The sound was disturbingly similar to Brohmin.

"Why do it then?"

"No choice. Once we realized what the Deshmahne were after, I knew our initial plan wouldn't suffice. This was the only option remaining."

Endric nodded, knowing they needed speed, but he had managed to find the storage room without accessing the teralin. There had been an element of luck, but had Novan truly needed to access the tainted teralin?

"What has it done to you?" Endric asked.

The historian shrugged, though Endric saw through the shadows surrounding him well enough to see the concern upon his face.

"I don't know. I had not thought it possible," Novan said.

Endric expected more of an explanation, but he didn't elaborate.

"I hold out hope that any effects can be reversed."

Endric swallowed. Thoughts of the darkness enveloping Novan as it had Brohmin were disturbing. Between that and the increasing burning sensation along his back—more painful than the last time he had seen the Deshmahne— he began to worry he wouldn't survive to warn the Denraen. What would happen if the Deshmahne accessed the teralin stored here?

"They will be here soon," he whispered.

Novan nodded, his breathing slow and steady. The teralin sword in his hand was held defensively and shadows seemed to swirl around him, enveloping him almost protectively. Did the teralin rod do the same for him? He still felt the warmth under his skin, almost flowing as if alive, but it was a distant sensation now. Endric's heart fluttering in his chest was more prominent; whether in anticipation or fear, he didn't know. Either was appropriate.

"Why Urik?" he asked quietly. There were so many questions he had regarding that betrayal. If only he had restrained Urik after incapacitating him, he would have had some answers. Now he was left only with more questions.

Novan looked over at him, the darkness to his face temporarily flaring before being replaced by sadness. "Urik was once a member of the guild. A great man whose intelligence was nearly unrivaled. Had he not lost his family, he likely would have risen to lead the guild. Their loss was nearly his undoing."

"Did the guild know he was Denraen?"

Endric wouldn't learn the answer. At that moment came a confluence of sensations. The burning along his back became nearly unbearable, a sharp and stabbing sensation. A loud explosion thundered into the room. The lanterns within the room seemed to dim, darkening. And a soft undercurrent of decay wafted into the room.

"Endric!" Novan yelled. "They must not acquire the throne!"

Endric chanced a look over his shoulder, looking at the solid teralin chair. "*That* is what they seek? What of all the teralin in the alcoves?"

"A bonus. The throne is the prize. If we survive, I will explain."

Endric stared at Novan a moment more before turning his attention down the length of the room. At first glance, nothing moved. The pain in his back continued to intensify. Staring deeper into the room, he saw subtly shifting shadows and overlapping darkness. Beneath that, dark-tattooed Deshmahne moved.

He couldn't count their numbers. The darkness that came with them, which he attributed to the teralin, oozed and flowed like a living thing. And perhaps it was.

"Stay near me," Novan directed. "Shift your focus beneath the shadows. They are just men. They die like any other!"

Endric nodded. He knew what Novan said was true but recognized that they were men who had gained attributes he didn't have. He had been lucky the last time he faced the Deshmahne. That had been but one. Now he would stare down possibly dozens.

There could be only one outcome.

He vowed to hurt them as much as possible before falling. He let the anger, the hatred he felt toward the Deshmahne well up within him and push back the hopelessness that threatened him. Faces flashed quickly through his mind. Andril. Olin. Senda. Countless others had fallen to them. Many more would likely die as well, but for today, he would do what he could to slow them.

"We should move back!" he told Novan. The shadows were nearly upon them.

Novan glanced at him briefly and then realized his intent: The room narrowed near the chair. Though the heat would be nearly intolerable, the Deshmahne would be less likely to get past them. They would fall quickly if they were surrounded.

He backed up, feeling the heat from the solid teralin chair almost pushing him forward. Novan stood to his right, holding forth the teralin-forged blade, its shadows encircling him.

Then came a flicker of movement. Endric parried, thrusting the teralin rod forward. Heat surged up his arm, slipping quickly through his body again. The sensation was not uncomfortable. The weariness and stiffness he had felt only moments ago seemed to burn away with the warmth. In its absence, he felt something unexpected, even a little frightening. He felt strengthened.

He thought fleetingly about the teralin contaminating him as it had Brohmin and Novan. A twinge of fear skimmed the edge of his mind, causing his heart to beat faster. For a moment, he worried about what would become of him if the darkness overwhelmed him as it had Brohmin. Only a moment.

Then the warmth surged again within him and those thoughts slid away.

The darkness surrounding the Deshmahne made following their attacks difficult. He could see at least two distinct men facing him, each coming at him with a teralin-forged blade. Both were skilled. He dared not glance over at Novan, hoping the historian could continue to hold his own with the sword. With the staff, the man was amazing, but there wouldn't have been space in the room for that weapon.

Endric attacked. He couldn't see well enough to defend, so he pressed forward instead, feeling somewhat giddy with the knowledge that he was only an errant strike from death.

Whipping the length of teralin around, he spun it through forms as he would his sword, moving as quickly as he could. The rod moved more fluidly than it had when he faced Urik, almost lighter. He felt each blow as the teralin blades blocked his attack. Endric fought more quickly than he had ever managed before. The effect of the teralin, he knew. Yet without it, he had no doubt he would already be dead.

When the first Deshmahne fell, he felt a small surge of pleasure. The sensation was brief. Another Deshmahne replaced the one who had fallen. Endric acted as if the first had not gone down, attacking with abandon. The heat beneath his skin continued to swell, growing to the point where he felt that he must glow. Still, there was no pain.

Another Deshmahne appeared before him. He didn't know how many he faced at once. At least three but possibly as many as five. There was no way he could maintain this. All it would take was one lucky strike and he would be slowed or killed. He would fall. The Deshmahne would win.

For a moment, he felt his movements falter, his attack slow.

In the distance, he heard a soft whistling. The sound was vaguely familiar, but he didn't risk shifting his attention to consider why. The fear threatening him dissolved with the distraction. The Deshmahne suddenly pressed with renewed frenzy, their dark swords slicing at him in a blur. The teralin rod managed to deflect each attempt. They moved more quickly than any man he had ever seen, but then—for now—so did he.

Endric didn't know when his vision had cleared, but the shadows had lessened so that he could clearly see the Deshmahne and their swords. Suddenly, one of the Deshmahne managed to get behind him. Then another. He sensed a dark satisfaction from them. The attacks now came from all directions. He spun, now only on the defensive, the saving grace his renewed vision and speed.

It was only a matter of time before he fell.

Then came a low growl and a snarling attack.

Endric recognized the sound.

Merahl. Here, in the tunnels.

Could the Antrilii have survived?

The mere idea was almost too much to consider, but why else would the merahl have come?

The Deshmahne were forced to press harder, faster.

Endric couldn't keep up. He had all that he could handle simply deflecting the now half-dozen teralin blades slicing toward him, synchronized like some deadly dance. The teralin grew warmer in his hand, and the heat spreading through his body intensified.

There was a flash of pain that left him quickly.

Suddenly, his mind felt freed. Fear of the Deshmahne left him, only contempt and hatred remaining. The pattern to the Deshmahne attack became clear, and he darted between their sword thrusts, stabbing with the blunt teralin rod before falling into his defense. Over and over, he attacked. The Deshmahne fell before him.

Still, it was not enough.

They had him surrounded. He felt as much as saw the dark blades streaking toward him. He had no idea if Novan still lived. The sound of his own heartbeat thumped loudly in his ears. Distantly, he was aware of the snarling merahl attack. He heard nothing else.

Through the heat of the teralin, the strength it lent him, fatigue set in. His reaction time slowed, and he suspected he had been cut at least once and probably more than that, yet he felt nothing other than the rolling waves of heat under his flesh. When two more Deshmahne joined the circle around him, he knew his time was short. Hopelessness pressed upon him like a physical presence.

"Novan!" he screamed, squeezing the teralin rod, almost welcoming the distracting heat into his body as he prayed the historian still lived.

With the scream, the warmth flared once more, hot and painful. Strength and speed surged through him again. The sensation was incredible, power unlike anything he had ever known and speed such that time seemed to slow.

The hopeless feelings fled and Deshmahne fell before him.

That still was not enough. The room was filled with Deshmahne, and more seemed to enter, replacing the fallen. Novan still stood, his sword moving more rapidly than Endric once would have believed possible, four Deshmahne held at bay in front of him. Several lay dead nearby.

When Endric was set upon by another circle of Deshmahne, he knew he and Novan wouldn't succeed. Whatever strength and speed the teralin lent was not enough. They would fail. The city would fall. The Deshmahne would win.

He sensed the dark satisfaction of the Deshmahne surrounding him, as if they knew his thoughts, his fears. Yet there was nothing he could do. He was beaten. The Deshmahne would win.

The Deshmahne suddenly attacked in a frenzy, like wolves sensing weakened prey. Endric had all that he could manage simply fighting them back. With each passing moment, the teralin-forged blades came nearer.

Somewhere, a door slammed open, a cool breeze coming with it.

He didn't look up, unable to spare a glance, thinking it only more Deshmahne.

A loud roar erupted from the open door. Even the attacking Deshmahne paused to look, giving Endric time to see who—or what—had arrived.

What he saw caused his heart to skip a beat. It was the last thing he had expected to see within the dark tunnels as he fought the Deshmahne for control of the teralin.

Dendril tore into the room, Trill spinning in a fury. Deshmahne fell back against the onslaught, many dying quickly. Pendin followed Endric's father. Behind him came others of the Denraen.

The Deshmahne fell back. And into the merahl.

The remaining Deshmahne around him attacked with urgency. Hope found Endric for the first time in hours. The warmth beneath his skin surged again, flaring hot and painful. He welcomed the sensation, lashing out with the teralin rod and dropping the remaining Deshmahne.

And then the room was silent.

Endric looked around. Dead Deshmahne littered the floor. At the far end of the room, flanked by two snarling merahl, stood Brohmin and two Antrilii. He couldn't tell if Dentoun was one of them. He blinked slowly, wondering if the others had died.

Novan still stood to his left. The historian was bloodied, his face and chest cut and oozing, but he was alive.

Then there was his father. Dendril stood with his sword tip resting on the stone ground. Nearly a dozen Deshmahne lay dead near him, killed in little more than an instant. How had he ever thought he was his father's equal?

Dendril's dark eyes scanned the room before settling on Endric. "Son."

Endric breathed slowly, his heart still hammering in his chest. "Father."

Dendril took a deep breath. When he exhaled, his features softened and he turned to Novan. "Thank you for your warning."

Warning? Endric thought they had traveled to the city to provide a warning.

Novan tilted his head in acknowledgement. "You almost didn't make it."

Dendril snorted. "If not for our guide, we wouldn't have."

Endric glanced at his friend, who only shrugged, then looked away.

"The miners still strike?" Novan asked.

Dendril flashed a wry smile before nodding. "Always questioning."

"It is my nature." Novan turned and gestured toward the teralin chair. "The throne must be protected. The rest"—he looked around the room—"must be charged. Find one who knows how."

Dendril nodded. "There are a few."

"It is time you return to the conclave."

Dendril sniffed. "I never left."

Novan narrowed his eyes. "Do not pretend I don't know what happened."

Dendril stared for a moment before backing down and looking away. "You're right. Much could have been avoided."

"We were all caught unaware, Dendril. But we must learn and move forward."

"You sound much like Listain."

"If he awakens, he will tell you the same," Novan said.

"You found him?" Dendril asked.

Novan motioned to the alcove Endric had set the Raen inside. "I don't know if he will live."

Dendril motioned and one of the Denraen moved past to look in the alcove.

"He lives. I'll get him to the healers."

Dendril shook his head. "Not the healers. Tresten. Have the Mage see to him. Tell him I sent you. Take the others."

The Denraen nodded and turned, pulling the others with him. Pendin gave Endric a searching glance before following.

When the Denraen left, the Antrilii and the merahl came to greet Novan. Graime and Hontin remained. Brohmin stood back, teralin-forged blade clutched in his hand. Dark shadows swirled around him.

"Dentoun?" Dendril asked.

Graime shook his head. "He dines with the gods now." The Antrilii smiled. "We delayed these Deshmahne as well as we could but were nearly overwhelmed. We withdrew and followed, harrying them along the way, trying to slow them."

Dendril reached out a hand and whistled softly, the sound so similar to what Dentoun had made. The merahl stalked over to him and sniffed his hand, then with wags of their long tails, sat so that he could scratch them. When he looked up, there was a tear in his eyes. "And then followed the Deshmahne into the tunnels, attacking when outnumbered." The young Antrilii shrugged. "Your father would be proud of how you fought today," he told Graime.

Graime nodded and smiled. The dark paintings upon his face were smeared and stretched. "Thank you, Uncle."

Endric looked over to his father suddenly. "Uncle?"

Dendril nodded once. "Dentoun was my brother."

"You're Antrilii?" Endric sputtered.

Novan laughed. Graime and Hontin nodded solemnly.

"You didn't leave me to die on the plains," Endric realized.

Dendril frowned. "You thought me capable of that? You were to learn from Dentoun." He shook his head. "And it seems you learned more than I intended."

Novan snorted.

Endric was at a loss for words.

"Now. There remains one question," Dendril said.

Endric shook his head. "What?"

"Are you ready to return to the Denraen?"

Endric closed his eyes, surprised by the warmth in his father's voice. Always that tone had been reserved for Andril. Now his father offered to take him back. After the years Endric had spent pushing against him, he knew he would need to earn his trust. But his father had been right. He had known little. Like a child. Now he knew more but realized there was a great deal more that remained unknown.

More than anything, he knew the Deshmahne had not been stopped. He would be a part of whatever the Denraen did to counter the growing threat.

"If you will have me."

"You're different."

Endric sat next to Senda. Much had happened since he returned from the tunnels. His skin itched, still warm. He had sheathed the teralin rod like a sword. Somehow, it felt right. If he found Novan, he would ask about the risks of carrying the rod, but for now, he kept it with him.

"I grew up when I nearly died."

Senda snorted and laughed, softly touching his leg with her hand. "It suits you," she said, catching his eye.

He stared into her dark eyes and smiled.

"Andril would be proud."

Endric closed his eyes. She knew him well. "Thank you."

"You have finally stopped fighting."

"I have fought enough for the day."

Senda laughed, soft and sweet. After thinking he would never see her again, he had not wanted her out of his sight since his return. She had happily complied.

"That is not what I meant."

Endric sniffed. "I know."

"The office suits you as well."

Endric looked around. Andril's office had been unchanged since his death. Sparsely decorated and tidy. So typical of his brother. Books stacked neatly along the walls. The desk uncluttered. "I didn't expect this."

Senda laughed. "He did, I think."

He looked up at her, furrowing his brow. Perhaps she was right and his father had expected his return. The promotion was still surprising, especially in light of their history. Endric had not fought this time, accepting the leadership his father offered.

A knock on the door interrupted. Senda stood and leaned forward, kissing him on his forehead. The sensation was warm and it tingled.

"I need to check on Listain," she said. "With Olin gone, he will need me."

Endric smiled. His distrust for Listain was gone. The man had been tortured by Urik, trapped in the teralin throne for a purpose they still had not determined. Urik had wanted Listain out of the way because he'd discovered what Urik planned and how he had allowed the Deshmahne into the city to force the Denraen to act, but there had to be more to it, some reason that he'd involved the throne. "I do too."

Senda walked to the door and opened it, pausing and turning back. "I know," she said before leaving.

The open door revealed Novan. The historian was cleansed and healed. He carried his staff in hand again. No evidence of darkness or shadows surrounded him.

"I came to tell you that I am leaving."

"So soon?"

Novan smiled. "I will return. The Magi will hate it, but your father granted permission."

Endric frowned but Novan didn't elaborate. "Is Brohmin—"

Novan smiled. "Healed. As am I."

"What of me?"

Novan shook his head. "I don't know how, but you were able to charge the neutral teralin."

"I don't understand."

"The teralin-forged swords were negatively charged. You managed to charge the rod with a positive polarity, and differently than any way that I know." He shook his head. "Be thankful for it. Otherwise, we would all have died."

"We haven't found Urik," Endric said.

Novan smiled, and a flash of the darkness returned, disappearing quickly. "That is my task now."

"He was Denraen."

Novan shook his head, his mouth a tight line. "He was of the guild first. That betrayal is the deepest."

"Why?"

"He lost a son, his family, to the Deshmahne, but his grief does not forgive his actions."

Endric didn't argue. He would discuss Urik with his father later. There were other questions he had for Dendril as well. The most pressing were those about his Antrilii heritage. Dentoun had been his uncle! Now that he knew, the resemblance became clearer. That made Nahrsin and Graime his cousins. He had gone from no other family to an exotic one in moments. And still had not adjusted.

"The chair?" he asked, turning his attention back to Novan. He couldn't quite call it a throne as the historian had, and still wondered at its purpose.

"Tresten and your father have it secured."

"What is it?"

Novan shook his head, tapping his staff on the stone floor. "Ask him to explain. The answer is long and complex. If he refuses, seek Tresten for answers. They will come, but you must earn them. Remain vigilant, Endric. Learn as much as you can. About yourself, the teralin, the Magi. Only through knowledge will we persevere." He paused, his face drawn and dark. He seemed to consider his next words carefully, weighing them before speaking. "What is stored in this city, the teralin in these caves, is incredibly valuable."

Novan paused again, and the weight of the next words made Endric shiver. He knew they were true, but hearing Novan speak them made the threat even more real.

"The Deshmahne were not defeated. Only slowed. And they will return."

ACKNOWLEDGEMENTS:

I want to thank all the people who helped me get this book together, including all my awesome beta readers, Victory Editing, West of Mars editing, Polgarus Studios for print formatting, my fantastic cover designer, and mostly, my family for allowing me the time to do the work!

About the Author:

New York Times and USA Today Bestselling Author D.K. Holmberg lives in Minnesota and is the author of multiple series including The Cloud Warrior Saga, The Dark Ability, The Endless War, and The Lost Garden. When he's not writing, he's chasing around his two active children.

Check my website for updates and new releases:
http://www.dkholmberg.com.

Follow me on Facebook:
www.facebook.com/dkholmberg

I'm occasionally on twitter:
www.twitter.com/dkholmberg

ALSO BY DK HOLMBERG

80281982R00188

Made in the USA
Lexington, KY
01 February 2018